Praise for *A Christmas Serenade*

"This collection of Victorian- and Regency-era Christmas romances is perfect for getting you into the holiday mood! You'll laugh, cry, and want to hug each of the characters as they try to figure out how to bring that extra something to their celebrations—and maybe find their perfect someone along the way."

—Jill Warner, author of *Of Jasmine and Roses*

"New loves, lost loves, family secrets, quirky characters, and a few Christmas miracles make *A Christmas Serenade* the perfect prelude to the holiday season."

—Josi S. Kilpack, author of *Summerhaven*

"'A Caroling Christmas' by Jennifer Moore is a charming and lovely salute to a holiday celebration, full of Dickensian delight! Her tale of a cozy house party with an insightful nod to the staff who make it possible had me smiling from beginning to end. Mr. Stanton and Miss Hopewell are my new favorite couple."

—Nancy Cambell Allen, author of *Protecting Her Heart*

"'A Carol So Bright' by Kasey Stockton hits all the right notes for a delightful Christmas novella: music, gifts, snow, and the recognition of a love that has been right in front of you all along."

—Esther Hatch, author of *A Proper Facade*

"'Christmas at Bellingham' brings emotional depth as Esther Harris learns the importance of family, healing, and making amends. Sometimes, doing the impossibly hard thing brings the greatest joys and peace that are such a vital part of the Christmas spirit."

—Jill Warner, author of *Of Jasmine and Roses*

"Rumors of a Christmas legend bring a duo of childhood friends together in Anneka Walker's 'Christmas in Amorwich.' This seasonal tale is full of second chances and heartfelt moments. Add in a cantankerous neighbor with a mysterious past and Christmas traditions common to the era, and Walker creates a recipe for holiday cheer in this delightful read!"

—Rachel Kelley Stones, author of *A Casualty of the Heart*

Praise for the Authors

"Anneka Walker is a master storyteller."

—The Power of the Page, Goodreads Review of *The Lady Glass*

"I don't know how Kasey Stockton does it. How does she write such phenomenal stories that leave me speechless the whole way through?"

—Heather, Goodreads Review of *I'm Not His Style*

"I've been reading Jennifer Moore's books since her first release years ago, and I've loved every one."

—Mindy, Goodreads Review of *Discovering Dahlia*

"[Katie Stewart Stone] is truly a master of romance!!!"

—Geri G., Deseret Book Review of *Scotland's Melody*

A Christmas Serenade

A HISTORICAL ROMANCE ANTHOLOGY

JENNIFER MOORE, KASEY STOCKTON,
KATIE STEWART STONE, ANNEKA R. WALKER

Cover images: *Christmas Frame* by Anna Nekotangerine and *Woman Silhouette* by Crazy Dark Queen; Adobe Stock

Cover design by Christina Marcano

Published by Covenant Communications, Inc.
American Fork, Utah

Library of Congress Cataloging-in-Publication Data

Name: Jennifer Moore, Kasey Stockton, Katie Stewart Stone, Anneka R. Walker
Title: A Christmas Serenade / Jennifer Moore, Kasey Stockton, Katie Stewart Stone, Anneka R. Walker
Description: American Fork, UT : Covenant Communications, Inc. [2025]
Identifiers: Library of Congress Control Number 2024945043 | 978-1-52442-854-9
LC record available at https://lccn.loc.gov/2024945043

Printed in the United States of America
First Printing: September 2025

34 33 32 31 30 29 28 27 26 25   10 9 8 7 6 5 4 3 2 1

Contents

OTHER BOOKS AND AUDIOBOOKS BY JENNIFER MOORE

Regency Romance

Becoming Lady Lockwood

Lady Emma's Campaign

Miss Burton Unmasks a Prince

Simply Anna

Lady Helen Finds Her Song

A Place for Miss Snow

Miss Whitaker Opens Her Heart

Miss Leslie's Secret

The War of 1812

My Dearest Enemy

The Shipbuilder's Wife

Charlotte's Promise

Romance on the Orient Express

Wrong Train to Paris

The Blue Orchid Society

Emmeline

Solving Sophronia

Inventing Vivian

Healing Hazel

Educating Elizabeth

"A Home for the Holidays" in *A Longing for Christmas*

Discovering Dahlia

"A Caroling Christmas" in *A Christmas Serenade*

Stand-Alone Novellas

"The Perfect Christmas" in *Christmas Treasures*

"Let Nothing You Dismay" in *Christmas Grace*

"Love and Joy Come to You" in *A Christmas Courting*

"To Love a Spy" in *Where Dreams Meet*

A Caroling Christmas

JENNIFER MOORE

Chapter One

1875, Three days before Christmas

"'Marley was dead, to begin with!'"

The theatrically eerie voice of Arthur Stanton's sister came through the keyhole into the laboratory. Heaven only knew why Cassie was quoting Dickens. Arthur, for his part, no longer asked why she did anything. She was unpredictable, to be sure, but Arthur considered it just one more reason to adore her.

The door burst open an instant later, and she stood there, grinning.

"Good morning, Cassie." Arthur carefully placed the specimen he was studying into its terrarium. Luckily, the creature did not appear to have suffered any trauma from a young woman's shouts—hardly surprising, though Arthur did intend to study its reactions to sound vibrations at some future point. He should make a note. He glanced around, located a pencil on the floor, and found a loose page on his desk, scribbling a reminder in the margin.

"Morning?" Cassie folded her arms, giving him the exasperated look only an eighteen-year-old young woman could manage. "It is three in the afternoon." She remained in the doorway, as was her habit, and pointed at the clock on the laboratory wall. "The guests will arrive at any moment."

Arthur knew better than to offer her a seat. She would not enter. "Guests?" he asked, scanning his memory to recall what guests were expected. "Are Reverend and Mrs. Bramwell coming to tea again?"

Cassie let out a dramatic sigh. "How can you be so obtuse? The guests for our *Christmas house party*. They are arriving today." She shook her head, making her blonde curls sway like seaweed beneath calm waves. "Surely you haven't forgotten."

"Of course I haven't forgotten. You and Mother have hardly spoken of anything else for months." He scanned the surface of his desk, hoping to find his calendar. He had been given a very fine one as a gift by an associate of natural science at Oxford, with drawings of Galapagos reptiles. "But the party is not for a week at least." He shoved aside a pile of books, but the calendar was not beneath it. He lifted a notebook, accidentally spilling some loose papers onto the carpet.

"A week?" Cassie made a sound that was both frustrated and amused. "Arthur, Christmas Eve is the day after tomorrow."

"So soon?" He bent to pick up the disordered papers, glancing at the contents. Notes on the Hassler expedition to the Galapagos Islands. He'd been searching for these. He set them on top of the books and turned to his sister. "Impossible."

"I take it you haven't tried on your costume for the Ball of Christmas Past?"

Arthur knew there was a garment bag hanging in his bedchamber, but he'd not even looked inside, even though his valet reminded him frequently. "Not yet."

"When were you planning to do it? The guests will be here tonight, and activities are scheduled throughout the next three days." Cassie scowled. "Miss Hopewell went to great lengths to ensure the costumes were delivered in time for alterations to be made if necessary."

He gave up on finding the calendar. "Who is Miss Hopewell?"

"Oh, Arthur, have you listened to nothing these past months? Miss Hopewell, Planner of Events, Parties, and Peculiar Festivities? She is the most sought-after celebration organizer in the country. We were very fortunate to engage her."

"Celebration organizer?" Arthur took off his spectacles and removed his laboratory coat, trading it for his wool jacket, which he tossed over his arm. He checked the hanging thermometer, noting with satisfaction that the new warming system was keeping the room at a steady temperature. "What is there to organize, aside from the meals? And Mother is completely capable of arranging those." He joined his sister in the corridor, closing the door behind him. "It is a Christmas party, not a royal jubilee."

"There is the matter of decorations, of course," Cassie said. "Invitations, food deliveries, and preparations for the various activities." She ticked the items off on her fingers. "Miss Hopewell is the one who came up with the theme: Charles Dickens's *A Christmas Carol*." She clapped her hands, grinning. "Is it not splendid?"

Now her earlier words through the keyhole made sense. "I thought the theme for a Christmas party was *Christmas*," Arthur said. He checked the laboratory door one more time to ensure it was closed properly. The latch did not always fasten.

"Oh, my dear brother." Cassie gave another sigh, this one making her long-suffering state clear. "A unique theme is what sets our party apart from all the others. Every holiday party in the country will have ivy on the tables and wreaths on the door." She shook her head, demonstrating the obvious inadequacy of such ornamentation. "But have you ever heard of a Theatrical Salute to Christmas Future or a feast with the motif of Christmas Present?"

"I have not," he said truthfully.

She gave a satisfied nod and took her brother's arm. "There you have it. People will be talking of our Christmas party for years to come." As they walked to the stairs, he could feel the excitement practically radiating from her.

They descended from the highest level of the house until they stood at the top of the grand staircase. Nearly every inch of the entry hall below was garnished with some form of Christmas embellishment. Garlands and bows were strung around the doorframes, wound up the stair banisters, and suspended from the chandelier. A wreath hung from every wall sconce. The table in the center of the hall held a large vase filled with red and white blossoms. Arthur blinked, amazed at the transformation. He hardly recognized his own house.

Cassie raised her brows and folded her arms in satisfaction, indicating that, as far as she was concerned, her point was made. The Stantons' Christmas celebration was already astounding even its own host.

Leaning over the banister, she reached out her hands dramatically. "'I will honour Christmas in my heart and try to keep it all the year.'" Her voice echoed through the entry hall.

Arthur laughed. He took Cassie's hand, holding it high as he led her ceremoniously down the staircase. "'I will live in the Past, Present, and the Future.'" He continued the quotation she'd begun, hand over his heart, calling out the words in a loud voice as his sister giggled. "'The Spirits of all Three shall strive within me. I will not shut out the lessons that they teach!'" At the bottom of the stairs, he flung his coat aside with a flourish and bowed over his extended leg.

Cassie's giggles continued, as he'd hoped they would, but they were cut off when a loud crash sounded behind them.

Arthur whirled. To his horror, the tossed coat had flown into a large pine tree, which stood just far enough behind the foot of the stairs that he'd not noticed it in his descent. Glass balls smashed on impact with the floor, and candles fell from the boughs. Thank goodness they were unlit. But, surprisingly, though the tree wobbled and tilted nearly to the floor, it did not fall.

The reason for the tree's extraordinary balance was made clear soon enough as a voice came from within—or, rather, beneath—the branches.

"Some assistance, if you please!" The voice was female, and it managed to sound alarmed and, at the same time, commanding.

Arthur rushed forward. He grabbed hold of the tree limbs, pulling the tree up and off the unfortunate woman. More balls fell, shattering when they hit the marble floor. A footman came to their aid, and the three managed to right the tree.

The woman stepped out from behind, brushing pine needles from her skirt. She was surprisingly small, wearing a plain dress and jacket in a fashionable yet not ostentatious style. Her eyes were the same color as her dress, a rather interesting shade of steel blue that one did not often see in the melanin pigment of the iris. She had arranged her hair in a practical twist with no curls, and the only adornments she wore were a pair of pearl earrings and a timepiece on a chain around her neck. She picked up Arthur's coat, gave it a firm shake that dislodged more needles, and handed it to him with a frown.

Arthur took it, feeling sheepish. His hands and arms were sticky with sap, and his shoes crunched on broken glass. "I beg your pardon, madam. I didn't see you there."

The woman made a small "Hmph" sound as she scanned the floor, taking in the broken glass, fallen candles, and scattered pine needles. Among the mess was a clipboard, which she picked up and held in the crook of her arm.

"What was that . . . ?" Arthur's mother stepped out of the downstairs parlor, panicked words trailing away as her gaze swept over her children, the woman and footman, the tree, and the mess beneath. "What has happened?"

"Just a small accident, Mother," Arthur began. "One I intend to repair immediately."

The unknown woman made the "Hmph" sound again. She straightened a bow on the tree and righted a candle.

"It is nothing at all," Cassie added, glancing toward her brother with a grimace.

Two other women came from the parlor as well. One was older, and the other he guessed to be near Cassie's age. They looked familiar; Arthur was sure they had been introduced at one time, but he could not recall their names.

"Goodness," the older woman said, pressing a hand to her chest. The younger woman took in the scene with wide eyes, her mouth forming an *o*.

Guests had already arrived. Arthur's heart sank. Appearances were so important to his mother, and he knew he'd embarrassed her.

Cassie hurried toward them, blocking the view of the wreckage as well as she was able. "Mrs. Wilcox, Imogene, what a wonderful surprise. You must have arrived while I was upstairs. How lovely to see you." She glanced at Arthur, then took each woman by the arm, turned them around, and walked them back into the parlor. "Now, let us have some tea, and do tell me all about the latest news from Bath."

Arthur's mother looked once more between the mess and her son and sighed before following the other ladies.

A pair of maids came into the entry hall with brooms and set about sweeping. Arthur and the woman with the clipboard stepped out of their way and toward the staircase.

"You must be Miss Hopewell," Arthur said.

"And you must be Mr. Stanton," she replied in a matter-of-fact tone. The way she looked at him made him feel as if he were a specimen being studied beneath a microscope. He glanced down and saw that not only was his waistcoat speckled with pine needles but one of the buttons was fastened in the wrong hole. He winced as he pulled his coat on and straightened his clothing as well as he was able, though the sap on his hands rendered the effort far from effective. His neck heated when the silk of his waistcoat bunched and adhered in a clump that did not permit the button to slide into the correct hole.

Miss Hopewell flipped over a page on her clipboard. Her sap-covered fingers stuck to the paper, but she smoothly removed them with a decisive twist of her hand that didn't tear the paper or even wrinkle it. She tapped the tip of her pencil on the page. "I've spoken to your valet, sir. You've yet to try on your costume."

"Yes," he said, resisting the impulse to hang his head and scuff his shoes on the ground. "I've been meaning to, you see, but the date quite snuck up on me."

Miss Hopewell made a note, shaking her head. In spite of a sprig of pine in her hair, another on her lapel, and the sap on her fingers and sleeves, she still managed to appear entirely in order. Arthur had known people like Miss Hopewell—schoolmarms, mostly. Organized, disciplined, tidy . . . all the things he was not. He half expected her to produce a ruler to rap on his knuckles.

"I will try it on," he said. "Be assured."

She tapped the pencil tip on the page again. "It would have been preferable for the tailor's business to have been completed a week ago when the costumes were delivered. Since you have put it off, any required alterations will be rushed." She looked toward the parlor doorway. "And I expect your time will be occupied now."

He followed her gaze, looking at the doorway as well. "I'm certain I will manage to find the time to try on the costume."

Miss Hopewell glanced pointedly toward a framed placard leaning on a stand at one side of the entry hall. Looking closer, Arthur saw that it was a schedule of events for the next three days, painted in a very fine calligraphy. As Cassie had mentioned, the Theatrical Salute to Christmas Future was to be this evening, the Feast of Christmas Present was to be tomorrow, and the Ball of Christmas Past would be held the day after, on Christmas Eve. In between these three main events were listed various other meals and activities. Arthur felt tired just looking at it . . . and irritable. When would he feed his specimens or document their growth based on rises in temperature? He had also been enjoying accounts of Louis Agassiz's zoological expedition to South America, but now he did not think he would have time to finish reading them until after Christmas.

"It isn't even in the correct order," he muttered, scowling toward the placard.

"I beg your pardon?" Miss Hopewell did indeed sound like a schoolmarm.

Arthur turned to her. "If the events are to follow the Dickens novel, they should proceed in the same order: past, present, then future." He gestured toward the placard. "This is reversed."

"It is a theme, Mr. Stanton," she said flatly. "Not a dramatization."

Arthur felt further chided. He scratched his head, wincing as the sap caught and pulled out hairs.

Mrs. Hopewell consulted the timepiece on her necklace. "The remainder of the guests are due to arrive at any moment." She glanced over him once again and lifted an eyebrow. "You should ready your presentation."

As if on cue, from outside came the sound of carriage wheels rolling up the gravel path. Arthur looked down at himself again. His clothes were a mess, hairs and fibers were stuck to his fingers and hands, and he hadn't even shaved today. He felt another burst of embarrassment and irritation. This woman had come into his home and made him feel like a naughty child.

The footmen went out to assist the new guests.

"Excuse me," Arthur said with a terse bow to Miss Hopewell before dashing up the stairs. His valet, Benson, would know how to remove the sap from his clothing, but what of the rest of him? There was a particularly sticky blob on his wrist, and the thought of tugging on it and pulling out more hairs made him grimace.

"Do not forget your costume, Mr. Stanton," Miss Hopewell said. "The window for alterations is closing."

Arthur took a page from the woman's book and replied with a "Hmph." When she was out of earshot, he muttered, "Humbug."

Chapter Two

Eliza Hopewell scrubbed at her hands, letting the harsh kitchen soap strip away the pine sap. She thought of the gorgeous tree, measured and chosen specifically for the space, now with broken limbs and bare branches. She frowned recalling the ornaments she'd found at a Whitefriars glassblower's shop now in pieces at the bottom of a rubbish bin. She breathed in, and on her exhale, she pushed out her frustration, imagining it dissipating with her breath.

In the five years since she'd begun the business of arranging extravagant festivities for exclusive clients, she'd come to learn that no matter how carefully she planned, how painstakingly she considered and prepared for various scenarios, nothing ever went precisely as intended. Thankfully, her best asset, and the one for which she charged her clients extra, was her ability to remain calm in the face of disaster and to adapt to new circumstances. Prepare for the unexpected.

She rinsed off the soap and accepted an offered towel from Mrs. Donovan, the Stantons' cook.

"A pity about the tree, miss," Mrs. Donovan said with a kind smile.

"It is a pity," Eliza agreed. "Fortunately, I brought some reserve decorations as a precaution." She handed back the towel. "Although, in my planning, I'd considered the possibility that one of the *children* might break an ornament. I hadn't thought . . ."

"That the master of the house would be the one to do it?" Mrs. Donovan laughed, and her eyes twinkled. "Bless him. I would not call him clumsy, but his inattentiveness does tend to lead him to break things. Teacups set too close to the edge of a table or a potted plant when the stack of books beside it becomes top-heavy. Do you know he once sat on a slice of Victoria sponge cake?"

"Oh dear," Eliza said. She could hardly imagine a mindset of such disarray. She waited, wondering if the cook would say more—perhaps she would express frustration at Mr. Stanton's careless nature—but Mrs. Donovan only smiled fondly.

"He is a good man," the cook said. "And I prefer a bit of eccentricity in an employer to cruelty." She set the folded towel on the food preparation table. "Now, shall we see what can be done for the tree?"

Eliza collected the box of decorations from her room and carried it into the entry hall.

Mrs. Donovan was already up on a stool, retying a ribbon that had been smashed. Eliza opened the box and took stock of the reserves, then assessed the tree. Most of the branches could be made presentable with a bit of trimming, but one of the larger limbs was snapped and hanging.

As if reading her thoughts, Mrs. Donovan reached out and tapped the broken branch with her fingers. "I have sent for the groundskeeper to chop it off," she said.

Eliza nodded her thanks. "If we turn the tree"—she held out her arms and shifted to the side to demonstrate—"the bare areas will mostly be hidden by the staircase. Creative arrangement of the decorations will cover up any other holes."

Once the tree was rotated and the limb removed, the women worked together to reattach candles, rehang ornaments, and retie ribbons.

Just as they finished, another carriage arrived. Based on the shouts of children outside the door, it was the Lind family, complete with their seven-year-old twin boys.

The women cleaned up the box and stool and moved out of the entry hall just as the front doors opened and the volume of the shouts increased. On her way to the kitchen, Eliza glanced back at the tree, trying to guess which ornaments would survive the day.

In the kitchen she washed sap from her hands again and retrieved her clipboard to glance over the list of tasks that still needed to be completed before the after-dinner events. She waited for the noise in the entry hall to taper off, imagining the footmen carrying the Linds' luggage, the maids taking coats and hats, and Mrs. Frasier, the housekeeper, showing the guests to their accommodations.

Once the sound of footsteps disappeared up the stairs, Eliza thanked Mrs. Donovan for her help, then took the box of ornaments back up to her bedchamber. The room Mrs. Stanton had assigned her was not on the lower floor with the guests and family, but on the top level with the nursery and some of the servants' quarters. Down at the far end of the corridor, behind a locked door, was Mr. Stanton's laboratory.

Although Eliza had asked, Mrs. Frasier had not given any information as to what sort of laboratory it was, and Eliza got the impression that neither the man's family nor the staff went inside. It was Mr. Stanton's realm alone.

She deposited the box in a corner of the room and started to leave. From the direction of the nursery came the children's voices. A woman—their nanny, Eliza assumed—spoke as well. A door closed, and she turned in the direction of the sound.

Mr. Stanton had just exited his laboratory. He twisted the knob and wiggled the door, ensuring it was indeed shut tightly.

For an instant, Eliza considered hurrying back inside her room before he saw her, but that idea was a silly one. That their initial meeting had been . . . awkward, to say the least, was no reason to hide from the man.

His gaze lifted to hers. "Miss Hopewell." His voice was polite as he strode down the corridor. His jaw was freshly shaved, his mustache trimmed, and his clothing pressed. Eliza was surprised by the transformation. He cut a very fine figure indeed.

"Mr. Stanton." She inclined her head.

A happy cry came from the nursery, followed by children's laughter.

Mr. Stanton glanced past her toward the sound, his brows knitting together.

"The Lind children, I believe," she said.

He nodded, but his confused expression did not go away. "I didn't realize there would be children." His gaze flicked toward his closed laboratory door.

"Yes," she said, not knowing how else to answer. She started toward the staircase, and Mr. Stanton joined her, walking beside her as they descended.

The silence felt strained. Eliza considered what to say to ease the discomfort. "You managed to extricate the sap from your hair, I see." She grimaced as soon as she'd said the words. Surely she could have come up with something less trivial.

Mr. Stanton glanced at her, blinking, as if just remembering she was next to him. "Ah yes. My valet recommended olive oil."

Eliza nodded, and unable to think of anything further, she accompanied him in silence down the final flight to the entry hall.

Outside the parlor, Mr. Stanton paused next to the doorway. He glanced inside and then drew back, standing to the side of the doorway, then pushed his fingers through his hair, making it stick up in tufts.

He was nervous.

Eliza patted his arm. This was not the first apprehensive guest she'd come across, and she took on the role of comforter. "Your mother and sister will be very happy that you're here," she said in a gentle voice. "As will your guests."

Mr. Stanton sighed and continued to look into the room. "A social gathering is not a situation in which I am at ease." Taking on a resigned expression and straightening his shoulders, he hesitated only a moment longer before stepping inside.

Upon his entrance, his mother immediately excused herself from her conversation and came to him. "My dear, here you are at last." She combed down his hair with her fingers and drew him into the midst of the gathered company.

Eliza remained in the doorway. It took only a moment to assure herself that all the guests were present and accounted for, but still she lingered.

Inside, old friends greeted one another, and new acquaintances were introduced. Listening to the affectionate welcomes and pleasant laughter, Eliza felt a familiar ache. Although she had planned this party for months—painstakingly arranging the menus, designing the decorations, and preparing the activities—she was not to be a part of it. Not really. Her role was to remain invisible, solve problems, and allay worries so the guests could fully enjoy the festivities. She wondered what it would be like to step inside and be welcomed, embraced by people who cared about her. In her thoughts, she had experienced myriad scenarios, from simply holding a plate of pastries while she gossiped to wearing a full-skirted ball gown and spinning around in a waltz. But all of that was in her imagination. And she remained, as always, outside of the doorway with her clipboard, watching and pretending her heart didn't long to be a part of it.

She drew in a deep breath and then exhaled, pushing those thoughts away. There was work to be done.

She took the pencil from her clipboard and made a small mark next to each of the names as she identified the corresponding person in the parlor. From Cassie's greeting in the entry hall, Eliza was already certain of Mrs. Wilcox, the widow from Somerset. Her daughter, Imogene, sat in a corner with Cassie and another young woman Eliza believed to be Miss Madeline Lind.

She studied the young ladies for a moment.

Cassie poured tea and chatted happily with the others, the picture of a gracious hostess.

Miss Lind took a sip and frowned at her cup, as if unsure what she had tasted, before setting it on the table. She was very slender, with blonde hair, wide eyes, and a small mouth that seemed to naturally purse in a frown, as if she were perpetually displeased.

The other young lady, Miss Imogene Wilcox, had beautiful fawn-like brown eyes surrounded by lashes so dark that they were noticeable even from a distance. Miss Wilcox seemed to be less at ease than the other women, her gaze darting around the room as she sipped her tea.

Two men stood near the hearth. Reverend Bramwell, apparent by his clerical collar, set his teacup on the mantel and clasped his hands behind his back as he listened to the other man, who must be Mr. Lind. The latter gentleman had a round belly and a thick mustache, which he wiped with a napkin between sips of tea.

Eliza made a mark next to both men's names. The Bramwells must have arrived while she was upstairs.

In the center of the room, Mrs. Stanton was introducing her son to the matrons of the group. In spite of his earlier reluctance to join the party, Mr. Stanton managed to conceal his discomfort. Mrs. Wilcox, Mrs. Lind, and Mrs. Bramwell all smiled as they asked questions, offered pastries, and giggled at every word Mr. Stanton said. By their scrutinizing stares, Eliza guessed that the women were sizing him up. And from their glances toward the younger women in the corner, their reasoning was apparent. The Misses Lind and Wilcox were here as prospective matches.

The realization needled Eliza. This reaction surprised her, but as she considered the reason for it, she decided it was because she'd seen Mr. Stanton's discomfort at the situation. The stiff way he stood with his mother and the other women was not at all an indication of his true nature. If they had heard his laughter and his jovial recitations with his sister while they'd descended the stairs earlier that afternoon, they would have an entirely different conception of the man. Eliza wondered, if the women had been in the entryway this morning, whether his behavior would have improved or damaged their perceptions of him.

How had it affected her own? If she were to be entirely honest, she preferred the happy version of Mr. Stanton. Even with the mess his exuberance had caused.

She had remained long enough. She made the final tallies on her guest list and started toward the suite of rooms on the other side of the entry hall. There were only a few hours until the Theatrical Salute to Christmas Future was to begin, and the performers had not yet arrived. There were last-minute decorations to see to, and when she'd last checked, the stage curtains were still not working properly. At least she did not have to worry about the food. Mrs. Donovan and her staff were entirely capable.

Someone called her name. She turned to see Mrs. Stanton approaching from the parlor.

"Is everything all right?" Eliza asked.

"Quite so." Mrs. Stanton's eyes twinkled. "The guests are delighted with the Christmas decor, and the tea is delicious." Her expression became more serious. "However, Miss Lind informs me that she simply cannot abide pastries unless they were made by a French chef." Her brow ticked, but that was the only indication the young woman's criticism irritated her. "Would you please ask Mrs. Donovan to send in some bread and maybe fruit?"

"Of course." Eliza jotted down the request. "And I will make certain there are options served at the other meals that will be more . . . agreeable to Miss Lind." Eliza had met plenty of Miss Linds among high Society, and the request did not surprise her in the least.

"Thank you," Mrs. Stanton said. A small frown pulled at her mouth. "And there is another thing." She glanced back and then stepped closer, speaking in a softer voice. "One of the guests, Miss Wilcox, is a bit . . . skittish."

Like a horse? Eliza was uncertain how to respond. "She . . . is . . . skittish?"

"Very." Mrs. Stanton nodded. "Her mother worries that she might be frightened by tonight's performance."

"I see," Eliza said. "You may tell Mrs. Wilcox to rest assured. The actors are aware that children will also be present and have prepared their dramatizations accordingly. While there will be ghosts in the tales, none will be malicious. I will remind the performers once they arrive." She made a note on her clipboard.

"I should have known you would have it managed." Mrs. Stanton gave a relieved smile. "We are all very excited for this evening. My guests are especially looking forward to having their fortunes told by Madame Sybil." Her eyebrows bounced. She smiled brightly, thanking Eliza again before returning to her guests.

Eliza watched her go. Mrs. Stanton and Cassie had been among her most enjoyable clients. Pleasant, grateful, nondemanding . . . and she was pleased to give all her effort to make this Christmas party exactly what they hoped for.

A moment later, she entered the dining room, halting in the doorway to admire the decor. A black tablecloth covered the table, and matching drapes veiled the windows. Candles and wilted flowers gave the table an eerie feel.

She and the Stantons had decided against a large supper, not wanting to keep the guests awake too late into the night on the day they'd traveled, so a smaller meal would be served here this evening. The gas lamps would be extinguished, leaving the candlelight as the only illumination.

Eliza followed the sounds of voices into the adjoining sitting room. The small table for the fortune teller was at one side of the room, and chairs were arranged in a row at the other, facing a raised platform that would serve as the stage.

The troupe of performers had arrived and were organizing their props and costumes. Eliza found the person she assumed to be their leader. "Mr. Carleton?"

"Call me Ben," the man said, sweeping off his hat and giving a bow. He was slender with wispy hair and a coat that appeared to be held together with different-colored patches. "You mus' be Miss Hopewell."

"Yes."

"Marvelous scenery you have 'ere, miss." He hooked a thumb toward the backdrop she'd commissioned, which was leaning against the wall behind the makeshift stage. The painted scene portrayed a darkened cemetery beneath a moon nearly completely shrouded by fog. A lone jackdaw stood on one of the crumbling gravestones.

"Thank you, Ben." She would make certain to convey his compliment to the artist. "Have you and your troupe been shown to your accommodations?"

"Aye, that we 'ave." He put his hands on his hips, looking up at the chandelier. "Fine place, this. And the beds are much better than our usual drafty barn. Housekeeper even invited us to supper in the kitchen."

The other troupe members nodded their appreciation.

"I'm glad." Eliza checked her list. "And Madame Sybil arrived with you?"

Ben grimaced, sharing a look with another member of the troupe. "Afraid I've a bit o' bad news on that front, Miss Hopewell. Madame Sybil has taken a fever. Sick in bed, she is. Left her behind in Bermondsey to recover with 'er ma. Thought she'd 'ave sent word."

"She did not." Eliza frowned. Why was this the first she was hearing of the fortune teller's illness? "Another of you will need to take her place."

"'Fraid not." Ben motioned to the men with him. "We're an all-male troupe, you see, miss."

A flare of panic lit in Eliza's chest, but she did not allow it to take hold. This was just another complication that she would have to surmount. A glance at the clock and then at her own timepiece told her she had over three hours before supper would be finished. Surely in that time she could find a replacement for Madame Sybil.

Chapter Three

Arthur squinted as he cut into the meat on his plate. It was difficult to make out in the dim candlelight, but he believed it was pork. The chunks in the gravy gave him pause . . . were they mushrooms? He wished he'd brought the spectacles from his laboratory, but he hadn't considered that he might need them for something as habitual as eating supper.

The other diners all appeared to be eating and chatting without any trouble. He listened to their conversations, wishing again for his spectacles as he buttered a piece of bread. At least, he hoped it was butter.

"Is this not thrilling, Imogene?" Mrs. Wilcox asked her daughter. "Dinner by candlelight!"

The young woman she was speaking to sat on Arthur's left side and had been particularly quiet since the meal began.

"You know I do not like to be frightened, Mother," Miss Wilcox replied in a loud whisper. "And this ambiance is . . . macabre."

Arthur picked up his glass, sniffing to make certain he was not surprised by the taste when he took a drink. He glanced toward his other side, where Miss Lind sat. She was picking carefully through the food on her plate, holding up each bite to study it before allowing it into her mouth. He wondered whether she, too, was having difficulty seeing in the darkened room.

Sitting next to Miss Lind was Cassie. She caught his gaze, utter delight twinkling in her candlelit eyes. His irritation with the presentation of the meal lifted. Fumbling blindly through his dinner was worth every moment if it made her this happy.

He imagined his sister and the stern Miss Hopewell planning the decor and was surprised to find himself much more kindly disposed to the woman. From what he'd seen so far, the arrangements she'd made must have taken up quite a lot of time and effort. He glanced toward the doorway, wondering whether she might be near, but of course, he couldn't see anything in the darkened room.

Arthur returned his attention to the table. Knowing he was expected to form an acquaintance with the young ladies, he considered what he might say. Small talk was not his strong point. But Cassie was close enough that she could smooth things over should he bungle a conversation.

"Miss Wilcox," he began, turning to the brown-eyed woman. "I understand your father breeds racehorses. Do you ride?"

The young lady's eyes widened, and she pressed her palm against her breastbone. "Goodness me, no," she said. "It is far too dangerous. The animal could spook and rear up. There is no telling what might happen."

"Ah, I see," he said. "You are wise to exercise caution in that regard."

"Do you know whether this hollandaise sauce was made with white pepper?" Miss Lind asked.

She did not look up from her plate, so Arthur wasn't sure whom she was asking. He glanced at Cassie, hoping for some sign as to whether or not he should respond.

"I do not know," Cassie answered. "I can inquire of the cook if you would like."

"I cannot abide hollandaise sauce with anything other than white pepper," Miss Lind said, putting down her fork.

Cassie motioned a server over and whispered to him.

Mrs. Wilcox elbowed her daughter, motioning with her chin toward Arthur.

He pretended not to notice.

"Do you ride, Mr. Stanton?" Miss Wilcox asked.

"Infrequently," he said. "But I do enjoy it when I do so."

"I do not care for it," Miss Lind said, shaking her head. "My riding habit makes my neck and wrists itch." She wrinkled her nose. "And horses have such an odor."

The server returned and whispered to Cassie, who reported that the hollandaise sauce was indeed made with white pepper.

Hearing it, Miss Lind returned to her scrutiny of her dinner, taking the occasional bite and looking displeased each time she did.

At last, dessert was served. Even in the poor lighting, Arthur recognized Mrs. Donovan's famous chestnut pudding. The dish was one of his favorites.

Miss Lind took a small bite, then pushed her plate away. If she had been his sister, Arthur would have taken it and eaten her portion as well. But he restrained himself, resolving to visit the kitchen later tonight for another serving.

Cassie leaned forward, speaking to all within earshot. "Did Mother tell you a fortune teller is in attendance this evening? Madame Sybil." She looked between the others with excited eyes. "We shall all have our futures foretold." Her smile was contagious, and even though Arthur could not think of an instance when the expression *bah humbug* was more appropriate, he smiled back at his sister.

Miss Wilcox gasped. "What if we learn a horrible accident is to befall one of us? Or an early and painful demise?"

Cassie blinked, her smile falling away, and the candlelight made the worried furrows in her brows look even deeper. "I don't think . . ." She glanced at her brother.

"It is just a lark," he said. "An entertaining diversion."

"Yes, you mustn't be worried," Cassie said. "There is nothing to be afraid of. Madame Sybil is very respectable."

Arthur met his sister's gaze and lifted his brow in question. *Respectable?*

She gave a small shrug meant only for him and continued telling the others about the entertainment for the evening.

The women withdrew, presumably to have their fortunes told, and Arthur breathed a sigh of relief, accepting a glass of port. Once the door between the rooms was closed, leaving only the men, he instructed the candles to be extinguished and the gas lamps lit.

Mr. Lind and Reverend Bramwell remained in their seats at the other end of the table.

"Another delicious dinner," the reverend said, raising his glass. "I shall convey my gratitude to Mrs. Donovan."

"Our cook is from France," Mr. Lind said. "My wife insisted upon it. In truth, I cannot discern a difference in the food quality—only the expense." He shook his head and took a long drink before setting his glass on the table and turning in his seat toward Arthur. "I understand you took a journey to South America, Mr. Stanton."

"Two years ago," he said with a nod. "A zoological expedition to Margarita Island."

"And you continue to conduct research of your own here?" the reverend asked, although Arthur was certain the man knew the answer. He was obviously forwarding the conversation.

"Yes," he said. "But, of course, I prefer to study creatures in their natural habitats rather than in manufactured environments. I hope to travel to Brazil to continue my research."

Mr. Lind's brow lowered, and he pursed his lips. "Much better to remain safely on British soil."

Arthur did not like the disapproval in the man's tone. Clearly, he couldn't understand the importance of the work Arthur and other zoologists were doing. "There is much to be learned about the fauna of the region. Millions of species remain undocumented."

"But what of your duties to your home and family?" Mr. Lind asked. "You should be worried about finding a wife, producing an heir, leaving a legacy. Or do you expect to leave a family for months on end to go traipsing around the jungle? It is a foolish notion, if you ask me."

Arthur's face was hot with indignation. Of course he'd considered such things. But to be expected to forgo his own interests for a life he may or may not one day have felt unjust.

"I—" he began.

"There is plenty of time for that, my friend," Reverend Bramwell interrupted, giving him a kindly smile. "No need to rush into anything. And a person can always make new decisions should circumstances change."

Arthur's frustration cooled, and he nodded to the reverend. He tipped back his head, emptying his glass and setting it on the table, and then pushed himself to his feet. "The ladies will be expecting us." He glanced at his pocket watch. "The dramatic presentation should begin any moment."

The reverend stood as well. "Oh, I do love a good ghost story."

Mr. Lind rose without saying anything. His displeasure was unmistakable.

The men entered the adjoining room, pausing in the doorway. It took a moment for Arthur's eyes to adjust to the sparse lighting. All of the usual furniture had been pushed to the walls. On the far side of the room, candles and hanging lanterns illuminated a raised stage. The Linds' two boys and an older woman who must be their nanny stood next to the stage, enthralled by a man in a colorful coat who performed tricks with a coin. Another of the troupe joined him, tossing up bits of cloth, which turned into juggling balls as soon as he caught them. The boys clapped their hands.

The two men with Arthur crossed the room to join their wives, who sat on chairs facing the stage. Arthur's mother sat with them.

From the corner of the room, Cassie caught his gaze, waving him over. She and the other two young ladies crowded around a small table with only one candle, where Mrs. Wilcox and a woman with a scarf over her hair sat facing one another. This must be the famous Madame Sybil. Arthur was skeptical of divination, mediums, ghosts, and any other supposed supernatural elements, but curiosity compelled him to at least observe.

He arrived at the table just as Mrs. Wilcox rose.

"I can't believe it," the woman told Arthur. "Madame Sybil saw straight into my soul." She gaped, looking back at the others. "She knew that I have a fondness for puppies and that my favorite flowers are roses." Mrs. Wilcox took her daughter's hand and pulled her closer to Arthur. "She told me the deepest desire of my heart: to see my only child happy. Now, how else would she know that if spirits from beyond didn't tell her?"

"I do not know," Arthur said, having no other answer. At least, no other answer that would not insult his guest.

Miss Lind joined them. "She knew I harbor a secret. I have many, of course, but last summer, Lenora Caldwell confided in me that she has developed an affection for Stephen Fortescue. I'm sure that is what Madame Sybil meant."

"And she told me that I will find happiness at the end of a journey," Miss Wilcox said. "She must be referring to the London Season. My cousin Molly is to have her debut this year, and I will be very happy to see her."

Her mother nodded, still holding her daughter's hand. "I believe you're right, my dear."

Arthur opened his mouth to point out that all of these predictions were deliberately vague and could apply to anyone, but he stopped when Cassie took his arm. His sister had a strange smile, one that implied she knew something he didn't.

"Arthur, it is your turn," she said.

He didn't protest, and as he was not eager to join Mr. Lind in the audience chairs, he allowed his sister to draw him to the table. While he sat, Cassie watched him, as if waiting for something.

Arthur sighed. He turned to the fortune teller. "Madame Sybil, I presume?"

Now that he was closer, he saw that not only was a silk scarf wrapped around her head, but large hoop earrings dangled beneath it as well. The shawl draped around her shoulders reminded him of a tablecloth.

"Yes." She spoke in a breathy voice that had a singsong lilt to it. "I am Madame Sybil. Have you come to commune with spirits from the beyond?" She kept her head bowed, and the candlelight cast her face into shadow.

Arthur gave Cassie a flat look. But seeing her encouraging nod, he confirmed in an equally flat voice that he had indeed come to commune with spirits from the beyond.

Madame Sybil extended her hand, and Arthur placed his own in it. The instant their skin touched, a charge jolted through him.

Madame Sybil gasped. She had felt it too.

She looked back down quickly, and Arthur fought to steady his breath, trying to make sense of what had happened. The reaction must have been a result of electromagnetism produced by the friction of his shoes on the rug. But that reasoning did not fully explain why his skin continued to tingle, nor why his heartbeat had sped up. For an instant, he wondered if it might have to do with the woman's cosmic powers, but he dismissed that inane notion immediately.

Madame Sybil turned his hand over, holding it while her fingers straightened his, spreading them out to make his palm flat. Arthur watched with fascination as her fingertips moved over the lines of his palm. "A stranger will arrive and change everything," she said in her lilting voice. She traced another line. "And you will lose something important."

"Will I find it?" He tried to sound skeptical, but in truth, he did not want her to release his hand.

"Perhaps," she said. Her fingers had stopped moving, and she rested her palm flat against his. "Or perhaps, instead, you will find something you cherish even more."

Heat radiated from his palm, and his heart pounded. He realized his breathing had stopped and drew in a sharp breath.

Madame Sybil pulled her hands away, ducking her head again.

"Ah, well, perhaps," Arthur said, trying to dispel the intensity of the moment. When had it become so hot in here? He tugged at his collar, which was suddenly too tight.

Cassie took his arm, pulling him from the table toward the stage on the other side of the room. "Is it not amusing?" she asked.

Arthur cleared his throat. "What? The fortune teller? Clearly, you can see through that phony blather."

Cassie leaned close, whispering into his ear. "It was Miss Hopewell."

Arthur stopped walking. He looked back at the little table, but the candle was extinguished, and the fortune teller was gone. "Miss Hopewell is Madame Sybil?"

Cassie put a hand over his mouth, glancing around to make certain none of the guests had overheard before she pulled it back. "Wasn't she wonderful?"

Arthur rubbed his hands. The tingling in his palm was faint, but it remained. The sensation stirred his anger. He had been deceived. He scanned the room, but she was not there. He took his seat, ready for the show to begin, but the anger did not dissipate. Miss Hopewell had some explaining to do.

Chapter Four

THE FOLLOWING DAY, ELIZA CRUNCHED through the snow, moving back to a distance where she could take in the view of the gazebo. Under her direction, the footmen had hung evergreen boughs and other greenery beneath the eaves of the stone structure. Holly wound up each column, interspersed with berries and red velvet bows.

Inside the gazebo, chairs and tables were arranged, the seats covered with cushions and fur blankets so spectators would have a comfortable place to enjoy warm refreshment while watching the ice skaters on the pond.

A small distance away, an outdoor oven was neatly screened behind a clump of trees, and stacks of firewood sat beside it, ready for use. The serving staff were arranging dishes on a preparation table nearby.

Distant sleigh bells jingled, and Eliza checked her timepiece. The party would arrive right on time. She cast a critical gaze around for a final inspection. The air was cold, but the sun was out, making the fresh snow sparkle. The pond shone like smooth glass. The scene could have come straight from a Christmas card.

She gave a satisfied nod and joined the servants in the trees, out of sight but ready to attend to any need. The oven warmed the area around it, and Eliza was glad the staff would be comfortable as they prepared refreshments. Although she would not be able to hear the guests' conversations when they arrived at the gazebo, it should be easy enough for Eliza to understand what was happening based on their body language and a bit of lip-reading.

The first sleigh arrived, carrying the Lind family. As soon as the horses halted, the two young boys bounded from the sleigh, rushing toward the pond. Eliza was impressed at the nanny's speed as she caught up with the lads and practically carried them to the gazebo. In only a few minutes, with the staff's help, the twins and their nanny were outfitted with skates, mittens, scarves, and hats, and they made their way out onto the ice.

The second and third sleighs drew to a halt, and the drivers and gentlemen helped the ladies alight.

Mr. Stanton climbed from his seat and assisted his mother as she stepped down onto the snow. Eliza had not seen him since the night before, when she'd held his hand across the small table, and the memory of it made her neck and cheeks go hot. Something strange had happened in that moment, something she could not entirely explain away no matter how much she'd tried. At his touch, a burst of energy had sent chills up her arms. Her heart had raced, and her mind had emptied. Eliza did not believe in magic or anything of a supernatural nature, but for this, she could not come up with a rational explanation.

She looked away from Mr. Stanton, watching Cassie instead. Upon seeing the decorated gazebo, the young lady clasped her hands together, grinning so brightly that Eliza couldn't help but smile too. She felt a great fondness for Cassie and her enthusiasm.

The reverend and his wife put on skates and were soon skating arm in arm slowly around the pond. Mr. and Mrs. Lind skated as well, apparently oblivious to their young twins, who fluctuated between tearing across the pond to escape their nanny or being comforted by the woman when they fell.

Inside the gazebo, Mrs. Stanton, Miss Lind, Mrs. Wilcox, and Miss Wilcox had taken seats, covering themselves with blankets. A server crossed the snow toward them with a tea tray.

Cassie laced up her skates, and her brother stood on the gazebo stairs. He appeared to be deciding whether to skate with her or remain with the women. His mother said something and motioned to a chair, but he did not sit, looking at Cassie. She waved him off, moving carefully to the edge of the pond and accepting Reverend Bramwell's assistance to step onto the ice.

Mr. Stanton hesitated a moment longer, watching his sister. Then he turned back, appearing to sigh as he stepped beneath the gazebo roof and took a seat.

Eliza had spent only a few moments with the young ladies the night before as she told their fortunes, and that was more than enough. She felt a burst of pity at the man's situation, and resentment that he should be expected to entertain such women when he clearly wished to spent time with his sister.

Eliza shook her head as if to dislodge the thoughts. What had gotten into her? Why were her thoughts becoming so consumed by a family she hardly knew? Perhaps the lack of sleep these past few days was responsible for her unpredictable reactions. She disciplined her feelings back to neutral and returned to the serving table for her clipboard. Tonight was the Feast of Christmas Present—the occasion she had felt most anxious about. The Stanton women had such high hopes for the meal, and she'd worried it would live up to neither her employers' expectations nor her own exacting plans.

But once she'd met the cook and housekeeper, Eliza's worries had turned out to be unfounded. Mrs. Donovan and Mrs. Frasier were creative and hard-working and capable, and Eliza had never known staff to go to such effort even when it meant more work for themselves. If the two women had not already been happily employed, she would want them to come work with her. They had understood her ideas immediately and built upon them, transforming this house party into something even more spectacular than she alone could have done.

Eliza tapped her pencil absently on the clipboard, looking back in the direction of the manor. She knew that right now, Mrs. Donovan, Mrs. Frasier, and their staff were cooking, polishing silverware, arranging furniture, and pressing linens. By the time she returned to the house, the majority of the work would be finished.

Two hours later, after the guests had had their fill of ice skating and merry discussions over tea, the sleighs departed, and the staff set to work. Footmen loaded the furniture into a wagon and drove it back to the manor, and servers packed up the dishes and remaining food. Eliza untied bows and helped take down the greenery, which they would reuse tonight for the feast. In only a few moments, everything was boxed up and ready to be hauled back to the manor house. But instead of waiting for the empty wagon to return, the remainder of the staff started back on foot, carrying the smaller boxes, and Eliza was left alone.

She finished tidying up the area, returning a forgotten mitten to the basket with the ice skates and adjusting the boxes of pine boughs. She sat on the gazebo stairs, which had been cleared of snow, and straightened the skates in their baskets, making certain each had a mate. One brown pair—they may have been the skates Cassie had worn—appeared to be her size. Eliza took a skate from the basket, straightening the laces. She considered it for a moment, and then, on impulse, she slipped it and its mate on before heading to the pond.

She had to waddle a bit before she was confident in her balance. It had been years since she'd skated. A moment later, she was gliding across the ice. The rush of wind on her face was cold, but after all the time spent beside the outdoor oven, it felt refreshing. The only sounds were the scrapes of her blades on the smooth ice. She closed her eyes, spreading her arms to the sides and feeling completely unburdened, if only for the moment.

Reaching the far side of the pond, she turned, following the shore in the paths left by the other skaters' blades. As she neared the gazebo again, she saw a figure. The wagon must have returned with the footmen, ready for the next load. Eliza considered, then decided she could make one more circuit of the pond before she would be needed, but as she neared, the figure stepped out onto the ice and skated toward her. It was Mr. Stanton.

He caught up to her, slowing to match her speed. "Good afternoon, Miss Hopewell." She couldn't quite decipher his tone, but it was not warm. Distracted, perhaps.

Eliza widened the space between them, fearing a brush of his hand would have the same effect as it had the night before. "Good afternoon, Mr. Stanton." Her voice was a bit breathless from the exercise. "You've returned."

"The opportunity to skate passed me by earlier," he said. He slid smoothly around a turn.

Eliza's turn was more of a shuffle, and she adjusted her weight awkwardly, then pulled her arms close to her sides.

"In truth," he said, once they were back on a straight path, "there is something about which I would speak to you."

"Oh yes?" Eliza was surprised. But, of course, it was not unusual for a host to make a request; she was simply accustomed to discussing such things with his mother or sister. She hoped it was not a complaint about his costume. Altering it or finding a new one at this stage would be difficult. She glanced at her companion, her stomach tightening when she saw his grim expression.

"I find myself questioning your intentions, Miss Hopewell."

"My intentions?" Worry and defensiveness rose up inside her. "Are you speaking of my borrowing your sister's skates?"

"No," he said. His voice had chilled considerably. "I am speaking of your deception of my mother and her guests."

"I beg your pardon?" Indignation heated her voice. How could he accuse her of such a thing when she had worked tirelessly for weeks to ensure this house party was everything the Stantons had hoped for? "In what way have I deceived anyone?"

"In posing as Madame Sybil," he said. "I know the fortune teller was you." He was watching her now.

Eliza was incensed at the ignorance of his accusation. "Of course it was me," she said. "I learned only yesterday afternoon that the real Madame Sybil was ill. And knowing how your mother and Cassie were looking forward to the palm reading, I took her place so as not to disappoint them." She wanted to give a haughty look, but as they were at another curve, she kept her eyes on the ice in front of her. "I told Mrs. Stanton of the plan before dinner, and she wholeheartedly agreed to it."

From the corner of her eye, she saw him look toward her. "Mother knew?"

"She did. And Cassie. I do not know which of the others, if any, they told."

He was quiet for a moment as he glided around another curve. "I did not know that."

"Perhaps you should have asked." This time Eliza did look at him, narrowing her eyes to show him that she did not appreciate his reproach.

Mr. Stanton nodded, but he did not appear to be regretful in the least for his accusation. "I am wary of charlatans," he said. "My mother is very trusting. I worry she could be easily taken advantage of."

Eliza didn't answer. Her muscles were unused to skating, and her legs ached. She measured the distance to the gazebo, wishing they were closer.

"What did you tell the guests? My family?" Mr. Stanton asked. "As the fortune teller, I mean."

The tone of accusation was gone from his voice, and now it seemed there was only curiosity, which made Eliza angry. How dare he reproach her unjustly, then simply pretend it hadn't happened! "I told them what I thought a fortune teller would say," she said. The skates were rubbing her ankles, and she predicted there would be blisters. "Simple things. I was careful to neither give offense nor inspire fear. But it was all nonsense."

"So you are telling me I will *not* lose something important and then find something I will cherish even more?"

Eliza glanced at him again, and her anger grew. "If you accuse people without cause, sir, and then neglect an apology, you *will* lose friendships. But I do not think you will easily find them again."

Mr. Stanton's head turned toward her, and she saw the moment realization dawned. "Oh, Miss Hopewell, I did not mean to—"

Eliza drove herself forward with a mighty push. She did not believe the injured party should have to request an apology.

Mr. Stanton caught up to her easily. "I was only concerned for my family," he said. "It was not my intention to offend. I did not think how my words would be received." He reached out, his fingers brushing her elbow. "Please accept my apo—"

Eliza pulled her arm away from his touch, but the movement, combined with her speed, threw her off-balance. She threw out her arms, attempting to correct herself and, in the process, struck Mr. Stanton in the chest. He caught her elbow, spinning her toward him as his other arm went around her waist.

Still sliding, Eliza grasped his lapels, holding on tightly as she fought to straighten out her skates and put her weight back on her feet.

"Steady on, Miss Hopewell." He held her against him until she regained her footing.

Once the panic had abated, Eliza lifted her gaze to find Mr. Stanton watching her. His brows were furrowed in concern. He was so close, and the way he held her was practically an embrace. Her face erupted in heat. Still clinging to his jacket for support, she scooted herself back, making space between them. She kept her gaze averted downward as she let go of his jacket and turned toward the edge of the pond. Mr. Stanton kept a hand at her waist as he led the pair of them to the side of the pond.

Eliza's muscles trembled, and her heart beat heavily. Her near-fall must have shaken her more than she thought.

"Are you quite all right?" Mr. Stanton asked, holding her arm as she stepped from the ice into the snow.

"Yes." Eliza's cheeks flamed with heat. Embarrassment added to her frustration, and she pulled her arm away, twisting from his hold and moving to sit on the gazebo steps.

Mr. Stanton sat next to her and traded out his skates for his low boots.

Eliza bent down to remove her own skates, but her gloves and shaking hands made the task impossible. She fumbled with the laces, wishing the man would just leave so her nerves could settle.

Seeing her struggle, Mr. Stanton knelt in front of her, untying the knots and loosening the laces. "Where did you learn to skate, Miss Hopewell?"

She wanted to tell him to go away, that she was perfectly capable of managing her own footwear. But a part of her wanted to remain, to allow him to perform the courtesy. "London," she said after a moment.

Mr. Stanton held a hand beneath her calf as he drew off a skate.

She didn't dare meet his gaze. He was simply being a gentleman, she reminded herself. She'd seen him assisting Cassie with her skates; this was no different. Eliza kept talking, trying to act as if she were not reacting to his touch. "The Thames froze a few times when I was young, and my cousin taught me." She did not add that it was a *very* few times. Mr. Stanton could no doubt tell by her lack of skill that she had not skated often.

He drew off the other skate, taking the sock with it. The cold air hit her bare toes, and Eliza snatched it from him and pulled it back on. She wondered whether the day could possibly get any more mortifying.

Once both skates were removed and sitting in the basket with the other pairs, Mr. Stanton set her boots beside her on the step and retook his seat next to her.

"I often speak hastily, Miss Hopewell," he said, clasping his gloved hands in his lap. "It is a fault of mine. I should not rush to a conclusion when I do not know all of the facts, but I am afraid when it comes to my family, I am very protective."

Eliza slipped her feet into her boots and fastened the buttons. Mr. Stanton being present while she did so felt intimate, and the private conversation only served to make it more so. She was glad when the sound of the wagon returning gave her an excuse to turn her attention away from him. She stood and dusted the snow off her clothes. "Thank you for your assistance." Her voice sounded strange, echoing in her ears. She cleared her throat.

"I should not have accused you, Miss Hopewell. Please accept my apology."

"Certainly." She still did not look at him. She picked up a wooden box filled with greenery and started toward the wagon.

Mr. Stanton brought a box as well, and Eliza tried to ignore the crunching of his footsteps and the way the warmth had dissipated when he was no longer sitting beside her.

Chapter Five

For Arthur, surviving the Feast of Christmas Present was a triumph of endurance. He found himself seated, again, between Miss Lind and Miss Wilcox, fumbling to find topics of conversation that would fend off the awkwardness of eating a meal in close proximity with near-strangers. Thank goodness for Cassie. Somehow his sister always knew precisely what to say, a talent that Arthur found more elusive with each passing day.

In spite of the discomfort of socialization, Arthur had to admit the feast was spectacular. Mrs. Donovan had quite outdone herself. She and the kitchen staff had prepared course after course, each unveiled to cheers by the diners, and all of it delicious. The dining room was entirely transformed from the night before; instead of a macabre darkness, the gas lamps burned brightly, illuminating displays created from every sort of food imaginable. A table in the corner of the room was piled high with cakes, pies, pastries, sweetmeats, and other confectioneries. Bowls and baskets overflowing with fruit covered the center of the dining table, surrounded by greenery and berries. Among them were platters of varying kinds of roasted poultry, sausages, and hams.

Arthur did not think it could all possibly be real, as he'd voiced to Cassie. She, grinning in delight, had whispered to him that, indeed, some of the cakes were actually frosted boxes, and much of the fruit was made of wax. "However, there is still more than enough actual food to satisfy the hungriest of diners," she added.

When the young Lind twins had entered, their eyes had gone wide and their mouths had dropped open in amazement as they gawked at the abundance surrounding them. Arthur could not blame the lads—he'd reacted similarly.

In spite of a meal that Arthur considered to be complete culinary perfection, Miss Lind still found reason to complain. The potatoes had too much salt, the pastry fillings were too sweet, and her soup was too hot. Arthur spent a moment explaining about the displacement of water vapor that occurs by blowing on liquid, thus bringing down its temperature, but the young woman wasn't interested.

Miss Wilcox did not complain about the food, but she returned more than once to the topic of the dramatic production the evening before, lamenting that the tales of ghosts had left her unable to sleep. Cassie took it all in stride, but Arthur thought it must bother her that the other young women constantly found fault with the things she had so carefully planned. He appreciated anew how much effort his mother, Cassie, and Miss Hopewell had given to the party.

The thought of Miss Hopewell brought the memory of her slip on the ice. Arthur had held her in his arms for just a moment, and in her eyes, he'd seen panic and the fear that she would fall. He'd had to stop himself from holding her close to his chest and whispering words of comfort. Such an action would most certainly have had the opposite effect than the one intended. Especially since he'd just insulted the woman.

There had even been an instant when he'd imagined kissing her. Arthur's face heated just thinking of it. Such an impulse was not one a gentleman ought to entertain. But even now, he could not entirely erase the thought.

He remembered how their hands had touched the night before, in the candlelight of the fortune teller's table. Had Miss Hopewell felt the surge of energy between them, or had he been mistaken before? And even if she had at one time possessed amiable thoughts toward him, he was certain he'd snuffed them out with his accusation. And his clumsy apologies had only made things worse.

Throughout the meal he glanced often at the doorway, occasionally losing the thread of the conversation as he thought—or, rather, hoped—that he might catch a glimpse of Miss Hopewell. She might just offer a smile or some sort of recognition that would assure him that her sore feelings had passed. But he was disappointed—she did not appear. And Arthur felt a twinge of discomfort in knowing that, as an employee, it would not be proper for her to do so.

"Oh, dessert, at last!" Cassie said, clapping her hands. "You will all enjoy this very much."

Her voice brought Arthur's thoughts back to the table. Cassie was grinning as she watched servers bring around trays of various puddings. Arthur's stomach protested at the idea of any more food, but he accepted a slice of cake covered with caramel sauce.

"As I said, I cannot abide a pastry made by any other than a French chef," Miss Lind said, waving away an offered plate.

Cassie's smile did not falter, but her eyes did tighten just a bit.

Once they'd eaten their dessert, the Linds' nanny came to take the twins to their beds.

Arthur watched them go with some jealousy. He glanced at the clock on the mantel, trying not to sigh aloud. He dreaded the hours of small talk that remained before the party would retire for the night. And his dread only increased when he thought of doing it all again tomorrow at the ball. He glanced toward the doorway once more, trying to recover his former train of contemplation. He had been thinking of Miss Hopewell. And just as he remembered, he asked himself why it was that he thought of her so often.

* * *

Two hours later, the party disbanded. Arthur bid the others good night, but instead of retiring to his bedchamber, he climbed the stairs to his laboratory. Opening the door, he stepped inside and slipped out of his dinner jacket, switching it for the white coat hanging on the peg. He checked the thermometer, relieved that the room had maintained its temperature. He would need to remember to thank Gus. The footman had taken it in hand to keep the fire burning, and he'd even attached a metal arm to the hearth's bricks, where he had hung a copper pot filled with water. This method of creating artificial humidity was simple but effective, and Arthur was pleased at the man's innovation.

He went to the first terrarium, peering through the glass to locate the specimen. The creature was in its usual hiding place inside a hollow log.

Arthur cleared a space on his desk, making room for his brass scales. He hadn't weighed any of the specimens for several days . . . four, at least. The house party had quite disrupted his schedule. He searched another table, next to one of the smaller terrariums, for the ledger where he recorded the specimens' measurements. The paper wasn't there, nor was it beneath the pile of books on the chair in front of his desk. After a few more minutes of searching, he located it atop a bookshelf. Some more searching turned up the ledgers with the feeding dates and quantities.

Arthur found a pencil, and now that his record-taking supplies were in order, he fetched the first specimen. The creature was docile enough to remain on the pan while Arthur added and subtracted counterweights. When the scales were balanced, he recorded the number, noting the very minute increase.

He picked up the specimen in one hand, holding a magnifying glass over it with the other as he studied it. He noted a few spots of thinning hair, a definite sign of growth. In the next week, he expected—

The laboratory door opened, and Miss Hopewell entered. "Mr. Stanton, I am sorry to bother you, but you still have not tried on your—" At the sight of the creature in his hand, her words halted, and she drew in a gasp. "Is that a spider?" Her voice was pitched much higher than her typical tone.

"*Avicularia avicularia*," Arthur said. "Commonly known as a pink-toed tarantula." He watched for the panic Cassie showed when she saw the arachnids, or for Mrs. Frasier's look of disgust. But he saw neither in Miss Hopewell's expression. She appeared wary but also curious.

"Would you like to see it?" Arthur asked. "It is truly a fascinating creature."

Miss Hopewell glanced around the room as if she were assessing whether any other creatures might be hidden away. Then she stepped farther into the laboratory.

"Close the door," he instructed. "It is necessary to maintain a constant temperature."

She did so and crossed to the desk, her gaze steadily on the tarantula.

Arthur gave her the magnifying glass and held the arachnid near the lamp to give her the best view. Miss Hopewell came near enough to see while still maintaining a good distance.

The tarantula crawled to the edge of Arthur's palm, and he rotated his hand as it continued along to the other side. Under the lights, various colors were visible on its abdomen. "Not to fear," he said, keeping his voice calm for both the arachnid's sake and Miss Hopewell's. "She is near to molting, and rather lethargic. She won't jump at you."

"She?" Miss Hopewell asked. Then she darted a look at Arthur. "They can jump?"

"Yes, this particular specimen is a female. And they do jump, but as I said, she will not."

Miss Hopewell took a step closer, learning forward to peer through the magnifying glass. "What does that mean? 'Molting'?"

He let the tarantula crawl into his other hand. "She is growing, so her exoskeleton—the hard exterior—will soon be too small. Arachnids shed their exoskeletons and form new ones."

Her mouth pulled into a small grimace. "Does it—*she*—molt often?"

He nodded, shifting his hands as the creature continued crawling between them. "A few times per year."

"She is so colorful." Miss Hopewell took another step, her stance relaxing a bit. "And her pink toes look like little shoes."

"Definitely one of the more charming varieties."

Miss Hopewell looked up at him now, and he felt as if she were scrutinizing him just as closely as she had the arachnid. "I did not know you were a . . ." She glanced at the tarantula, at the scale, and then back at him, as if searching for the word.

"Naturalist," he said. "I am a student of zoology."

"And of all the creatures on the planet to study, you have chosen spiders?" There was no accusation, but the slightest hint of a tease lightened her voice. Her sudden unguardedness made him feel as if he could be honest—vulnerable, even.

He smiled, shrugging. "I find they are of the most interest to me."

"Why?" Miss Hopewell's eyes were wide, curious. The steel-blue color of her gaze was bright in the lamplight.

He tipped his head, considering as he watched the creature start up onto the cuff at his wrist. "There are thousands and thousands of species of arachnids, living on nearly every corner of the planet. So very little is known about them." He carefully lifted the tarantula from his jacket sleeve. "Most people are either afraid of or repelled by the creatures, associating them with evil or seeing them as a sign of death, but with little reason aside from their appearance or perhaps the strange way they move."

"You believe they are misunderstood," she said.

"I suppose I do."

Miss Hopewell studied his face before her gaze dropped back to the creature in his hands. "What does she eat?"

"Insects," he said. "Crickets in the summer and, in the winter, whatever can be found. One of the footmen, Gus, has taken it upon himself to supply sustenance for the arachnids."

Miss Hopewell tipped her head to the side, and Arthur turned over his hand again to keep track of the pink-toe's explorations.

"Would you like to hold her?" he asked.

Eliza was quiet for a moment, but then she set the magnifying glass and her clipboard on the desk, nodding.

Arthur lifted his brows, surprised. Aside from Gus and a few visiting colleagues, nobody had ever shown the slightest bit of interest in the creatures other than to flee in fear. "Are you not afraid?"

"A little," she said. "But I trust you."

Her words were simple, but their effect, combined with the faith in her eyes, was anything but. Arthur's thoughts flashed to when he'd caught her on the ice. Had she trusted him then too?

"It may shock her if your hands are cold," he said, taking her hand in his free one. Her soft skin was warm to his touch. He nodded. "Now, remain calm. She senses vibrations and may become agitated if you are nervous. If you become frightened, don't jerk or drop her. Just tell me, and I will take her away."

He could feel her hand shaking. Before he could place the tarantula on her palm, she pulled away with a gasp and took a step back. "I'm sorry. I . . ." Her breaths were coming quicker and her face had gone pale. "I just can't."

Arthur nodded, giving a smile that told her he understood.

"I did not mean to disappoint you," she said, her forehead creased in worry. "I really do trust you. It's just . . ." She grimaced, and a shiver went over her as her gaze went back to the tarantula.

"It is not necessary to hold the creature to observe it," he said. In truth, his only disappointment came at the withdrawal of her hand from his.

Now that there were a few feet between herself and the arachnid, Miss Hopewell's forehead relaxed. "I do enjoy watching it."

"That is more than can be said for most of this household," Arthur told her. "Poor Cassie will not even enter the room. One of the tarantulas, a small specimen from Brazil, escaped its enclosure a few months ago, and she was terrified it would drop on her or appear in the bath."

Miss Hopewell shivered again and directed an apprehensive look at the terrariums. "Did you find it?"

"Yes, it was at liberty for only a few hours. And Cassie need not have feared. The creatures will always find a warm, dark place to hide in. Gus located him underneath the sofa."

She glanced toward the sofa and then at the door. "I did not mean to interrupt your work."

"It is a welcome interruption," Arthur said, worried that she would excuse herself. He had always enjoyed the privacy of his laboratory, but surprisingly, he wasn't ready to return to solitude tonight. "Would you like to see the others? They each need to be weighed."

He returned the pink-toed tarantula to its terrarium. Arthur pointed out the thick web at the bottom of the enclosure. "An arachnid will often make a mat when it is near to molting." He wondered whether he was mistaking Miss Hopewell's politeness for interest. But as she hadn't made a visible effort to leave, he continued to explain about the creature, finding it extremely enjoyable to have such an attentive audience. He used a perfume atomizer to spray water onto the plants inside the terrarium, and satisfied, he moved on to the next one.

Miss Hopewell followed, bending down to peer through the glass.

"In here is a Costa Rican zebra tarantula," Arthur said. He searched beneath the table before finding a jar and a lid. "He is smaller than the pink-toe and quite fast moving, so I keep him contained while he is weighed."

He looked through the glass, located the arachnid, and opened the terrarium's cover. After catching the zebra tarantula in the jar and fastening the lid, he offered it to Miss Hopewell.

"Zebra," she said, peering through the jar glass. "Because of his striped pattern."

"Precisely."

They returned to the desk. Miss Hopewell placed the jar carefully on one of the scale's pans, and Arthur located the ledger where he recorded the zebra tarantula's weight. He checked the contents and realized it was outdated. There was a more current version somewhere. He dug through a stack of papers, relieved that it was among them.

"You need a more effective system," Miss Hopewell said.

He nodded, knowing she was right. "I find myself rather caught up in my work," he said, placing counterweights on the scale's other plate. He searched for a pencil before remembering it was behind his ear. "And I lose track of things." He held out the ledger. "Care to do the honors?"

Miss Hopewell took the book, and Arthur pointed to the space where the weight was to be recorded. She made a note of the date and time, and once the zebra tarantula's weight was established, she recorded that as well.

Arthur typically wrote beneath each entry observations about the specimens' general appearance and behavior, but tonight, Miss Hopewell volunteered to take dictation. They settled into a routine until all of the specimens had been observed, weighed, and watered. He took the opportunity to describe each of the arachnids and some of their unique features and behaviors.

Once the final tarantula was in its terrarium, Arthur straightened, rubbing the small of his back. Miss Hopewell had taken the ledgers back to his desk. After transferring the pile of books from the chair to an empty corner of the desk, she sat and flipped through each page of the ledger they'd been working in, making certain all of their work was documented.

"It appears that all of the spiders are due for a meal tomorrow," she said.

"Gus will bring a fresh batch of beetles from the garden compost in the morning."

"You have a sleighride in the morning," she reminded him, yawning. "Do not forget." She set the ledgers in a tidy pile with the pencil and magnifying glass on top, then glanced at the timepiece around her neck. "Oh, I had no idea it was so late." She stood, grabbed her clipboard, and started for the door. "I apologize, Mr. Stanton, I truly did not intend—"

"Miss Hopewell." Arthur caught her by the elbow just as she opened the door.

She turned toward him, her fingers still on the handle.

"You mustn't apologize," he said. He hadn't intended for his voice to drop low, but he spoke seriously, earnestly. It was imperative that she understand. "Your company was welcome—it was more than welcome. It was a gift." He realized he was still holding her arm and loosened his grip. "It is not often that I am afforded the opportunity to share my enthusiasm with such an agreeable party."

Miss Hopewell tipped her head, as if considering what he'd said. "Thank you. I really did enjoy myself." A small smile lifted her cheeks. "I am not often surprised, but seeing you tonight with an enormous spider in your hands . . . it was a shock, to say the least."

"You surprised me as well." Arthur returned the smile. "And I find myself very happy in your company."

"The feeling is shared, Mr. Stanton." Miss Hopewell's color had heightened. Her eyes were bright, and Arthur thought he could stare at them forever. Did anyone else possess eyes of such a stunning gray-blue color? He'd never noticed. His gaze dropped to her lips.

"Good night." Miss Hopewell's voice had softened to hardly more than a whisper. She hesitated, as if she had more to say, but she must have changed her mind. She turned and walked with quick steps down the corridor.

Arthur warched her go, feeling as if he'd been shaken awake and his knees had turned to jelly. He blinked and steadied himself against the doorframe. He scratched his chin, considering the evening, and a delicious warmth spread over him, one that his vast knowledge of science could not explain.

Chapter Six

THE NEXT MORNING, ELIZA WOKE late. She'd been unable to fall asleep for hours after leaving Mr. Stanton's laboratory. Her thoughts would not still, and as much as she wished to blame the room filled with giant spiders, in actuality, her disquiet came not from the creatures but from the man who owned them. The gentle touch of his hand, his earnest explanations of the creatures' behaviors, and the depth of his gaze as his eyes had held hers—they were enough to elevate her heartbeat. It was silly, really, this reaction. And she was frustrated that it was one she could not bring under control.

She dressed and descended to the kitchen, where she ate breakfast as she looked over the list of tasks. In another household, preparing for a ball might be a daunting chore, but Mrs. Donovan and Mrs. Frasier managed their duties and their subordinates effectively. The food preparation was already underway, and the cleaning staff were hard at work polishing woodwork and sweeping floors. They would wait to move furniture and hang decorations until the family and their guests were gone for the day.

Satisfied that the arrangements were well in hand, Eliza set out for the stables to make certain the sleighs were suitably outfitted for the day's excursion. The estate's outbuildings were tucked away from sight, down a hill and past a copse of trees. She walked slowly, enjoying the fresh air. The opportunity to leave behind the coal smoke and noisy streets of London was one she did not experience often. The Stantons' estate was not remote, but on this quiet morning, with only birdsong for company, she could well imagine there was not another person around for miles. She paused before descending the hill, taking in the view. From here, she could see the town's rooftops in the distance, wisps of smoke from chimneys the only indication of inhabitants. She turned slowly. Mr. Stanton and Cassie must have had idyllic childhoods, playing amongst the trees or rowing across the pond. Had Mr. Stanton first developed his interest in crawling things in this very forest?

A coldness washed over her at the thought, a sadness she'd been unprepared for. She was leaving tomorrow, never to return to this place she'd become so fond of in so short a time. The house was well situated, its residents amiable, and a general feeling of happiness exuded throughout the estate. Eliza thought it a nearly perfect home. And Mr. Stanton . . .

She shook her head, bringing her thoughts back to her reason for being there. She was an employee of the household, not a member of the family. It was foolish for her to feel this need to belong.

She continued on down the hill, smiling when a white rabbit bounded across her path. Such a sight was still a delight to a woman who had lived her entire life in a city.

When she reached the stables, she saw that the sleighs and horses she'd engaged were ready for their excursion. Ribbons and wreaths adorned the rears of the conveyances, and sleigh bells hung from the harnesses. Mrs. Stanton and Cassie had been eager to give their guests a tour of the countryside and villages around their home. With the sun shining brightly over a fresh layer of snow, it could hardly have been a more picturesque day for the outing.

Eliza spoke for a moment with the stablemaster, who affirmed that the extra hands she'd retained for the day were already hard at work and, he believed, would be sufficient to tend to the horses and carriages that the ball's guests would bring.

She surveyed the sleighs one last time, making certain there were enough furry blankets inside. Mrs. Frasier had already set bricks by the hearth for the guests to warm their feet during the ride.

For just an instant, Eliza imagined Mr. Stanton standing beside one of the sleighs, holding out his hand to help her step inside. She blinked hard and scolded herself for the thought, frustrated at how easily it had come.

She returned to the house. This time she did not pause to enjoy the scenery or consider the pleasant situation of the manor and its inhabitants. She kept her gaze in front of her and her thoughts firmly on the tasks ahead. Letting them stray would only invite disappointment.

The family and their guests were eating breakfast in the dining room. Eliza slipped past the open door, allowing herself only a quick peek inside as she did.

Mr. Stanton was speaking with Reverend and Mrs. Bramwell. He looked up, his gaze meeting Eliza's for a heartbeat. His eyes twinkled amiably.

She hurried on, hoping nobody would see her blush.

When she stepped into the kitchen, Mrs. Donovan set down the spoon she was holding. "Miss Hopewell, your cheeks are so red—it must be very cold outside." The cook poured a cup of tea and brought it to her.

"Thank you." The notice of her cheeks only made them grow hotter. Eliza took a sip of the tea, looking with especial interest over the lists on her clipboard. "You've sent word to the refreshment room in town with Miss Lind's dining requirements?"

"I have indeed," Mrs. Donovan said, blowing out a breath. "The young lady is certainly . . . particular, isn't she?"

"That is putting it lightly," Eliza said, smiling at the woman. "But take heart. You will have to endure her fastidiousness for only a few more meals."

"Unless she becomes mistress of this house." Mrs. Donovan frowned. "From what I've heard, Mr. Stanton has already requested her company for the first set."

"Has he?" Eliza feigned disinterest, unprepared for how the information stung.

Mrs. Donovan nodded. "And the supper dance with Miss Wilcox." She offered Eliza a tin of biscuits to go with the tea, sighing as she did. "It was his mother's motivation in having a house party, finding the master a wife. But I do wish Mrs. Stanton had friends with more agreeable daughters." She cocked one of her brows, giving a good-natured smirk before returning to the pot she'd been stirring.

Eliza swallowed hard against the lump that pressed inside her throat.

* * *

Later that afternoon, the ring of sleigh bells sounded outside, drawing near as the party returned from their excursion to the village. Footmen opened the front doors, and the company shuffled inside, shivering and chattering. Furs, coats, gloves, scarves, and hats were tossed to waiting servants, and the Stantons and their guests retired to their bedchambers to rest before dressing for the ball.

Eliza watched from the kitchen doorway, glad when they were gone and the house was quiet again. She stepped across the entry hall and into the dining room.

If anyone deserved a nap, it was the staff, who had worked for hours turning the adjoining suite of rooms on the main floor of the manor house into a Christmas paradise. The dining tables were set with candles, greenery, and artfully arranged fruit. Wreaths hung in front of windows and candles were everywhere. Eliza rubbed her hands where pine needles had scratched her skin. Her arms ached from lifting holly boughs and tying endless ribbons, but as she walked through the rooms, admiring the bows, garlands, and artificial snow adorning the space around the dance floor, a swell of pride grew inside her. The spectacle was extravagant and beautiful and entirely worth the months of planning. She straightened a fold in a drape and fluffed up a bow as satisfaction filled her chest.

A gasp sounded in the doorway behind her. Eliza turned to find Cassie walking slowly, almost reverently, into the room. Her hands were clasped in front of her as her gaze traveled around the room. "Oh, Miss Hopewell," she whispered. "It is splendid."

"Thank you," Eliza said, crossing the floor to join the young woman. "I am very pleased with how it all came together."

Cassie continued to stare wide-eyed around the space, taking it all in. A grin spread over her face. "It is so much better than I imagined."

"Come see the rest." Eliza motioned to the adjacent room.

Cassie took her arm as they walked, squeezing it. "Mother said I should nap, but I am much too excited to sleep. I have never attended a ball. And my mind is besotted with foolish romantic imaginings." They stepped into the ballroom, and Cassie sighed. "Miss Hopewell, if there were ever a setting ideal for falling in love, it would be here." She moved to the center of the room and spread her arms, twirling slowly around with her eyes closed.

Eliza couldn't help but smile at the young woman. "I hope the night is simply magical."

Cassie danced to the corner of the room and brushed a hand over the flower arrangement on the refreshment table as she admired it. She looked past the decor, through the window. "I only wish the same for my brother."

Eliza joined her, straightening a few of the punch glasses on the way. "I imagine Mr. Stanton will enjoy himself," she said in a neutral voice. "The Misses Lind and Wilcox seem pleasant enough."

Cassie groaned, then slapped a hand over her mouth. "I beg your pardon, Miss Hopewell. That was very rude of me. But in truth . . . they are so onerous. And I am an awful person for thinking it."

"Not to worry." Eliza patted the young woman's arm reassuringly. "You are only worried for your brother's happiness."

"I am at that. I want him to find love," Cassie said. "He spends so much time alone in his laboratory." She shook her head. "But I would not wish him to settle in order to please Mother. Maybe one of the other ball guests, a woman from town, or . . . well, there will be plenty of young ladies here tonight."

"And plenty of gentlemen for you," Eliza teased, attempting to change the course of the conversation without making herself too obvious.

Cassie's smile returned and her eyes shone. "True. I hope—"

A scream cut off her words. Eliza and Cassie hurried into the entry hall. Mrs. Frasier and a young maid were already there. "Did you hear that?" the maid asked. "Someone must be hurt."

"I think it came from upstairs," Mrs. Frasier said.

As if to confirm her conjecture, the scream came again, and it most certainly originated from above.

Eliza rushed up the stairs, and the other women followed. At the top of the flight, they encountered guests peering from their bedchambers and crowding into the corridor. Confusion and worry clouded every face, and each person was trying to speak over the others. When it was clear that the scream had not originated on this floor, the mass of servants and guests choked the staircase as the group pushed onward to the upper story.

Eliza was buffeted by the crowd as they climbed the steps. At the top level, they paused, and Eliza scanned the corridor. Her gaze landed on the open door of Mr. Stanton's laboratory and the source of the screams. She pushed her way inside with the rest of the crowd close behind, and found Miss Wilcox with her hands covering her eyes. On the other side of the room, Mr. Stanton and a footman stood frozen. The footman held a large glass jar that appeared to be filled with insects, and Mr. Stanton, wearing his white laboratory coat, held a pair of long-handled tongs. A beetle of some kind twitched between the tips of the instrument.

Mrs. Wilcox broke free from the throng and went to her daughter, taking the young woman into her arms.

"Mother, it is horrible. Grotesque." The young woman's words were a shriek.

Mrs. Wilcox patted her daughter's back in an attempt to console her. "There, there, Imogene."

Mrs. Stanton joined them, looking worried. "There is nothing to be afraid of, my dear. Nothing at all." She darted a look at her son.

"How can you live in a house surrounded by such monstrosities?" Miss Wilcox pulled away from her mother to face their hostess. Her face was pale, her hands shaking.

"We may need smelling salts before long," Eliza said to Mrs. Frasier in a quiet voice.

The housekeeper sent the maid away to fetch them.

Eliza stepped farther into the room, staying near the wall and away from the confusion.

"What is the meaning of this?" Mr. Lind asked in his booming voice. He took a few steps into the room and stared between the weeping young woman and the master of the house. He put out his arms, blocking the doorway, as if to protect his family and friends from the dangers within.

Cassie remained in the corridor, peering inside with the rest of the chattering onlookers. She was biting her lip—Eliza couldn't tell whether it was out of fear or amusement.

Miss Wilcox continued to weep as her mother and Mrs. Stanton tried to comfort her. Miss Lind and her little brothers argued with their father as they attempted to see around him.

Mr. Stanton's brows were pulled together in a look of dismay. His gaze met Eliza's, and she grimaced in solidarity with his frustration at the invasion of his space.

The Lind twins managed to maneuver past their father and rushed to the pink-toed tarantula terrarium. One of the boys pressed his nose to the glass, and the other attempted to open the latch.

Mr. Stanton gave the tongs and beetle to his assistant and approached the crowd in the doorway. "If you please, these creatures are quite sensitive to vibrations," he said, his voice remarkably steady. "Noise can make them very uncomfortable, and they may behave erratically."

Instead of having the calming effect he was likely hoping for, his words only succeeded in ratcheting up the noise.

"Erratically?" Miss Wilcox shrieked. "Mother, what will they do?"

"They will do nothing if everyone will simply leave the laboratory," Mr. Stanton said. He grasped one of the boy's hands to stop it from tapping on the glass. "And do so quietly, if you don't mind."

The nanny ducked beneath Mr. Lind's arm and took the boys' hands to draw them back. "Theodore, Bernard, come away from there."

"Yes, come along," Mrs. Stanton said, motioning to the boys. "I believe Mrs. Donovan has baked biscuits this afternoon. Doesn't that sound nice?"

The children whooped and bounded after her, the spiders forgotten. Mr. Lind stepped aside to let them through.

While he was distracted, Miss Lind scooted past her father into the room. "Oh, I feel as if they are crawling on my skin!" she cried, apparently tired of Miss Wilcox getting all the attention. She brushed at her arms and shook her skirts.

Mrs. Stanton hesitated, then left Miss Wilcox and came to comfort Miss Lind.

Mrs. Lind, meanwhile, moved behind her husband, one hand on his arm as she peered over his shoulder.

Mr. Lind folded his arms across his chest, his frown making his mustache droop. "This is very poor form, sir." His loud voice silenced the others. "Very poor form indeed. A deception. We have been duped, believing we were invited here to a home when it is in fact . . ." He cast his eyes around as if looking for the right word.

"A horror," Miss Wilcox said.

"Quite so." Mr. Lind nodded.

Mr. Stanton's mouth constricted into a line. "This is my laboratory, sir. My private domain." He kept his voice low, but the anger in his words was apparent. "The door is kept closed. The creatures are contained. You are in no danger here."

"It is unacceptable," Mr. Lind continued as if he hadn't heard the man. "Improper. We could have been attacked—bitten in our sleep by these deadly creatures."

The Misses Wilcox and Lind each put a hand over her mouth, and their mothers both went pale.

"There is no danger whatsoever," Mr. Stanton said. His own skin was flushed, and Eliza was impressed that he could keep his manners under control despite the affronts and betrayal of his privacy. But she could tell that no manner of argument would convince Mr. Lind of anything. It was time for the festivity planner to step in.

Eliza clapped her hands together. "Come along, ladies," she said in a voice that was both cheerful and practical. "You are all in need of a cup of tea and a rest before the ball." She held out her arms, much as Mr. Lind had done moments earlier, but instead of blocking the doorway, she was herding the interlopers toward it.

"Now then," she continued, not leaving any chance for argument as the group started out into the corridor. "Miss Wilcox, is your costume pressed and ready?"

"Yes," the young lady said, shivering as she was shepherded forward. "But I shan't be able to rest knowing those . . ." Her voice trailed off as she flicked her eyes back toward the laboratory.

"Mr. Stanton will close up all of the terrariums and fasten the door," Eliza said. "You will be perfectly safe. And hasn't this adventure heightened the color of your cheeks? You shall both look perfectly lovely this evening." She gave both of the young women a gentle push through the doorway, then turned back to close the door behind her.

As she grasped for the door handle, Mr. Stanton caught her hand instead. "Miss Hopewell, I cannot thank you enough for—"

"You must prepare for the ball as well, sir." Eliza extracted her hand from his. She was tired, both physically and emotionally, and surprised at the rush of anger she felt. "I do hope your costume fits." She gave a quick curtsy and started down the stairs, walking slowly to give herself time to discern the reasons for the emotion.

It took only a moment of analysis to understand. She was angry that the laboratory had been discovered by the house party guests. The late-night rendezvous between herself and Mr. Stanton had felt like something special, a secret she shared with only him. But with the others invading the space, the magic was lost.

She sighed, glancing upward toward the laboratory, which of course she couldn't see. If she were being entirely honest with herself, she had no right to share a secret with the man.

She had been treasuring these moments, these small encounters, storing them away deep in her heart, and of course, it was all foolishness. The entire purpose of the house party and the ball—her entire reason for being here in the first place—was to ensure that Mr. Stanton found a wife. A lady suitable for his station. There would be plenty of women in attendance this evening who fit the bill. And she, a working-class spinster, was not one of them. Though the knowledge was not a surprise, it still stung. She held on to the feeling, facing it head-on and not allowing it to slip away, lest she forget.

Once she'd confronted the truth, Eliza knew her anger was directed neither at Mr. Stanton nor at his guests, but at herself.

Chapter Seven

Arthur stared into the mirror. Dread, heavy and cold, wrapped around him like a wet towel as he took in the full effect of the ill-fitting costume. He was expected down in the entry hall to greet guests straightaway . . . and he looked like a complete fool.

"If the sleeves were too long, we might have folded them," Benson said, frowning at Arthur's wrists, "but there is no time to add length." He tugged on the velvet sleeves, as if doing so might stretch them; the action only served to pull the doublet's already strained buttons across Arthur's chest, creating gaps. The lace-bordered cuffs of the shirtwaist hung at least three inches too long, all but obscuring Arthur's fingertips while making the velvet doublet look even smaller. The breeches seemed to have been made for a person twice Arthur's size. He had to hold on to the waist lest they slip off and join the stockings sagging at his ankles. How had the costumer managed to send some items that were too small and others that were too large?

Benson set to work sticking pins into the waistband. "Take care when you sit, sir."

Arthur lifted his chin, noting the reddened patches on his neck where the starched ruff had already begun to chafe. It didn't seem possible that the day could get any worse, but that was what he'd thought during the sleighride. Listening to one young lady complain about the scratchy furs, the pork served at the refreshment rooms in the town, and the brightness of the sun on the snow while the other worried about bandits or wild animals in the woods had left him feeling wrung out and eager to retreat to the quiet of his laboratory.

Feeding the specimens always brought with it a measure of satisfaction. Watching the arachnids capture their prey was naturally fascinating. And knowing the creatures would continue to grow and thrive in his care as he studied them was immensely gratifying. Not to mention, the pink-toe was close to molting, and he was eager to document the process.

But the calm of his sanctuary had been shattered when Miss Wilcox invaded and screamed and the other guests had quickly followed. Arthur had almost dropped the beetle he had been readying to feed the zebra tarantula.

He rarely became as angry as he'd been this afternoon. A closed door was the opposite of an invitation. What sort of houseguests didn't understand that? If anyone should have received a reprimand, it was Miss Wilcox and rest of the intruders who had so rudely invaded his domain and then accused *him* of indecorum.

He winced, remembering the dismay on his mother's face, and his anger became tinged with shame.

Benson attached a thin cord around the top of the oversized breeches and tied it tight. "That should hold," he said. He tugged down on the doublet and grimaced when he found it too short to cover his handiwork. If Arthur bent over or lifted his arms, the separation would become even more evident. Benson hurried away and returned with Cassie's lady's maid, who brought a basketful of fripperies. Soon a scarf was tied around Arthur's waist, and two ribbons beneath his knees to hold up the loose hose.

Arthur took one look at the slippers that had come with the costume and insisted upon wearing his own shoes. Dancing was difficult enough without his feet being pinched.

From the costumer's box, Benson drew out a soft velvet cap with a large feather, and even the breeding of generations of valets could not prevent the tug of his mouth as he avoided making eye contact with the other two in the room.

Once Arthur's attire was complete, the servants stepped back, looking him over.

"Very nice, sir," Benson said in a voice that he tried to make convincing.

The lady's maid pressed her fingers to her lips, nodding.

Arthur sighed, left his room, and started down the stairs.

When he reached the foot of the staircase, his costume woes were forgotten. The entryway was aglow with candles. The large pine tree had been joined by two others, all covered with shining baubles and bright bows and lit by even more candles. Greenery was strung over every doorframe and window. There was even more artificial snow on the sills. Servants rushed through the space, carrying trays of food. A maid swept up a few wayward pine needles.

Dickens's words came into Arthur's head. *"He was conscious of a thousand odours floating in the air, each one connected with a thousand thoughts, and hopes, and joys, and cares long, long, forgotten!"*

Arthur wished he felt as excited as the occasion and its preparation warranted, but between the costume failure and the dread of small talk with the two young ladies who were his guests, the ball loomed—a night to be endured, rather than enjoyed.

The voices of his guests and the sounds of their footsteps came from overhead. He glanced into the dining room, hoping to find Miss Hopewell, but she wasn't there.

Arthur's mother came from a side room, the top of her Marie Antoinette wig barely clearing the doorway. "Oh, my dear . . ." She grimaced at the sight of his costume but forced the expression into a smile. "Mr. Shakespeare, how do you do?"

"Madame," he responded, kissing her cheek.

The sound of horses' hooves on the drive signaled that the first ball guests had arrived.

Cassie rushed into the hall in a flurry of orange and black taffeta. Ornate wings extended from the shoulders of her gown, and delicate antennae were woven into her hair arrangement. Arthur smiled. A monarch butterfly.

"It is time!" Her bright smile faltered when she saw him. "Oh, Arthur . . ." Her gaze traveled down his attire.

"You look beautiful," he said, taking his sister's hand and feeling a stirring of happiness at the sight of her shining face. At least she would have a wonderful evening.

Her smile returned. Even his mess of a costume couldn't take away the excitement of her first ball. She squeezed his hand, and the three Stantons took their places at the entrance, ready to greet their guests.

Once the attendees had been properly welcomed, he accompanied his mother and sister into the ballroom, and his steps almost faltered at the sight awaiting them. Miss Hopewell had created an elaborate tableau throughout the suite of rooms. The attention she'd given every aspect of the space was apparent. There were, of course, the spectacularly lit trees and the greenery adorning the doorframes and wreathes at the windows, but he also noticed smaller details, such as the arrangement of the furniture to allow for maximum dancing space while still providing comfortable areas for guests to rest and visit. The refreshment table was laid out elegantly with orderly rows of punch glasses and plates of pastries, and between the food, artificial snow was sprinkled over floral arrangements. Past the refreshments, an orchestra sat on the raised stage beneath swaths of garlands. Baubles and decorative berries and holly hung from ribbons on the backs of their music stands.

As he'd promised, Arthur danced the first set with Miss Lind, who was dressed as a cat. She wore a black dress with a fur collar and fingerless gloves with fur on the backs of her hands. As the two of them moved across the floor, he listened with half an ear to her stream of complaints regarding everything from the pinching of her cat-ear headpiece to her worries that spiders could be hiding in her wardrobe.

He nodded and made the occasional sympathetic noise, but his attention was captured by the setting around him. The more he looked, the more amazed he was by Miss Hopewell's efforts.

Arthur considered how important the special details were to his mother and Cassie, how unique they made the party, and he felt a rush of warmth as he thought of the woman who had not only created this for them but had gone to so much additional effort.

"Mr. Stanton, did you hear me?" His dancing partner's tone was frustrated.

"I beg your pardon, Miss Lind," he said. "I was admiring the decorations. What did you say?"

Her eyes narrowed and her lips pursed. "I merely reminded you that I am owed an apology."

The young lady had his full attention now. He tried to remember what she had been talking about. "An apology, Miss Lind?"

"For the spiders," she said. "A young lady should not be exposed to such horrors."

The idea of apologizing when Miss Lind and the other guests had barged into his personal space uninvited was so ludicrous that Arthur was tempted to laugh. But the absurdity of the request only emphasized the frustrations he'd felt since the houseguests had arrived, and he ground his teeth. If anyone deserved an apology, it was the Stantons.

The music stopped, and Arthur took the young lady's hand, leading her back through the crowd toward the edge of the room.

When they reached the wall, Miss Lind halted but held on to his hand so he couldn't escape. She watched him with brows raised, waiting.

Well, she had insisted.

"I apologize, miss," Arthur said. "I am very sorry that you did not follow my housekeeper's instructions regarding your safety and my privacy. I am sorry that you have found nothing during your stay here to your satisfaction and that you are apparently unable to be happy."

Now that he'd begun, Arthur had more to say about the young woman's behavior and her family's rudeness, especially toward his mother and sister, but feeling the sash at his waist slipping, he decided to cut his apology short before his breeches slid down and entirely ruined the effect. He released Miss Lind's hand and held up his waistband, and after a quick bow to the stunned young woman, he walked quickly across the ballroom, through the entry hall, and into the drawing room, hoping for a bit of privacy so he could adjust his costume.

The music was softer in here, the sound of voices muted.

A few lamps were burning, but this room wasn't lit as brightly as the others, so it took a moment before he saw Miss Hopewell. She sat in one of the drawing room chairs, writing something on her clipboard in the light of a gaslamp. When she looked up, her eyes widened, as if she had not expected to be interrupted. Her gaze moved over Arthur's costume, and she sighed, a small smile tugging at the edge of her mouth. "I see you did not try on your costume in time to have it tailored."

He gave a sheepish smile, untying the sash and pulling his breeches higher.

"Allow me." Miss Hopewell stood and took the sash, shook out the creases, then reached her arms around his waist to retie it.

Feeling her arms around him made Arthur's heart race. The air in the room felt charged, as if lightning were near to striking. His mouth went dry, and he cleared his throat, searching for something to say that would ease the tension.

"The entire purpose of the Ghost of Christmas Past showing Scrooge the Fezziwigs' Christmas party was to remind him that happiness did not require a great expense," he said, trying very hard not to think about her proximity. "The Fezziwigs were poor, but the holiday celebration was a joyful memory because of their genuinely good-hearted efforts."

Miss Hopewell pulled the sash tight, knotted it, and then stepped back. "You resent the money spent on this Christmas celebration." She folded her arms, her expression pinched. "You feel it was unnecessary."

"Oh no, that is not what I meant," he said. "I intended to pay a compliment." He winced, wishing he knew better how to put his thoughts into words. "This ball, the days of events, they have all been wonderful. And I am grateful to you. Everything you have done has made my mother and Cassie so happy. The guests are impressed." He scratched his neck where the ruff was itching. "It is just that none of it was necessary." Seeing that he had offended her again, he scrambled to explain. "To me, I mean. I would be just as happy at a small gathering with only people I care about in attendance."

Miss Hopewell's expression was stony. "You are saying I should have not come. That you wish none of this"—she waved her hand toward the ballroom—"had happened."

Arthur knew he was only making it worse. He shook his head. "No, not at all. I am sorry. I am not explaining myself well. I . . . what I meant . . ." He scratched his neck again. "I meant to thank you." Why couldn't he just tell her that what made all of this perfect was *her*? Not all of the extra details and planning, but the way *she* made things special. Why couldn't he say that he didn't need any of this if he could only spend time talking with her in his laboratory or perhaps skating again or—?

"Excuse me." Miss Hopewell picked up her clipboard and started for the door.

Arthur felt a burst of panic. "Wait. Don't go. I—" He needed to fix this, but he could not think of the words to explain. Instead, he asked, "Would you like to dance?"

Her face hardened further, but he thought he saw tears in her eyes. "Mr. Stanton, are you having a laugh at me?"

"I am not." He held out his hand. "It is not fair that you did all of this work, planned and executed this party, and yet you sit in here, alone. You should at least have one dance."

"Mrs. Donovan isn't dancing," she said. "Nor are any of your other servants."

"You are not a servant."

"I am employed by you, sir. I see little difference."

"Do you want to know what I see?" He stepped toward her. "I see that you are a woman, I am a man, and there is music playing. It is very simple." He took her clipboard and set it on the sofa.

"I do not think it is appropriate," Miss Hopewell said. Her cheeks colored, and some of the stoniness left her face, replaced by embarrassment. "Besides, I am not a very good dancer. I might step on your toes."

"If you will remember, I crushed you with a Christmas tree at our first meeting," he said, taking her hand and drawing her closer. "Your feet could hardly do more damage than that."

Miss Hopewell gave a soft laugh and rested her other hand on his shoulder, but she still seemed to hesitate.

"The song is nearly at an end," he coaxed. "Just a few turns."

She nodded, and he placed a hand at her waist. Together, they stepped into the dance.

The space between the credenza and the table in front of the sofa was small, so the pair moved in a tight circle. Without the distraction of other dancers, Arthur's full attention was on the woman in his arms, and she consumed his senses. He was acutely aware of the softness of her hand in his and the curve of her hip where his fingers rested. She smelled like pine needles and cinnamon. When she looked up at him, the lamplight glowed in her blue-gray eyes.

Arthur's heartbeat was strong, sounding in his ears to the point that he could barely hear the orchestra. His thoughts took on an ethereal haze, and reality blurred around Miss Hopewell. Nothing mattered more than this moment, this woman. The music swelled to a close, and before he could question the wisdom of the action, Arthur pulled her into the circle of his embrace and kissed her.

Reality hit him at that instant, and he pulled away, ready to apologize. But there was no offense in Miss Hopewell's face. She may even have looked pleased, but Arthur didn't know whether he could trust his perception just now.

She held his gaze for a moment longer, and Arthur was just about to lean in for another kiss when a noise came from the entry hall, startling the pair of them apart.

She grabbed her clipboard just as Mr. Lind—dressed as Napoleon Bonaparte—entered the room.

"Ah, there you are, Stanton," he said. "I've something to discuss with you."

His voice dissolved the last of Arthur's fuzzy thoughts, jarring him back to the reality of the Christmas Eve ball.

"Thank you, Mr. Stanton," Miss Hopewell said in a businesslike tone, not looking up from her clipboard. She made a quick note and then curtsied. "Excuse me, gentlemen." She left the room without a backward glance.

Mr. Lind hardly gave her so much as a look as he mumbled some sort of farewell, and Arthur drew in a breath, bracing himself for the reprimand he knew was coming from the father of an affronted daughter.

Chapter Eight

Eliza's lips tingled as she hurried from the drawing room. Her skin was hot, and her heart raced. Instead of returning to the kitchen, she went up the stairs, closed herself in her bedchamber, and leaned back against the door. She shut her eyes, letting her thoughts return to the drawing room. To the dance, to the kiss . . . to *him*. The memory of being in Mr. Stanton's arms spread from her heart, filling her up with warmth. She sighed, even though just doing so felt overly dramatic, and let the feeling overtake her. Before today, all poetry had seemed silly, but now she understood how time could stand still, how her mind could go blank, how her entire world could exist in another person's eyes. She sighed again, holding on to the feeling, allowing it to wrap around her for a moment longer before willing herself back to rationality.

It was all foolishness. Mr. Stanton was a gentleman, the holder of this grand estate and the acres of surrounding land. His family moved in elite circles, while she . . . This time Eliza's sigh was one of resignation. She was an employee, a paid laborer. Allowing her emotions to be swept away, believing herself to be in love . . . was utter foolishness.

Now that she was thinking clearly, she realized Mr. Lind's insistence on speaking with Mr. Stanton must have concerned the latter's relationship with his daughter. They were even now likely to be discussing marriage arrangements. Eliza's heart went from floating to sinking.

She splashed some water onto her face from the basin next to her bed, then patted herself dry with a hand towel. The simple action cooled her skin and focused her thoughts back on her responsibilities. Dinner would be served in a quarter of an hour, and while the guests ate, she and the staff would need to refresh the dancing rooms for the remainder of the evening. She considered the tasks that still needed to be done, hoping she hadn't forgotten anything.

Once she was certain her emotions were tamed, she stepped out of the bedchamber, surprised to find the young twins and their nanny in the corridor. The three were talking in low tones, their voices tinged with panic. When they saw Eliza, all of them froze, staring at her with wide eyes.

"Good evening," Eliza said tentatively. As she drew closer to them, she noticed that one of the twins seemed to be crying. The nanny's face was pale. Had someone taken ill? "Is everything all right?" she asked.

One of the boys looked at the nanny, his eyes rounding even further. The other glanced toward the door of Mr. Stanton's laboratory.

Eliza followed the boy's gaze but didn't see anything amiss.

The nanny's breath hitched. "Miss, we have a . . . predicament."

One of the boys shook his head, as if he might quiet her.

Eliza's stomach tightened. "What is it?"

"Go on, then." The nanny nudged one of the boys. "Bernard, tell her."

"We lost Mr. Stanton's spider," Bernard said in a rush.

Eliza's mouth went dry. "You lost it? Where?"

Bernard didn't respond.

"Theodore." The nanny nudged the other boy.

"We just wanted to play with it," Theodore said, looking down at his feet. "We opened the cage, but it jumped out and—"

"And it was gone," Bernard said.

"When did this happen?" Eliza pushed the words through a constricted throat. She looked down the corridor, half expecting to see a spider creeping toward her. Or perhaps it was on the ceiling and would drop down onto her hair. She darted a glance upward, her skin prickling at the thought.

"Perhaps twenty minutes ago," the nanny said. "The boys were supposed to be preparing for bed, but when I went to check on them, they weren't in the nursery." She gave the children a scolding frown. "I found them in the laboratory, and the spider was already missing. We looked, but—"

"It could be anywhere," Theodore said. "What if it has gone down the stairs to the ball?"

"The dancers will surely trample it," Bernard said.

"Or it will bite someone," Theodore said.

The nanny put her face in her hands. "What are we to do?"

"Well, we must find it," Eliza said. This was the exact reason she had thrived as a planner of festivities. Eliza could improvise. She often handled difficult situations. She worked well under pressure. Managing the unexpected was what she did best, and this calamity was no different from when the ice sculpture had begun to melt at Lady Montague's garden party or when the flowers that had arrived for the Cavendishes' musicale performance were the wrong colors. The fact that this particular predicament involved a creature that sent shivers across her skin made no difference. The spider was important to her employer, and as such, it was important to her.

A memory of Mr. Stanton's kiss flashed into her thoughts, but she pushed it away. This was purely a business decision.

She considered for a moment how best to go about finding the spider. The creature would not have gone far—at least, she didn't think so. Based on the story Mr. Stanton had told her when she first visited the laboratory, it may have just hidden itself away. She would begin the search inside Mr. Stanton's laboratory. She shuddered.

"Boys, you are to return to the nursery," she said, deciding the likelihood of the creature being crushed was only magnified with each additional person in the search party. "And I will hear no argument to the contrary."

She waited for their assent before turning to the nanny. "There is a footman named Gus." She glanced at her timepiece, pursing her lips when she realized dinner was already being served. "He should be in the dining room. Please ask him to come to the laboratory at his earliest opportunity. But do not allow anyone else to hear. We do not want to cause any alarm to the guests." She could only imagine the panic the news of a rogue tarantula would cause.

Once the nanny was on her way and Eliza had seen the boys safely to the nursery, she turned back toward the laboratory door. The corridor leading to it wasn't particularly dark, but the shadows in the corners seemed deeper than they should. Each looked like just the place to conceal a furry little beast. She stepped carefully, scanning the walls and ceiling as she did. Her heartbeat accelerated as she turned the doorknob.

Eliza pushed open the laboratory door and paused to take stock of the situation. The gaslights were already lit—most likely by the twins—and it was immediately evident which spider had been released. The lid to one of the terrariums was unfastened and folded back on itself. The table holding it was at the far side of the room, nearly to the wall, and it was lower than the others. The boys must have chosen it based on accessibility.

Eliza drew in a deep breath and let it out slowly. She closed the door behind her and held up her skirt as she stepped across the room on tiptoe. When she reached the low table, she braced herself and peeked inside the open terrarium, holding on to a shred of hope that the spider hadn't escaped at all, that it was sitting in its enclosure and all she had to do was close the lid. But aside from plants and rocks and strings of web, the terrarium was empty.

She held her skirts tightly against her legs and looked around the laboratory. She did not remember what this particular spider looked like, but she was certain she would know it when she found it. She had hoped it wasn't one of the jumping varieties, before the boys had told her otherwise.

She lit a lamp from the desk and began a slow circuit of the room, holding the light close as she peered into corners, into spaces beneath the furniture, and even behind the books. There were so many places the creature could be hiding.

The sound of the door opening startled her, but instead of Gus coming to assist her, the nanny had returned.

"I'm sorry, miss. The footman cannot leave his station until after the meal is finished. But he will come directly when he can." The nanny scanned the floor apprehensively.

"Do you know what the spider looks like?" Eliza asked.

The nanny shook her head. "I didn't see it, but the boys told me it moved quicky." She grimaced. "When I told Gus which cage was empty, he said it will find a dark place to hide and go completely still."

Eliza nodded. She motioned toward a lamp. "Come along, then. You can assist. Just watch where you step."

The nanny pulled back. "But, miss, what if it should jump on me? Or bite?"

Eliza kept her face from revealing that she shared those very fears. "The spider can sense vibrations, so step softly," she said, remembering Mr. Stanton's words. "Keep your voice low."

The nanny hesitated, then lit the lamp and joined her, looking every bit as terrified as Eliza felt.

Eliza directed the older woman to the desk. There were endless places a small creature could hide among the papers and books and equipment. Once she was satisfied that the nanny was making a thorough search and not just glancing over the top of the clutter, Eliza returned to the bookshelves.

Each book she moved sent a dart of fear through her, but she carried on, shuffling aside stacks of notebooks, lifting loose papers, and peering into dark corners. The constant tensing as she braced herself again and again was wearing her out, and her muscles started to ache. But when she considered giving up, leaving the laboratory, and closing the door behind her, she thought of Mr. Stanton.

She didn't entirely understand why she felt she must do this. He was undoubtedly more qualified. As a naturalist, he understood the creatures' habits and would probably find the runaway much quicker, as well as know what to do when he did. But Eliza wanted to do this for him, to show him that the things that were important to him mattered to her as well. She cared about him. There was not much she could do for him—in fact, she would be gone by tomorrow—but this was one thing, one small gesture she could make, a Christmas gift. Even if he was likely never to know it had happened at all.

After the bookshelves had been completely searched, Eliza got down on her knees, leaned down, and put her cheek to the floor to look beneath the bookcase. She moved the lamp as close as she was able, squinting to see deeper into the shadows.

Something caught her eye. Or, rather, the lack of something did. The shadows in one area seemed to be thicker, blocking the wall behind. Her pulse throbbed through her ears and her breathing sped up. She moved the lamp from side to side, trying to judge whether it was merely a trick of the light. But after a moment she concluded an object—or creature—was definitely there.

"I may have found it," she whispered to the nanny. "Bring your lamp."

With both light sources and two sets of eyes, the women were certain they were looking at something, but whether that something was a tarantula was less sure.

"I think I see a shine on its eyes," the nanny whispered, adjusting her lamp.

Eliza squinted but could not make out anything. "Perhaps it is merely something that has rolled beneath the bookcase."

She sat up on her knees, looking around. "Even if it is the tarantula, neither of us can reach it." Not that either was prepared to grab it. Eliza fetched a rolled-up map from the desk, as well as a jar with a lid. "I am going to try to guide it from the corner," she said. "I'll bring it closer so you can catch it in the jar."

The nanny's face went even paler than before, and her brows rose.

"Don't be afraid," Eliza said in a voice that was at odds with her own trepidation. "I will just move it gently. You must be ready with the jar."

The nanny picked up the jar, but her expression did not relax. "I don't think I can do it, miss."

"Simply scoop it up and put on the lid," Eliza said. "Surely that is easier than caring for twin boys." She tried to sound warm and inflict a bit of understanding in her tone, but in truth, she was so frightened that her hands trembled. She twisted the map until the tube was long and narrow, then leaned down again and reached the tube slowly forward.

The object in the corner didn't move.

Taking a breath, she moved the roll closer until it bumped the mass in the corner. The object did not roll away, nor did it scamper. Perhaps it was a cloth. She scooted the roll again, using it to push object from the shadows.

As soon as it came into the light, the spider came alive, scuttling directly toward the women. It was larger than Eliza's palm and covered in coarse brown hair, and its long legs and frightening appendages on its face wiggled as it moved.

Eliza jumped to her feet.

The nanny screamed and dropped the jar. She rushed to the sofa, sprang up onto it, and hugged her knees to her chest.

Eliza's instinct was to join her, but summoning every bit of self-control, she knelt again and felt for the jar on ground behind her without taking her eyes from the spider. The creature did move fast. Eliza again used the map to block its escape, not allowing it to return beneath the bookshelves. The spider shifted direction, coming toward her. She twisted around on her knees, scooting backward. She placed the jar on its side in the tarantula's path, praying the creature would simply climb inside.

Of course it didn't.

She used the map again, sweeping it to turn the spider back toward the jar, but it passed by once more.

She would have to pick it up.

Just the thought made her feel as if a thousand spiders were crawling over her skin. She could hear her pulse in her ears as her chest rose and fell quickly in panic, and her fingers and toes prickled as she imagined how it would feel to touch the creature. What if it ran up her arm? Got into her hair? How could she possibly do this?

Mr. Stanton's voice came into her thoughts. "She may become agitated if you are nervous," he'd said.

Eliza used the map again to block the spider, redirecting it. She drew in a breath and let it out. She must calm herself so that the creature would also be calm.

The tarantula was moving toward her again. Her thoughts flashed back to the things Mr. Stanton had said. He'd mentioned that some spiders shot coarse hair from their bodies as a defense. She squinted to protect her eyes, reached out slowly, braced herself, and caught up the tarantula in her hand.

Its feet tickled as it crawled over her palm, but the feeling was not a pleasant one. Its hairs were bristly, and the creature was much bigger up close. She repressed a shudder at the sight of its black eyes.

The nanny whimpered.

Eliza forced her breathing to remain even. She turned her palm down as she'd seen Mr. Stanton do, letting the creature crawl over the back of her hand while she brought the jar slowly toward it. With a gentle twist, she shook the spider from her hand, dropping it inside. The lid was too far away, so Eliza used a book to block the opening. Her hands were trembling so badly that she feared she might lose her grip as she set the jar carefully on the desk. She sat for a moment, closing her eyes and letting her heart rate slow.

Seeing that it was safe, the nanny came to join her. "That was so brave, miss," she said with awe. "I'd never have the courage to do that."

Eliza was still too shaken to reply.

Once she could trust her knees to support her, she got to her feet, bringing the tarantula back to its enclosure. She tipped the jar, and the creature crawled into its terrarium, moving down to the darkest spot, beneath the leaves.

The nanny closed the lid, and they both made certain the latch was fastened.

Footsteps sounded in the corridor, and the laboratory door opened. "I came as quickly as I could." The footman, Gus, approached them and the terrarium on the low table. "Ah, the Chilean rose. One of the larger ones. Shouldn't be too difficult to locate."

"Miss Hopewell already found it." The nanny gestured toward the enclosure.

"And you recaptured it, miss?"

Eliza nodded, feeling physically and emotionally exhausted. She was still shaken and didn't trust herself to respond.

Gus gave her a worried look. "Perhaps you should sit for a moment, miss. I'll send for tea once I'm certain all of the creatures are where they should be." He took the jar and book from her hands. She had not realized she was still holding them. "Where did you find it?"

Eliza sank into the sofa, shuddering. The back of her throat felt tight, and she was glad she hadn't eaten in the last hour. She rubbed her eyes, listening with half an ear as the nanny recounted their adventure.

Gus listened, glancing occasionally at Eliza.

Once the nanny's account was finished, she excused herself to return to her charges, and Gus inspected the laboratory. In a few moments, he declared with relief that all of the specimens were in their proper places. "Thank you for your help, miss. Mr. Stanton would have been very upset indeed should he have lost one of his specimens. They are rather difficult to replace."

Elize could still only nod.

"I'll bring some tea to calm your nerves," Gus said. "And perhaps something a bit stronger."

At this, Eliza smiled. "Tea will be fine."

While she waited for the footman to return, she glanced down at her dress, realizing for the first time that it was covered in dust from kneeling on the floor. She brushed her hands over her skirts and allowed her gaze to travel around the room. The room felt brighter and much less frightening now that she knew the creatures were all where they belonged.

Mr. Stanton's laboratory really was terribly inefficient. Remembering how he'd searched for the misplaced ledger when they had weighed the tarantulas, she considered ways to organize the information, both for ease of documentation as well as location. A glance at her timepiece told her the ball would not end for hours, giving her plenty of time for implementation. By the time Gus returned, she had a plan in place.

Chapter Nine

Christmas morning arrived faster than Arthur expected. The sky was dreary, and he'd had far too much to eat and drink the night before. His inclination was to remain in bed, but he knew the effort Reverend Bramwell had put into his Christmas sermon, and Arthur would not miss the service no matter how much his stomach and head ached.

He was disappointed that Miss Hopewell was not among those gathered in the entry hall to meet the carriages, but he figured she'd most likely been awake far later than any of the guests while the remnants of the ball were cleaned up and the house returned to order. It was likely most of the servants had not slept at all, and he was glad they would have both Christmas and Boxing Day to recuperate from the extra work the house party had required.

Arthur rode with his mother and Cassie in one carriage, while Mr. and Mrs. Lind, the twins, and their nanny rode in the other. The other guests were apparently still recovering from the late night.

In spite of his red eyes and occasional yawn, Reverend Bramwell gave a pleasant sermon, though at times it was difficult to hear his words over the Lind twins' bickering. Even though the nanny sat between them, the boys would reach over or lean around her to poke at one another and hiss insults. The nanny did her best to keep them distracted, encouraging them to sing the Christmas carols with the choir or pointing out various stories in the stained glass windows, but her efforts did little to dissuade them.

Arthur's mother found some peppermints in her handbag and handed them down the pew in hopes that the sweets would keep the boys' interest, but the gesture only led to more squabbling.

For the parents' part, the Linds seemed content to allow the nanny to manage the situation, contributing little more than disappointed glares toward the poor woman when the boys were particularly loud. By the end of the service, the nanny was flushed and disheveled. She led the boys out of the church, and Arthur sighed at the thought of returning home with the little rascals. Not to mention their father.

The man had not been pleased with Arthur's reprimand to his daughter, and he'd made it very clear that the young woman was owed an apology—in addition to the apology she felt she was already owed due to the existence of his laboratory. It had apparently been too much to hope that the Ghost of Christmas Past had spirited the entire Lind family away in the night.

While Arthur's mother and sister chatted with the reverend and his wife, Arthur wandered through the churchyard. Although the morning had not warmed, the brisk air was still a pleasant change from the smell of incense and the press of bodies. He stepped around a crumbling headstone, taking a different path to avoid the tussling boys and their exhausted nanny.

When he glanced back toward the church doors, he saw a young man had joined his sister—Mr. Warner, if Arthur remembered correctly. The man had come costumed as an American soldier the night before and had danced with Cassie. Based on the color in his sister's cheeks, the occurrence had been more significant than Arthur had realized. Feeling it was his brotherly duty to be present for their visit, he turned back toward the church, moving again past the nanny and children.

"Come along, Bernard, Theodore," the older woman was pleading as she tried to separate them. "It's Christmas. We shall return in just a few moments to the nursery, and then you can play with your new toys."

"I do not want to play with him," one of the boys said, pointing at his brother. "He has eaten all of the buttermints. They were gone before I even woke up."

"I did not!" the other boy yelled, lunging at his brother. The two fell to the ground, rolling in the snow as they continued to quarrel.

"Yes, you did! And I am going to tell Mother."

"If you do, I shall tell her about the spider."

Arthur stopped walking. He turned toward the boys just as their heads snapped in his direction. Fear replaced the anger on their faces as they stared at him.

The nanny went pale.

A sick coldness poured into Arthur's belly. He remembered the nanny coming into the dining room the night before and whispering to Gus. At the time, the exchange hadn't seemed important, but now, looking at the three frightened faces of the boys and their nanny, Arthur knew something had happened.

"Are you lads speaking about my spiders?" He smiled and forced his voice to sound casual, not wanting to frighten the children into silence.

The boys looked at each other, clearly still afraid.

Arthur turned his attention to the nanny. "Did something happen?" he asked. "Perhaps in the laboratory?" Just saying it aloud made his throat dry.

The nanny nodded. "I'm sorry, sir. I . . ." She looked at the boys and then back at Arthur, grimacing. "Theodore and Bernard were supposed to be changing into their nightclothes, but when I went to the nursery to put them to bed, they were gone." She lowered her eyes, her voice turning to a whisper. "I found them in your laboratory."

"We only wanted to see it," one of the boys said, a hint of defiance in his voice.

Arthur clenched his fists, reminding himself that they were only children. "What happened?"

"The spider escaped," the other boy said. "Theodore opened the lid."

"You told me to!"

Arthur's pulse sped up as anger and panic took over his thoughts. He needed to return home immediately. He looked around for the children's parents and the carriage.

"No harm was done, sir," the nanny said. "Miss Hopewell recaptured the creature and returned it to its pen."

The sound of her name jarred Arthur, briefly distracting him from his apprehension. He felt his ears and neck go impossibly hot at the sudden memory of their kiss, but instead of allowing himself to relive the moment, he stopped short, realizing what the nanny had said. "Miss Hopewell caught the spider?"

"She did, sir." The nanny nodded heartily. "She picked it right up." She pantomimed scooping up the spider with her hand.

Arthur thought of how frightened Miss Hopefull had been when he'd suggested she hold the pink-toe. He was impressed and overwhelmingly grateful. But just hearing that the tarantula was returned to its terrarium did not fully ease his worry. If the laboratory door had been left open for too long, the temperature could have fallen, endangering all of the specimens. If the boys had dropped the spider, it could have been injured. There were so many factors, so many things that could have gone wrong. Arthur was anxious to return and assess the damage.

"You won't tell, will you?" one of the boys asked. His wide eyes were shining with tears.

"We are very sorry," the other said.

Of course Arthur wanted to tell the boys' parents. He thought of how extremely satisfying it would be to inform Mr. Lind of his children's transgression, especially after the dressing-down the man had given him the night before. But it wouldn't do any good. The information would not replace an injured specimen or repair any damage to the terrarium and would, if anything, only get the nanny into trouble—and very likely the boys as well. Mr. Lind in a foul temper was not something Arthur wanted to set upon children.

"I won't tell," he said at last.

"Thank you." The nanny's words came with a heavy exhale.

Half an hour later, the carriage was silent as Arthur finished telling his mother and Cassie what he'd learned in the churchyard. The women stared at him, disbelieving.

"I can't believe they would do such a thing," Cassie said after a long while.

His mother rubbed her forehead. "Our house party guests have been . . ."

"Trying," Cassie finished for her. She closed her eyes, leaning her head back against the seat. "Must we go home? We could take rooms at the inn."

Arthur and his mother laughed.

"Though it is very tempting to abandon our guests, they will only be with us until tomorrow," their mother said. "Chin up, my dears."

In spite of his dread of spending yet another day with the Linds and Wilcoxes, Arthur was impatient to return. Not only did he need to check on his laboratory, but he was eager to see Miss Hopewell again. They had danced, had kissed, but they had been interrupted before Arthur could ascertain her feelings on the matter. Did he owe her an apology for taking that liberty, or had she felt what he had?

As soon as the carriage reached the manor, Arthur excused himself and hurried up to the laboratory. He put on his white coat and immediately checked the room's temperature, relaxing a bit when he found it was just where it should be.

He did not know which of the specimens had escaped, so he planned to examine each. The nearest terrarium was the one that held the pink-toe tarantula. Arthur bent down and peered through the glass, locating the creature beneath a rock. She appeared sluggish, her coloring dulled, but this was typical before a molt, and after a few moments of observation, he concluded that the creature was healthy.

He straightened, and as he did, he noticed his desk. Gone were the papers scattered across it, tucked inside stacks of books, and left on shelves. Now the ledgers were organized by date, his mass of scribbled notes were assembled in a neat pile, and a few papers were gathered neatly on a clipboard near the pink-toe's terrarium. When he examined the papers, he found them to be the weeks of documentation he'd collected about the pink-toe's weight, eating habits, and information related to her molting process. There were other clipboards, too, laid out on the tables next to each terrarium and holding the rest of his documentation papers, which had been divided according to specimen type.

There was only one person who could be responsible for such order.

As Arthur moved through the room, inspecting the specimens and their corresponding clipboards of information, a bubble of happiness expanded in his chest. Miss Hopewell had not only saved one of his arachnids but also must have spent hours sorting and organizing the data, making a simple-to-use and maintain system, a skill that Arthur sorely lacked. It was the perfect Christmas gift.

Where he had entered the laboratory half an hour earlier on the verge of panic, Arthur now could not hold back his smile as he left the room. He passed Miss Hopewell's bedchamber, but an unanswered knock suggested the room was empty, so he descended the stairs to search for her.

Hearing voices in the parlor, Arthur peeked inside but saw only his mother, Cassie, and their guests. He continued on, thinking that perhaps Miss Hopewell was putting away party decorations in the chambers that had hosted the ball. But it appeared the rooms had all been restored, the furniture put back where it belonged. The only indication of the previous days' festivities was the greenery around the windows and doors. And, of course, the single grand Christmas tree in the entry hall.

In the dining room, Mrs. Frasier and Mrs. Donovan were setting out a cold luncheon on the sideboard. They would leave soon to spend the remainder of the day as well as Boxing Day with their families, but for now, the women chatted happily, likely relieved the house party was finally ended.

"Happy Christmas," Arthur said when he entered. He was feeling much more jolly than he had an hour earlier.

Both women curtsied and returned the greeting.

"Shall I prepare a plate for you?" Mrs. Donovan asked.

"No, thank you," Arthur said, although he couldn't stop his stomach from growling at the delicious smells. "I wondered, have you seen Miss Hopewell today? I did not have an opportunity to thank her last night for all of the work she did."

"I'm sorry, sir," Mrs. Frasier said, shaking her head. "She is already gone."

"Gone?" His heart dropped.

"She left early, before dawn," Mrs. Frasier said. "She rode into town with the domestic servants once everything was cleaned up and put back to rights after the ball."

Arthur looked toward the window as if he might see all the way into town and discover her.

"I did invite her to supper at my daughter's," Mrs. Donovan said apologetically. "But she insisted that she needed to catch a train."

The two women returned to arranging the meal, and Arthur left the room. Trains did not run from the town on holidays, so why had Miss Hopewell left so soon? Was it because of the kiss? The thought that she'd taken offense and rushed off into the cold on Christmas Day made Arthur ill. But if she had been angry, why would she have put his laboratory in order? Could she have left for a different reason? If so, what?

Not wanting to join the others in the parlor, Arthur remained in the entry hall, gazing up at the Christmas tree as he contemplated. He didn't notice his mother had joined him until she spoke.

"I am sorry, Arthur." She frowned, her gaze also on the tree.

"Sorry?" he asked. "For what?"

"For choosing so poorly. Mrs. Lind and Mrs. Wilcox were both delightful in their youth, and I assumed their daughters would be the same." Her frown turned sad as she looked at him. "I want you to be happy, my dear, and I had hoped this party . . ." She waved her hand. "I hoped this would be just the thing. I truly hoped that you would fall in love."

Arthur turned to face her, and as he did, everything became clear. "Mother," he said slowly, "I think I have."

Chapter Ten

EVEN THOUGH SHE WOULD BE there for only one night, Eliza hung her dresses in the wardrobe of the rented room. It not only gave her something to do but seemed a better idea than leaving them folded in her traveling bag. Around her, the inn was quiet. In fact, the whole town was quiet. Earlier, Eliza had heard noises in the street as the townsfolk made their way to the church for the Christmas service, then the same noises an hour later as they returned to their homes. She imagined joyful families gathered for Christmas dinner or sitting around a piano, singing carols, and her loneliness grew so intense, she actually ached.

Eliza sat on the bed, letting the feeling overtake her. She breathed in jagged breaths. It would pass soon enough. Christmas would be over, and then she would return to London, and life would continue just as it had before. There would be new parties to plan, vendors to meet, supplies to purchase, and plenty of tasks with which to occupy her time.

She rose to look through the window. The glass in the old inn was warped, making the scene outside unclear, but she could still see the row of buildings on the high street, with drifts of snow clinging to their roofs and evergreen wreaths on doors. A blurry carriage came up the road, and she was surprised when it stopped right outside the inn. Eliza had been told she was the only guest and no others were expected, and she couldn't imagine it was a delivery. Not today. More likely the innkeeper had a Christmas visitor. Another carriage came up behind the first, extinguishing Eliza's hopes of a quiet day in which she could be alone with her melancholy. She imagined the dining room below her bedchamber filled with the innkeeper's friends and family, and the thought made her even lonelier.

Eliza returned to sit on the bed, considering how to pass the remainder of the day. The inn's sitting room had a bookshelf, but she did not feel like reading, nor did she want to go down the stairs where she might be expected to interact with the company. In the end, she took out her clipboard, turned to a blank page, and listed the coming events that she would be arranging. There were three this spring, and she knew that once the Season began, there would be more.

A knock sounded at the door, and Eliza's heart sank. Though she was certain the innkeeper's intentions were kind, she did not want to spend the day making conversation with strangers who took pity on a lonely spinster.

She put on a smile and opened the door, ready to make a polite excuse. But she froze when she saw Mrs. Stanton and Cassie standing in the corridor.

"Happy Christmas, Miss Hopewell," Mrs. Stanton said with a gracious smile. "May we come in?"

"Of course." Eliza stepped back, allowing the women to enter. "Forgive me. I would invite you to sit, but as you can see . . ." She motioned to the small space. The bedchamber didn't even have a chair.

"That is not necessary," Mrs. Stanton said. "We will be brief."

Eliza studied the woman's face, trying to discern her intention, but Mrs. Stanton wore a pleasant expression that gave nothing away. Cassie, for her part, simply smiled.

"Miss Hopewell," the older woman began. "Our working arrangement has come to an end. We are very satisfied, but we have no more need of your services."

Eliza was taken aback. The words weren't particularly rude, but she still felt as if she were being dismissed. The house party was ended, so why had the Stantons felt the need to officially terminate their partnership? "Thank you." She was uncertain of what else to say. "I very much appreciated this opportunity."

Mrs. Stanton gave a nod. "Now that's done." She moved aside, and Cassie stepped forward. The young woman's smile widened.

"Miss Hopewell, now that you are no longer a business associate, we would like to invite you to Christmas dinner."

"Oh," Eliza said, scanning her mind for reasons to decline. "I—"

"As our *friend*," Cassie interrupted, taking her hand.

"I really do not wish to intrude," Eliza said. "Your house is quite filled with company already."

"Not at all," Mrs. Stanton said. "In a . . . fortuitous . . . turn of events, our dear friends Reverend and Mrs. Bramwell have invited the Linds and Wilcoxes to spend Christmas at the rectory." Her smile twisted into the smallest of smirks, and her brows flicked upward. "It will be just the four of us this evening."

"Please say you'll come." Cassie squeezed her hand. "Arthur will be very disappointed if you do not." As soon as she said it, her eyes widened and she darted a look at her mother, wincing. "Of course, I mean, we will all be disappointed."

Mrs. Stanton sighed and shook her head the slightest bit, but her smile did not dissipate.

Eliza's heart somersaulted at the mention of Mr. Stanton's name. Knowing that he was aware of the invitation—not only aware of it, but in favor of it—made it difficult to catch her breath. She felt her cheeks heat up as she nodded. "I would be delighted to come."

"Very good!" Cassie clapped her hands. She moved around her mother to open the door into the corridor, where a young woman stood holding a garment bag over her arm. Eliza recognized her as one of the Stantons' staff—a lady's maid, she assumed.

"I thought you would not have traveled with a party gown, so I brought one of mine—we are close to the same size, I think." Cassie motioned for the woman to enter. "Marta will help you dress and arrange your hair, and when you are finished, Gus will bring you to the house." She held open the door, waving for Mrs. Stanton to follow. "Come along, Mother, we must get ourselves ready too." Her smile was bright. "We will see you soon, Miss Hopewell."

The Stanton women were gone in a flurry.

When Marta opened the bag, ruffles of red satin spilled out, and the sight struck Eliza with a mixture of excitement and terror. In only a few moments, she was fastened into the gown, and she sat on the edge of the bed as the lady's maid twisted and braided her hair into an intricate style, which she finished off with sprigs of holly and berries. Marta, bless her, didn't seem to mind silence, so Eliza was left to her anticipation of Christmas dinner with the Stantons—with Mr. Stanton.

Once Eliza's presentation was complete, the women descended the inn's stairs and found Gus in the dining room with a mug of something warm. Seeing them, he raised his mug in a toast, drank the remainder, and wished the innkeeper a happy Christmas. Marta left to return to her family's home, and Gus assisted Eliza into the waiting carriage.

As they drove, Eliza's anticipation became tinged with nervousness. She had not seen Mr. Stanton since their kiss the night before. What would she say to him? How would he act? She twisted her gloved fingers together as she rode, watching through the window as the manor house drew near.

A moment later, Cassie opened the door, and the young woman's bright smile eased Eliza's worries. "Welcome!" She drew Eliza into the entry hall with a warm embrace, as if they had not seen one another for months instead of merely an hour. She stood back, holding Eliza at arm's length as she inspected the dress. "You look absolutely beautiful."

"Thank you." Eliza felt beautiful. She'd never worn such an extravagant gown, nor one in such a vibrant shade, and she had felt self-conscious. But seeing that Cassie's green dress was every bit as covered in ruffles and ribbons, she felt entirely appropriate.

"Mother and Arthur are arranging everything now," Cassie said. "Dinner will be cold and rather a small affair. I hope you don't mind. And then we shall play games and sing carols and feast on Christmas pudding."

Cassie's excitement was contagious, and Eliza smiled back at her. "It all sounds wonderful." And it did. A thrill of anticipation tickled over her skin.

Mr. Stanton and his mother came from the dining room.

Eliza's blush returned with a vengeance when she met his eyes.

"Oh, don't you look lovely," Mrs. Stanton said. She wore an elegant golden gown, and her son a smartly tailored coat and a red necktie.

"Thank you," Eliza said. "It was so thoughtful of Cassie to allow me to borrow this dress."

"It looks as if it were made for you, my dear." Mrs. Stanton said warmly.

Eliza met Mr. Stanton's eyes again. His gaze was thoughtful. She looked away quickly, to the Christmas tree.

"Cassie," Mrs. Stanton said, "I was hoping you might assist me with something in the dining room."

Cassie gave her mother a puzzled look.

"Come along." Mrs. Stanton linked arms with her daughter, pulling her from the entry hall and leaving Eliza and Mr. Stanton alone.

He stepped toward her, his hands clasped behind his back. "I hoped you would come."

His voice was deep and soothing and momentarily drove all reason from Eliza's brain. She could not think of anything at all clever or interesting to say. She gave a small curtsy, then felt silly at the gesture. "Thank you for the invitation."

Mr. Stanton scratched his neck. "Your . . . dress is very beautiful."

"It is Cassie's." Eliza resisted the impulse to twist her fingers as the awkwardness between them turned into a nearly physical presence.

"Oh yes, so you said. I've never noticed it before." He grimaced. "I apologize. I am dreadful at small talk."

Eliza allowed a small laugh, relieved that he had spoken aloud exactly what she was feeling. "I am as well."

Mr. Stanton stood beside her, admiring the tree. The candles were lit, their light making the glass baubles glow. The effect was every bit as stunning as it had been the night before.

"I've learned that I owe you a debt of gratitude, Miss Hopewell," Mr. Stanton said, his gaze still upon the tree. "For the rescue of one of my arachnids last evening."

"Is that why your family invited me tonight?" Eliza asked. She felt silly for having assumed there might have been a more personal reason.

"No," he said. "But I would thank you anyway." He pushed a hand through his hair, glancing at her, then back at the tree. "What you did . . . I know it must not have been pleasant for you—you may have even been frightened, which makes your effort all the more appreciated. I know most people do not understand how important those specimens are to me, but you seem to understand." He turned fully toward her and this time held her gaze. "And for this, I thank you."

"You are welcome."

"As to why you are here," Mr. Stanton went on, "I have spent the past three days with people I would not be sorry never to see again in my lifetime. I wanted to spend Christmas Day with people I care about—and you are one of them."

He reached out and took her hand, much like Cassie had done at the inn. But the effect was entirely different. Energy shot through Eliza at his touch, just as it had that first night when she'd told his fortune.

"I am odd, Miss Hopewell," he said. "Awkward. I have strange hobbies. I am clumsy, absent-minded." He shrugged, giving a crooked smile. "But when I am with you, I feel as if none of that matters. You are a remedy to my shortcomings. You make order out of chaos, you beautify, you set systems into place. The way you organized my laboratory—my mind does not operate in a linear fashion; it is messy and scattered—you did what I am incapable of."

"I did not mean to presume—"

"You saw what was needed and knew how to put it into order. Thank you."

Eliza was pleased her gesture had been so well received, and a flush crept over her skin at his praise.

Still holding her hand, Mr. Stanton motioned to the tree. "Last night at the ball, I realized all of the effort you'd given to this house party. The beauty, the festive atmosphere, the details—they were all created by you. But you did so much more. When the guests were upset, you calmed them. Whenever there was a problem, you solved it. You made all of this possible, but you did not get to enjoy any of it."

Her heart beat faster. Was he truly so perceptive?

"I wished you had been by my side listening to ghost stories or eating the delicious meals or riding over the countryside in a sleigh. But you were here, laboring to make all of this for the rest of us."

"I enjoyed the part I played," Eliza said. "Although, it would be an untruth to say that I would not have wished to be a part of the festivities." She glanced up at him. "I have never actually danced at a ball . . . aside from last night with you . . ." The memory of that moment—the feel of his arms, the way the very air had felt alive—made her heartbeat speed up. "But I was not here as a guest," she reminded him. "My position in your home was as the festivities organizer."

"But not anymore," he said in a firm voice. "I hope my mother and Cassie made that abundantly clear. You are no longer Miss Hopewell, Planner of Events, Parties, and Peculiar Festivities. You are Eliza Hopewell, guest and dear friend of the Stanton family." His gaze held hers. "Guest and dear friend of *mine*."

He stepped closer to her and took her other hand. A twinkle came into his eyes. "A wise woman—a mystic of sorts, I suppose—once told me a stranger would arrive and change everything. That I would lose something important and then find something I cherish even more."

Eliza chuckled at the memory. "She may not have been totally reliable."

"On the contrary. She was exactly right." He put an arm around her waist, drawing her near, and crooked a finger beneath her chin to lift up her face. "Last night, we were interrupted. I thought we might continue?"

He paused, holing her gaze and allowing Eliza to make the decision.

She did not hesitate. She put an arm around his neck, pulling his face to hers and letting herself get lost in his kiss. He pulled her tighter until the entire world was only the two of them.

A gasp and a giggle startled them, and Eliza's eyes flew open as she broke their kiss. She started to pull away, but he held her close, touching his forehead against hers. "Cassie . . ." His voice was a growl.

The giggle sounded again, and Cassie approached them. "It is a happy Christmas after all! Especially for you, Arthur."

He sighed, loosened his arms around Eliza, and scowled good-naturedly at his sister. "Don't you have somewhere to be?"

Eliza's face was aflame, both from the kiss and from being discovered. She took a step back, untangling herself from Arthur Stanton and trying to school her face. But it was impossible to know what expression to land on. Arthur gave her a sheepish grin, which she returned. Even the embarrassment of being caught in such a situation could not dampen the happiness filling every part of her.

"It is time for our Christmas celebration." Cassie linked her arms with both of them and led them toward the dining room. "If you'd like, once we've eaten, I will leave the two of you alone beneath the kissing bough."

Arthur spoke before Eliza could comment. "Yes, we would like that."

Eliza allowed herself to be escorted into the dining room, where a warm fire sparked and a simple table was laden with sliced breads, meats, fruits, and cheeses.

The four of them chatted happily through the meal, then played games, ate desserts, and sang carols late into the night. For the first time since Eliza was a child, Christmas once again meant family, happiness, laughter, and love.

After the other women had retired to bed, Eliza and Arthur remained on the sofa, watching the fire burn down into embers. Eliza looked up at the man sitting beside her, and the softness in his eyes made her heart swell.

He leaned down and kissed her softly. "Happy Christmas, Eliza Hopewell."

"Happy Christmas," she said, nestling closer and leaning her head on his shoulder. Dickens's famous words had never seemed more appropriate than in that moment. "'And God bless us, every one.'"

About the Author

Jennifer Moore lives with one husband and four sons, who produce heaps of laundry and laughter. She earned a BA from the University of Utah in linguistics, which she uses mostly for answering Jeopardy questions. A reader of history and romance, she loves traveling, tall ships, scented candles, and watching cake-decorating videos. When she's not driving carpool, writing, or helping with homework, she'll usually be found playing tennis. Learn more at authorjmoore.com and on Jennifer's social media.

Facebook: Author Jennifer Moore

Instagram: jennythebrave

OTHER COVENANT BOOKS AND AUDIOBOOKS BY KASEY STOCKTON

STAND-ALONE NOVELS

I'm Not Charlotte Lucas

I'm Not His Style

NOVELLAS

"A Carol So Bright" in *A Christmas Serenade*

A Carol So Bright

KASEY STOCKTON

for Mom and Dad, for teaching me the best way to enjoy the Christmas season: through selfless love, giving, and music

Chapter One

Lillian

December 1852
Cheshire, England

LILLIAN HARTLEY WAS DEAD, TO *begin with.* What a ghastly, morbid thought. Charles Dickens first wrote a similar line for Old Marley, but the character began that story as a ghost. Upon further recollection, I felt it was suitable for my own story as well.

Not that I had a story of my own to tell. Were I important enough for it to be written, I should have liked for it to claim a striking beginning. As it stood, I was hardly worth noticing, my life an unceasing string of keeping silent and out of the way, so it was up to me to devise my own exciting tale. Though, at present, it would have been more accurately stated that my *heart* was dead. The rest of my body was very much alive and at that moment tucked into one of the window seats that lined the enormous entry hall of my grand house, where I could neither bother anyone nor be bothered, entirely hidden from view.

Now, to write the second line.

> *Nestled into the hilly countryside of the Peak District, Lillian Hartley lived out her days overcoming the loss of the only man she had ever loved. For how could a heart live when the love it gave was never returned?*

Hmm. That was no good, regardless of the truth it held. A bit too theatrical for my taste. Evidently I was just as awful at writing stories as I was at reading them. I had not even finished an entire page of the book I'd brought to this window seat, and my mind had already wandered into the dramatics of my sad, unrequited romance. The man had left three years ago. It was a testament of my pathetic nature that I thought of him now.

I closed the red bound book and set it on the cushion beside me, leaning my head against the wall. A group of rabbits hopped up a white-frosted hill just outside, leaving green-tinted prints in their wake. They were much more interesting than Old Marley, anyway. Even if he was dead to begin with.

Mama's voice filtered into the entry hall, echoing in the cavernous room. "We've yet to find a tree." Her steps clicked down the marble floor as she drew closer. "I also need something to decorate the children's tables with for the tea. Have you ordered the beef for the servants?"

"Yes, ma'am," someone replied. Likely our housekeeper, Mrs. Cole. "Ages ago."

"Very good." Mama stopped, growing still. "Why is it so dark in here?"

I pressed my lips together, holding my breath.

Fingers clutched the edge of the drapes that had kept me hidden and pulled them to the side, revealing Mama and Mrs. Cole in dark gowns, though Mama's was a fashionable arrangement in ruby and Mrs. Cole wore black. Mama's eyebrows rose, her head tilting to the side. "Goodness, Lillian. Are you hiding?"

"Reading." I lifted my red bound copy of *A Christmas Carol.*

"You do not read."

"Ada lent it to me. It is . . . interesting." The entire half a page I had endured. My dearest friend loved the story and had promised I would too. Thus far she was wrong.

"Lovely." Mama started to walk away.

I scrambled down from the window seat. "Mama, is there anything I can help with?"

Mrs. Cole looked at me sharply, but my mother took longer to give me her attention. "It is best if you leave us to it, Lillian. We have much to do before your papa returns from Town. He's due at the station in four hours."

I tried not to let that sting. The rejection was quickly overshadowed by my father's schedule anyway. *Four hours* and the Christmas season would truly begin. Only, our home looked decidedly lacking in festive spirit. "We need a tree."

Mother gave an exasperated sigh. "I am aware, but Archibald is occupied and Papa is not here. It'll have to wait."

"I can find one."

Mama looked past me to the window, a line forming between her eyebrows. "We'll wait for your brother to finish with the boughs, dear."

"I do not propose cutting and carrying the tree myself, Mama. If I locate a good one, surely Mr. Sterling would bring it to the house."

"Is that a good idea, darling?" Her eyebrows pulled together. Did she realize her foot was tapping anxiously? I was twenty years old, for heaven's sake. I was not a child.

My instinct was to retreat, to silently agree I would somehow find a way to ruin my task. But how was I to prove my capability if I did not insist? Besides, it was only selecting a tree. How could I possibly ruin that? "Mama, I would like to try."

"Oh, very well," she said with a tremulous smile, waving a hand toward me. "Bundle up though. It is very cold outside."

I pulled her in for a quick hug. "I will not let you down."

A look passed between her and Mrs. Cole that did not inspire any confidence.

It did not take long to layer a warm cloak, mittens, and a scarf over my exposed skin. I made my way outside, past the Italian garden, and up the hill toward the nearest trees. Frigid air bit at my nose as I trudged through the snow, my boots dragging through the soft powder.

> *Lillian Hartley was an underestimated young woman who only wanted to prove herself, even though no one had any faith in her at all.*

Though, to be fair to my family, I *was* rather clumsy. I hardly left the dinner table without a drip of something on my dress, but I never knew entirely how it got there. I was no longer allowed to pour the tea after one too many steaming-hot mishaps, though I could not entirely blame Mama for that rule either. My brother, Archie, forbade me from riding after my horse tripped and tumbled to the ground—where the ground had been entirely flat. Some people were prone to accidents. Try as I might, I could not avoid them.

But selecting a Christmas tree? I felt safe in this task. Once I found a suitable tree and pointed it out to Mr. Sterling, I would return to the house and be perfectly out of the way, watching them bring it in from a safe distance.

It was a foolproof plan.

Only, finding the perfect tree seemed to take longer than I'd anticipated. Queen Victoria's tree in the image I'd saved from the *Illustrated London News* a few years ago had looked perfectly symmetrical, but none of our trees were quite right.

Lillian Hartley failed her family by choosing the worst Christmas tree in all of Cheshire County.

Frustrated, I blew out a breath and looked along the horizon, scanning the woods in the distance. The trees were much better on *that* side of our property, but I avoided the memories they still carried.

Snow fell in thick, fluffy flakes around me, melting on my cheeks. I glanced around one more time, but no trees stood out to me. It was getting colder, and I would soon become an ice sculpture if I did not remove to the house to thaw.

To Pine Woods it was. The woods were not named for the tree but for the Pine family, whose house was nestled just on the other side of the small forest. They weren't home just now, and I had not seen their only son, my brother's dearest friend, in three years. But that did not ease the ghostly memories that lingered there.

My boots dragged long prints over the hill as the snow fell harder. Lynton Park rose behind me, beckoning me to its warm great hall and blazing fires. But I could not return without a tree—that would be a failure.

I reached Pine Woods and was rewarded for my efforts. Multiple trees stood out to me as sufficiently symmetrical. Perhaps if I searched deeper, I would find the *perfect* tree. I could imagine Mama's face, glowing from the candles on a well-balanced Christmas tree that rivaled the Queen's, proud I had not ruined my one task. I would be the reason we had the smell of pine in the hall. I will have done something good and worthwhile.

The tree appeared just before me, and I made a soft squeal of delight. It was perfect. The right thickness of branches, tall but not unwieldy, no bald patches. I pulled my red scarf from around my neck and reached up to tie it to a sturdy branch so Mr. Sterling would be able to find it with some ease.

Only, it was difficult to tie with such stiff fingers. I pulled one mitten free of my hand and held it in my teeth, using my fingers to weave the scarf into a loose knot.

Motion caught my eye from the side, and I turned to find a man coming around from the back of the tree. I screamed, catching my mitten as it fell from my mouth and chucking it at the intruder. His hair grew past his ears, unkempt, and a short, scraggly beard bushed around his face. There was a slight moment in which his countenance tugged at my awareness as if I recognized him, but I knew no men with such ungainly facial hair.

He reached for me, and I screamed louder, pivoting away. My foot slid on the slick ground, and I fell forward, my face burying in the icy snow.

I scrambled to my feet, letting out another scream.

"Wait!" he yelled, running toward me.

"Do not come closer!" I picked up a broken branch and held it toward him. It was small, thinner than one of my archery arrows, and could easily snap between my fingers, but I had nothing else.

He stopped and rested his fist on his waist, the other hand holding an instrument case of some sort. "That is your weapon of choice?"

The faint mocking in his tone tripped another feeling of recognition. I peered at him closer, my eyes narrowing as I tried to make out his face behind the sunburned cheeks, long hair, and bushy brown beard. The twinkle in his blue eyes was familiar, reaching through my chest and commanding my heart to beat more rapidly.

"Theo?"

A smile broke across his mouth, revealing a slightly crooked front tooth I recognized so well. Good heavens, *this* was Theodore Pine. I had not seen him in three years, and despite his unkemptness, he had aged well—evidenced by the shape of his cheekbones, the breadth of his shoulders, and the fact that I had mistaken him for a man.

Theo was no longer the boy who had left. Now he was a man fully grown, with a beard like a goat, who was grinning at me like he forgot that we had not spoken in three years—that I had not gone to bid him farewell before he left us.

"Still getting into scrapes, I see." His smile only widened as he ran his gaze down my snow- and mud-covered cloak. "My, how you've grown, little one."

Little one? "I am twenty years old, Theo."

"You can't be." He took a step back, shaking his head. "You couldn't have been more than thirteen when last I saw you."

His words buried themselves in my chest like a blunt dagger. "Seventeen."

"Impossible." Twisting the dagger.

I had been in love with the man for most of my life, and he considered me a child. I tried to wipe the snow from my face, but it only felt as though I'd smeared mud over my skin.

"You are making it worse," he said, smiling affectionately at my muddy cheek. He leaned down and scooped up a handful of snow. "Here, allow me to help clean—"

I took another step back. "No, I thank you. You needn't bother."

His dark eyebrows pulled together. His hand dropped to his side, and the snow fell to the ground. "Come, Lily. Are you not glad to see me?"

"Glad?" I scoffed. I was *thrilled.* I had missed him so dearly, but mortification pecked at me. I was drawn to him, but my mind kept pulling me away, tugging and teasing with snippets of a memory set in these very trees. Of coming upon him and my dearest friend, Ada, kissing beneath the shade of an elm tree not far from where he and I stood now. It had been utterly humiliating, believing he'd cared for me when, really, he'd only ever seen me as a child or a sister—unfair, when Ada was only two years my senior. I'd loved Theo for forever, but he had never loved me.

After three years of nothing—no letters, no visits—he'd forced me to glean information about him through my brother or Ada or Mrs. Pine. And now he was simply reappearing, pretending he cared for *me*?

I tossed the stick at him, turned on my heel, and marched away.

Chapter Two

Theo

What the devil had gotten into Lillian Hartley? I turned around and picked up the pink mitten she'd thrown at me, then jogged through the snow to catch up to her. "You forgot this," I said, reaching toward her.

She looked down at my hand, then took the mitten. "Thank you," she muttered quietly.

I walked alongside her a moment longer, searching my mind for something I might have said or done to so greatly offend her. I shifted my violin case to the other hand. The Lillian I recalled was never cross. She embodied the brightness of tulips and the warmth of the summer sun. I thought of the delicate blue-gray necklace in my bag now. It was the only gift I'd brought home with me, and I'd bought it solely because it reminded me of her. But this angry creature? This was not my dear little Lillian.

We broke through the trees, and Lynton Park came into view, its large Palladian front overwhelming from its raised position at the top of the hill. I never approached the house without feeling simultaneously inferior and loved. The Hartley family cared for me; I knew they did. But their prestige was sometimes suffocating.

Lillian, however, did not have a prideful, conceited bone in her body. Or so I had previously thought.

"Is it the beard?" I asked her, running my fingers over the coarse hair on my chin. I had not intended for anyone but my mother to see me in this state.

She shook her head. Mud smeared over her cheeks and forehead, but her hair was the same rich brown as before, from what I could see peeking out of her bonnet, and her eyes were just as gray as they always had been. "The beard makes you look like a goat."

Hmm. Not what I'd expected. "I meant to shave before coming to see your family, but things did not work out as I intended."

"Then, perhaps you ought to come another time."

"So you can find yourself absent?" I asked, if for no other reason than to test her. Lillian had never before treated me in this manner, and I couldn't find a reason for it.

She opened her mouth, then closed it again.

That was troubling. "I came home to surprise my mother."

Lillian looked at me swiftly. "Mrs. Pine is not home."

"I gathered as much," I said wryly. From the way the house was utterly locked up, the windows dark, and no one answering, I had assumed no one intended to be home for quite some time.

"She is down in Dorset staying with her sister until Twelfth Night. We were to see her next in London when we go to prepare for the Season."

"What of Mrs. Gherkin?" I asked. "O'Toole? Hampstead?"

"Your mother took her servants with her. Though, Mrs. Gherkin chose to visit her son for Christmas, I believe."

Everyone was gone? It explained the dark house. "Who is caring for the animals?"

"A neighbor. I cannot recall which."

My breath clouded before me when I released a long sigh. After traveling all the way from Vienna by train, boat, then train again, I was utterly exhausted. I'd walked a good deal of the way from town to reach my mother's home, and the very last thing I wanted to do now was travel to Dorset—let alone to Aunt Frye's house. It was a ghastly place full of the most pigheaded children I'd ever met. Last time they came here to visit, one of the boys had cut all the strings on my violin. I would not trust myself around him were he to do it again.

"You can stay with us tonight," Lillian said, snapping me from my black mood. She must have sensed my displeasure and taken pity on me.

"I wouldn't wish to impose."

She started walking again. "Archie won't hear of you leaving again so soon and you know it. Come up to the house."

I caught up again, her swing in mood making me wary. I still could not reconcile her age. She was a woman now. By her account, she had been for quite a while. "Have you become changeable, Lily?"

"Far more constant than you could know," she muttered.

I stole a glance at her from the side. Her nose was the same as ever, small with a slight slope, and her voice had not changed. My breath caught, excitement flowing through my veins. That was one thing I had most heartily missed from Lynton: Lillian's angelic voice. Three years in Vienna studying music, and nothing had come close to the clarity and perfection this girl—no, woman—could produce.

She slipped through the stone archway and into the inner courtyard. I followed her, aware that Lynton Park looked precisely how I'd left it. The front door swung open to reveal my closest friend, Archibald Hartley. "Theo?" he called, standing at the top of the split staircase.

At least some people could recognize me instantly.

I doffed my hat and bowed with a flourish before proceeding to the door. I hurried up the stairs to greet him when I realized Lillian wasn't beside me but halfway across the courtyard, heading toward the stables.

"Where are you going, Lily?" Archie called.

She looked back at us but did not slow her gait. "To find Mr. Sterling. I will be in shortly."

Archie paid her no more mind. "Come in, Theo. It's blasted freezing out here."

I slipped into the house and watched Lillian disappear through the other stone archway before I set my violin case on the floor near the wall.

"Theodore Pine?" Mrs. Hartley said, her feet clicking across the marble floor in the large entry hall. A row of marble pillars cut through the middle of the room, creating a sort of corridor that led to the staircase on the far end, but the fires blazed on either end of the hall, and the room was warm. It was the type of space that would have once housed an enormous table and medieval spit roasting above the fire, but now it was just a large room with a row of window seats on one side and a group of chairs and sofas before the hearth. In essence, it was a glorified drawing room.

Mrs. Hartley pulled me into an embrace, her arms coming warmly around me. "Your mother isn't here, Theodore. She's gone to Dorset."

"Lily told me so," I said, stepping back.

Mrs. Hartley looked over my shoulder. "Kemper, come take Mr. Pine's coat, please." She looked back at me. "You must be hungry. I'll send for something to hold you until dinner." She turned to relay her instructions to a servant while I followed Archie.

The assumption that I would remain here since my house was empty was what made the Hartleys feel like family. The grand entry room we stood in, though, reminded me how distant we were in station.

"How long are you staying in Cheshire?" Archie asked, leading me toward the grouping of chairs near the fireplace.

"I don't have a plan, really."

He paused, his dark eyebrows rising. "Does this mean you are finished in Vienna? You've come home for good?"

My chest constricted. The idea of never returning to Vienna—never again sitting by the Danube and playing my violin where great men had played before me—hurt my soul. But my home and my family were here. "I will return eventually. For now, I would like to spend time with my mother."

There were other responsibilities waiting for me in Cheshire, of course. Ada was here. Her letters had grown more and more sparse over the last year, and the time had come for me to return and fulfill the promise I had made. I'd spent long enough hiding in a foreign city, running away. It was time to face the things I'd been avoiding.

Archie looked at the fire and sighed. "I do not blame you. Vienna is a brilliant city. It was one of my favorite places we visited on my Grand Tour."

Mrs. Hartley returned and claimed a seat on the end of the sofa. "Food will be up shortly. I want to hear everything, Theodore. Is the . . . beard a Viennese style?"

I grinned. "I planned on being rid of it before greeting your family, Mrs. Hartley, but I did not anticipate that my mother would be gone when I arrived. I suppose I've learned my lesson about surprising her."

"She does not know you're in England? You may stay with us for as long as you wish, but I imagine you are eager to be on your way to Dorset."

I cringed, inciting laughter in my oldest friend. "You may stay here until your mother returns, Theo. I would not wish those blasted cousins on you for all the world."

"Are they very spirited?" Mrs. Hartley asked.

"Yes. But I will write to my mother, and if she wishes for my company, I will go. Though, I may leave my violin here for safekeeping."

"You've brought it?" Mrs. Hartley asked, her body straightening, a smile filling her lips.

"I have." I gestured to where it sat on the floor near the door. "Most of my things are waiting on the front steps of my mother's house, but I did not want to leave my instrument out in the cold."

"I will send Sterling to fetch your trunks," Archie said, rising. He crossed the room to speak to a servant before returning to his seat across from me.

"Mr. Hartley's train arrives in a few hours," Mrs. Hartley said. "We will not eat until seven tonight. Mrs. Cole is preparing a room for you, but it will not be ready for some time yet, so I directed her to bring your refreshment here. I will request hot water for your room."

"Thank you, Mrs. Hartley. That would be wonderful. I do not know how I might repay your kindness."

"Easily, dear. You can play for us." She rose, smiling. I had always had a captive audience in Mr. and Mrs. Hartley. Not everyone appreciated music, but they both did.

I smiled back, feeling my beard shift with my expression, my skin itching beneath it. I was anxious to be rid of it now. "I will play if Lillian agrees to join me."

"Oh," Mrs. Hartley said, her brow creasing in uncertainty. She cleared her throat and looked at Archie.

He shrugged. "Sorry, chap. Won't be possible."

Not possible? Lillian and I had performed together many times. It wasn't an unreasonable assumption that she might be willing to do so again. She was older than I realized, but that should not preclude her from performing. Singing was a perfectly acceptable lady's accomplishment. "Whyever not?"

Archie looked at his mother before leaning back in his seat. "Lily doesn't sing anymore."

"Perhaps she might," she said hopefully. "Now that you are here to accompany her again."

Archie looked doubtful.

"I have much to do at present, so I will leave you." Mrs. Hartley reached out and squeezed my shoulder softly. "Welcome to Lynton, Theodore. We are always glad to have you."

I smiled my gratitude until she left the room.

Archie leaned closer to me. "So was it a wager?"

I lifted an eyebrow. "What do you mean?"

He swirled a hand in front of his mouth. "The beard. Why is it so long?"

A wager? No, it was a mixture of laziness and thinking it would be a lark to surprise my mother this way. "Your sister told me I resembled a goat."

Archie leaned forward, laughing from his gut. He looked at me and laughed harder. "She is not wrong, my friend."

I couldn't help but grin. "I never intended for anyone of my acquaintance to see it, save for my mother." I ran a hand down the hair, hoping to smooth it. "Now I fear my hair will not be trimmed for some time."

"You do not travel with a valet?" he asked, sitting up a little.

"No." Last I'd known Archie, he hadn't had a valet either.

"I cannot live without my man. His shoe polish is exceptional, and he keeps my hair trimmed. You can borrow him while you are here."

He spoke as though the servant were a pair of shears or a shaving blade—something to borrow, use, and return. "I can cut my own hair."

Archie sighed. "Suit yourself."

The door opened and closed again, letting in a whoosh of cold air with a young woman.

"Lily, come here for a moment," Archie called.

"No, thank you," she said politely, her face turned away from us.

"What is it now?" He chuckled. "Slipped in the mud again?"

She had done exactly that, and I'd been witness to it.

"I must change, Archie," she said without slowing.

"You can change later. Theo is here—"

"Let her go," I said.

Lillian had already slipped from the room and up the stairs, out of sight, so it was just as well. She'd been covered in a fair amount of mud and slush. I imagined she only wanted to be clean.

Archie frowned, watching the doorway his sister had walked through. "Odd."

"She was wet and muddy. I am certain she wants nothing more than a warm, dry gown."

Archie nodded. "That I understand, but it felt like she was avoiding us." His countenance cleared. "You know, the last time she sang was with you."

I looked at him sharply. "She hasn't sung in three years?"

He shook his head, his lips pressed together. "No."

"Why did she stop?"

"That's the rub." Archie settled back comfortably on his seat again. "No one knows why she stopped."

The timing was strange, but more than that, it hurt my sense of justice to think that something had put itself in the way of her desire to sing. If no one knew her reasons, then Lillian was hiding something. I was going to find out what it was.

Chapter Three

Lillian

I WAITED FOR BETTY TO finish refreshing the curls beside my temples before she slid silk flowers—violet and pink to match the embroidery on my deep golden-yellow gown—into my coiffure. No one could expect Theo to leave Lynton immediately, but if he intended to spend Christmas with his mother, he would need to catch the train tomorrow afternoon, at the latest. Which meant I had to endure only one day in his company.

It would be easier this way. Any longer than that, and I was sure to succumb to the girlish love that had once consumed me. I closed my eyes and drew in a breath. *I am older and wiser now, and much more mature.* If I repeated that enough, I would come to believe it.

Betty slid my necklace into place and clasped it behind my neck.

"Thank you." I straightened the silver pendant in the mirror. I was a little early for dinner, but I wanted to look in the entry hall and see if Sterling had managed to collect my Christmas tree. It would be a boon to have it ready in time for Papa's arrival—to show I was capable.

The staircase at the end of the corridor was darkening, the sun having already made its early winter descent. I rounded the corner and halted, surprised to find Theo waiting at the bottom of the steps, looking up. He smiled when he caught sight of me. The candles burning in the sconces along the walls lit his gleaming teeth and clean-shaven jaw. His hair was pomaded and tamed, brushed to the side except for a stray curl that chose to remain on his forehead. This was the Theo I remembered, but he'd matured and lost the boyish softness to his cheeks and jawline.

My answering smile was immediate, but I tamed it. Theo's joy radiated in such a way that I could not doubt his happiness to see me—as he would be were I his younger sister. It was an important distinction to remember.

Holding my head high, I came down the stairs sedately, forcing myself not to hurry so I would not trip in front of him a second time today.

Theo's smile slipped as I approached him, though his gaze never wavered. A soft line formed between his brows, a gentle shadow betraying its existence.

The shift in his demeanor was subtle but unmistakable. I paused on the step above him. "Are you . . . that is, are you well?"

"Yes, quite well." He gave his head a small shake, and his smile returned. He bent his arm, offering it to me. "Can I escort you to the family drawing room?"

"I need something from the hall first."

"All the better."

"Were you not waiting for someone else? Archie, perhaps?"

Theo tilted his head back to better look at me, making his blue eyes shimmer in the candlelight. "He mentioned his desire to speak to me privately, but I wager it will keep."

I let him escort me toward the entry.

The hall was dim, only the central hearth burning a fire that glowed against a Christmas tree in the center of the room. The evergreen was set up on a table, which gave it the effect of looking taller than it had in nature. "They've done it," I whispered and dropped my hand from Theo's arm.

"I did not realize you'd adopted the custom," Theo said, admiring the tree. "This is a delightful surprise."

"It is only our third year bringing a tree inside. I quite love it though." I liked the symmetrical nature of the tree and the spaces that would soon be filled with shiny ornaments and dried fruit.

He peered at me through narrowed eyes, humor on his lips. "Is this what you were doing in the woods when I found you?"

"I chose the tree, but I had no part in its retrieval. Mama would never trust me with something so potentially dangerous. She hardly has a task she *will* trust me with."

Theo's laugh rang out in the hall, springing through the room and coiling in my heart. I had missed that sound so deeply; it buried itself in my chest and gave me the grounding feeling of home.

"I am quite happy with it," I said, grinning. "I think it is the most beautiful evergreen on Lynton property."

"Many things have changed in the time I've been away," Theo said. When I turned to look at him, I found him watching me.

My cheeks pinked. I hoped I didn't seem too immature by my appreciation of the tree. I tried to temper my enthusiasm. "Shall we go through to the drawing room?" I started moving toward the window seat I had occupied earlier. "I only need to fetch something I left here."

"Of course." He followed me, and I tucked *A Christmas Carol* to my chest before taking his offered elbow. He led me back up the stairs toward the drawing room.

No one waited for us there, so I released Theo's arm once more and moved to sit on the sofa away from him, placing the book in my lap.

"I have much to share with you," he said, standing near the fire, his hands resting lazily behind his back. "You would have loved Vienna, Lily."

"It was easy to fall in love with the city through your letters."

"Archie shared them with you, I presume?" Theo said.

"Yes, he read snippets to me. Sometimes to Ada as well."

His face was impassive, not a flicker of emotion at her mention. I'd watched closely for any sign of how he might feel, but he'd disappointed me by giving away nothing.

Theo cleared his throat. "How is Miss Marcote?"

"Eager to see you, I imagine." I'd spoken clearly, my voice unwavering. It was incredible that all these years later, I could still feel such a surge of jealousy when I remembered finding them kissing in the woods. What a blessing I'd been successful at masking it.

Theo could not hold my gaze. He looked away, then ran his fingers over his smooth jawline. "Between you and me, I am not as confident in that as you are."

"What do you mean?"

He gave me a sad smile. "If I am to take you into my confidence, I might request you do the same in return."

"That would depend on the nature of the secret you wish for me to share." My heart raced. If he intended to ask about my feelings for him, I could never respond with the truth.

"It is nothing of an intrusive nature, I hope." He paused. "I have been told you no longer sing."

My breath caught. Footsteps clicked across the floorboards leading into the drawing room, and Archie arrived beside my father before I had an opportunity to reply. I stood, setting my book on the cushion. "Papa! You've come home. Did you see the tree?"

"I did." He reached for me, pulling me into an embrace. "It is perfect."

I beamed. "It will look better tomorrow once we have dressed it."

He smiled, his gray whiskers quivering. "It is good to be home," he whispered as if imparting a secret.

"Is your business concluded to your satisfaction?"

His smile widened, and he rocked back a little on his heels. "That is for you to determine."

"What do you mean?"

He pressed his lips together and shook his head.

Oh gracious. I hated secrets.

Papa *tsked.* "Do not look so glum. You shall soon be well aware of what I mean. I have brought you a Christmas present."

"Christmas is not for three days."

"This present will not keep." He winked at me. "But we must wait for your mama." He gave me a squeeze on the shoulder and passed me to approach Theo. "You look well, son."

Theo dipped his head in acknowledgment and reached to shake Papa's hand heartily.

"You must help me convince him to remain over Christmas," Archie said.

"What's this?" Papa asked, looking between Archie and Theo.

"He believes it is his duty to go to his mother," Archie said, motioning to his friend. "At this rate, he'll hardly make it in time for Christmas anyway. If he remains with us, he can go to her after the holiday, when she is in London. This way Theo can spend a few days with us."

Theo cleared his throat. "I would never wish to be an imposition—"

"You could not be. We have missed you these last few years." Papa looked at me, forcing the other men to turn my direction. "Lillian most of all, I am sure. None of us have any great musical talent, you know. I fear being relegated to our company has been a great challenge for her."

My smile stretched awkwardly over my teeth. "Do not listen to Papa. I do not rate the measure of a man on his ability to play a musical instrument."

"More pity for me, then," Theo said.

Father laughed, but Archie looked uncomfortable. "Mother is here."

Mama came in, her violet gown swishing with each step. "Shall we give Lily her gift before dinner or after?"

I grinned. "You cannot make me wait an entire meal."

Papa tapped his finger against his chin. "Yet we do not wish for the meal to grow cold. What do you say, men?"

"Give it to her now, or she'll be unbearable during dinner."

I lifted my eyebrow toward Archie. "I choose to believe that was in no way a criticism of my behavior and you are purely on my side."

He delivered a dramatic bow. "Always, dear sister."

Mama crossed the room and slipped her hand around my father's arm. "Now is best. Come with us." She looked very pleased with herself, and together my parents led us from the room, through the dining room, and into the small antechamber on the other side.

In the center of the room sat a wide tower with a domed top, a cloth draped over it. It stood as tall as me. Mama and Papa waited beside it, watching me approach. Archie and Theo followed me, waiting on my other side.

"Lift the drape," Mama said.

I pinched the fabric between two fingers and lifted it to reveal a gold cage. Thin bars ran vertically in a circle from the bottom to its domed ceiling. Intricate scrollwork lined the door and the roof, and the entire thing was nearly as wide as my gown, hoops and all. Resting on a perch in the center was the most beautiful bird I had ever seen, its talons curled tightly around a wooden rod. Bright green, so vibrant that it looked unnatural, bled down to blue and white feathers in the wings, with bits of yellow near the head, like a necklace.

"Is he a parrot?" I asked.

"*She* is," Papa said. "With perfect pitch."

I looked at him swiftly. "The bird sings?"

"Indeed." He approached the cage, and his arm went around my back. "She learns by listening to you sing, and then she can repeat it."

My stomach sank. Had he bought the pet as some sort of enticement to compel me to sing again? After three years, were they not aware that perhaps I had decided to cease because the act itself brought me pain? That it filled me with embarrassment and shame and reminded me of exactly how clumsy and ridiculous I was?

That I wanted to be valued for more than how well I could carry a tune?

I looked at Theo and found his blue eyes regarding me softly, a line between his eyebrows again.

The small room grew inordinately stuffy. I took a step back from the bird, forcing my father's hand to drop.

"You do not like it," Papa said.

"No, of course I love it." The blue-tipped wings were incredible. Were I an accomplished painter, my first order of business would be an attempt to capture the beauty in this golden cage. "She is entrancing."

The silence then was thick, but Mama brought us around again with her cheery tone. "Let us enjoy dinner before it grows cold."

Chapter Four

Theo

I HALF EXPECTED LILLIAN TO return to her parrot when dinner concluded, but she surprised me by following her mother to the drawing room instead. She opened the little red book she'd brought up earlier and had not put it down for the last half hour.

But I had not seen her turn the page once.

Archie snapped a finger, stealing my attention. "You are not listening to me." He followed my gaze toward Lillian. "What the devil has my sister done to capture your attention so fully?"

"I was thinking." I looked to where Mr. and Mrs. Hartley were seated together near Lillian. They were on the other side of the room—far enough not to have overheard Archie, I hoped. "She is merely in my line of sight."

"You are brooding," Archie said quietly. "Has any trouble followed you home from Vienna?"

"No, nothing of the sort."

"Are you angry that I want you to remain here? You can go to your mother if you choose."

"You're saving me from an extremely uncomfortable holiday. I would much rather see my mother when she goes to London next week. Perhaps I will hold off on writing and surprise her there." I shook my head. Those details could be sorted later. "What is it you wanted to speak of?"

Archie flicked his head to where his family was seated on the other side of the room. "We need more privacy than this."

"Understood." I sighed. "Maybe I *should* have gone to Dorset. If I remain with you, I will see Miss Marcote much sooner than I am prepared for."

Archie tucked his chin. "Why do you say that?"

I let out a sigh and ran a hand over my mouth. If I spoke these thoughts aloud, they would no longer be an inkling of worry in my mind. They would be real, and the notion was frightening. But if I could not speak to my closest friend about my concerns, they would only eat at me further. I glanced at where the rest of the Hartley family was sitting, but they all appeared otherwise occupied.

"We've written to one another over the duration of my absence, but her letters have grown increasingly sparse of late."

"Women become busy," he said with a shrug.

"Yes, but it is more than that. The letters have also changed in tone. I fear she has had a change of heart." Or beyond that . . . but no, I could not even think it. I passed a hand over my forehead and sank a little in my chair, lowering my voice. "No one but you knows of our promise. What if she has decided that it no longer suits her?"

Archie swallowed, shaking his head softly. "Ada is honorable. She is a good woman, and she would not renege on any promise she has made."

Her character wasn't in question, just how she felt about me. "Something doesn't feel right anymore. I have a feeling I will know why as soon as I see her."

"Which might be tomorrow," Archie said quietly. "My mother invited the Marcotes to participate in the children's tea."

"Brilliant." If our reunion was heading in the direction I predicted, it was better not to put it off any longer than necessary. That did not mean I relished the oncoming conversation though. I did not want her to jilt me, but neither did I want to marry a woman who had fallen out of love with me. Especially not when my own feelings had entered a stage of uncertainty. Surely that would be righted when I laid eyes upon her again.

"Will you play for us, Theo?" Mrs. Hartley asked.

Lillian focused on her book. If I peeked over her shoulder, would it still be on page one? "I would love to play, if Lily will sing."

Lillian looked up, closing her book with a snap. "I'm afraid I have other plans this evening."

"Other plans?" Mr. Hartley said, laughing.

"We do not have any centerpieces for the children's tea. Do we, Mama?"

"No." Mrs. Hartley narrowed her eyes at her daughter. "How did you know that?"

"I heard you telling Mrs. Cole earlier today. Shall I create something?"

Mrs. Hartley's gaze shifted away, searching the room as if it would provide an answer to the question. Heavens, what was her reason for refusing the help? Lillian could not have meant it when she'd said earlier that her mother didn't want her assistance in any matter, surely. Mrs. Hartley was the kindest of souls.

"It is too late tonight, darling. We will sort it in the morning."

Lillian reached for her book again.

Mrs. Hartley frowned. "Will you not join Theo as you used to do?"

"No, I thank you. I shall not."

The room went silent. Mrs. Hartley looked at me.

I stood. "I suppose we'll have to put off the performance, then. I am rather tired, so if you'll excuse me, I think I will turn in for the night."

"Of course, dear," Mrs. Hartley said, rising. "We are so glad to have you here. Please ring for Kemper if you find yourself in need of anything at all."

"Thank you, ma'am." I bowed to each of the Hartleys. Archie dipped his head to me but remained seated, much to my surprise. He'd mentioned wanting to speak to me, and I assumed he'd walk out with me for that purpose, but he stayed in his chair. I turned back and looked at him before slipping from the room and found his attention on his parents. Lillian was the only person watching me leave. I sent her a soft smile, and she returned it briefly before I slipped out.

Darkness had crept in and stolen a little of her joy, and I did not like it in the least. Something needed to be done to reinstate her light.

* * *

Perhaps my somewhat early night could be blamed, but I woke with the sun and could not find sleep again. I dressed and helped myself downstairs, but no one else had awoken yet. Or if they had, they no longer breakfasted in the morning room, for it was empty.

My stomach made a loud rumbling sound. I looked through the window to the long building at the back of the house. If there was one thing I could count on, it was finding ripe, juicy oranges in the orangery, even in December. Mr. Hartley's gardener had always prided himself on the way he had trained the trees to produce fruit just in time for Christmas. Receiving the citrus from the Hartleys each year was among my fondest memories from my childhood holidays.

It also meant I could have breakfast without bothering anyone in the kitchens. If the children's tea was today, the maids were likely elbow-deep in cakes and tarts and would not appreciate the interruption of a hungry guest.

I regretted forgoing my greatcoat the moment I stepped outside. The air was frigid, seeping through layers and chilling me to the bone. I jogged from the courtyard, under the domed stone walkway, and around the side of the house. The exercise warmed my blood, though my trousers were not made for it, and they tugged awkwardly with each step.

The orangery was long and slender with glass windows lining the entirety, broken by columns of stone. The door in the center was set in a large bay window, and I pushed it open, glad for the warmth inside. A mosaic floor created a pathway around the fountain straight ahead of me, and I bypassed it, turning toward the orange trees lining the building to the side.

"Good morning," a sweet voice called from high in the branches.

I looked up to find Lillian at the top of a ladder, her face peering out from between full green branches. "Is it safe for you to be up so high?"

She glanced down at her feet. "It was a little difficult to find my footing, but I feel secure."

My feet carried me to the bottom of her ladder. "Allow me to guide you down."

She stood above me, looking down with a quizzical expression. "I am not stuck, Theo. I am in the middle of completing a task."

"Which is typically the job of a gardener, is it not?"

She tilted her head. "The longer you distract me, the longer it will take for me to finish."

"By all means," I said with a flourish toward the tree. "You may continue."

Lillian faced the tree again, reached for an orange, and plucked it before dropping it into the basket hanging from her other arm. She reached for another when her hand stalled, and her attention turned once again to me. "You are distracting me."

"I have not spoken another word."

"But you are hovering at my feet."

"So I might catch you if you slip."

"I have come up and down this ladder three times already this morning with no accident."

"Why? There are many oranges closer to the bottom that have yet to be plucked."

Her gray eyes sparked. "But those are not as ripe. The best oranges are up here."

I noted the larger basket near the wall, half full of oranges. "Why do you need so many?"

"I thought to place one on each of the children's plates. Most of them are orphans. I imagine they do not have the opportunity to eat many oranges." Lillian turned away again, plucking another fruit.

Her ladder tottered a little, and she froze. My arms went up, ready to brace her, but she settled.

"It frightens me each time it does that," she admitted.

"Gads, Lily. Climb down and let me gather the oranges for you. I will climb as high as you wish."

"I am nearly finished. I need only six more." She plucked another.

"But if you were to fall—"

She scoffed. "Why must you underestimate me? I am only gathering oranges, for heaven's sake."

My stomach jolted at the same time as she took hold of a stubborn orange and tugged hard. Her arm flew back too far, and she lost her balance. The basket of oranges plummeted to the ground, the fruit rolling every direction as Lillian let out a squeal and flailed her arms, falling from the ladder.

I put out my arms to catch her, but she didn't fall into them perfectly, and we both crumbled to the tiled floor. I cushioned her fall, and she landed on top of me, knocking the wind from my lungs. Lillian's hair was near my mouth and her weight distributed over my chest. I sucked in a breath, inhaling a faint floral scent with the sweet aroma of oranges.

She groaned, the sound bouncing from the glass walls and amplifying. I tried to help her stand, but she wouldn't let me, instead pulling herself up and finding her basket.

"Are you hurt?" I asked breathlessly, my heart thudding.

"No."

I got to my feet and started picking up oranges. I tossed a few into the basket near the base of the tree.

Lillian removed them. She moved toward a pile of empty baskets and lifted one, dropping the bruised oranges into it. "We cannot use these now."

"Surely one fall will not ruin them entirely."

"Not by my standards, but I could not bear it if one of the orphans received a bruised orange. This might be the only one they have all year." She returned her attention to gathering the spilled fruit. She'd caught my attention, and I had difficulty tearing it from her. When had little Lillian turned into a woman? She had claimed as much, but it was hard to reconcile until last night, when she was walking down the stairs toward me before dinner. She was beautiful. Striking. But I'd immediately pushed all attraction from my mind. I could not look at her in this way. It was wrong. I had already pledged myself to Ada Marcote.

I continued helping Lillian pick up oranges. "How is your parrot settling in?"

"I've yet to put her in my room."

"Does she have a name?"

Lillian looked down at the orange in her hand with a soft smile. "Clementine, I think. She looks like a very elegant bird."

"I like it." The oranges were nearly all picked up, so I took an empty basket and climbed the ladder, plucking more fruit to replace the ones that could have been bruised in their fall. If I harvested them fast enough, maybe Lillian would stop trying to climb ladders.

She took up shears and another basket and moved to the other side of the orangery to cut flowers instead. Her skirt swished as she walked, its stone blue almost the color of her gray eyes.

"Have you always been an early riser?" I asked.

Her voice came from behind a large rosebush. "No. I wanted to surprise my mother with centerpieces when she woke up, so it was a necessity today."

I climbed down from the ladder and transferred my oranges to the largest basket before joining her. "That is kind of you."

"Is it? I think it is my pride wanting to prove I can accomplish small tasks without ruining the event."

"You did fall from a ladder."

She cut a rose and laid it in her basket. "Because you distracted me."

"And you fell in the mud yesterday."

"*Again*," she said, snipping another rose with extra force, "because you distracted me."

I crossed my arms over my chest. "You cannot blame everything on me, Lily. Next you will try to claim that I am the reason you no longer sing."

She flashed me a frank look before crossing the mosaic path to the flowers on the other side. Her silence seemed an answer in itself.

My mouth hung open. "You cannot mean that."

"I said nothing."

"Your expression did all the talking necessary."

She shook her head, snipping away flower stems like she was venting her anger on them.

So something *had* happened? "If I did something—"

The door opened, bringing a fresh wave of cold air with it. I spun to find Archie stepping inside, his eyes widening in shock. "What are you both doing here?" he asked.

"Collecting oranges and flowers for the children," Lillian said with a slight edge to her tone. I'd done something to vex her—that was certainly clear—but *what*?

"Oh." There was a breath of silence, broken only by the trickling water in the fountain. "Well, the Marcote carriage was seen coming up the drive." Archie looked at me. "Ada will be here soon."

"Good. She can help me with these flowers," Lillian muttered, passing me a basketful of a variety of blooms. She returned to the overly large basket of oranges and looked at us. "Can you carry these to the great hall?"

"I had planned on . . ." Archie cleared his throat and looked at me, then away. "Yes, I can help."

"Thank you." Lillian swept past us with her basket of flowers, moving the floral and citrus scent under my nose again before leaving the orangery.

"Shall we each take a side?" Archie asked, looking at the oranges dubiously.

I nodded, positioning myself on the opposite side of the basket and taking a handle. It was heavy, but we lifted and carried it toward the door. "What were you going to the orangery for?" I asked.

"To inform Lily of the Marcotes' arrival."

I did not say another word, but something about his answer rang false. If he had gone there to speak to Lillian, why was he surprised to find her there?

Archie nearly dropped the basket, and we both readjusted our holds on the handles. Lillian walked ahead of us, but all I could think of was the expression she'd worn and how clearly it had stated that I carried some of the blame for her refusal to sing.

But how could I, when I'd been gone?

Chapter Five

Lillian

Ada and her mother swept into the great hall as I was dividing the flowers into groups of ten. I laid the last of the roses down and wiped my hands on my apron before moving to greet my friend. Servants had begun setting tables with plates and cutlery, and two footmen were putting chairs around each of the round tables.

"You look marvelous," I said, leaning forward to kiss Ada's cheek as her mother met Mama near the pianoforte. Ada wore a gown of hunter green that balanced her copper hair perfectly. She was easily the most beautiful woman in Cheshire, but her humility made her even lovelier. I appreciated that I could call Ada my friend.

She looked over my shoulder. "Is it true?"

My heart thundered. She had already caught word of Theo's return?

Ada's blue eyes widened. "I heard whispers that your mama invited the rector to speak to the children."

"She did." Relief sluiced through me. I was not yet ready for her to take Theo's attention captive again. "I think we might plan on the sermon portion taking a good deal longer than it did last year."

"As long as we are prepared, it shan't be too bad." Ada grinned.

"It is a *Christmas* tea, so we would be remiss if there was not some mention of Christ's birth, I think."

Ada nodded. "I heartily agree. But the rector? A more long-winded man does not exist."

Her smile was so genuine, so kind, my stomach sank. It occurred to me that whether I wanted it to happen or not, Theo and Ada would see one another this morning. How would she feel if I allowed her to discover his return without any warning at all? Seeing him yesterday had been an utter shock for me, and I had never kissed the man. Whatever was between Ada and Theo, I knew they had some sort of understanding. They had to. One did not allow a man to kiss one without a promise of some sort.

"Ada, I must tell you something." I took her hand and pulled her farther away from our mothers. "I do not wish for you to have a fright, but we have a visitor."

"Who?" She looked up when the door opened to Archie and Theo carrying in the heavy basket of oranges, and her face paled.

"Theodore Pine has returned," I said, a little late.

Ada stared at him, her gaze frozen. The expression that flashed in her eyes appeared more akin to fear than joy, which tugged at my conscience. Something did not add up.

Theo glanced up and saw her, surprise parting his lips.

But neither of them looked exceptionally happy. For those who didn't know better, they would assume this wasn't a joyful reunion. But, of course, I did know better.

Ada quickly shuttered her expression, a smile transforming her face. "You've returned!" She crossed the room, gathering attention from all, until she reached his side, with the entire room watching closely. Theo set down his side of the basket and took Ada's hand, bringing it to his lips to kiss her knuckles as he bowed over it—the greeting between an interested man and woman. Quite unlike anything I'd ever received from Theo. My mood fell. Mrs. Marcote watched this interaction with joy, her smile wide.

Archie left them, lifting the large orange basket on his own and bringing it to my side. "Where do you want this?"

I tried to cover my disappointment. I gestured to where he'd set it down. "You may leave it there."

He gave me a brief smile and walked from the room. I bent my attention to the flowers, filling the ten vases and arranging them to my satisfaction. They were interspersed with sprigs of greenery and looked festive with red roses and berries.

Ada laughed, her voice melodic, and I did my best to ignore her and Theo.

Carefully carrying each vase to a different table, I set them down gently so they would not break or spill. Ada's laugh rang through the room again, followed by Theo's chuckle. The sounds pierced my heart like tiny daggers.

I supposed I should have noticed their connection on my own all those years ago, but it was difficult to see clearly when one's mind was clouded with affection. I never realized that the way Theo flirted with me was never flirting—it was the teasing affection of an older brother. His calling my voice angelic was not from attraction but an unbiased opinion of sound.

The day I'd gone to his house for the purpose of working on a song to perform together at his farewell party, I had worn perfume, done my hair with particular care, and prepared myself to tell him how I felt. He was about to leave for Vienna, and I didn't want him to go without knowing of my love for him. He had given me cause to think he could return my feelings—or so I'd believed. But when I turned the corner in the path and found him and Ada kissing beneath the elm tree, her giggle piercing my false ideals of Theo, I had been crushed. When he'd followed the kiss by telling her that her laugh was the most angelic sound in the world, my feelings had crumbled to dust.

I'd left before they saw me and had hidden in my room, feigning illness in order to be excused from any obligation to perform. In reality I was ill from a broken heart. Ada eventually took me into her confidence, but only so much as to tell me they had a shared affection for one another so she could speak freely to me of his letters. Looking back, I knew I'd been blind.

Now I didn't want to see them together—to know they were steps away from announcing an engagement or some such thing. I had done my best to forget Theo, but my silly heart had yet to agree with my mind. I bent my focus to the task of being happy for Ada instead. I could not count myself her friend if I felt anything less.

And perhaps I would sing again someday, but I could not do it yet. Not when all it did was remind me that I was not good enough. It was far more than the shame and embarrassment of realizing Theo didn't love me like I'd hoped, that he loved someone else. It was everyone in my life who had only appreciated me for my voice. I was more than a lovely song. I wanted to be appreciated for *me*.

Mrs. Marcote approached me, admiring the vase of flowers I was arranging. Her auburn hair was styled high above her head, intricately braided and pomaded into a complicated coiffure. "This is lovely, Miss Hartley."

"Thank you."

Mama joined us but paused by the large basket of oranges. "What is this, Lillian?"

"I thought it would look festive if we placed an orange on each plate."

She blinked at me. "You retrieved all these oranges yourself?"

"Yes . . . well, mostly. I did have some help."

Mama nodded as if to say she believed that to be the case. It irked me.

"But I had done nearly all of it myself. I clipped and arranged all the flowers, and I've yet to break a single vase."

"Of course," Mama said, smiling kindly. "Thank you, darling. They're lovely. You can leave the rest of the work to the servants if you'd like to visit with Ada."

I looked to where my friend was talking quietly with Theo, and my heart cramped. I pasted a bright smile on my face. "I think I will fetch the decorations I made last year for the tree, actually."

"Allow the servants to assist you," Mama said, worried.

I swallowed my hurt, avoiding giving her a response for fear that my voice would break. I left to retrieve the decorations before I could say something I would later regret.

* * *

Theo

I had been correct. Something was not quite right with Ada. Seeing her again after three years was . . . perfectly lovely, of course, but nothing more. The connection between us was missing. The trouble was, I could not discern whether it was her feelings that had undergone a change, or my own.

"Will you go to Dorset to see your mother?" Ada asked, peering up at me from beneath a fan of lashes. Her copper hair was vibrant, her skin pale and unblemished. She was beautiful, but she did not set my heart to a rapid beat.

If only I had been more patient before pledging myself away. Now there was nothing I could do but see it through.

"My plan is to spend Christmas here and travel to London next week to see my mother. I need to write to her and confirm her plans before I attempt another surprise though. I can see now how foolish my idea was."

"Not foolish in the least," she argued. "It would have been wonderful had your mother been home to receive you."

"I've been too long away. She hardly ever traveled to Dorset before. It appears now she goes to see her sister frequently. I suppose she must have grown less wary of the train."

"That is a fair assessment." Ada grinned. "Quite the modern woman, Mrs. Pine."

I laughed. Never before would I have believed that descriptor, but now I wondered how much Mother had changed in the last three years. I'd stayed away in part because being in my house after my father died was too painful.

Had that been more harmful or helpful to my mother? Now she was the only family I had. Guilt flowed through me like the Danube in springtime.

Lillian passed us, carrying a small crate. I moved to take it from her. "Allow me to help you."

She pulled it away, giving me a tight smile. "I can manage."

I wanted an excuse to breathe away from Ada for a moment. "It is no trouble, Lily."

Her eyes flashed. "I agree." She turned away and headed straight for the Christmas tree in the center of the room, leaving me behind. What had I done now?

My feet stalled halfway between Lillian and Ada. I knew which direction I wanted to move, but it wasn't the way I was supposed to go. I rubbed a hand over the back of my neck and turned back to Ada, surprised to find her directly beside me.

"Shall we help Lillian decorate the tree?" Ada asked, watching me closely.

"Yes." I offered her my arm and led her toward the center of the great hall. A footman had brought a small ladder for Lillian, and she was climbing onto the second rung, making me nervous. "Shall I be the one on the ladder, Miss Hartley? You can direct me from a better vantage point."

Lillian didn't spare me a glance, her focus remaining on the string of dried-orange triangles she was untangling. "I am happy where I am."

Ada reached into the crate and pulled out a paper-wrapped parcel, unfolding it to reveal thin strands of silver. "These are lovely."

"They reflect the candlelight and make the tree appear as though it sparkles," Lillian said, her attention on weaving a strand of dried oranges through the branches. She leaned forward to wrap the twine about a branch, and I stepped beneath her, prepared to catch her should she fall.

"Shall we wait and add these last?" Ada asked, setting them back in the crate. She looked about the room. "You seem to have this well in hand. I will place oranges on the plates."

The space Ada provided me was a relief, which pecked at my conscience. I'd given her my word that we would someday be married, and now I was relieved when she walked to the other side of the room? It felt like I'd crawled into the parrot's cage and locked myself inside. Shaking myself, I watched Ada's slender hand reach for an orange and place it gently on a child's plate. She truly was lovely. A life with her would be satisfying, surely. I was no longer plagued by the boyish infatuation that had once ruled my thoughts, but that did not mean I could not find a way back to that.

It hardly mattered, for I'd given my word, and I would not break my promise.

I pulled another strand of dried-orange slices from the crate to untangle, angling myself to remain beneath Lillian.

Without looking down at me, she spoke. "I know what you are doing."

"You cannot expect me to forget the last time you were on a ladder." I glanced up to find a blush bleeding slowly into her cheeks. She was already pretty, but this made her glow.

"How unkind of you to mention it," she muttered.

"Would you prefer if I did not care at all for your safety?"

"My safety is not in jeopardy. I would prefer if you had faith in me." Lillian stepped farther up the ladder to reach the next layer of branches.

"Faith is not the issue, Lily. It is the sheer width of your skirts." I gestured toward her feet.

Lillian looked down, shaking her head. She stepped up another rung and leaned forward to weave the garland through the higher branches. Her body angled dangerously away from the ladder. I watched with trepidation. It was evident she felt underestimated and was doing her best to prove the opposite.

But she needn't prove anything to me.

"Is that not high enough?" I asked.

Lillian gripped her skirts and pushed them to the side so her feet could step up one more rung, without so much as glancing my way. When she reached for the branches to string the garland, however, she lost her balance and fell forward, toppling into the Christmas tree. I grabbed the skirt of her dress, pulling her toward me before she could go down with the tree. I held tightly around her legs, then slid her down my chest and set her softly on the floor, but I could feel her body trembling.

"No," she whispered, her gray eyes wide. "The children's tree."

Children's? Not Christmas? The evergreen was on its side, needles covering the nearby tables and marble floor.

"Are you hurt?" I asked.

Lillian raised her face, her cheeks flushed bright red. She shook her head as she extricated herself from my grasp.

Mrs. Hartley hurried toward us. "Oh dear. I asked you to let the servants help. We cannot afford any mishaps this morning. We haven't the time."

"I will fetch a broom."

"No, darling." Her mother shook her head. "You go ready yourself for the tea. Where is Kemper? Tilly can clean this, and John will manage the tree."

The servants mentioned must have heard her, because they sprang into action, doing as Mrs. Hartley requested. They effectively pushed Lillian away, and it was unfair.

"I am to blame, Mrs. Hartley," I said. "Had I not hovered—"

"Nonsense, darling. Lillian knows that she is not to climb ladders in that gown."

A look of forlorn misery passed over Lillian's face, piercing my heart. She gave one brisk nod and turned, walking elegantly from the room. Her shame and disappointment were so thick, they were nearly palpable. She paused at the mouth of the corridor that led to the stairs and turned to glance at us over her shoulder. When she caught my eye, she looked away quickly.

I needed to find a way to make this right. Regardless of what Mrs. Hartley believed, it was entirely my fault.

Chapter Six

Lillian

I'd ruined the children's Christmas tree, and it ruined the rest of my day. Mortification had bled through my limbs and lingered. I could not trust myself around any more preparations for the children's tea, so I made myself absent. I had tugged a chaise longue in front of the squint in the drawing room upstairs and settled myself there, cracking one of the doors open so I could see out over the entire great hall below me.

I was not *spying*, exactly. The purpose of the squint was to be able to look down over the room.

We never had the doors open in the squint. If anyone did look up, they would see me immediately, but no one thought to. From this vantage point, I could watch the entirety of the children's tea without being there to ruin it.

Mother and Mrs. Marcote had welcomed all the children before Mrs. Cole seated them and the servants brought out the food. My favorite part of the annual children's Christmas tea was approaching. I watched with disappointment niggling in my stomach as Ada held a basket and walked from child to child, distributing a paper-wrapped parcel to each of them. That had usually been my task, and it was the highlight of the season for me to watch their small faces light with joy.

This year Mama and I had selected dolls for the girls and wooden soldiers for the boys. Last year we gave them the cup-and-ball game. The year before that a set of genuine marbles. Most of these children were orphans or from poorer families in the village. This would likely be the only toy they received this year, so we did our best to choose one that would be universally enjoyed.

The longer I watched their faces while they received their gifts, the larger my heart swelled. Ada made her way between the tables, distributing joy and receiving the widest of grins in return. I pushed the door open a little more to better see and rested my elbows on my knees in a distinctly unladylike manner. I did not care. I only wanted to soak in the joy and allow it to eclipse my embarrassment.

I made a special effort to avoid looking at the tree. Its broken branches and naked spots made it decidedly less magical than it had been this morning.

"You could go down and help, you know," a deep voice said from just behind me.

I startled, turning to find my brother standing there, Theo just beside him.

"Why are you up here?" I asked.

"We always watch the tea from here," Archie said. "Though, usually it is you distributing the gifts."

I hadn't known that. I shifted to watch Ada distribute the toys once again. "Mama has banished me. I've ruined too many things."

"You know that is not the case," Archie said. "Mother only cares that you are not hurt."

I lifted my hand to stop him. "It is too soon for your platitudes, Archie. Let me be sad."

"You would not need to be sad if you joined them," Theo said.

I shot him a look, but he did not back down, instead holding my gaze. It was too heavy, and I was forced to look away.

"Do you know what would be a great trick?" Archie asked. "If we taught the bird a song without Mother or Father knowing and surprised them at dinner tonight."

I leveled him with a look. "You are not as sneaky as you believe."

The blood drained from his face, making his skin chalky white. Genuine fear flashed in his eyes.

"Are you unwell?" I asked, rising from my seat.

Archie shook his head, looking at Theo and then back at me. "What did you mean by that?"

"Only that you cannot trick me into singing with the pretense of tricking our parents."

His shoulders deflated at once, and he ran a hand over his forehead in relief. What was he hiding from me? He couldn't have been more obvious had he tried to give himself away. He was holding on to a secret.

"Shall I fetch us something to drink?" he asked. He was already walking away, and I imagined he wanted a reason to leave for a minute and catch his breath.

"That was odd," I said when he walked from the room. "He knows we're to take tea with the Marcotes as soon as the rector finishes his speech."

Theo approached me slowly. "I, for one, am glad he left."

My heart kicked up speed. "Why?"

"So I can apologize."

I turned away from him and sat again on the chaise longue in front of the open squint doors. "You've nothing to apologize for."

"It is my fault you fell into the tree."

"Don't be absurd."

He sat beside me, shifting the weight of the cushions. I felt our solitude immensely, yet anyone who looked up from the great hall would see us together, watching them from above. We were alone, but we were also entirely on display.

"If I had not pushed you into feeling you must prove yourself, you never would have fallen."

"Good heavens." I gave a soft laugh. "You cannot blame yourself for my clumsiness, Theo. It is very chivalrous of you to try, but you sound ridiculous."

"You do not accept my apology?"

"It is not necessary." I made the mistake of turning toward him and found him watching me, his face far too close for comfort. His blue eyes were soft, revealing a thread of confusion while he searched my face. What was he hoping to find? "Tell me of Vienna instead," I requested, looking away. "Distract me."

Theo was silent for so long I wondered if he heard me. I looked at him again, and he was still watching me. I mapped the faint lines beside his eyes etched from laughter, the creases bracketing his lips from his easy smile. His presence was heavy, close, and I needed to put distance between us somehow.

I tried again. "Could you feel the presence of Mozart? Were there musicians everywhere?"

Theo swallowed. "Yes. It was incredible to be where so many great men were before me."

"You must have felt vastly inspired. Have you returned with an abundance of new music to share with us?"

He looked away. "Not as inspired as one might think after walking the same streets as Schubert and Beethoven."

"But you remained for so long."

"The first year was incredible. The people I met were inspiring and talented. I worked under Mr. Hollander's cousin, who had a gift for combining instruments, and I learned the art of duets."

Mr. Hollander was our old vicar who'd invited Theo to go to Vienna and introduced him to his family there. It had been a boon, proof that Theo possessed the talent we'd all imagined he had. But when Mr. Hollander returned to England a few months later, Theo had remained, learning from the masters there. I'd thought it was good for his career, at the time.

"What of the last two years?" I asked.

He wrinkled his nose. "I spent those looking for the inspiration that filled my first year in Vienna."

Two years searching? I couldn't imagine the toll that must've taken on him or the constant disappointment it must have provided. "Why did you choose to come home now?"

He gave me a crooked smile. "Aside from missing steak and ale pie?"

I chuckled. "Aside from the food."

He looked out over the great hall below us, the children sipping their tea and munching on cake. I didn't know if he was watching Ada finish her task of distributing the gifts, but I imagined that was where his gaze had traveled. I stood abruptly, deciding I did not need to hear from his own mouth that he had returned for her. My heart could not take it.

"Forget I asked." I took a step back. "That was intrusive."

"Hardly," he argued, rising to follow me. "If anyone has the right to question me about my music, it is you."

I felt a blow to my heart, as though it had been delivered physically, and stared at him. "How can you say that? I can have no more claim than any other woman." I *knew* I had no more claim than Ada, though Theo was unaware of my knowledge in that regard.

"It is not your status as a female that gives you any privilege."

"Precisely." I scoffed lightly. "While you have pledged yourself to another, you cannot permit me to believe *we* share any special connection, Theo. It is not appropriate."

He stared at me, his blue eyes unyielding. Did he wonder how I knew of his relationship with Ada? His gaze shifted away before landing on me once again. "You are correct. I do not know what I was thinking. No, that is untrue. We have always shared a connection with music, Lily, have we not?"

"I thought so once, but it hardly matters." Not when he was soon to be married. I looked to the great hall but no longer saw Ada.

"What happened, Lily?" he asked softly. "I gather I had a part to play in it, but I cannot understand why you will not sing anymore."

Will not? "I *cannot*. It is not by choice." I thought back to the time after he'd left when I had attempted to sing alone in my chamber, and the pain had been too great to continue. My barriers were of an emotional origin, yes, but no less real.

He looked startled. "Cannot? Then, you must have suffered greatly in some way."

How could he see through me so easily? I tried to soften my tone. "That is a dramatic way of looking at things."

"Is it not the truth?"

It was, but I could not admit so to him.

"Talk to me," he said, nearly pleading. "Perhaps I can help you."

"You can do nothing," I said hoarsely.

Theo shook his head. "You cannot mean to deprive the world of your voice, Lily."

It was on the tip of my tongue to admit to him that I would choose to be wanted for myself. His blue eyes watched me. I could tell this was important to him. As a composer and connoisseur of beautiful music himself, he appreciated and admired a pure tone. But I did not want Theo to admire my voice alone—and with Ada involved, he could not admire me in any other way. It was a truth I had long since accepted, but that did not make it hurt any less.

"It hardly matters," I said.

"It does. To me, it—"

"It should hardly matter to you," I snapped quietly. "Your attention ought to be elsewhere entirely. You are not free to say such things to me, even if they are only about music."

He appeared chagrined. "How did you know? Did Ada tell you?"

"That is not relevant," I whispered.

Theo looked down at the great hall, searching the room. The rector had been introduced and begun to the story of Christ's birth. "Has Ada left?"

"I am not sure. You can look for her in the morning room. That is where my mother planned to hold the tea for us once the rector finishes his sermon."

Theo stared at the floor before lifting his gaze to me. "I have only been home for one day, and already I feel as though it would have been better had I not come home at all."

"Do not speak in such a way." I reached for him out of impulse, squeezing his forearm before dropping my hand to my side. "We are all glad you returned, Archie especially. I wager no one is as glad as Ada though."

Theo met my gaze, though his remained troubled.

"Everything will settle soon; you will see," I promised. "Shall we go down for tea? A bracing cup is known to cure many ailments, you know. I imagine that is another thing you must have missed while abroad."

"They do have tea in Vienna, Lily," he said. The smile had returned to his voice.

"But it is not *English* tea."

"Very well. You have persuaded me. I will go down if you accompany me."

If I did not, I would only be prolonging the discord between us. It was better to swallow my disappointment than to prolong it. "Very well."

Theo dipped his head softly before offering me his arm.

Chapter Seven

Theo

It was Christmas Eve, and Kemper had not spared a moment clearing out the tables and chairs from the children's tea to make room for the family's celebration. Archie had stolen me from the breakfast room in order to find a Yule log for this evening's fire. We bundled up and trekked out to Pine Woods, as the Hartleys affectionately called the trees between our properties.

"We have an easy time of it this year," Archie said, trudging through the snow beside me and tugging along a sled. "That old oak tree fell recently, so I thought to cut a portion of it."

"Lead the way," I said, eager for this task to be completed so we could return to the warmth of Lynton Park. We reached the edge of the trees, their bare branches glistening from melting ice. "Has your father relinquished any of the estate control since you returned from Cambridge?"

"Not exactly. When I first came home, he told me he wanted to give me time to settle. That was two years ago." Archie shot me a wry smile. "You would think I have had sufficient settling time by now."

"Perhaps he meant it literally. He wants you to settle down with a wife, and then he will give you serious responsibilities."

Archie rubbed a hand over the back of his neck and wouldn't meet my eyes. "Perhaps."

The man was more averse to marriage than I'd realized. I used to feel the same, but I couldn't afford to put it off any longer. It was time to follow through on my promise. I tugged on his arm, forcing him to stop and face me. "Did you think Ada behaved strangely yesterday?"

"I couldn't say."

"No, I suppose you wouldn't have noticed the nuances of her actions toward me." I stepped back, shaking my head. "Has she been strange in my absence? Something is not quite right, but I cannot identify exactly what it is."

Archie leveled me with a frank look. "Have you asked her?"

"That would be best, but broaching the subject hasn't been easy. I do not know what to say."

"The truth, Theo. Tell her how you feel, and she will undoubtedly do the same."

It was sound advice, though I couldn't help but feel that Archie was uncomfortable offering it.

"The Marcotes were invited to dinner this evening," he said, starting on the path again. He looked at me briefly over his shoulder. "I'm certain my mother did that for your benefit, you know."

My body went cold, and it was not from the frigid temperatures outside. "Does everyone know?"

"About your secret engagement? I doubt it. But even a simpleton could detect that there was something between you before you left for Vienna. Your behavior yesterday, searching her out straightaway, likely only confirmed my mother's assumptions."

"Blast."

"You are not happy with everyone knowing?"

"I do not know myself what is between Ada and me. How can I? I've been away for too long and have yet to ask whether her feelings have changed. It certainly feels as though they have."

Archie ran a hand over his dark hair before putting his hat back on his head. "Why do you say that?"

I shook my head, noticing the felled oak tree ahead of us. "You are wanted back at the house soon to help distribute the beef to the tenants, I think."

"Father mentioned it."

"We must hurry if we are to return in time."

Archie didn't mention Ada again, much to my relief. We used a saw to cut a large portion from the oak tree for our Yule log and loaded it onto the sled, tying it in place with rope before we pulled it back up the hill to deliver to Mr. Sterling. We each took a rope attached to the sled and pulled together.

"Is this not usually a family affair?" I recalled searching for a Yule log many times before, but never with such a small hunting party.

"I invited Lily to join us, but she didn't want to come. Wretched girl."

"We will choose to believe she wanted to stay warm and not that she was avoiding me, though I fear the latter to be the case."

"Why would she avoid you?" Archie asked.

"I am the reason she fell from the ladder yesterday and missed her favorite part of Christmas."

Archie stopped pulling the sled and turned to face me. His thick, brown eyebrows pulled together. "What is her favorite part? And how the devil do you know of it?"

"Giving the gifts to the children at the tea. It always has been." Didn't everyone know this about her?

Evidently not. Archie stared. "Did she tell you so?"

"No, I assumed." He did not look convinced. "We've always watched her do it. Have you never paid attention to Lily's face? She lights up like a freshly burning Yule log. She loves to hand out the gifts and watch the children light up in return."

Watching Lily from the squint in the drawing room had always been a highlight of the season for me. Her joy was infectious.

"But she stayed away yesterday," Archie said. "My mother asked Ada to step in because Lily was nowhere to be found."

How could he not see what was so plainly before him? "She did not feel wanted after ruining the tree. Where did we find her, Archie? Up in the drawing room, watching Ada deliver the gifts. She could not bear to miss it, even if she was not the one distributing the toys."

Archie studied me. "You have always been better at reading her moods than I ever was. I used to wonder if one day there would be a connection between the two of you that transcended music."

"She is a child," I said defiantly. But she wasn't, was she? I'd noticed that from the moment I'd come to Lynton two days ago. I was only fooling myself if I continued to pretend otherwise.

"She's twenty," Archie muttered. "Ada is only two years her senior."

Not a child at all, as I well knew. I was appropriately chastised. I started walking again, tugging my rope, and Archie fell into step beside me. "It almost sounds as though you still hope for a connection of some sort," I muttered. The cold was doing strange things to my head.

Archie grinned. "I wouldn't refuse having you as a brother." It seemed an odd thing to say after our conversation about Ada.

We pulled the log all the way up to the house and passed it off to Mr. Sterling to carry into the hall.

Archie brushed his hands together to remove the dirt. "I'm glad that sled is good for something. We haven't used it properly in ages."

"Perhaps we ought to rectify that."

He laughed, leading me through the courtyard and down a set of steps toward the tunnel that ran beneath the house. It went from the kitchen to the other side near the stables, where the icehouse was located, and it was where the tenants and servants lined up to collect their joint of beef for Christmas. "Father would certainly not trust me with estate business were he to find us playing in the snow like children," Archie said.

"That is where we disagree, my friend." I slapped him on the back when we entered the tunnel, making our way past the families lined up to receive their beef. "I do not think sledding is a sport for children alone. We ought to invite your parents along as well."

"I did not realize we agreed to this," Archie said, raising his eyebrow.

"You look like you could use a diversion." We rounded the bend, and torches lit the way through the domed underground tunnel until we reached the entrance to the kitchen. I pulled up short, surprise stalling my steps. Lillian stood beside her father at the head of the line, the parrot resting on her forearm. She was leaning down to a little boy and talking about the bird. Her gown was tight at the waist before it flared out around her legs, making it impossible to deny that she'd grown into a beautiful woman.

I swallowed, pushing the attraction down and covering it with mud, like one would to suffocate a fire. It was dangerous and odd and needed to be eliminated at once.

"Gads," Archie said, stepping up to his father's side. "Is she not afraid of losing the bird?"

"The bird likes her," Mr. Hartley said proudly. "We need not fear her flying away."

"But the tunnel is open at the end. If she were to escape—"

"Lillian intends to remain just here and show Clementine to the children as they pass. They will not go near the opening of the tunnel."

Archie nodded, but he was clearly skeptical of the wisdom of this plan.

I could easily see this situation for what it was: Lillian wanted a way to give to the children since she was unable to do so yesterday. The parrot was unlike any of the birds we had in Cheshire. It was a rare treat.

The family at the front of the line received their joint of beef, wished Mr. Hartley a happy Christmas, and left the way they'd come. The next family approached, and Lillian stepped forward to show the little girls her parrot. Her face lit up, joy exuding from her in palpable waves. Her gray eyes shone despite the torchlit dimness in the tunnel, and her smile was radiant. She spread her light to others with such ease; I yearned to have some of it for myself. If I could bottle her light, I would never be adrift in darkness again.

The family collected their beef and filed out, making room for the next group. I tucked myself against the rough stone wall behind Mr. Hartley and Archie, watching them take the time to query each family about their health and wish them the compliments of the season.

When my father died, leaving Mother and me alone with only one another for company, I had done my best to be the companion she had missed. I'd remained home when Archie went off to Cambridge, teaching myself all I thought I needed to know and forgoing university or any occupation that would take me from the house. Until the opportunity to travel to Vienna with our old vicar had presented itself.

Mr. Hollander had not remained in Vienna above three months, but I had fallen in love with the people and the city and obtained my mother's blessing to stay and study further under Mr. Hollander's cousin. Watching the interactions between the Hartleys now, however, made me question the wisdom of leaving my mother for so long on her own. She had plenty of servants and a bailiff to manage the estate, small as it was, but she did not have companionship in the form of family. It was no little wonder she had taken to visiting her sister more often.

Guilt swept through me, building steadily with each interaction I observed between the Hartleys and their tenants. They were a good example to me of prioritizing family and service—Mrs. Hartley with her children's tea, Mr. Hartley and his gifts of beef. In each of their projects, Lillian and Archie participated in some way, shifting the events into family affairs. If anything, their actions made it clear that I needed to pack my things and go to my mother as soon as I'd settled things between Ada and myself.

Once the last of the tenants had collected their joint of beef and left, Lillian turned to face her father and froze when her gaze landed on me. "How long have you been here, Theo?"

"We arrived at noon," Archie said defensively.

She looked between her brother and me, nodding. It was no surprise she had been so wrapped up in the children that she hadn't noticed my presence.

"Have you taught the bird to say anything yet?" I asked.

"Clementine," she reminded me. "Not yet. Though, she did greet me with a 'Good day' earlier, so I imagine someone else must have taught her that."

I laughed. "Good day, Clementine."

"Good day," the bird repeated, her voice high and nasally.

Archie laughed, clapping, and Mr. Hartley grinned. Lillian looked happy.

"Greeting all those children must have been stimulating for her," Lillian said. "I should return her inside so she can rest."

We all fell into step, following Lillian through the kitchen and into the house.

"Theo wants to take the sled up the hill," Archie said.

"You haven't done that in years," Mr. Hartley said.

"Would you care to join us, sir?" I asked.

Mr. Hartley laughed. "I am afraid I would not be able to stand for a week if I did. My back is not what it once was. You ought to enjoy your young backs while you have them."

Archie looked surprised by this. I clapped him on the shoulder.

"We shall, Father," Archie said.

"Will you join us?" I asked Lillian when we mounted the stairs and entered the great hall.

"It'll take me a moment to find enough warm clothes for two, but I think I can manage."

"Two?"

She pointed ahead to where Ada waited on a chair between the Christmas tree and the fireplace. "Ada will want to join us, I am sure."

"Will I?" she asked, rising to meet us. "Oh, you have your parrot."

"Clementine."

"Good day, Clementine," Ada said.

"Good day," the bird repeated to everyone's delight.

"Clever girl! Now, what have you volunteered me for?" Ada asked. Her copper hair was styled immaculately, with a large bow-like structure high at the crown. She did not appear dressed for any such active pursuits, and I expected her to refuse.

"Sledding on the hill," Lillian said.

Ada's sleek eyebrows rose, and a smile curved her lips. She directed it to me. "That sounds like a lark. Count me in."

Apparently, I did not know the woman as well as I thought.

Lillian left to put her bird away, and Ada went with her to find warm clothes for the snow. I watched them leave and settled in a chair, disappointment weaving its way through me. Oh, blast. That was not good at all.

Chapter Eight

Lillian

Ada and I walked up the hill arm in arm, doing our best not to freeze. It had taken a while for Betty to style Ada's hair again in a way that supported the use of a warmer bonnet, but she'd achieved it in the end. I'd lent Ada a fur-lined cloak, gloves, and boots, but even in those layers, she looked as cold as I felt.

Archie and Theo pulled the sleds up the hill for us, dragging grooves through the inches of powdery snow.

"Shall we race?" Archie asked.

"Of course," I said. "Is there any other way?"

Theo handed the ropes of his sled to me. "The ladies can go first."

"I see no reason we cannot all ride together." Ada peered at the long wooden planks that made up the beds of the sleds. "They look plenty long enough."

Archie and Theo exchanged a dubious glance.

I tried to measure the length of the sled. "Do you think so? Our skirts are certainly longer than the last time we brought these out."

Ada shot me a challenging gaze. "If you do not think you can—"

"Of course I *can*; I only wonder at the wisdom of it." Or the potential for disaster that awaited this scheme.

"We will not know until we try." Archie beckoned me over. "Come here, sister. Let's try."

"Very well." I handed Theo back the rope of the sled he had pulled and sat on the front of Archie's while he held it in place, then tucked my skirt around my legs the best I could.

Archie positioned himself behind me, much as he had when we were children, then scooted us to the edge of the hill, holding us in place with his booted feet. He looked up. "Are you joining us?"

"Of course," Ada said. She watched Theo hold the second sled beside ours, then perched on the front, Theo sitting behind her.

I looked away so jealousy would not mount and overshadow my enjoyment. Theo and Ada together were a sight I would need to grow used to if they were to be married.

"Ready?" Archie called loudly near my ear.

Theo agreed and they counted off, pushing from the hill at the same time. "Go!"

Archie's arms tightened on either side of me as he held the rope, leaning this way and that in an effort to steer. Wind flew past us, cold and bits of snow stinging my face in the rush. A laugh tore from my chest, lost in the wind while we sped down the hill. We reached the bottom and slowed, coming to a stop in a thick bank of snow just before the hill rose in the other direction. Our sled landed on a slant, and Archie hopped up, taking my hand to help me stand before we could topple onto our sides.

My brother grinned, looking from me to where our friends had landed some distance from us. It had been exhilarating to move at such a speed. I wanted to do it again.

Ada laughed, rising from her seated position with Theo's help.

"Shall we do it again?" I asked.

"Yes. Give us an opportunity to win," Theo said, grinning. His wind-slapped cheeks were red, but his smile was no dimmer for it.

Ada shook her skirts out. "I cannot remain in this cold for another minute. You'll have to excuse me, I think."

Disappointment settled in my stomach. "I can return to Lynton with you."

"Stay. I can see the house from here. I will await you all inside with a pot of fresh, hot tea."

"Allow me to escort you back to the house," Archie said. "You should not return alone."

Ada dipped her head. "Thank you, Mr. Hartley. That is most kind."

Archie offered his arm, and she leaned against it while they made their way toward the house.

Theo looked at me with an overly bright smile. "Shall we start up the hill?"

Was it not strange for us to continue alone? What had seemed to be mere fun a minute ago now felt far more significant. But I could not walk away from him without making it clear that being alone with Theo felt significant to me. If I was going to swallow and suffocate my feelings, I ought to begin now. I nodded, clutching my skirts with both hands to raise them so they would not gather moisture and drag snow on the way up the hill.

We climbed in silence, Theo dragging one of the sleds behind him. I tried to watch him surreptitiously, holding my skirt up so I would not trip. Cold air slid up my stockinged legs, making me shiver. I sent Theo another glance and missed my footing, my shoe sliding backward and sending me sprawling on the ground. Snow met my face in a jarring rush. Could I never accomplish anything without a misstep?

"Lily!" Theo said, reaching for me. He took my hand, and his own foot slipped, causing him to pull me down the hill beside him. We rolled downhill for a few rotations before coming to a gentle stop, my body resting alongside his.

A blush stole up my neck, bleeding into my cheeks, while I pushed up and tried to stand. Theo climbed to his feet, looking me up and down. He grimaced, likely at the state of my dishevelment.

But he also looked like a snowman, white powder clinging to him everywhere. A laugh tore from my chest. "You're covered, Theo."

"As are you," he shot back, hitting the snow from his trousers and wiping it from his face.

I did my best to remove the snow from my clothes.

"Ready?" he asked.

"I believe so." I turned to start back up the hill when he stopped me with a gentle hand on my shoulder.

He turned me to face him and removed his glove with his teeth before reaching up to wipe the snow from my cheek. My blush intensified, bleeding hot down my chest. It suddenly didn't feel so frigid anymore.

"There. Much better," he said, stepping back and slipping his glove on once again. He fetched the discarded sled, and we started up the hill again, my heart refusing to pulse at a normal rate.

When we reached the top, we stood beside one another and looked out over the white countryside. The back of Lynton Park was just over the next rise, and we could see Ada and Archie nearing the house. Pine Woods was visible in the distance beyond, and the tips of Theo's roof were evident through the bare branches of the trees. He should be there, with smoke puffing from the chimneys and his mother bundled in her favorite tartan blanket.

I looked at Theo. His tanned cheeks still carried the red hue of a sunburn. His hair was tamed into a style and not quite so long as when he'd arrived. He smiled, revealing his slightly crooked front tooth. My nose stung from the cold, but my chest was warm.

"This was not quite the Christmas you imagined, was it?" I asked.

Theo's blue eyes granted me all the attention he possessed. "I had been imagining a quiet Christmas alone with my mother, so no, it is nothing like I was expecting. I would not say that makes it anything less, however."

"How gallant of you. You need not dress up your feelings on my account. I do not take offense that you prefer to be with your mother."

"Then, you will understand that I wondered if I would have been better off traveling to Dorset?"

I grinned. "But all those cousins!"

Theo laughed. "It would have been the sacrifice I paid to see my mother." He was quiet for a minute, his brow growing serious. "I should have gone to her. I have been running for three years, Lily. I left her on her own for far too long and failed to be the son my father expected me to be. She certainly deserves better."

I turned to face him fully. "How can you say so? You know your mother supported your music; she always has. Your father did as well."

"Had I stayed away merely for studying, it would be understandable, but I *was* running."

"From what?"

He looked away. "Myself? Memories? Responsibility? I am not certain. Likely a little of each." Theo ran a hand over his face and turned a hesitant smile on me. "But I am back now. I hope that counts for something."

I reached for his hand, squeezing his gloved fingers with my own. "Exactly. And it is what you do now that will count."

Theo regarded me closely, his eyes narrowing in contemplation. His focus was acute, resting on me for so long that he made me nervous. I dropped his hand and looked away, over the rolling hills, when my gaze alighted on the second sled at the bottom of the hill.

"I didn't bring the other sled," I said. "The thought didn't cross my mind."

"Nor mine," he said quietly. The silence was perfect, the earth padded and insulated with snow so we could hear nothing but one another. "Well, shall we? I am quite looking forward to that tea."

He held the sled while I sat on the front. He sat behind me, cocooning me with his arms when he reached for the rope. I had shared sleds with my brother many times, and never had he felt so close. I could feel Theo against me from all sides.

His arms tightened around mine, and he leaned forward. "Ready?"

I could not speak. I could only nod.

He waited a moment before pushing us off, and his hold on me tightened even more. We flew down the hill. The air whipped past us, bringing out my laugh once again. I could feel the rumble of Theo's laughter through his chest against my back and could hear him close to my ear. It was simultaneously wonderful and painful.

When we came to a stop at the bottom of the hill, we landed on our sides and rolled off the sled. Theo's arms went around my waist, and he lifted me, helping me stand. He had given me the taste of an embrace, and it was as lovely as it was impossible. I stepped out of his hold at once and began wiping the snow from my gown.

"Again?" he asked.

"I think we should return to the house." My heart would not be able to endure that again.

Theo nodded. He stacked the sleds and held both ropes, tugging them along as I fell into step beside him.

We crested the top of the next hill, coming upon the back of the house. I saw a rustle of burgundy skirts and auburn hair before a woman disappeared into the orangery. "Did you see Ada just there?" I asked, pointing. "I think she went into the orangery."

Theo shook his head. "I didn't notice."

I'd seen only a flash of the woman, but it had been Ada, unmistakably. No one else in this household possessed such vibrant copper hair. But why would she find refuge in there when the house was so near, unless she wanted to warm herself quicker? "It *is* very warm inside."

"Perhaps they requested the tea to be brought to us here," Theo said. "It would not be the first time."

"Shall we join them?" I asked, noticing the second set of boot prints that led into the building.

"It does sound rather enticing." He smiled at me, and we followed the path toward the orangery door. Theo opened it for me and held it while I stepped through a wall of thick heat, stomping my boots to remove the snow. I looked up and drew in a quick breath. My brother and Ada stood close on the other side of the fountain, their hands clasped and their conversation serious. They jumped apart, but not soon enough.

I turned to stop Theo from witnessing what my eyes had just seen, but I was too late.

He stood staring on the threshold, his jaw hard and his eyes unyielding. "Would someone care to explain?"

Chapter Nine

Theo

Anger coursed through me unchecked. If Ada and Archie's position had not already betrayed them, the guilt painted over each of their faces certainly would have. The anger heating my blood was expected, but that it was coupled with relief was too strange to give much credence to.

"I will," Archie said calmly, stepping forward. His hand was raised in a silent plea that fell flat against my ire. It was not Archie I had entered into a secret engagement with, and thus it was not him who owed me an explanation.

Ada put her hand on his arm, and as if she'd heard my thoughts, she said, "No, it should be me." She raised her gaze to meet mine, steadier and stronger than I'd ever seen it before. She had always been kind but never as stalwart as she seemed in this moment, stepping forward to protect her beau. It was telling that I had never inspired this sort of behavior in her.

"This certainly explains why your letters changed," I said, unable to help myself.

Ada's cheeks flushed, and she lowered her gaze.

Lillian cleared her throat. "Archie, should we give them privacy?"

He nodded, stepping past me. I had forgotten Lily was here, just behind me, and I did not like that she'd heard my snide remark.

The Hartley siblings slipped from the orangery, leaving Ada and me in silence.

"I intended to honor our agreement." Ada spoke quietly but firmly.

"You did not think I would wish to know that you've developed a sort of . . . *something* with my closest friend?"

"I love him, Theo," she whispered. "We planned to tell you. Archie wanted to do so immediately, but I thought it best to wait until after Christmas so we would not ruin your holiday."

Which explained why Archie had wanted to speak privately to me but hadn't done so after seeing Ada. And his appearance in the orangery yesterday? Gads, had the man been coming to meet her in secret? I shook my head, prepared to manage only one falsehood at a time. "You thought it was preferable to lie instead?"

"No one lied. We only chose to *wait* to tell the truth."

"Doing so makes it a lie, Ada." How many times had I spoken to Archie about my relationship with her? About the changes I had felt between us? I was foolish not to have seen the signs before now. His discomfort, the way he'd left the room when I first greeted her, the way he avoided speaking of her. I gave a quiet scoff. "You could have written to me about this."

"I'm sorry." She looked at her feet. "I made a promise to you, Theo. I would not go back on my word."

"You would not jilt me, but you would marry me despite falling in love with my closest friend? How polite."

Her chin trembled.

I regretted my unkindness immediately. "You needn't fear that I will hold you to any promise, Ada. We were young when we entered into the engagement, and it ought never to have happened in the first place. We must be glad that we never informed our parents of our plans."

Ada frowned. "That is all? You simply release me?"

"What more is there to say?"

"You might accept my apology." She took a step forward, beseeching me with widened eyes. "I did not intend to fall in love with him. I am sorry for any pain I have caused you, Theo. I care for you a great deal."

"It is no great surprise that your affections have altered, only to *whom* they were transferred. It was obvious from your letters that you'd had a change of heart, so do not believe I am overly alarmed. Did it occur when Archie returned from Cambridge?"

Her silence was answer enough.

"I thought so," I muttered. "When will you announce your engagement?"

She shook her head. "We will wait a respectful amount of time."

How long was that, I wondered. I closed my eyes and drew in a breath for patience. I was being unfair. Had I not felt attraction to Lillian since returning home? Would I have suppressed those feelings as far as marriage as well? I smarted from the pain of Ada and Archie's dishonesty, but I needed to be reasonable.

"Can we remain friends?" she asked, her tone hopeful and sad.

"We have been friends for most of our lives before we fell into a romantic relationship. I do not think our friendship is unsalvageable, but I need time."

"Of course."

I dipped my head toward her in a semblance of a bow and walked away.

No sooner had I stepped outside than Archie pushed away from the stone column and came toward me. "Can we discuss this?"

I kept walking toward the house. "It would be in all of our best interests if I were to leave."

"Theo, wait. We must speak."

"There is nothing more to say."

"You deserve an apology and an explanation. I have never kissed her, Theo."

My feet stalled, and I turned to face him. "That is not my concern." Indeed, it hadn't crossed my mind. It was an odd relief all the same that I could count on the nature of Archie's character to remain good and unchanged. He'd given me no reason to doubt his word. I looked at my friend, at the sadness in his eyes, and was hit with a profound truth. I had been less hurt by Ada's dishonesty than Archie's. He was my friend. He had been granted the opportunity to speak to me a handful of times since I'd returned home, yet he had done nothing. It angered me, but more than that, it hurt.

"I did not try to fall in love with her."

I kept walking. "And yet, when you did, you did not tell me."

He caught up to me. "I begged her to write to you, but she would not jilt you, and it was not my place to do so on her behalf." Archie took my sleeve and pulled. "Listen to me, Theo. I had no choice but to keep silent. What was I to do but beg her to make a clean breast of it?"

"Which is what you were doing in the orangery?"

"Yes. I could not bear to have this secret between us. You are more than a friend to me; you are a brother. I will not sacrifice that for anything."

"Have you not already done so?'

"Is that the way of things?" Archie asked, stepping back and dropping my sleeve. Sorrow splashed in his eyes. "You will leave and never speak to me again?"

He had always been the more dramatic of the two of us. I was hurting, but this pain would not last. Our friendship was not ruined forever. "All I know at present is that I need some time."

"I can give you that. Please understand I never meant for it to happen. I never meant to hurt you. I have wanted to tell you from the moment I saw you again, but I tried to respect Ada's privacy and the preexisting arrangement between you."

Archie had not been placed in an enviable position, but I would not do him the honor of agreeing out loud. I merely nodded. "Enjoy your Christmas," I said, walking past him.

"Christmas is tomorrow!" he called after me. "Where will you go?"

"Home."

* * *

My actions might have been a tad hasty. I stood on the porch of my mother's house and leaned back, searching the windows for the best entry point. Each door was locked tight, and I did not possess the skill to unlock them without a key. Entering through an upper window was my best option, but only if I could find one that was unlatched. Knowing my mother, that would not be the case.

But I would try.

I blew out a heavy breath and watched it cloud before me while I rounded the house to fetch a ladder from the barn. I'd been too quick in leaving Lynton. It was late afternoon on Christmas Eve, and I had no way to enter my childhood home without breaking something. I ought to have remained and swallowed my frustration until Christmas was over and I could take a train to Dorset.

The ladder was waiting beneath a layer of dust and dirt. I pulled it free and carried it outside, leaning it against the house. When it felt steady, I climbed to the window on the upper floor and tugged, but it did not give way. Blast.

I moved the ladder and tried three more windows before leaning back and gazing over the treetops toward Lynton Park. The orangery was hidden from this viewpoint, but I could easily see the hill behind the house where we had taken the sleds. Flying down the snowy incline, my arms around Lillian, had been an unexpected pleasure. It was more rewarding than it ought to have been, and I enjoyed it far more than I needed to.

My stomach sank, and I leaned against the house, looking at Lynton. How was this situation any different from my prolonged visit to Vienna? I was running again, and I needed to stop. It was time to face the things that mattered to me, despite how difficult that might seem. I needed to return to Lynton.

The sound of a horse's hooves clomped on the packed snow and pulled a gig down the road in my direction. Mr. Hartley drove, his cheeks already red from the cold. I lifted a hand in greeting, surprised when he slowed in front of my house. "Have you found an open window?" he asked, easily surmising my attempts.

My neck heated. "Not yet."

"Come down from there, son."

I obeyed, climbing down the ladder and crossing the garden toward Mr. Hartley's gig. If I asked him for a ride back to his house, would he think me foolish?

He held the reins, looking down at me plainly. "I do not pretend to know what has occurred between you and my son, but given the way Archibald is moping in my study with a bottle of brandy, I take it he carries much of the blame."

I said nothing to condemn Archie, but my silence alone was condemnation.

Mr. Hartley still peered down at me. "Come back with me. It will not be Christmas without you, Theodore. I am not asking you to forgive sooner than you are able, only that you put aside your grievances for Christmas. I will drive you to the station myself as soon as you'd like on the twenty-sixth."

It was what I'd wanted, but now that I faced the opportunity, I reconsidered the situation. Could I sit at the dinner table with the Hartleys and not feel anger toward Archie? My heart had already cooled toward Ada, further proving that I had accepted the change between us long ago. I had suspected as much already, or I would not have been able to feel such attraction to Lillian.

I swallowed those thoughts.

"The Marcotes have left already, if that helps," he said, misunderstanding my hesitation. Evidently he understood far more about the situation than I'd realized.

"Because of me?"

"No. Miss Marcote was unwell."

Then, yes, it was because of me. Though, the argument could be given that she could have been honest with me months ago, if not yesterday.

Mr. Hartley shifted the reins in his hands, softening his voice. "Come home with me, Theodore. Spend Christmas with family."

His words warmed my stomach and formed a longing in my chest. Outside of my mother and her sister's brood, the Hartleys were the closest thing

I had to family. Archie had always been as much a brother as a friend, Lillian like a younger sister. And, regardless, it was time for me to cease running and hiding so I might face my problems directly.

I inhaled the cold, biting air. "Let me fetch my trunk."

Mr. Hartley gave a brisk nod, a smile that made his graying side-whiskers quiver spreading over his face.

I hurried to put the ladder away in the barn and retrieve my trunk, placing it into the back of the gig.

We drove up to Lynton Park, and the closer we drew to the house, the better I felt. I'd run away for the last three years, staying away from the house and responsibilities that had waited for me here. If I was being honest, I would admit I'd remained in Vienna in part because I knew Ada and marriage waited for me in England, and like hers, my heart had undergone a change. It had not clung to the boyish love and attraction that had been so consuming before I left.

When I saw Ada with Archie, my relief had been as strong as my hurt. That did not lessen their dishonesty or my injury from being lied to, but I had served Ada poorly as well. I could not deny the feelings Lillian had stoked in my chest, subtle though they had been. Stepping back into this house knowing I would see her again made my pulse increase speed with anticipation.

Mr. Hartley pulled into the courtyard. A groom ran to stand at the horse's head, and Mr. Hartley tossed him the reins and climbed down. "Take Mr. Pine's things back to his room," he requested.

I followed him up the steps and into the great hall, where Mrs. Hartley and Lillian were seated before the cold fireplace. Had they been waiting for me before lighting the Yule log?

Mrs. Hartley crossed the marble floor toward me, her smile warm and welcoming. "If you would like to change into dry clothes, we will wait for you in the drawing room, dear. It is nearly time for dinner."

I nodded, the emotion in my throat suddenly too thick to allow words. I'd had a disagreement with her son, and still this woman and her husband did not consider me any less important to them. I glanced up and caught Lillian's gaze across the room, her serious gray eyes watching me, her brow bent in concern. She wore a gown of crisp white with emerald embroidery that made her skin look smooth, her rich brown hair framing her face in curls. The worry over her brow was disheartening though, and I felt the temptation to inform her that she need not be anxious over the state of my heart. I turned instead to go to my room to change out of my cold, wet clothes.

One thing had nestled securely in my chest alongside the image of Lillian standing beside the hearth, the candlelight dancing over her skin. I had made the right choice by returning to Lynton Park.

Chapter Ten

Lillian

Dinner had thus far been a quiet affair. Theo and Archie must have agreed to some sort of peace treaty, for neither of them spoke much, but neither did they ignore one another completely. It was an odd reconciliation—one that did not feel altogether healed. Perhaps Theo had slapped a plaster over his wound and hoped it would hold. I wished he would heal it more thoroughly than that.

It had hurt to discover my brother and dearest friend keeping a secret of that magnitude, but I had not allowed Ada to be privy to the contents of my heart, had I? In that way, I could not hold anger toward her. Indeed, I only wished I had seen the signs earlier. Surely they were there.

An orange-colored soup was placed before us, the sauce likely derived from tomatoes to achieve this color. I glanced down at my white bodice. It would take great effort, but I would *not* spill on this gown. Sometimes I wondered if I spilled so frequently simply because I was constantly making an effort not to do so.

Mama must have had the same worry. She requested Kemper to approach her and said something quietly to him. The butler left the room and returned shortly with an additional napkin, which he handed to me. I looked up, catching Mama's eye. She gestured to the front of my gown with her eyebrows raised, as if to tell me to tuck it over my bodice so I could protect the white fabric. The napkin hung limply from my hand, my gaze flicking to each of the gentlemen at the table, and I was unsurprised to find all of them watching me.

Theo cleared his throat and turned toward Papa. "You have added a lemon tree to the orangery, I noticed."

"Yes, but it does not flower in tandem with the oranges. We have lemons earlier in the autumn."

"Does it yield fruit already?"

Papa described the tedious process he'd endured to achieve lemons. I tucked the napkin into my gown to save the fabric, my cheeks burning from the embarrassment of being treated like a child. I knew I spilled often, but for Mama to have the butler fetch an additional napkin in front of a *guest* was nothing short of mortifying. I spent the remainder of dinner focused on my plate and paying little heed to the conversation going on around me.

When our meal was complete and we rose from the table, I pulled the napkin down, chastised to find two drips of orange soup in the center. I hated that my mother had been right.

We convened in the great hall, and I brought *A Christmas Carol* in an attempt to read it once more. Ada had spoken so highly of the story, but I could not bend my attention to the task very well. Father had John bring Clementine and her cage down to the hall so she might join us for the festivities. I would admit her gold cage looked festive beside the evergreen Christmas tree spangled with silver tinsel and dried-orange garlands.

"Shall we light the Yule log?" Mama asked once we had all gathered in the seats around the unlit fireplace.

I set my book on my lap and looked up, catching Theo's eye from the seat opposite me.

"Will you help me, Archibald?" Papa asked.

The Yule log was already in the hearth, prepared and ready to light. Archie helped my father strike a match, and they set it to the tinder beneath the log. The flame grew quickly before leveling out, casting a warm glow over the immediate circle in front of the hearth.

Mama stood. "We must have a carol, or it will not feel like Christmas Eve." Her footsteps clicked across the floor until she sat at the pianoforte and lifted the cover from the keys. Her fingers warmed up to the tune of "Joy to the World," and she heartily avoided my gaze.

I followed everyone as they made their way over to stand around the pianoforte. Mama ran through the accompaniment one more time before looking up at each of us flanking the sides of the pianoforte, a three-armed candelabra sitting atop its center. She seemed nervous and hopeful when her gaze passed over me, sending a jolt of guilt through my stomach.

Was I being stubborn by keeping quiet? Was it silly to refuse my voice when it seemed to be the only thing anyone appreciated about me? I looked down at the smooth wooden pianoforte and exhaled. I did not have to sing loud to participate in this activity and join my family in celebrating Christmas. It was no performance, after all.

Mama played the beginning of the song again and everyone joined in. I did not amplify my voice, but it was clear all the same—if a little rusty from such disuse. Avoiding looking at anyone in particular when I sang, I chose to feel the music and its purpose of bringing in the Christmas season. I found a smile curving over my lips as the song went on, my body filling with warmth. It was impossible not to feel joy at this musical appreciation for the Savior's birth.

As it drew to a close, Mama seamlessly shifted into playing "O Holy Night." We followed along, five voices blending in a lovely harmony. Theo held my gaze across the piano, his eyes full of appreciation that swam into my stomach and filled me with warmth.

The last note rang out in the immense hall, and the room drew quiet. The log caught fire and crackled behind us, sending a bright orange light over everyone as smiles lifted each face. Archie and Theo nodded at one another vaguely, though I did not know what the gesture meant. I assumed it was some sort of secret male agreement. Perhaps the furthering of their peace treaty.

The Christmas carols had done a little to heal the discord in our family.

"Shall we read the story from the Bible now?" Papa asked.

"Do we not normally do that on Christmas Day?" Archie asked.

Papa gave a soft shrug. "Usually. But I feel it would complete our evening nicely."

"Go and fetch it for him, dear," Mama said to Archie, who left at once to retrieve the Bible from the library.

I reached for the candelabra on the pianoforte to carry it back to the chairs so Papa could use it to read. My hand hit it at an odd angle, pushing the candle holder over instead of grasping it. Two of the candles rested against the top of the pianoforte while the other flew from the holder, rolling onto the floor.

Mama screamed, rising and reaching to correct the candelabra and put the candles back.

"The carpet!" Papa yelled.

The flame on the floor had caught hold, smoldering slowly along the Aubusson carpet beside Theo's feet. He sprang into action, running to the chair set against the wall and pulling the cushion from it. He dropped to the floor and hit the cushion down against the flame, suffocating it until it went out and smoke rose from the charred floor.

Theo's gaze rose, his chest heaving from the effort of putting out the fire. He sat back, pulling the cushion away to reveal a dark, angry mark on the carpet.

Mama's hand splayed over her heart. "Darling, what were you thinking?"

I swallowed, my throat dry. "Only to move the candles so Papa could read—"

"Leave it to me next time, Lillian," Papa said, patting my shoulder. He lifted the candlestick and walked around the pianoforte to where Theo was still kneeling on the floor. Theo handed him the last candle, and Papa relit it and placed it back into the holder. My chest heaved, tears threatening to break free while Papa took Mama's arm and led her toward the chairs in front of the fireplace.

I drew in a shaky breath, commanding my heart to calm, my fingers gripping the edge of the pianoforte for stability. It was nothing to lose my composure over, especially not in front of Theo.

He stood, coming slowly around the pianoforte until he stopped just beside me. "Would you care to sit down?"

"I am in no danger of fainting, I assure you."

"That was not my concern."

"Of course not." My grip on the instrument tightened. "Surely your concern was more to do with whether or not I just nearly burned the house to the ground."

"You and your brother are quite the dramatic pair." Theo gave a soft chuckle, taking my fingers and prying them gently from the pianoforte. "The house was in no danger, Lily."

I faced him fully. "How can you say that? Only moments ago, you put out a fire that was started by my clumsiness."

"Anyone could've made that mistake."

"But *anyone* didn't, Theo. I did." My fingers tingled as the blood rushed back into my hands. "I do not know any other way."

"You shouldn't speak as if your actions are inevitable."

"Some of us recognize we are not graceful creatures, and we have accepted our fate." I shook my head, dislodging the embarrassment as best as I could. What were my feelings compared to his after all he had gone through today? I was being selfish, worrying only about myself. "Pay me no mind."

"Impossible," he muttered.

I looked up quickly, finding him watching me. Time seemed to slow, and I wondered at his purpose in regarding me so directly. Could his mind have been opened to me? Despite my need to wear a napkin like a child, did he now see me as an equal? My chest hitched. "I am glad my father convinced you to return."

"Your father merely saved my pride from suffering further. I had already decided on my own to return."

That gave me an unaccountable feeling of relief. Theo *wanted* to be here. "It cannot be easy for you to share a meal with Archie so soon."

"He is not a villain." Theo gave a soft smile. The fire was far from us, but his handsome face was lit with a soft glow anyway. "I cannot appreciate the way he chose to handle the situation, but I do not blame him for it entirely. Were I in his shoes, I'm not sure I would've done things differently."

"That is charitable of you."

"I offer him no charity, only my honest feelings. I did not appreciate his secrecy, but I can understand his belief that Ada needed to speak to me first. It was she who needed to end our engagement, regardless of her claim that she had no intention of doing so. She knows me well enough to believe that once she informed me of the change in her feelings, I would have released her from any obligation. Archie could not have done that. It had to be her."

I watched his blue eyes for any sign of pain but found nothing there. His gaze was direct, his voice calm. It was not the way I would have expected a jilted man to act.

"Lillian," he said, his voice soft. He leaned toward me. "I wanted to—"

Archie swept into the room, Bible in tow, stealing the remainder of Theo's sentence.

I waited, hoping he would continue. Could he mean what I hoped? That he had undergone a change? That perhaps he could see me as a woman and not a child any longer?

But Theo said none of that. He merely offered me his arm. "Shall we join the others?"

"Of course."

We gathered around the fire again. My father opened the Bible and read to us from Luke while Mama pulled out her knitting basket to occupy her hands. I sat on the end of the sofa beside Archie, Theo directly across from me. Mama and Papa took the chairs closest to the fire, the candelabra on a small table beside Papa's chair to lend him more light.

When he was finished, he closed the large book with a deep thud. "Let us all remember the true purpose of why we celebrate Christmas. It is through our service and charity that we can better serve the Lord."

"Did everyone seem happy to receive their beef?" Mama asked, her brow furrowing at the mittens she was knitting. She was likely considering the ways we had been charitable and, knowing her, additional ways we could be so.

"They did."

"What of the Larsens?" I asked, realizing we had not seen them today.

Papa leaned back in his chair, pushing out his chin in thought. "They did not come to the kitchen."

"Strange," Mama said. "We'd best take care of that in the morning."

"Did anyone mention why they might not have come?" Archie asked.

"I did not think to ask," Papa said. "The Stevensons would have informed us if something were wrong, surely. The families have been neighbors for a decade now at least."

I agreed with him, and the Stevensons hadn't said anything. That was something of a relief. "Mrs. Larsen is with child. If her husband was working, perhaps she did not feel well enough to walk all the way up the hill to our house."

"Could be," Papa mused. "We'll go first thing tomorrow. Theodore?"

"I'd love to join you," Theo said.

"I will bring these mittens for one of the children if I can finish them in time," Mama said.

Papa rose, lifting the heavy tome. "I will turn in, then. Good night, my dear family."

We all bade him a good night. I lifted my book and turned to the second page. *A Christmas Carol* had such a negative beginning, all this talk of Old Marley being dead and Scrooge being perfectly aware of it. I had thus far struggled to see the appeal of the novel—except for its shortness of length, perhaps.

Mama tugged at her yarn and frowned. "Wretched basket is always making a tangle of things."

"Allow me, Mother." Archie took Papa's empty seat, dragging it closer to Mama's, where he bent his attention to the task of untangling the yarn in the basket so she could finish the mittens.

"What are you reading?" Theo asked, rising from his sofa to come sit beside me.

I lifted the red book, turning it over to show him the cover. "Ada lent it to me." I cringed.

"You needn't fear speaking her name around me. This was not as much a surprise as you'd imagine."

Not a surprise? He had expected a break in their understanding? I looked down at the gold-embossed cover, hope sprouting within me. "My discomfort was more for how much I dislike the story than for who recommended it to me. It will be awkward when I return it unread."

"How far have you read?"

My smile grew. "Two pages."

Theo laughed, the sound full and rich. "You cannot judge the book on so little. It is a worthwhile story, I assure you."

"You like it?"

"I do. Though, I admit that when it was first recommended to me, I did not believe I would appreciate a Christmas ghost story. I was wrong." He smiled. "And I am no great reader."

"Of that I am aware."

"Neither are you, if I recall correctly." He studied me. "Or have you changed so very much?"

"Not at all." I looked down at the slim novel. "I will give it another effort."

We fell into silence, the cracking of the fire and soft clicks of Mama's needles breaking the quiet.

Reading was impossible with Theo so close. I rose, holding the book to my middle. "I will bid you all a good night."

"Good night, darling," Mama said, her head bent toward her mittens. I said good night to Clementine and started across the room when I heard Theo speak.

"It is time for me to retire as well."

I glanced back, unable to help myself. Was he following me out for any particular reason, or was it only a coincidence? I slowed my steps. Archie looked up from where he'd been focusing on a large multi-yarn knot. "Meet me in the library first, Theo? I would like to speak with you."

Theo gave one precise nod before following me from the room. He caught up at the stairs, walking beside me. "Lily."

I stopped on the landing, suddenly more breathless than the few steps warranted, the long, narrow corridor stretching ahead of us. "Yes?"

His lips formed a small smile. "You sang tonight. I did not wish to make anything of it, but I wanted you to know how much I have missed your voice."

My voice. Not *me*. Realization fell over me like a bucket of icy water. This man did not see me as a woman—he saw me as a singer. "Thank you, Theo."

He tucked his chin. "Why do you sound disappointed?"

"It was a kind compliment."

"That was not an answer."

I was overwhelmed with the same tired feeling that had lived in my heart for years—only ever appreciated for the beauty of my tone. Otherwise, I ruined things: burnt carpets, needleless Christmas trees, my own nearly stained gown.

But I did not wish to be wanted and appreciated merely because I could produce a lovely song. I wanted to be wanted for myself, to be missed for my own company. If Theo could only see me as a young girl with a powerful song, it was time I placed a lock on my heart and forbade it from wanting anything more from him.

"Good night, Theo."

"I've offended you," he said unhappily.

"Not in the least." I turned away, heading down the corridor.

He followed me. "How can I make this right?"

"You have done nothing wrong. I just . . ." I faced him, looking up into his sad eyes. The poor man did not need a young lady throwing herself at him the moment he was jilted by another. It was best I kept my mouth closed. "I am tired. That is all."

He nodded. I could tell he did not believe me. Still, he let me walk away.

Chapter Eleven

Theo

Lillian was not telling me everything. She was holding back, and I did not know how to convince her I was worth trusting. I frowned as I made my way to the library. She'd been bothered by my complimenting her singing, that was clear, but the confusing thing was *why*? Why would it be a negative thing for me to enjoy her voice, to say I'd missed hearing her sing? There was no understanding women sometimes.

The fire in the library was banked, smoldering low so it could easily be restarted. I stoked the coals, adding a log before I dropped into one of the chairs. Heat emanated slowly from the building fire as the log caught and the flames grew. I leaned my head back against the chair and closed my eyes.

"Thank you for coming," Archie said, drawing my attention. He closed the door behind him and took the seat near mine. "You had every right to deny my request."

"I am not a spiteful person."

"I know." Archie ran a hand over his face and let out a long sigh. "Brandy? Or I can fetch some Madeira?"

"No, thank you."

Archie did not stand, so I assumed he did not want anything more to drink either. His troubled eyes rested on me. "Can you ever forgive me?"

The man had tormented himself longer than I'd been aware of his role in this—probably for months now. It was no wonder he'd asked in the last few letters he'd sent me when I was planning to return home. He wanted the business dealt with. Did it not say in the book of Matthew that we ought to forgive others their trespasses if we expect God to forgive ours? It was nearly Christmas, after all, and if nothing else, that was a timely reminder of what truly mattered. I was not perfect, by any means. Regardless of the pain Archie had caused me, I knew his heart and saw evidence of his remorse.

I took stock of my own feelings and recognized a lightening in my chest. It was not Archie and Ada and hurt that filled my thoughts and feelings anymore—it was Lillian.

"I already have forgiven you," I said. "In all honesty, it was the lying that hurt more than anything, but I do understand why you felt you couldn't be the person to speak to me about Ada's feelings. If you'd known I had a similar change of heart, perhaps you would have been more at ease, but I also felt I needed to speak to Ada about it first."

Archie ran a hand over his eyes, weary. "Shall we put it behind us?"

"That would be preferable. When will you announce your engagement?"

Archie looked at me with suspicion. "You cannot have moved on so rapidly."

"There was nothing rapid about it. I have already mentioned to you that I have felt a shift in Ada's letters for the last year. I believe that was when I allowed myself to recognize the difference between love and infatuation. The feelings I had for her before I left were real, but they were not lasting."

"It is not painful to think of her marrying someone else, then?"

"Far from it," I said, glad to realize I meant the words. "I am happy for you both. It is a blessing we never publicized our attachment, for now you have no dark shadow overhanging your own announcement."

Archie nodded slowly. "Is there someone else?"

Lillian popped into my head unbidden.

"There *is*," Archie said, sitting up. A boyish grin stole over his face. "Who is it?"

"I hardly know what you mean."

"Don't be absurd." He gestured toward my face. "You've given yourself away. Do I know the lady?"

I looked down at the fire, avoiding catching his gaze.

Archie fell silent. Moments passed with the popping of the wood and the crackle of the fire the only sounds before he spoke again. "It is my sister, isn't it? You've always had a special connection with her, but I believed it was a brotherly sort."

"It was."

He lifted his eyebrow. "*Was?* But no longer is?"

I could not meet his gaze, unable to speak the words that I'd yet to decide for myself. "I hardly know how I feel."

"That cannot be true. You are acting strange."

I ran a hand over my face. "She has always been special to me, but I never saw her as anything more than a younger sister."

"Until you came home?"

"Yes," I admitted with feeling, flinging my arm to the side. It felt relieving to speak my feelings out loud, if only so that I might try to understand them better. "I thought of Lily often when I was away, but my feelings were never romantic. I never wrote to her."

I considered the necklace I'd brought home for Lillian—how it was the only gift I'd purchased in Vienna. It was proof I'd thought of her often, that I'd missed her.

"But you did." Archie gave a chuckle. "Did you really not know? All those letters you wrote to me . . . they were never entirely meant for me."

"What do you mean?"

"Do you think I cared about where composers dined or the concerts you enjoyed or how many violins were in the orchestra? I cared to hear about what you were doing, but you did not write those details for my benefit. You did not write of Vienna in depth so I might appreciate it—I've been there during my Grand Tour, and you knew that. You were writing to Lillian, and I was merely the reason it was proper for her to read those things."

Was he correct? I sat back and thought about it. Most of the things I'd conveyed in my letters were things I knew Lillian would appreciate and hoped were passed on to her, but I never thought— It had never occurred to me that anyone else would notice.

I did not think even I truly realized what I'd been doing.

"Do you want to hear something funny?" I shook my head, unable to stop my smile. "When I packed up my trunk earlier, it occurred to me that the only person I brought a gift for was Lillian."

Archie laughed. "You brought nothing home for Ada?"

"It wasn't intentional. I just saw something and thought of Lily, so I bought it for her. I've been carrying it around for nearly a year now, actually."

"I think your heart has been hers for quite a while, even though it took your brain some time to catch up."

"Do you think so?" Was that even possible? To love a woman without realizing it? I had loved her for years, of course, but not in this capacity. I'd loved her because she was important to me.

Now I wondered if that love had shifted long ago to encompass more than a brotherly and sisterly affection.

"Well, how do you feel around her now?" Archie asked.

I blew out a heavy breath through puffed cheeks. "Lily is who I want to see. I want to hear her sing. I want to hear her laugh. I want to sit beside her while she pretends to read the little book she has no interest in."

Archie was silent, watching me. "I think you do have feelings for my sister."

I recalled how she'd looked tonight, standing by the pianoforte, singing, her face bright, her eyes sparkling. There was no use trying to deny it. "I think I have for a long time." I rubbed my eyes. "But she might not feel the same."

"There is only one way to find out." Archie grinned. "You can talk to her."

"I tried to do that tonight. She averted our conversation."

He cringed. "Perhaps she does not feel the same way."

"I need to find a way to be alone with her so we can speak plainly to one another. But that is near impossible."

"Not necessarily." Archie looked thoughtful. "If you want to draw her toward you without being obvious, you know what you need to do."

"What?"

He smiled. "Play your violin."

Chapter Twelve

Lillian

THE INTERLUDE IN THE CORRIDOR last night had left me so unsettled that attaining a restful state in which I could fall asleep had been nearly impossible. Instead I opened *A Christmas Carol* with a renewed desire to give it a chance, and I had not been disappointed. It had taken two candles and all night turning pages, but I'd finished it. The story was just as good as both Ada and Theo had led me to believe, and the timing was perfect regarding Christmas.

I stood by my earlier statement of stealing the first line for my own book, though with a little addition: *Lillian Hartley's* heart *was dead, to begin with.* I would follow that line with, *She was a fool.*

It was true I'd allowed Theo's special attention to give me hope that his feelings for me might have undergone a change, but he was no different now than before he went to Vienna. Kind, caring, attentive, interested. He had been all those things before, and just like then, I'd allowed myself to believe his attention indicated a higher regard for me.

All it meant was that Theodore Pine valued me as one would a sister. He valued my voice. He cared if I was sad, but not so his arms could comfort me. No, that would be silly.

I dropped my head back onto my pillow and groaned. Had not the last three years given me ample time to mature? I felt like the same seventeen-year-old girl who had her heart broken and felt duped and ridiculous.

The distant strains of a violin broke through the silence, making me sit up in my bed. It had been so long since I had heard that sound in this house—over three years, in fact. I swung my legs over the side of the bed and closed my eyes, listening to the long pull of the bow across the strings while the instrument was tuned and warmed up.

My gown was already laid out, and Betty was at the fire heating my curling tongs. I dressed quietly in the early-morning light, listening to Theo finish tuning his instrument and move on to playing songs. I was in no great hurry, enjoying the music while I waited for Betty to finish pinning my hair. She positioned dark ringlets at both of my temples and pulled the rest of my hair back into a curly knot at my crown.

I smoothed my hands down the waist of my emerald-green gown, fighting the temptation to go to Theo and hear him play. I was afraid he would entice me to sing with him . . . but oh, that sound. Surely I could listen to him play and refuse to join.

It was not difficult to find him in the library, even with the door closed. The music bled through the walls and down the corridor, leading me directly to him.

For the last twenty minutes at least, Theo had played music I did not recognize, and I longed to ask him about it—who the composer was, whether it was something he had learned in Vienna or written himself, whether Englishmen would recognize it.

I pushed the door open and froze. Theo stood near the window, white Christmas light pouring through the glass and bathing him in brightness. He did not slow his playing for the interruption but continued the melody while his gaze found me immediately and did not let me go. I was caught in his attention, unable to move. The beauty of the song was so rich I wanted to close my eyes and bask in it, but Theo's attention kept me alert.

He did not stop playing, so I stepped into the room and closed the door behind me in case anyone happened to still be asleep. He looked with meaning at the wingback chair near the blazing fire, his eyebrows lifted. I took that as an invitation, though he did not speak. He could have, but his concentration must have been on his music.

The violin looked no different from the one he'd had before—perhaps it was the same instrument. It rested against his shoulder, his arm holding it up, his other hand moving the bow across it in smooth, flowing motions. His coat was missing, draped over the other wingback chair, allowing his arms to move more freely.

This was my favorite state to see him in—casually dressed and completely lost in his music. He drew the final note out, then lowered his bow, looking at me. Light from the window haloed around him, giving him an ethereal glow.

"That was lovely," I said quietly, afraid speaking too loudly would break the magical atmosphere in the room.

"Mr. Hollander taught it to me before he returned to England," he said softly. "It is an old favorite of mine."

"It is a *new* favorite of mine."

Theo moved to sit near me, leaning back in the chair his coat was draped over. He rested his violin on his knee and looked at me, his blue eyes bright from the sunlight streaming into the library. "I hope I did not wake you."

"I was already awake. You might have hurried along my morning routine though."

Theo grinned. "I cannot be sorry for that."

"Wretched man."

"You do not truly think so."

"Of course not."

His gaze dropped to the violin. "I had thought to play a song for your parents as a Christmas gift."

"They will love that."

He lifted his eyes to meet mine. "I was hoping you would join me."

My body stiffened. "I do not perform any longer."

"But you still sing?"

"Not for an audience."

"Your family does not constitute an audience, surely."

"Why not?"

"Because they are your family." He blinked at me. "What happened to you?"

"Nothing—"

"Tell me," he pleaded with compassion. "I cannot help you move past this if I do not know what caused it."

"What gives you the impression I need help?" Or that I could move past the pain my singing brought me, though I would not add that aloud.

Theo raised one dark eyebrow. "You used to confide in me often."

"That was a long time ago." I looked down at my hands. "So much has changed since we were younger."

Theo loosened the bow. He bent forward and laid his violin and bow in their case, then closed and fastened it. He straightened, giving me his full attention. "Were you embarrassed? Sang a wrong note in front of a group?"

I let out a drawn-out sigh of frustration, repositioning myself on my seat. "You are making this into something it is not. No one has bothered me about it in some time now—"

"Except when your mother asked you to sing with me shortly after I arrived or your father bought a bird specifically to entice you to sing or your mother played Christmas carols with the express purpose of forcing you into singing."

"Thank you, Theo; I do see your point," I said dryly. My parents had been trying to persuade me to sing in indirect ways. This had been going on for ages.

"Then, you must see how deeply they miss your voice. Likely almost as much as I have."

"Missed my *voice*," I said, holding his gaze directly.

"Yes."

"Not *me*."

He was quiet, his eyebrows drawing together as he watched me for a long moment. I'd forgotten how comfortable Theo could feel in silence, allowing his thoughts time to form and settle. It was disconcerting. "Is that what this is all about? You believe we love your accomplishments more than we love you?"

"Am I wrong?" I stood and crossed to the window, allowing it to bathe me in light. I could no longer sit and be analyzed in that manner. It caused me to as though Theo could see through me and read the words written on my heart—my longing to have worth outside of my voice.

He scoffed lightly. "Of course you are wrong. No one loves your voice more than they love you." He was closer now, standing directly behind me.

"Singing is the one good thing I have, Theo. I spill every time I eat. I fall from ladders and slip in the snow. I knock over candles. I trip on flat ground and twist my ankle when there is no pock in the road. I am clumsy and silly, and I do not have much to recommend me except for my ability to sing prettily."

"*Prettily* is a vast understatement, but you are so much more than a beautiful voice." Theo stepped forward and turned me to face him, looking into my eyes until I met his. "We do not desire that you sing so we may have enjoyment, Lily, but so we might watch you light up with song. Have you not considered that you are misreading our motivations?"

My heart hammered as I pushed his hands away from my arms. "How can I when my mother is pushing napkins at me and you are begging me to step down from ladders? No one trusts me, and they are right not to. I *did* spill the soup last night, and I *have* fallen from ladders." I gritted my teeth in embarrassment. "More than once."

"You also put yourself into some of those situations merely because of your need to prove yourself, did you not? Your mother was trying to help you, to save your gown, and I was trying to save you from hurting yourself. It is not a lack of faith that led to either of those instances, Lily. It is that we noticed a situation that could be unsafe—whether to your white fabric or your person—and hoped to help you."

"That *is* a lack of faith. Were you not making those choices because you believed I would fail?"

Theo looked stunned.

"When you treat me like a child, you do not give me the respect to decide for myself what is safe or necessary. I did not fall from the ladder in the orangery until you stood beneath it. And is it truly so awful if I spill on a gown?"

He stared at me, his blue eyes unblinking. "No. It's not." He shook his head, never removing his attention. "You are correct, Lily. I am trying to tell you that you matter so much that we would never wish to hurt you, but all I have done—your parents have done—is underestimate you. It was misguided from our love for you, but misguided all the same."

Our love for you.

"You mean, *my parents* love for me."

"No. I meant what I said." He stepped closer, looking down at me, his blue eyes clear and his gaze direct.

My breath suspended, growing shallow. He was much too close for me to think clearly. *Our love for you*, he'd said. "Much the same way Archie feels," I said for clarity.

Theo gave the slightest shake to his head. "I assure you, Lily, my feelings are in no way similar to what Archie must feel for you."

The implication was as clear as the Christmas morning sun, but still, I could not credit it. I leaned back, but my shoulders bumped into the cold window. "I saw you," I blurted, unable to keep it in any longer. "The day before you left for Vienna, I was walking to your house to practice our song for the party, and I saw you and Ada kissing."

"But you were sick that day."

"After that, I was. I had . . . believed that perhaps you felt a certain way for me, and when I saw you together, I realized how wrong I had been."

"Oh, Lily—"

"Do not pity me. I have had years to understand where I erred. The point is I realized that what I thought to be affection from you was nothing more than an appreciation for my voice."

He watched me, his eyebrows pulling taut. "So you decided not to share it with anyone again."

"Yes," I said, the word escaping on a breath. He was still so close, I could not think clearly. If I had, I would not have revealed such an embarrassing piece of information.

"I was a foolish young man then."

"And I was a veritable child."

"So we have both matured."

I swallowed. Why was he not stepping back? Why was he remaining so close, looking at me with such intent?

"You have long been the subject of my thoughts, Lily. It hurts me to think that you've been suppressing your talents merely because you thought that was the only way others saw any worth in you. I assure you I have noticed and appreciated your worth far longer than I've valued your talent. What you once thought to be affection was exactly that, only I was blinded by your youth and Ada's charm. I've grown in these last few years, and the distance has given me leave to recognize who my heart truly belongs to."

"What are you saying?" I asked, my voice hardly above a whisper.

"I love you. *All* of you—the talented and the clumsy bits." His smile slipped, the serious nature of the conversation evident in his eyes. "The way you light up when you serve others, your smile when you planned the oranges for the children and introduced your parrot to them. You are a beacon of light, and you are perfect exactly as you are, Lily. Your light shines no less brightly for your imperfections."

My heart stuttered, filling with warmth.

He dipped his head. "Is there any chance you might feel the same?"

Chapter Thirteen

Theo

WAITING FOR AN ANSWER WAS torture. Lillian stood pressed against the window, silent. She was the most beautiful woman I'd ever seen, and it was not merely because her rich dark hair framed her smooth skin perfectly or because her gray eyes were alert and attentive. She was beautiful for the light that exuded from her, the care and tenderness she had for others, even when no one was watching. It was in her desire to give each child an orange for Christmas and the way she watched them receive their gifts, the way she'd brought her parrot to the kitchen entrance so the tenant children could see the exotic bird. It was her knowing of Mrs. Larsen's pregnancy and her quietly stepping back when she thought—when I thought—I was in love with someone else. She always thought of others, and it did her credit.

"I do not know what to say," she whispered, her voice so quiet I could hardly hear her.

"The truth. How do you feel?"

She held my gaze. "I am still as much in love with you now as I was when I was seventeen."

A soft smile bent my lips. "You have long honored me with feelings I did not deserve."

"I suppose only time will tell if *your* feelings are of a long-standing nature or—"

"They are." I reached into my pocket and pulled out the necklace. The blue-gray backing of the silhouette was the same color as her eyes, a white lily spreading behind the outline of a woman. "I saw this in Vienna, and it reminded me of you. I've held on to it for more than a year, waiting to give it to you."

Lillian inhaled a quick breath. "It is lovely."

"Will you accept it?"

I could see from her hesitation that she understood the importance of my question. She could not accept such a gift from a gentleman without first agreeing to an understanding. It just wasn't done otherwise. On some level, I must have understood when I bought it for her that it would never be appropriate to give to her unless she had agreed to courting me, at the very least.

"Do you mean it?" she asked.

"You are the only person I have a gift for, Lily. Somewhere deep inside, I must have known my heart always belonged to you." I swallowed against a suddenly thick throat.

Lillian turned around to face the window, putting her back to me. "Will you clasp it for me?"

My heart kicked up speed, a galloping team of horses in my chest. I unhooked the clasp and placed the necklace around her graceful neck. My fingers brushed her skin at the nape, securing the necklace in place. Raised gooseflesh ran over her skin from her neck down to her shoulders. I leaned down, pressing a kiss to the soft skin beside the necklace clasp. She turned her head to face me, her eyes bright, and I lifted my lips to meet hers in an eruption of heat and shivers.

Lillian turned her body to face me without breaking contact on our lips. Her arms went around me while I pulled her closer, understanding for the first time how light could fill me from a kiss. I felt vibrant and warm and worthy, as though I could conquer anything.

She pulled back, looking up at me. Her fingers found the silhouette at her throat and pressed against it. "I love you, Theo. I always have."

My joy burst. I leaned down again, kissing her with abandon, giving freedom to the emotions that had felt restricted and pent-up these last few days.

A throat cleared in the doorway, and we broke apart at once, turning to find Mr. and Mrs. Hartley wearing equal expressions of surprise. Blast. Kissing their daughter in the library was no way to repay them for taking me into their home.

"I suppose this means you have something to tell us, darling," Mrs. Hartley said, her voice excruciatingly calm.

"After Theodore asks me a question, I think," Mr. Hartley added.

Lillian's hand found mine, her fingers threading between my own.

I cleared my throat, my neck heating from embarrassment. I should have begged his permission to court his daughter before confessing my feelings to her. I'd done things out of order, but we would sort it. "I would appreciate a moment of your time today, Mr. Hartley, at your convenience."

"My morning is entirely free, son."

"But first, shall we all visit the Larsens together?" Mrs. Hartley asked, her eyes darting to her daughter while a soft smile curved her lips, affording me a measure of relief. "I finished the mittens."

"Oh yes," Lillian agreed. "I thought we could take them a basket of oranges as well."

"Cook is already preparing a basket of food. Adding oranges is an excellent idea."

Lillian started away from me. "I can fetch them—"

I tugged her hand to stop her. "Only if I can help."

"Indeed, only if Theo helps you, darling. We do not want you to fall."

Lillian's shoulders straightened, and I felt her resolve grow thick and solidify. "I am not a child, Mama. I know my limits, and I would appreciate it if you would trust me to discern when I need to exercise caution. You did not raise a simpleton."

Mrs. Hartley's mouth opened and closed again while shock permeated her features. "We only worry for your safety. We know how wise and thoughtful you are."

"Then, I would appreciate it if you would treat me that way."

Mr. Hartley gave his wife a nudge and a gentle nod, a look passing between husband and wife that made me wonder if they had privately had this conversation before.

Mrs. Hartley swallowed. "Of course, darling. If you are to pick oranges, please do so now. We must hurry if we are to be home in time—" She stopped abruptly, and silence filled the library.

"Home in time for what, Mama?" Lillian asked.

"Just home." She turned to walk away. "I must wrap these mittens. Gather the oranges and meet us at the carriage."

Mr. Hartley winked before following his wife from the room.

I waited until the way was clear before pulling Lillian back toward me. I pressed a lingering kiss to her lips.

"Shall we fetch those oranges now?" she asked, grinning.

"Will you let me climb the ladder?"

"I *like* climbing the ladder."

I closed my eyes and shook my head, then returned my gaze to her. "I will not stand in your way if it is what you'd like to do."

Her smile grew. "I will climb the ladder, but you may hold my waist so I do not fall."

I pretended to think this over, glad we were finding a way to meet in the middle. I did trust her to know what was right for her. "That sounds like an agreeable arrangement." We made it to the corridor, and I tugged on her hand, pulling her back for one last kiss.

"Please tell me this is not going to be the view that greets me every morning now," a wry, deep voice said, pulling our attention. Archie stood in the corridor, his arms crossed over his chest, his eyebrows raised.

"Not *every* morning," I said, pulling Lillian along again. When we were out of earshot, I added, "Your family is everywhere."

"Yet none of them were upset at finding us together."

"I think they have long guessed this would be the result of our friendship."

Lillian sighed. "Luckily for me."

"And me."

* * *

After a visit to the Larsen family, the Lynton party rode to the Marcotes' house to sing a carol and wish them a happy Christmas.

Ada stood at the door between her parents, her expression hesitant. I did my best to give her a warm smile. When we finished singing, Mr. and Mrs. Marcote fell into conversation with Mr. and Mrs. Hartley.

Ada descended the front stairs to the gravel drive, where we stood, her green gown swaying with each step.

Lillian took her hand, squeezing it. "You will likely be spending Christmas with us next year, I think."

Ada looked at Archie sharply, then to me again. I smiled, but understanding seemed to pass between us. It was enough.

Archie slapped Theo on the back. "You'll be interested to know that Theo and my sister have discovered feelings of their own as well."

Ada's eyebrows lifted, her hesitancy gone. "I wondered, though I didn't . . . Anyway, I am happy for you both."

Lillian blushed. "You aren't angry?"

Ada smiled at Archie. "How could I be?"

It was too cold to remain outside any longer, so we bade the Marcotes farewell and filed into the carriage to return to Lynton. Thus far, Christmas had been nearly perfect. My soul craved mended relationships, and it had been mostly satisfied.

The carriage pulled up to the house and came to a stop. I followed Archie out and turned to offer my assistance to Mrs. Hartley and Lillian, the latter of which I had difficulty releasing. We needed to have a long enough courtship to grow together in our newfound relationship, but I hoped it wouldn't be of too great a length.

"Would you care to accompany me to the library, Miss Hartley?" I asked. "I was hoping to practice my Christmas gift."

"You need Lillian's help to do so?" Mrs. Hartley asked, her eyebrows lifted. She paused, looking from Lillian to me. "Does this mean you are singing for us, darling?"

She looked at me, then her mother. "If I answered you, it would ruin the surprise."

Mrs. Hartley nodded, her smile growing. "Go, and keep your secrets, but I would like for you to come to the morning room first so we might have breakfast together." She looked at me. "All of us."

"Of course, Mrs. Hartley." How could I refuse her anything? She had no qualms about me paying court to her daughter.

We removed our cloaks, coats, hats, and gloves near the door, handing them off to Kemper. Mrs. Cole appeared at the foot of the stairs. "Breakfast is awaiting you, ma'am."

"Thank you, Mrs. Cole." Mrs. Hartley started toward the morning room, the rest of her family following. When we reached the door, I was the last to step inside, surprised to find the entire Hartley family watching me closely.

I turned to Archie to ask what was happening when my gaze lit upon a woman standing near the hearth, her gown a rich, dark purple and her eyes shining bright with unshed tears. She appeared to have aged in the last three years, her face more finely lined, the brown of her hair having faded to a less vibrant hue.

"Mother?" I looked from her to Mrs. Hartley and back. "What are you doing here? I thought you were in Dorset."

"Mr. Hartley sent for me. I had no notion of you coming, or I would have remained at home." She opened her arms to me, and I stepped into them, overwhelmed by how glad I was to see her.

"I should have come to Dorset, but I was hoping to meet with you in London after Christmas."

"I recall the last time my sister visited us while you were still home. Young Henry cut your violin strings, did he not?"

It felt a foolish, childish reason to avoid my family now that my mother spoke it aloud. "Yes. But I do love Aunt Frye. I wasn't quite ready to leave the Hartleys though."

"The Hartleys? Or *Miss* Hartley?"

I looked at Archie, but he shrugged. "I said nothing," he claimed.

"You have no faith in a mother's intuition if you believe I would rely on Archibald for my information," Mother said. "The vast number of times you asked after her in your letters made it plain to me."

My cheeks warmed, and I felt my neck heating. I caught Lillian's smile and returned it. Finally seeing the necklace adorn her after my holding on to it for so long brought me unaccountable joy. In truth, I was glad my feelings were no great surprise to anyone else. It made the business with Ada far less troublesome. She and Archie could be happy together without the pall of scandal hanging over them.

"We will leave you and take our breakfast in the drawing room," Mr. Hartley said. "Welcome to Lynton, Mrs. Pine, and happy Christmas."

The Hartley family left me alone with my mother. I guided her to the small table that had been set for only two. Evidently this surprise had been planned exactly. "I am glad to see you, Mother."

"England is glad to have you home. Tell me, how long do you intend to remain?"

"Forever. If I can convince Lillian to be my wife, I have no reason to be anywhere else."

"She won't need much convincing," Mother said, patting my hand. "That poor girl has been in love with you for years."

"I have been blind."

She did not argue that point. "This is all well and good, son, but you need to sort things with Miss Marcote first."

I leaned back, surveying my mother. "You ought to work for the Crown, you know. How are you receiving your information?"

She lifted her tea and took a sip. "Observation, darling. You ought to try it."

"Well, you need not worry about Miss Marcote. Archie is well on his way to proposing."

She gave a distinct nod of satisfaction before cracking into her egg.

"Happy Christmas, Mother."

She smiled warmly. "Happy Christmas, my son."

Chapter Fourteen

Lillian

"Do you feel prepared?" Theo asked, leaning close and whispering into my ear. It sent a volley of shivers down my neck in an entirely pleasurable way.

I looked back to face him, but the corridor was mostly dark, and I could only make out his outline with the wall sconce just behind him. "Had I been given more time to practice, I would. As of now I fear I shall ruin the entire performance."

"You could not possibly ruin anything. If you forget the words, make up your own. No one will know."

"Both Archie and my father understand Latin. They will know."

Theo grinned. "You will do splendidly."

I drew in a breath. It had been so long since I stood before a group and sang anything—let alone a new song. My heart was beating unusually rapidly, my breath frustratingly shallow. I was nervous, which was silly. This was my family.

Theo took hold of my silk-gloved fingers. "We have practiced, Lily. You know the song. You will do well."

I nodded. This was not the first time we had practiced this song together. We had been working on it to perform at his farewell party before he left for Vienna. I had refused to so much as look at it since then, but now it felt a fitting way to begin our first performance together in so many years. "I only wish I'd had enough time to learn the song on the pianoforte. It would sound so lovely paired with your violin."

"Next time," Theo whispered. He leaned forward, pressing his lips to mine softly, a mere whisper of a kiss. Would I ever grow used to the joy his affection brought me? "I will be right beside you."

I leaned forward and kissed him again, tightening my hold on his hand. "Always."

We filed into the great hall to find our families all seated on the sofas waiting for us. Mama, Papa, Archie, and Mrs. Pine watched us expectantly. Theo stood between the Christmas tree and Clementine's cage, giving me space to stand directly in the center of what we had deemed to be the stage area, holding the music in front of me.

He positioned his bow and closed his eyes, beginning the first few drawn-out notes. Sound filled the vast hall, the emotion so vivid and full in the pull of the notes. I looked down at the music and opened my mouth, singing the first few words of "Ave Maria." It was a beautiful song, made lovelier by its meaning.

I did not focus on the Latin or the act of singing, instead letting my voice ring out in the room. The beginning of the song was about Mary, the mother of Jesus, and that alone made it feel worthy of Christmas evening.

The longer I sang, the more my body relaxed, allowing the music to unwind and release the unhappy parts of me, replacing them with goodness. Music was healing, and in this moment, it was a choice I had made to appreciate my talent and gifts that came from God and to recognize that no one loved me any less for the parts in which I lacked. My imperfections did not lend my talents extra worth—I was worthy just as I was.

Our audience sat rapt, hanging on to every note until the song came to a close. The room remained silent for a moment while our mothers wiped away tears, likely both equally glad to see their children perform after such a length of time.

Clementine trilled, filling the silence. "Ave. Ave Maria."

Laughter bubbled from my chest. "Ave Maria," I sang back to her.

She repeated it again, dragging out each of the words as I had done.

"Well done, Clementine!" Archie said.

She repeated her song again. "Ave Maria."

"May we have another?" Mother asked.

"Perhaps 'O Holy Night'?" Mrs. Pine requested.

Theo nodded, positioning his bow. "I know that one by heart."

As did I. We sang the carols, my soul and heart brightening with the power of music, love, and family. When Theo put his violin away, I sat on the empty settee and waited for him to join me there. It did not take very long. He took my hand, holding it tightly in his own. "Happy Christmas, love."

"Happy Christmas."

Author's Notes

Franz Schubert originally wrote "Ave Maria" in 1825, but it was titled "Ellens Gesang III" ("Ellen's Song" in German) and was based on text from Sir Walter Scott's poem *The Lady of the Lake*. Given its opening line, "Ave Maria," the song obtained that nickname and in the 1850s was altered, applying the Latin Hail Mary prayer to Schubert's melody. For the purpose of my story, I used the song as we know it today, but in truth, it was another six years before these characters would have sung "Ave Maria" religiously. If someone in 1852 sang this song, it would have been political in nature, following a portion of the story in Sir Walter Scott's poem.

Lynton Park is an imaginary house, but it is based entirely on Lyme Park, which some of you might recognize as Pemberley from Colin Firth's *Pride and Prejudice*. On a trip to visit the estate, my husband was invited to play the pianoforte in the great hall (which doubled as an entry room). I have no musical talent, but when I heard my husband playing and the beautiful acoustics in the room, this story was born. The same room also features a squint, which is a door high up on the wall that could be opened from the family's drawing room so they could peek down to the front door and see who was calling, making it possible for them to decide whether they wanted to greet their guests or make themselves absent. I thought that was a fun feature of the house that needed to make its way into my story as well.

About the Author

Kasey Stockton is a staunch lover of all things romantic. She doesn't discriminate between genres and enjoys a wide variety of happily ever afters. Drawn to the Regency period at a young age when gifted a copy of *Sense and Sensibility* by her grandmother, Kasey initially began writing Regency romances. She has since written in a variety of genres, but all of her titles fall under clean romance. She loves reading, chocolate, and period dramas, but nothing tops her very own prince charming, their three children, and their sweet goldendoodle.

Learn more about Kasey at kaseystockton.com and follow her on social media.

Facebook: Author Kasey Stockton

Instagram: @authorkaseystockton

OTHER COVENANT BOOKS AND AUDIOBOOKS BY KATIE STEWART STONE

STAND-ALONE NOVELS

Coming Home to Bellingham

Scotland's Melody

NOVELLAS

"Christmas at Bellingham" in *A Christmas Serenade*

Christmas at Bellingham

KATIE STEWART STONE

Acknowledgments

THIS STORY WAS MADE POSSIBLE by such talented and amazing authors. Thank you to Bri Stephens, Liz Lowham, Allison Matthews, and Kasey Stockton for your help in making this novella stronger in every way! Thank you to my readers who loved my first book, *Coming Home to Bellingham*! Thank you to Covenant Communications for giving me the opportunity to be a part of this Christmas anthology! And thank you to my fellow Covenant authors for being so welcoming and kind; you make this writing community extraordinarily special.

Chapter One

It was two weeks before Christmas, and I sat in the music room of Bellingham Hall, tinkering with my variety of instruments. I collected them and attempted to learn each one. I enjoyed the challenge to master each discipline, but that was not all; the range of emotions that could be communicated with each instrument fascinated me. I'd already practiced conveying poetry with my violin, joviality with my lute, and mysticism with an instrument called the sitar, given to me by one of the dowager countess's four sons, Admiral Hollis Alexander. He'd brought it back from one of his trips to India.

As I set down the sitar, the Dowager Countess of Bellingham, Lady Amelia Alexander, entered the room and smiled brightly at me. "Don't mind me, dear. Play on," she said. A servant followed her with a writing desk so she could answer correspondence. She often accompanied me while I played. In return, I accompanied her while she planned the many parties she hosted at Bellingham Hall and the nearby village of Lynsfield.

"You're just in time," I told her. "I'm moving on to the pianoforte next." It was her favorite of all the instruments.

"It's always more agreeable when I do not have to force you to play it." The youthful lilt in her speech was accentuated by the gleam in her eye. She was nearly seventy, but even with a fair number of wrinkles, she maintained her exuberance for all things frivolous and humorous. She especially loved teasing.

One would never imagine that underneath it all, the doctor's grim prognosis told a different tale.

My careful smile didn't betray my worry at the thought as I sat on the bench.

The familiarity of the pianoforte had me closing my eyes in order to fully enjoy the feeling of the smooth ivory keys.

"Esther Harris, that sounds bee-yoo-tee-ful," I heard a voice say from the doorway.

I didn't have to open my eyes to know who had said the all-too-familiar phrase; it was the first thing I'd ever said to her as a child. I opened them anyway and smirked at Lady Bellingham, whom I called Aunt Anabelle, though she was only an aunt through affection, not blood. I had been seven when she first visited my three siblings and me in our tiny home in Lynsfield. Back then, before she became Lady Anabelle Alexander, Countess of Bellingham, she had simply been a close friend of my elder sister, Lucy.

"You say that far too often for me to believe you," I replied. "Besides, I don't play half as well as you."

"Well, your tutor has been much more lax than mine was," she replied ironically; she was that very lax teacher. "Never mind my own failings, however." She grinned at the dowager. "I have brought an invitation from my sister-in-law."

Her excitement sent ripples through the air, tantalizing my curiosity. The dowager and I didn't have to wait long for Aunt Anabelle's news. She waved a letter in the air, presumably from the wife of Admiral Alexander, my sitar benefactor.

"Katherine wants us to visit her in London before Andrew arrives there. We can surprise him!" she announced.

The dowager turned fully in her seat to face Aunt Anabelle. Her face shone bright with excitement.

My heart threatened to jump from my chest, so I stood along with it. My best friend since childhood, Andrew Lawrence, was due to return from his Grand Tour before the Christmas festivities. I had been awaiting news of his arrival for weeks.

"What an intriguing invitation!" The dowager countess laughed, full and rich. "All of Katherine's friends must have left Town for Christmas," she mused about her daughter-in-law.

Aunt Anabelle laughed too. "You know her well. I imagine the admiral has some business he needs to take care of before they travel here and she's feeling lonely."

"Being an admiral has made that boy such a bore. Katherine should just come here by herself," the dowager said. "But it might be fun to see London covered in snow." She looked at me thoughtfully, perhaps wondering how I felt about London, considering my elder sister's awful experience with it. Lucy, like Aunt Anabelle, had married far above her station. She'd visited

Town soon after marrying Robert Alexander, the youngest of the dowager's sons, and had been badly ridiculed by Society. It was due to how the *ton* had treated Lucy that I had never had a Season, even at one and twenty.

The dowager continued to observe me. "What do you think, Esther?"

I should have been more hesitant, but the thought of surprising Andrew tugged fiercely at my sensibilities. London didn't frighten me in the face of finally having a chance to pay back all those times he'd startled me growing up. His penchant for hiding in the bushes and sneaking up on me had never ceased to amuse him. The possibility of retaliation awoke the embers of mirth that had been cooling in Andrew's absence. My heart pumped with greater force, as if it were spurring me on.

"I would love to go," I answered easily.

The dowager nodded decisively. "I think it a splendid idea as well. Little Andrew will be pleased beyond measure to see us, I think."

"My cousin Andrew isn't so little anymore, Mother. Or so he tells me in his letters." Aunt Anabelle smiled. "It's settled, then. Let's leave tomorrow. I'll go tell Aunt Lawrence." She set off immediately for Bellingham Cottage to tell Andrew's mother, Rachel Lawrence, of our plans. A note would have sufficed, but I knew Aunt Anabelle enjoyed the walk to the quaint cottage on the Bellingham property. It was the steward's residence and where she had once lived with her aunt, uncle, and cousin Andrew before she'd won the heart of the heir to the Bellingham earldom.

She had moved in with her aunt and uncle after being orphaned and became a catalyst for the unions between the Alexanders, the Lawrences, and the Harrises. The unique family unit at Bellingham all began because Lord Peter Alexander fell in love with Aunt Anabelle. It was a match that surprised even her. I was certain becoming Lady Bellingham had never been her ambition, but she now owned the title nonetheless.

Andrew and I owed our good fortunes to Aunt Anabelle's and Lucy's marriages. Without his cousin becoming Lady Bellingham, it was unlikely the son of a steward would have been able to receive the benefits of high Society—including the Grand Tour from which he was returning. As for myself, use of expensive instruments was only a fraction of the luxuries I had access to.

Setting a precedent, such as marrying far below one's station, was never easy. And as my father and brother reminded me frequently, such a change in station didn't sit well with most of Society, whether it be high or low.

* * *

Later that day, the dowager dragged Aunt Anabelle and me into her extravagant bedchambers so that she could help me try on my newly arrived gown for the Christmas ball. She knew how much I loved pretty things, and she never wasted an opportunity to spoil me. Part of me wished she wasn't quite so attentive, but after getting to know the dowager, one would never wish to deny any pleasure of hers—and doting on others was her greatest pleasure.

Aunt Anabelle placed a hand on my shoulder as we looked into the mirror at my reflection. "Lucy will not recognize you." We exchanged a look of longing for my sister. I knew Aunt Anabelle missed her almost as much as I did.

I hadn't seen Lucy in over eighteen months. Her husband, Captain Robert Alexander of the British Army, was stationed in the South of England. Rather than stay at Bellingham Hall with me, she had opted to follow him. Unsurprising, considering they were remarkably in love.

The dowager countess inspected the dress, tugging it this way and that. She stood back for a better view. "It brings out the green in your eyes," she said with appreciation.

"That's quite a feat, considering it's purple," I replied with teasing. I agreed with her though. My hazel eyes did tend to show signs of green when contrasted with certain colors. This dress accentuated those hues and even complemented my sometimes-dreary straw-colored hair.

The two countesses stood laughing with each other as I stepped away from the mirror and inspected the choices for hair adornments the dowager had set aside for me. I fingered the pieces delicately. From a very young age, I had harbored a deep affection for all things lovely. Perhaps because as a child I had worked in a draper shop and handled items I knew I would never own. Of course, a twist in fate had brought me into this house and given me access to those luxuries I coveted. It was all thanks to my kind, sweet, and beautiful sister for catching the eye of the youngest son of an earl, even though she was merely a maid. I was certain stranger things happened in this world, but not many.

Three children burst into the room then, their distraught nurse quickly following with a baby in her arms. Aunt Anabelle's four children disliked being away from her for too long. She sighed through her smile. "There you are, my babies." She walked over to them and took as many of them into her arms as would fit. "Were you looking for me?"

"Mama, Phillip pulled my hair," the second child and only girl, Rene, complained about her elder brother.

"Mama, Mama, Mama!" the second to youngest, James, babbled in his newfound speech.

Aunt Anabelle took them out of the room as she answered all of their complaints and questions. The dowager countess and I laughed together at the familiar but comical scene.

She then held up one of the hair ornaments and folded it around my hair, testing its placement. "I think this one perfectly accents the purple in the gown. Don't you agree?"

I grinned at her, then took the piece to view it in the mirror. The amethyst jewels glittered in the bright sunlight, making them look more like diamonds against my hair. "As expected, the dowager countess has impeccable taste."

She nodded. "Well, I'm pleased with the dress. How do you feel?"

"It will do nicely." It fit just as I wished, complementing all of my best features. I smiled at myself as I wondered whether those attending the party would notice how mature I looked in it.

"What's that expression?" the dowager asked.

I gave a single laugh. "What expression? I don't know what you mean." My smile couldn't be hidden, so I stepped away from the mirror and placed the hair accent back on the table.

"Are you that excited for the Christmas party? Is there someone attending you wish to look well for?" Her tone was full of hope. She wanted to see me happily married. Many times in the past two years she had introduced eligible young men, all of whom I'd rejected. Thankfully, she'd never asked why.

The truth was I didn't know the reason. Perhaps I was afraid. Perhaps I had no interest. Perhaps I didn't feel I deserved to marry too far above my station.

"I don't want to disappoint you, but there's no such person."

She nodded and beckoned me to follow her out of the bedchamber while she changed the topic. "I believe this will be one of the most spectacular celebrations Bellingham has ever hosted. Everyone has been away for so long; we must make it extravagant, no?"

Every celebration was the most spectacular celebration, each one better than the last. "Of course, Dowager."

"How I love when you humor me, Esther. I think you're my favorite daughter of them all."

She was old enough to be my grandmother, so calling me a daughter was her way of making me feel more at home, making me feel as though I truly belonged. I hugged her arm affectionately. "You tell me so quite frequently. I hope your daughters-in-law don't resent me for it."

Her laugh rang out through the echoing corridors as we walked. "Raising four boys certainly was worth it once I gained so many daughters."

My thoughts hitched as they did each time she mentioned having *four* sons. I knew only three of them. The eldest was Lord Peter Alexander, Earl of Bellingham; the third son was Admiral Hollis Alexander in the Royal Navy; and the youngest was my brother by law, Robert. The second son, rarely spoken of, had been exiled from Bellingham almost fifteen years ago. I'd heard his name only once: Nathan Alexander. There'd been some falling out between him and the eldest brother. I'd never touched on the subject, but I'd always wished to. I had an inkling that the dowager countess wished to speak of him as well but held back due to the rift between her sons.

She looked around us. "Speaking of young women who have joined the Alexander family, where did Bethany run off to? I thought she was going to try on her dress as well."

"She took her dress and escaped to her bedchamber. You know how she dislikes everyone looking at her." My younger sister wasn't taking to Bellingham Hall as well as I wished, though she'd been here only a few months. It disappointed me more than I could say. It had taken us weeks of coercion for her to agree to move in, and although I'd given her time to adjust, she didn't put forth effort to make the manor house her home. It was almost as if she disliked the endless luxuries available to her, which I couldn't fathom no matter how hard I tried. Then again, she didn't appreciate lovely things as much as I did.

The dowager clicked her tongue. "What can we do to help that girl overcome her timidity?"

Rather than speak my mind about my true concerns, I decided to make her laugh. I disliked worrying the dowager. She already had so much to occupy her mind. "Must we help her overcome it? She's much prettier than me. It would be a shame to be overshadowed by my little sister." While I meant it to be a jest, I admitted to myself Bethany's beauty outshone mine without effort.

The dowager chuckled and poked a finger at my shoulder playfully. "And you, Esther. What can we do to help you overcome your need for attention and admiration?"

I lifted my chin. "Some people cannot be fixed."

"'Tis true. There have been many who wished to fix my meddlesome tendencies."

We entered her favorite parlor, where she planned all of her parties. Papers, books, and quills were strewn over a large table. She was known for her intricately planned parties, not for her organization. Aunt Anabelle used to be the dowager's assistant, but when I moved into the house five years ago, I had assumed the role. Likely to Aunt Anabelle's relief, considering the many responsibilities she had as Countess of Bellingham.

I sat in my usual seat and picked up the book I was perusing about French music. The dowager had encouraged me to plan the entertainment for the family gathering after Christmas dinner. Deciding to stray from tradition, I'd opted to look to France for ideas. I had yet to solidify a schedule. I paused and looked up over the spine of my book, curious to know how many to expect in the party. Arranging entertainment for a handful of people versus two dozen people would determine the number of songs and instruments to use.

"Will all the Alexanders come?"

Seeing the dowager's reaction, I regretted having asked the question. Her eyes widened in surprise, and then, within a few seconds, she corrected her features. I had unintentionally alluded to her estranged son.

I wanted to frown, sympathize with her, and take her hand. When would she open up to me about her heartbreak? Surely she wished to speak with someone about it.

She forced a smile. "Yes, of course. Who would miss their mother's most important party of the year? They wouldn't dare." I hated that she brushed past it. I knew she missed him.

But if she wished to ignore her feelings, I would go along with it. I nodded and sent her a knowing smirk. "Certainly no one would wish to disappoint you."

She chuckled and riffled through a stack of papers. "Have you seen a response from the Timmonses?" She was focused on planning the Christmas ball, which would take place on Christmas Eve. "I know Mrs. Timmons often goes to Bath this time of year."

I returned my gaze to the book while recalling the note I had read from Mrs. Timmons earlier that day. "They'll be going there again this year, it seems."

After a few moments of papers shuffling and a quill scratching, she spoke again. "Oh, will you read Andrew's letter? We need to know when to expect him in London."

Upon hearing my childhood friend's name, the book I held suddenly seemed unimportant, even though it was for his sake I'd decided on French music to begin with.

I found the letter immediately because I wished to read it again myself. He'd addressed the letter to Aunt Anabelle, but once she'd relinquished it to me, I'd read it as if it were always meant for me. "He'll arrive in London on Wednesday. His plan is then to arrive here on Thursday, just in time for Christmas Eve on Friday."

That wasn't the only information in the letter, however. He also spoke of his traveling companions. Two men—Mr. Stenton and Mr. Beaumont—and . . . a woman by the name of *Miss* Beaumont. Had Andrew been traveling with them for an entire year? Not that such information was important. Why would I care whether he'd been traveling with an unmarried lady for thirteen months, two weeks, and three days? I wondered again about the lady's age and physical appearance.

I pushed the letter away from me with a sigh, then asked the dowager, "Did Lucy say when she was arriving?"

"She will be here on Christmas Eve."

I couldn't prevent my childish pout. "I wish she were coming today."

"I know, dear. I miss them too." She clucked and then looked up at me as if just remembering something. "Will you go see Bethany and ask what she thinks of the dress? We need to be sure everything is tailored before the ball."

I didn't wish to have another frustrating conversation with my little sister, but I knew it was inevitable. "Yes, Dowager," I said with another sigh.

"Don't sound so excited. I'll think you wish to be doing anything but helping me with planning." The dowager raised an eyebrow. I knew she meant to reprimand me, despite her teasing sarcasm.

I smiled at her before heading upstairs.

Upon entering Bethany's room, I found that she had packed most of her things. She had not come with much; only one carpet bag lay on the floor in front of the armoire.

I tensed, and my words came out with an edge. "What's going on here?"

Chapter Two

Bethany saw me and sank slowly into the chair in front of the vanity, effectively avoiding my scrutinizing gaze as she bent her long neck to study her feet. "I'm leaving. I cannot stand it any longer," she said without meeting my eyes.

I looked at her perfect ball gown hanging on the armoire.

She must have noticed my attention turn toward it. "I hate it," she pouted.

I scoffed. "Why? Is it *too* beautiful?" I walked over to the dress and touched its luxurious folds, admiring it.

When I looked at her again, she wrinkled her pixie nose. The gesture was a habit we'd learned from our father when we disliked something. "The colors don't suit me at all."

"You mean they don't allow you to hide in a corner and blend into the wallpaper?" The pale-green gown had accents of pink, which would make her look even more like a woodland fairy than she already did.

She stood. I watched her curl her dainty fists as if trying to summon all of her courage. It only made her seem younger to me. "You don't understand how unhappy I am here, Esther. This is paradise for you, but the dowager makes me miserable with her constant meddling."

I sighed slowly. My feelings about Bellingham were more complicated than paradise, but it didn't matter. I took her hand lightly in an effort to connect with her. "She means well. She wants to draw you out, to help you be less timid. Has Aunt Anabelle never told you about her first year at Bellingham?"

She pulled away from me, wrapping her arms around herself. "Well, I'm not Aunt Anabelle."

Appraising her, my lips turned down in sympathy. "That's true. While the dowager countess was able to make her feel comfortable and accepted, her tactics only drive you into hiding. I'll talk to her about it. Try to endure, Beth. We have a chance here to make a life for ourselves. I know you haven't lived here as long as I have, but you'll see that our old life was beneath us."

Bethany's eyes turned severe, as if she not only wanted to rebuke me for my words but was deeply offended by them.

She misunderstood me; I could tell. I held up my hands. "I mean we deserve more than living in that old cottage or marrying mere farmers. We can aim higher while taking advantage of the chances Lucy's marriage has brought us." Hadn't I told myself this a hundred times? If I repeated the words enough, they would ring true to both of us.

She narrowed her eyes. "You think our cottage is beneath us? What do you think of our father and brother, who still live there?"

My arms fell to my sides, and I looked away from her. How could I get her to see logic? "They're still my family, of course. But we don't have to settle for their life. You should accept the dowager's generosity and leave Satchell Cottage behind."

I was only being realistic. We may have come from humble origins, but things had changed after Lucy's marriage elevated us. I would take full advantage of it, even if my father and brother disapproved. Even if Bethany disapproved. Even if deep down I didn't believe I deserved it.

Her chin quivered and tears pooled in her eyes. "I cannot leave my home, my family, behind."

"Am *I* not your family? Is *Lucy* not your family?"

Bethany swiped at the quick tears that spilled over and sniffed once before responding resolutely. "You've chosen to disregard us while following Lucy into the Alexander family. You'll always be my sister, just as she is. But Papa and Sam still need us. I think you've forgotten your duties as a daughter and a sister."

I folded my arms. "If that's how you feel, then why did you agree to move in here?"

Several vulnerable emotions crossed her features as she looked for something in my face. "I've been noticing it over time, but, Esther, you've changed. You've grown further and further apart from us. From *me*. I've tried to understand you, but I can't do it anymore." She shook her head at me, letting out a noise of disbelief. "You truly think you're above us."

For a shy girl just barely into adulthood, she certainly could make me feel small.

With that, she took her bag and left the house. I didn't follow her; I was too surprised by her callous words. And too angry by her accusation that I'd become pretentious. I paced the empty room, speechless.

Very well. Let her leave if she wanted to. If she didn't appreciate all of this, I would do it enough for both of us.

Even as I thought it, however, my heart ran after her. I loved the manor house and those within it, but nothing could replace the comfort of a sister. I'd thought having her here would complete my happiness. But if we didn't see eye-to-eye, what comfort could either of us give the other?

When I returned to the parlor, the dowager wasn't there. I sat heavily in my chair and noticed a note she had left me.

> *Please visit Satchell Cottage to invite your family to Christmas dinner.*

I laid my head on my folded arms. It was only a few minutes' walk through the forest, yet it might as well have been across the sea. If only my family would accept the generosity of the Alexanders, then we could live in harmony. They were so exhaustingly stubborn.

* * *

My father peeled potatoes and listened to my halfhearted invitation to Christmas dinner. No matter how kindly I invited them, they wouldn't attend. I knew I wasted my breath. My elder brother, Sam, wasn't interested, if his blank stare communicated anything. Bethany avoided my eyes as she sat in the corner of the room.

My father barely looked at me when he replied, "The Alexanders may have become your family, but they still aren't mine." His reaction did not surprise me; his unwillingness to visit Bellingham Hall was a point of tension between us and had been since I'd moved into the manor house. I could've quoted his response verbatim to the dowager before coming here, for as many times as I'd heard it.

My tone of voice turned bored. "Papa, they are your family by *law*. Lucy's an Alexander. The dowager treats me as if *I'm* her daughter. Surely you feel at least beholden to the Alexanders for treating your daughters like their own kin, enough to show your face at holiday gatherings." My father's wrinkled nose mirrored mine but for different reasons. He disliked my accurate assessment of his situation, even if he didn't admit that it was, indeed, accurate.

Sam spoke up. "Of course we're grateful to them. You have luxuries that Father and I could never provide. But they've also made you vain and selfish. There's a cost for a sudden change in station. That much is certain while looking at you."

That stung.

This was why I never came to Satchell Cottage. They never failed to make me feel defensive. "There's nothing wrong with changing my standards to match my circumstances."

Sam's blond eyelashes were so like Lucy's, and yet his glare beneath them was vastly different from her gentle gaze. If she were here, we wouldn't be arguing. I was a poor substitution for our eldest sister.

"Well, your circumstances changed far too much, too quickly," he said. "It's not natural. Everyone in the county believes that the Harris family are upstarts. Maintaining relationships with those on our level is more difficult each year as you overlook all the eligible men nearby because you have set your gaze too high."

I sputtered. "What? Can I help it if I don't wish to be courted by *Levi Halverston*? He's a balding widower with three children. Certainly I should have the ability to choose whom I'll accept, whether he's deemed a good match or not."

Sam glanced at our father before saying evenly, "Levi Halverston is an honest man who could provide a comfortable living. Father has been close with him for years, and you've ruined that relationship."

I pointed to the two of them. "Don't forget that Lucy's union with Robert Alexander has benefited you as well. We would still be living in Lynsfield trying to survive if not for Robert giving us Satchell Cottage."

Sam laughed bitterly. "You don't understand because you've been at the manor house for too long, but we've lost more than Levi Halverston. People Father has known from childhood are beginning to scorn us because *you've* made us into upstarts. They could accept Lucy's sudden rise in Society and even our move to the cottage. But after your multiple slights to suitors—"

I interrupted. *"Multiple?"*

Sam raised his eyebrows higher as he spoke over me. "Your pretentiousness has soured our relationship with the whole village. Who'll want to purchase our crops or assist us during the harvest if they think we look down on them?"

I had to look away from his disappointed gaze to take in his explanation. The unfairness of it made me angry. "Is it my fault that the villagers are narrow-minded?"

As soon as I said it, I regretted it, but I was not one to recall my own words. I waved a hand to ignore it. "We are straying from the point. The Alexanders have done nothing to deserve your derision."

My father sighed and threw down the potato he was working on with a huff. "Yes, yes. We're all filled with undying gratitude toward the Alexanders.

It still doesn't mean I like eating with them." He left the cottage in a decisive retreat.

I scowled at my brother. "The truth is both of you feel so inferior to the Alexanders that you dislike being around them. *They* don't look down on us; they welcome us as family, so why should *we* feel intimidated by their status? Are you so embarrassed by your humble roots that you cannot feel comfortable in the home of an earl?" I cringed inwardly. If only I would stop letting these things fly from my lips, but it was as if I were also speaking to myself.

He sighed, then cast his unwavering blue eyes on me. "You would think that, wouldn't you?"

"You're being childish." I heard the irony in my own words; who sounded more childish than I did in this moment?

"I expect nothing more than insults from you," Sam replied sharply.

Bethany continued sitting quietly, knees to her chest as she watched me argue with our brother. I shifted my focus on her. "You have to come back to the manor house. What will I tell the dowager? She'll be greatly offended by your departure."

She bit her lip and bent her head. "I'm sorry to disappoint her, but I have to be true to myself. Tell her I'd rather live simply than extravagantly."

I had to acknowledge Bethany's constant nature. Though timid, she wasn't easily persuaded. If only that trait weren't getting in the way of her seeing things how I did.

"Do you think she'll accept that?"

"It's the truth. I don't intend to return."

That simple sentence pierced me more than I thought it would. She wouldn't return. She would rather stay in this cottage than live in luxury with her own sister? I closed my eyes and let out a long breath. It didn't help. I wasn't accomplishing anything with this visit. My patience had waned—admittedly it hadn't been very fortified to begin with.

"All right," I said shortly. I turned back to Sam. "If you all don't come for Christmas, I'm never inviting you again." I curled one fist, holding back any childish name-calling, which so easily slid off my tongue. "I will no longer waste my time on you. I know you don't like that I've benefited from the Alexanders' generosity. You think I'm a haughty upstart." I shifted my weight and brought up the one thing we could agree on. "But you can at least be supportive of Lucy."

Sam and Bethany both cast their eyes down at mention of our eldest sister. The sister who had taken the place of our mother. The sister who held our family together.

"She doesn't ask much of us; don't offend her by abstaining from dinner with her family. It's not hard to come and have a Christmas meal at Bellingham Hall."

"If Lucy wants to have a meal with us, she can come to the cottage. And if you can lower yourself to eat at our table, you're welcome too," Sam said quietly but firmly.

My father entered the house again and sat down, picking up another potato. He cleared his throat as if he would say something but stayed silent. His son and youngest daughter followed his example, each picking up a potato and ignoring me.

I threw up my hands. "Peel your blasted potatoes and completely ignore your family members who have moved on to a better life, leaving you all"—I pointed to each of them—"behind."

I stormed out and made my way back to the house, muttering angrily under my breath. My boots crunched in the snow, leaving deep footsteps in my wake. I imagined if someone followed me, they'd know exactly how I felt simply by seeing the overly pronounced indents.

I knew my family didn't exactly dislike the Alexanders. No one who knew the Alexanders could truly dislike them. But my family's aversion to the manor house began with the hardships Lucy had endured after her rise in Society—apparently it was an affront to the hierarchy for the son of an earl to marry a maid—and had ended with my rejection of men my family considered suitable. It wasn't as if I wished to belittle anyone, but the fact was that I *could* set my sights higher now, even if I had yet to feel worthy of it.

When I came into view of the manor house, I let out a long breath. The towering beauty of the building brought imaginings of fairy tales and girlish fantasies. It was bright, cheery, grand, and picturesque.

While lost in my muddled thoughts, I heard a clear voice call out to me. "Esther!"

It was Andrew's mother, Mrs. Rachel Lawrence. Her kind smile thawed my icy mood.

"Good day, dear," she greeted. She was walking toward Bellingham Hall with her husband, the steward of the Bellingham estate. He wasn't one to make conversation, so he simply nodded his hello.

It took only a handful of long strides to reach them. "I am so pleased to see the two of you. I meant to come visit yesterday, but the dowager took up the whole of my afternoon."

Mrs. Lawrence laughed and pulled my arm through hers. "No need to apologize. We understand better than anyone how the dowager countess can take up one's time."

"I'm sure you do. How are you? I imagine you're comforted to know that Andrew will be home soon."

Mr. Lawrence cleared his throat. Mrs. Lawrence nodded, somehow understanding what he meant by the gesture. "My husband and I are of the same mind on this point. Andrew has been away for far too long."

"I absolutely agree. And to think we'll have the chance to surprise him in London! Are you as thrilled as I, thinking about his face when he sees us there?" I grinned at her with mischief.

"Absolutely thrilled!" Her thin lips certainly could produce a warm smile.

"Aunt Lawrence!" Aunt Anabelle called out to Mrs. Lawrence, who let go of me. They embraced. One wouldn't guess they'd already seen each other today.

I heard Aunt Anabelle and Mrs. Lawrence laughing as I lagged behind and kept pace with Andrew's father as we entered the manor house. Mr. Lawrence glanced at me and smiled softly, the sight of it making me miss Andrew. His son took after him in several ways, from his kind brown eyes to the shape of his smile. Andrew didn't, however, take after his father's calm nature. He enlivened every gathering with his spirited good humor. I smiled back at Mr. Lawrence, and we walked down the corridor together in silence until I came to the staircase that led to my bedchamber. I still had to dress for dinner.

As I ascended the stairs, I saw Lord Bellingham greet Mr. Lawrence below me. The earl was almost as quiet as his steward. They got along well because they were of the same temperament. Of course, the earl had an air about him that intimidated me much more than Mr. Lawrence, but that was to be expected of someone with his title. Perhaps that perception was due to my upbringing.

After I came down appropriately dressed, we sat around the table like a complete family, though many members were missing.

"Where is Bethany?" The dowager countess looked around the dining hall in confusion. "Did no one call her down for dinner?" she asked a servant beside her.

The young man bowed. "She wasn't in her room, my lady. Her things were gone as well."

Everyone's attention fell on me.

"What's this about?" the dowager asked, worry creasing her brows.

I cleared my throat guiltily. "She's decided to return to Satchell Cottage. She said she felt needed by Papa and Sam."

The dowager frowned. "I thought she was beginning to feel comfortable here. But I suppose not everyone can leave their home easily." Her eyes softened when she noticed my expression, though I didn't know what emotion I'd let slip through. Did she see my disappointment or my lingering irritation at my family? "Perhaps she needs another year or two before she warms up to the idea. Let's work on her a bit more." Her eyes lit up conspiratorially, and I answered her with a slight smile. Eventually I would have to explain to her how that line of thinking was what had led Bethany to flee.

A general agreement passed across the table, and the conversation soon turned elsewhere. I was glad we didn't dwell on the topic that had been bothering me all day. Instead, a topic was brought up that fully distracted me.

"What day is Andrew supposed to reach London?" Aunt Anabelle asked Mrs. Lawrence after the first course was served. As Andrew's elder cousin, she doted on him. She once told me that meeting him had made her feel right at home when she'd come to live with the Lawrences sixteen years ago. It had been the same for me when I'd moved into Satchell Cottage at the age of eight; Andrew and I had become fast friends. He had that way about him, that inexplicable quality that made one feel comfortable in his presence.

"He'll arrive on Wednesday." Mrs. Lawrence's eyes shone with glee. Then something dawned on her face. "Oh. That's right." She turned to me. "Esther, I just remembered. Andrew asked me to tell you to expect the perfect Christmas present."

I raised my eyebrows. "My expectations have been set. If it disappoints, he must take responsibility for his words."

Mrs. Lawrence laughed. "I'm sure you have every reason to look forward to it."

I nodded, and she turned back to her niece while my mind wandered over her announcement about Andrew's Christmas gift.

Not simply a present, but a *perfect* present. Inwardly, I chuckled at the preposterous claim. What did he know about gift-giving? All of his presents in the past had been underwhelming at best. When we were nine, he'd given me a rock. At twelve, reins for my borrowed pony. At seventeen, a book about fishing with a purple flower pressed between the pages. At nineteen, nothing at all. At twenty he'd left Bellingham, and me, behind. What could I expect from such a boy? Despite all rational thinking, however, my lips curled up of their own accord.

He likely thought the most perfect gift would be seeing his face again. That would be quintessentially Andrew. I could imagine his wry smile as he handed me an empty box. I laughed privately at the thought.

Once supper ended, we retired to the drawing room and played cards. The children came down to say good night, which caused all sorts of beautiful chaos and had us laughing. After cards were strewn about the floor and more than one drink was spilled by their reckless behavior, Lord Bellingham gathered his children and took them to bed himself. Despite his reserved demeanor, he was a caring and involved father. I saw his wife's adoring expression while she offered to help. He told her to stay and enjoy herself. Somehow, I thought she'd predicted his response. She sat down without a fight.

I was left at the card table while Mrs. Lawrence and Aunt Anabelle began speaking. I practiced shuffling while unabashedly eavesdropping. Being so much younger than the rest of the party had its drawbacks, as I wasn't always included, but that didn't mean I wasn't diverted by their conversations.

"I cannot believe it has been fifteen years since you two fell in love. If I hadn't been here when it happened, I would never have believed it possible. I remember how you thought him quite frightening at first." Mrs. Lawrence chuckled.

Aunt Anabelle's wide smile in response spoke of her fond memories, ones she dearly loved to revisit. "He was so intimidating! As soon as we met, I felt like all the air had left the room."

"And yet he loved *you* at first sight," the dowager countess interjected. She laughed from the other side of the room as she scribbled at her portable desk.

Aunt Anabelle held up a finger to correct the misconception. "He loved me the first time I played the *pianoforte*." That explained why she'd never lost her talent in music after marriage. Lord Bellingham must have supported her accomplishments, unlike many husbands in high Society. Of that I was grateful, for I had a countess as an in-house music tutor. Because of Aunt Anabelle, I had the opportunity—and the desire—to become accomplished in music.

"Peter's nothing if not a lover of music," the dowager countess said about her eldest son. She met my eyes. "Perhaps we can have you exhibit your talents at the ball, Esther. It would be a wonderful way to entice young men to your side."

I laughed, unsure how to refuse the offer. I wasn't shy like Bethany, but I didn't have an urge to attract a husband with my talents either. "I don't think

Aunt Anabelle played the piano as a way to snag herself an earl," I responded with humor, hoping to turn the attention away from me.

It worked. The adults laughed and continued speaking of the past, leaving me free to escape to my room for the evening.

Chapter Three

It was half a day's drive to London, but the time went by swiftly in the oversized and jovial carriage. The four of us ladies sat together inside, and Lord Bellingham rode outside of it. I was certain he could hear our laughter from his horse. Mr. Lawrence might have been able to hear us from Bellingham Cottage as we drove away. He'd stayed behind to care for the estate in Lord Bellingham's absence.

The dowager never tired of talking, and her stories were always amusing. Mrs. Lawrence's quiet ha-ha's added harmony to Aunt Anabelle's throaty chuckle and my unchecked cackling, while the dowager's laughter filled every open space and reverberated off the walls. By the time we reached the Alexanders' London town house, we were nearly out of breath. Mrs. Katherine Alexander greeted us at the door with warm embraces and much laughing. Although only related by marriage, she shared many similarities to the dowager countess. They were both lively and talkative.

After unpacking my trunk, I waited to be called down for dinner. I opened the curtains and stared out over my limited view of London. I had only been to Town once before, and briefly. It had not been this busy then. This time we were here during the height of the Season, and not even the heavy snowfall deterred those hunting in the Marriage Market.

I smiled at the young ladies walking arm in arm across the street toward a park. I saw several gentlemen coming toward them, and the young women put their heads closer together as if whispering.

I hadn't a clue what it would be like to have so many female friends, nor what it would feel like to be courted by eligible young men. I had a limited number of suitors in Lynsfield but none I felt would match both me and my unusual position in Society. Levi Halverston indeed. Goodness. What did my brother think of me? Certainly he would never push Bethany into a marriage to such a man.

I let the curtains fall closed, and a few minutes after I collapsed onto the bed, a maid came to call me for dinner. The conversation there was just as lively as it had been in the carriage.

"Tomorrow we shall go for a ride in Hyde Park. Won't that be fun, Esther?" Mrs. Katherine Alexander's eyes gleamed. Her excitement rivaled that of the dowager, who immediately agreed and waited for my answer.

I nodded easily. "I have often wished to do so."

"What of the weather, Dowager?" Mrs. Lawrence asked. "Will it not bother you?"

With her failing health, which we never openly discussed, we all worried about her condition.

The dowager waved a hand. "Not to worry. We shall bring ample blankets and sit closely together to ward off the cold." She leaned toward Mrs. Lawrence, pretending to whisper about me. "One cannot bring a young lady to London and *not* go for a ride in Hyde Park."

The plan was set, and the next day we were freezing in an open carriage ride through the park. The ground was covered in a heavy layer of snow, and the trees were sparkling white. The scenery was lovely. There was a surprisingly high number of other carriages just like ours, their occupants shivering and laughing at the absurdity of their choices. Of course, our purposes for the ride were not to be seen. Strictly speaking, we were not here for the Season and therefore had no investment in the Marriage Market. I did wonder, however, as I watched everyone passing by, what kind of suitor would be interested in a girl like me—not considering only my ambiguous station in Society but also my personality and appearance. What sort of man would I attract, if I participated in the Season?

"I'm surprised you decided to come, Mother. I thought you would not leave Bellingham while planning for Christmas!" Mrs. Alexander observed, carefully covering her mother-in-law in a thick wool blanket.

The dowager tutted and playfully swatted away her daughter-in-law's hands. "I have all the fine details ironed out; it simply lacks execution. I would only have been waiting all week. A little diversion never hurt anyone. Isn't that right, Esther?"

I nodded, teeth chattering.

The chill did not merit being outside for too long. I felt no disappointment in returning to the town house, even if we had been out for less than an hour.

Once we warmed ourselves by the fire, the dowager, Mrs. Lawrence, Aunt Anabelle, and Mrs. Alexander visited with each other. I went into the music room and began playing the pianoforte.

After I played through two pieces, Mrs. Alexander and Aunt Anabelle entered the room.

"Esther, what say you to an outing that is both social and not social?" Mrs. Alexander grinned at Aunt Anabelle, who was watching me.

"I'm intrigued. When do we leave?" I stood.

"Right now, if you're ready."

Aunt Anabelle took my arm and hugged it. "I'm very glad you are not as timid as I was at your age. It makes things much more enjoyable when one is open to new experiences."

Mrs. Alexander laughed. "Do not be self-deprecating, Anabelle. You were mourning when you first met me. I don't hold your behavior against you."

"You may not, but I often think of it with embarrassment." Aunt Anabelle met my curious gaze. "Just after my parents passed, I came to London on my way to Bellingham. Katherine was being generous to me, but I did not make it easy. My emotions were brittle and my mood was foul. I'm afraid I didn't present myself well upon our first meeting."

I'd heard most of the history before from Andrew, as he'd heard it from Aunt Anabelle. I let myself go over the whole story in my mind. Aunt Anabelle's appearance in the Alexanders' life sparked many things to happen. From what I could piece together, it seemed that Mr. Nathan Alexander's disownment was also connected to her. The mystery of the second son was the only story left for me to hear. All other tales from that time fifteen years ago were told and retold at Bellingham.

As much as I wished to understand it, I didn't have the courage to ask. Perhaps someday, hopefully not too late. The dowager didn't have many years left before she succumbed to her illness, and before that happened, I wished for nothing more than her heart to be full.

We rode in an enclosed carriage this time, thankfully, on our way to our mystery destination. I watched the city pass by with fascination. When the carriage stopped, I couldn't help but feel disappointed.

"The Circulating Library?" I frowned at Aunt Anabelle.

Mrs. Alexander laughed at my expression. "See? She is not so agreeable as you think, Anabelle. She's honest and forthright, just like you."

"Come along, Esther. I'm certain you'll find something of interest here." Aunt Anabelle went ahead of Mrs. Alexander and me, practically skipping into the building.

Mrs. Alexander sighed. "She does love her books. She's grown to love them more since she married that bore, Peter." Her eyebrows rose when I gave her a surprised look. "What? Can I not use my own brother-in-law's Christian name?"

I laughed. "Certainly you can, but to call the earl a bore doesn't seem very appropriate."

"What else should I call him? A great reader?"

"Well, he is a great reader." I shrugged. "And there's nothing wrong with books. I'd simply rather play music or go for a ride."

"Or attend a ball!" Mrs. Alexander said in a singsong voice. "You have to help me convince the old ladies that we must attend at least one ball while you're here. You've never been to Almack's, have you?"

"I assume that's a rhetorical question." She knew as well as anyone my history with London.

We walked into the building, and I was accosted by the smells of parchment, dust, and musk. It wasn't unpleasant, but I didn't relish the scents either. "It seems Aunt Anabelle has disappeared," I observed.

"Oh! I see someone I know. Go ahead and find Anabelle. I'll meet you both here later." Mrs. Alexander made her way toward her friend, and I walked farther into the library. My jaw dropped when I realized the magnificence of the space. Books lined the walls clear up to the ceiling. Ladders were the only way to reach most of them. It seemed there was even a second floor with more books.

"Twenty thousand books! That cannot be true," I heard a lady say to my right.

"I read it myself in an advertisement just yesterday," the man she spoke with assured her.

I cast my gaze over the room again, this time with new appreciation. I would never be near so many books again in my lifetime. I'd never imagined so many books existed in the world, much less in London.

A sudden thought of Bethany made me sigh. She loved books. If only I could see her face when she beheld this place.

I began to look for Aunt Anabelle. The place was crowded, and although I was tall for a girl, I struggled to see through the throng. If she was browsing the shelves, she could only be on one of two sides of the room or upstairs. I made a wide circle, searching.

Suddenly, I turned and went crashing into the form of a man. I bounced off him and began to apologize before I froze.

"Esther." Andrew's naturally cheerful eyes laughed before his mouth did. "What is that expression? Do you not recognize your oldest friend?"

Chapter Four

I BLINKED SEVERAL TIMES BEFORE saying slowly, "How are you here?"

"Have you become slow-witted, dear Esther?" His smug, playful, endearing smile sparked something inside of me.

Annoyance, probably. How in the world had he turned the tables and surprised *me*? After such carefully laid plans . . . the gall of Andrew Lawrence.

I tried to scowl but could only laugh incredulously. "What on earth are you doing here?"

"London?" His smile traveled farther up his face, creasing his eyes.

Crossing my arms, I took a different approach with one raised eyebrow. "The library. Aren't you nearly illiterate?"

He took it as a challenge, clearly. His smile turned devilish, and I had a difficult time not mirroring it. "I may be illiterate, but I'm relieved to see you here and not at Almack's. It's no place for a lady who dances like a foal who has yet to find its legs."

The absolute glee in his eyes set my nerves on edge. Curse his quick wit. "It appears time did not grant you maturity," I told him.

"Nor you a sense of humor," Andrew retaliated.

I prepared myself to walk away from him, but he held me back with a feather-light touch on my arm. My exposed skin tingled at the point of contact. His fingers were unfamiliar, as if they'd become heavier. Had he become a stranger in just a single year? I turned to look into his curious brown eyes before they searched the room around us. "Who have you come with?" he asked. "Is my mother here?"

"Yes. And no. She remained at the town house." Just then I caught sight of Aunt Anabelle and waved her over. I smirked at him. "Just wait until you are reprimanded by Aunt Anabelle for not telling anyone of your early arrival."

Andrew spun right when she reached us. She took a step back when she saw him, placing a hand over her heart and dropping her jaw. Rather than rebuke him, however, she gifted him with a wide smile and a hand on each cheek. "Little Andrew!" she exclaimed. Then she looked him over with surprise. "How you have grown in just a year!"

"Aren't you angry at him for keeping his arrival a secret?" I asked her with a pout.

"Cousin Annie could never be angry with me," Andrew threw over his shoulder at me. "Right, Annie?"

She laughed and dropped her hands before lifting an eyebrow. "I should be, but it's so wonderful to see you, I can't remember why."

Perhaps I was the only one truly looking forward to shocking him. Everyone else would simply be happy to see him. I was happy too, much more than I'd anticipated. It was as if I had taken a full breath for the first time in over a year.

Aunt Anabelle pressed her lips together as she looked at Andrew, shaking her head. "How long have you been here without writing a word? If you say longer than two days, you'll truly be reprimanded."

From my vantage point, I could tell Andrew did not take that as a reprimand. His shoulders remained upright and confident.

"We were all supposed to surprise you when you arrived. You've ruined it now," I told him.

He turned to me, and Aunt Anabelle threaded her arm through his, both of them laughing at my irritation. His eyes connected with mine. "But here I am, surprising you." I didn't miss the flash of victory in his eyes.

My smile was thin. "I reject your conclusion. We surprised each other."

"True. It's a great curiosity that we should meet here, of all places, considering neither of us enjoys reading."

"I enjoy reading."

"Since when?" He raised an eyebrow and a corner of his mouth.

"Since you left and I had no one to amuse me." I tried to hold back a smile but failed. He enjoyed that reaction.

Aunt Anabelle cleared her throat. I had forgotten her presence completely. "Let's not bicker so soon after our reunion. We should be celebrating. Let's find Katherine so we can go back to the town house together."

That led Andrew to begin looking around as well. "Then, I should find Stenton," he said. "Let's go to his house first and invite my friends to come with us. Wait here for a moment." He took off through the crowd to find his friend, whose name I recognized from his letter.

Aunt Anabelle chuckled and touched my shoulder before she, too, left to find Mrs. Alexander.

Alone now, I clasped my hands in front of me and waited for everyone to return. Unfortunately, I was in a walkway. While I managed to dodge most of the figures, an older gentleman and I bumped shoulders as he passed by. He met my eyes and bowed briefly with a "Pardon me, miss." His startling blue eyes reminded me briefly of my brother-in-law, Robert, and in my confusion, I nearly forgot my curtsy.

There was another Alexander brother who might possess those eyes. My heart stopped, and I sucked in a breath. Could it be Mr. Nathan Alexander?

Before I could stop the man, he had disappeared into the crowd. I stood on my tiptoes to catch another glimpse, but to no avail.

"What are you looking for?" I heard Andrew's voice beside me.

"Oh, um, nothing. I just thought I recognized—never mind," I said, planting my feet again and facing him.

He smiled and lifted a hand to present his friend to me. "This is Eric Stenton, my friend and traveling companion. He kept me alive for a whole year, if you can believe it."

The young man next to him was of average height, wore modest attire, and had an extraordinarily handsome face. His smile made him even more admirable. He bowed. "Miss Harris, it is a pleasure," he said.

I glanced at Andrew before bobbing a curtsy in response. "You know me?"

He nodded, and in that smooth gesture, I noticed his movements were confident and calm. "Andrew rarely speaks of anyone else from home." His voice brought to mind a deeply rooted tree, steady and sure. I enjoyed listening to it.

Andrew cleared his throat. "Well, that is not *strictly* true. Don't inflate her ego, Stenton. She already thinks enough of herself."

Before I could respond to Andrew's typical inclination to make fun of me, Aunt Anabelle and Mrs. Alexander came to greet Andrew and Mr. Stenton as well. Introductions were made. We were all quickly ushered into two carriages. Surprisingly, Andrew made a point to sit next to me in Aunt Anabelle's carriage.

"Are you making your friend ride alone in his carriage?" I asked, raising an eyebrow.

He waved a hand. "Oh, he's perfectly well. I've seen him enough for a lifetime. It has been too long since I've seen you, however. I wanted to have a few minutes to catch up." He scooted closer to me. "How have you been? How are all the Harrises?"

I tilted my head. The usual answer of "Very well" tattered on my tongue, but this was Andrew. If there was one person with whom I could be entirely transparent, it was Andrew. I spoke softly so as not to be overheard by Aunt Anabelle and Mrs. Alexander, who were in conversation together. "To speak truthfully, my family and I are at odds. They refuse to come to Bellingham for Christmas."

He didn't seem surprised. "They are still having trouble including themselves in the Alexander family?"

"You know my father and Sam." I folded my hands in my lap. "And Bethany moved into the house—"

"Did she? I hadn't heard—"

"And then promptly moved out." I frowned at him. "It seems she dislikes the manor house and wishes to live in Satchell Cottage instead. It is unfathomable to me."

"Hmm," Andrew responded. Surely he did not understand her. "I think it is possible not everyone would love living in Bellingham Hall as you do. I've never moved in, though Annie has asked me several times if I would." He shrugged. "There's nothing so comfortable as being at home, after all."

I lifted a corner of my mouth. "I suppose that's one way to see it."

"Sometimes you're too obstinate for your own good, Esther. Perhaps try seeing things from a new perspective. You don't need to push your values onto others."

I turned my attention abruptly away to look out the window, effectively cutting off our conversation. As much as I'd wished to have matured over the past year, I still disliked being told I was in the wrong. And by Andrew, of all people. I felt embarrassed that he could speak of my faults with such an air of wisdom. That had never been the case before.

We made our way first to Mr. Stenton's town house to meet the other two of their party. A slight nudge disturbed my stomach, thinking of meeting Andrew's French friends, especially the unmarried sister.

We arrived in front of the town house, and to my surprise it was nearly as grand as the Alexanders'. I paid more attention to Mr. Stenton, trying to deduce his monetary worth. Was he as wealthy as his home suggested?

We were led into the drawing room, where a roaring fire burned in an immense cavern-like hearth. On either side of the mantel stood two extravagantly dressed young people. A man, whose attire was even more elaborate than the woman's, came over to us immediately upon our entry. The young woman, however, stood leaning against the mantel, simply watching us with an expression I could only interpret as one of apathy.

"This is Monsieur Lois Beaumont," Andrew said in a mockingly French accent. Mr. Beaumont laughed with good humor and gave us all a bow, as if he'd just performed on stage.

"Good grief, Beaumont." Mr. Stenton snorted a laugh. "Can you do anything halfway?"

The Frenchman grinned at us all. "Indeed not. I must make an impression on as many pretty English ladies as possible."

Andrew then introduced us, and I was a bit startled when Mr. Beaumont's lips met my hand. "Miss Harris, I am most pleased to finally meet you. Andrew has—"

"And here is his twin sister," Andrew interrupted Mr. Beaumont before he could finish what I assumed was "Andrew has told us much about you." I wanted to laugh at the idea that Andrew had spoken of me to his friends, and often enough for them to feel as if they knew me already. Surely he had not said anything in my favor. Perhaps they were all anxious to meet the girl he spoke so ill of.

Andrew continued. "Miss Vivianne Beaumont."

Miss Beaumont finally walked over to meet us, and I was able to take note of her full beauty. Just her name brought to mind a heroine in a gothic novel. Her appearance, too, matched that same sort of elegance. I admitted to having a reason for suspicion. If Andrew had traveled with such a lovely Frenchwoman for an entire year, it was highly likely they had formed an attachment. His attention did not linger on her, however, so if they indeed had a close relationship, he was skilled at hiding it.

My heart wavered with an emotion I'd grown to dislike over the past few months since learning of her existence. Jealousy.

"Lady Bellingham, Mrs. Alexander, Miss Harris," Miss Beaumont said in a lovely French accent. "It's a pleasure." Her curtsy would have made the Queen envious of its grace.

Andrew explained the situation to his friends. "My mother has accompanied Lady Bellingham to Town. She and the Dowager Countess of Bellingham are at their town house. I wanted to bring everyone there, if you are willing."

It was agreed that we would leave together. We took two carriages again—I begrudgingly took note that Andrew decided to ride with his friends this time—and upon our entering the Alexanders' town house, Mrs. Lawrence came quickly out of the drawing room to meet her son. He caught her tightly in an embrace. I couldn't see her face, as she had buried it into his shoulder, but I suspected tears were falling down her cheeks. Andrew began rocking side to side, causing both of them to laugh. She pulled back and took a good look at him. She must've noticed how much his face had matured, along with his inexplicable growth. He must have grown four inches taller somehow. Or perhaps I'd remembered him shorter than he was. I would've been blind if I didn't also notice the fit of his jacket and how well it showed the change in his physique. Did traveling require so much heavy lifting that it would significantly increase the size of one's muscles in only a year's time?

I had to look away before anyone noticed my appreciation for his changes.

No. Not appreciation. I was simply observing what a year had done to his appearance. That was all.

We made our way into the drawing room, and after another excited greeting, this time from the dowager, we sat around the fireplace and separate conversations began, as often happened in large groups.

Andrew sat next to his cousin and patiently let her ask him a hundred questions, smiling the whole time. The two of them had always been very affectionate, like brother and sister—perhaps even more like mother and child, like my relationship with Lucy.

Mr. Stenton came to sit next to me. "How long are you all in London?"

"We had planned to stay until Thursday in order to surprise your friend, but it appears we are no longer needed here, so we may return Wednesday instead. We have much to accomplish at Bellingham before the Christmas ball on Friday." I spoke as if he understood what planning for a party might entail. He had yet to know the dowager countess, however, and had no inkling about the scale of her celebrations.

"I see." He nodded. "Andrew had planned to leave on Wednesday to surprise you all as well."

I huffed a laugh. "Typical Andrew."

Mr. Stenton smiled. "It is rather like him, isn't it? I suppose you were disappointed you could not surprise him?"

"How did you guess?"

He lifted one shoulder. "I know a little of your relationship."

"And what has he told you of it?" I scooted forward in my seat, very curious.

Mr. Stenton's eyes turned thoughtful. "Childhood friends, closest confidants, a special type of relationship that cannot be duplicated."

I pressed my lips together. How did one respond to such insightful words? I had been expecting a clever anecdote about my childhood. Instead, with just a few words, I was reminded of cherished memories. My heart warmed, and I suspected so did my cheeks. Mr. Stenton made no mention of it, however.

He changed the topic entirely. "What have you done since your arrival?"

I answered his question vaguely. "We only arrived yesterday, so not much."

"London does not suit my tastes, in general. I am much more thrilled by books than Society," Mr. Stenton told me.

"There you and I differ. I have never been overly fond of reading. My sister, Bethany, however—"

"Ah ha!" Andrew said from across the room.

I made a face at him. "Oh, don't make a fuss."

"I knew you could not have changed so much as to *like* reading now." His tone spoke of a challenge, of victory.

I sighed and shrugged. "I don't *dis*like it. I simply prefer other things." I tried to force him out of my conversation. I asked Mr. Stenton, "How do you feel about music?"

"I—"

He was cut short by Andrew coming to sit on my other side, leaning forward to see Mr. Stenton. "Don't answer that, Stenton. Whatever you say will be wrong." Andrew placed a hand on mine, and I looked down at his casual touch. A tingling sensation began at the contact and traveled up my arm. I had to push down a shiver, which made me shift in my seat.

Andrew took his hand back and met my eyes; whether he noticed my discomfort, I couldn't tell. "You adore music because it is fun, but you have no interest in studying it," he said. His teasing expression could have moved the most apathetic heart. He looked at Mr. Stenton again, shaking his head. "She's full of contradictions. When she asks you questions like that, just ask her right back."

I scoffed. "Don't pretend to know everything about me. I *do* study music. It is why I am so talented at it. Don't listen to him, Mr. Stenton. He likes to pretend he knows every thought I have, when in truth, he cannot fathom them all."

He grinned. "You speak as if your thoughts are so complicated," he said quietly. Our gazes held for a moment longer than was comfortable. A swirl of nerves went through my belly at the idea that he could actually read my mind.

I continued speaking to Mr. Stenton. "As I was asking before Andrew interrupted, do you like music?"

He cleared his throat after glancing at Andrew beside me. "I enjoy it, but I admit I have not studied it."

Nodding, I leaned back. "Then, you and I shall get along splendidly."

"I believe I shall like that," he responded.

Smiling at his kind reply was easy, but one glance at Andrew made it more difficult. Why was he looking at me like that? As if he were displeased by my conversation with his friend? I almost asked him but was interrupted by Mr. Beaumont. Then his sister joined the conversation, and for the first time in a while, I participated in a party with people my own age.

Chapter Five

BEFORE THE END OF THE evening, plans for the next day had been set. Mr. Stenton invited us to a party a friend of his was hosting. He assured us that there would be plenty of room and his friend would be more than happy to host the Earl of Bellingham and his family.

"What say you, Mother?" Lord Bellingham asked after hearing the invitation upon his entry just five minutes before.

She formed an excited *o* with her mouth and clapped her hands. "I do love a party!" It was quickly settled that we would all attend, for the dowager countess held the first and final say.

I had brought plenty of dresses. Thank goodness for my propensity to overpack. I picked a green gown with delicate beading around the sleeves and neckline. When I moved, it glittered as if I wore diamonds. Who could help but smile at their reflection when draped in such finery? It was not that I was truly vain; I just appreciated beauty in all its forms. A lady's maid, the timid one who usually assisted Aunt Anabelle, came into the room and helped me finish my hair before I went to meet the family at the bottom of the grand staircase. Everyone complimented my dress, and it helped me lift my head a little higher.

We piled into the carriages. The distance was short, but the winter was so bitterly cold that none of us had any inclination to walk the few blocks it would take to get to the party. As it was, I pulled my cloak as tightly as possible around me in the closed carriage.

When the Bellingham group—the earl; the countess; the dowager countess; Admiral Hollis Alexander and his wife, Katherine; Mrs. Lawrence; and me—arrived, we entered the party. Our appearance caused quite a stir; it was not often that an earl and nearly his entire family showed up at a small party like this. Whispers began, and all eyes were on my aunt Anabelle and Lord

Bellingham first, then on each of us in succession. My searching gaze found Andrew, who was already looking at me. His open mouth and lifted eyebrows could have been interpreted as surprise or . . . appreciation? My face heated at my absurd belief it might be the latter. His attention was latched on to me so strongly, though, that I noticed Mr. Stenton nudging him before he did. When he turned to his friend with a jolt, they were approaching Lord Bellingham. There was another man on the other side of Mr. Stenton, who I assumed was hosting the party.

Introductions were made, and then the earl, Aunt Anabelle, and the dowager countess were announced to the entire party. The building was abuzz with excitement. Being in London made Lord Bellingham seem even more formidable to me. His rank truly inspired awe, and his presence itself could not be overlooked. Aunt Anabelle, on the other hand, wore a welcoming smile and made the earl altogether more approachable.

It wasn't long before the dowager countess came to my side. "Esther, shall we find a place to sit?" she said as she took my arm and laced it through her own.

She maneuvered around a few groups to find a seat in the middle of everything. Leave it to the dowager to find the most ostentatious seating arrangements. There were people all around us, but none dared approach due to not having been formally introduced to the illustrious dowager countess. Then Andrew appeared with Mr. Stenton and Miss Beaumont as well. I vaguely noted that Miss Beaumont had her hand on Mr. Stenton's arm, as though they were engaged for the next set.

"Do you mean to dance, Miss Harris?" Andrew addressed me like this only in public or in jest. This time I could not be sure whether he meant to be comical or polite. His smile betrayed only a hint of teasing.

I made a face. He knew I danced poorly. If I had one shame in life, it was my two left feet. Surely I would never be taken seriously in Society if I could not even dance properly. "I—"

The dowager took my hand. "Of course she shall." She raised her eyebrows at me. "It is a party, after all. One must never turn down a reel."

Andrew grinned at us. "They have set up for a dance in the next room," he said, holding out his arm for me to take.

I stood, took it, and turned back to the dowager to complain but saw she was staring toward the entry. She stood slowly. The look in her eyes made my heart clench. Following her gaze, I noticed a man staring back at the dowager with a matching expression. Recognition tugged at the corner of my memory.

He was incredibly handsome, from his blue eyes and full head of hair to his impressive height, and seemed to be in his early forties.

Those blue eyes . . .

The library! I knew I'd seen him before.

"Nathan," the dowager breathed out.

My mouth hung open at the revelation.

The man took a step forward, paused, bowed in a manner that spoke of sorrow, and then—too quickly—turned to leave. The dowager struggled to rush after him, and I panicked at the sight. I let go of Andrew's arm and followed.

I made it to her just outside the entry door, and we watched together as a carriage pulled away, a silhouette of a man and a woman inside. The dowager swayed, and I held on to her. She began to cry. She cried as if something inside of her hurt tremendously. I wrapped my arms around her, and she put her head on my shoulder as she shook with sobs. Those who passed us by did not interfere but were understandably curious.

Andrew came out, and after seeing the dowager's emotional state, he met my eyes with concern. "What . . . ?"

I shook my head at him as the dowager continued to cry. I rubbed her back. After a few moments she calmed and pulled away from me, her face a mess of tears. "I'm sorry, Esther. It's just that it's been so long since I've seen his face. He looked well, did he not?" She looked into my eyes with hope.

I smiled softly at her. "He did indeed."

Andrew stepped up. "Are you all right, Dowager?"

He handed her a handkerchief, which she used thoroughly before nodding. "Let us return. We cannot let a perfectly fine party go to waste." Her light tone sounded forced, and I felt a pang of sympathy for her. She walked ahead of us, giving Andrew and me a moment to exchange matching expressions of worry.

Aunt Anabelle joined us when we came inside, her expression equally worried. She carefully held on to her mother-in-law's shoulders and led the dowager away.

Before they crossed the ballroom, however, the dowager saw her eldest son and rushed over to him. She grasped his sleeve, and in a voice filled with agony and desperation, she pleaded with Lord Bellingham to find Mr. Alexander. "Please, Peter. Please let us go find him."

Shock ran through me at the sight. If I thought her crying was out of character, this absolutely did not suit her. "I know he made many mistakes, but it has been so many years."

I had never seen anger on Lord Bellingham's usually placid face, but it hardened his features as he avoided eye contact with his mother. She pulled on his arm, muttering, "Please, Peter. Let us go find him."

He looked around, noticing the scene they were making, and finally turned to face her. He reached out a hand to soothe her, but let it fall when she backed away. He kept his voice low, but with the silence of the ballroom, everything carried. "We have nothing to gain from acknowledging each other. Please, Mother. Let it be." His face showed his regret. "I am sorry." He leaned closer to his mother and said something quietly. She looked into his eyes and nodded slowly, seemingly to show her understanding. Then they left the room together, apologizing to the party as they passed.

It took a moment for me to calm myself, and I took a few shaky breaths. Never had I seen the dowager in such a state. I had suspected but had underestimated how much she missed her estranged son.

"Shall we dance or eat?" Andrew asked at my side, interrupting my thoughts. His voice lacked the joviality to match his words.

I looked up at him. I could tell he, too, was out of sorts. His brows knitted together uncharacteristically, and he swallowed hard, as though trying to hold back tears.

He would do his best to improve our moods, as was his way. The smile that pulled at my lips came so naturally, it was as if he'd bewitched me. "Both, if you'll join me."

A smile lit up his face and he nodded. We went to sit next to his friends at the table and ate first, then danced afterward. Historically I had only enjoyed dancing if Andrew was my partner. While this time was no exception, I found that after having the strongest woman I'd ever known cry in my arms, I stumbled even more than usual. It did not improve my mood to fail so much in front of the entire ballroom. I apologized multiple times during the half-hour reel.

"Since when are you so apologetic?" Andrew said, grinning. "I'm not saying it's a bad change, only that I'm not used to it. Your manners have improved."

I snorted.

"There. That's more like you."

My eyes narrowed, and I didn't have to say anything to communicate my irritation. He pulled up a corner of his mouth. Words were unnecessary for him as well while we stood by the refreshments; it was clear he felt pleased to have accomplished his goal to annoy me.

The party had recovered quickly, but a buzzing like none I'd ever heard before hummed. Rumors began circulating like books in a library.

I paid little heed to the whispers behind fans, but I heard them nonetheless. The scandal had occurred fifteen years ago and had happened in Bellingham; needless to say, no one knew the truth. Some whispers said the second son had tried to kill the heir to the earldom or that he had gambled away his inheritance and was asked to leave when he wanted more. Some said he had fathered a child out of wedlock or that he'd fallen in love with the now Lady Bellingham.

Andrew spoke quietly to me, saying that all he knew was that Mr. Alexander had caused Aunt Anabelle some harm and the late Lord Bellingham had cut him off from the family. I wondered if the late Lord Bellingham had had any idea that his son would still be ostracized from his family fifteen years later, or if he had planned to bring him home someday. The dowager seemed to believe a reconciliation was possible . . .

The beginnings of an idea formed in my mind.

"Do you think she'll be all right?" Andrew asked me as we walked to the carriages together at the end of the evening.

"I cannot say." I frowned. "I've never seen her like this before."

Andrew nodded and helped me into the carriage, and he watched us pull away. I watched his form shrink into the distance as I pondered the events of the evening with growing anxiety. What on earth was Nathan Alexander's unforgivable wrongdoing?

When the Bellingham family entered the town house, silence seemed to reach the high ceilings, almost like a chilled breeze had followed us in, rustling the window drapes and flickering the candles. Aunt Anabelle helped the dowager up the stairs to her bedchamber. She did not look well. My heart nearly broke watching her struggle up the stairs. It seemed she had aged a decade in just a few short hours.

I lay in bed mulling over the situation and came to a conclusion. The dowager countess desired to meet with her son again but did not wish to go against the earl. While I could not understand the earl's persistence in keeping his mother away from her other son, even with her current health, I knew the dowager had to respect his wishes. Perhaps what they needed was a catalyst. Something or someone to change the narrative. If no one else had the courage or inclination to grant the dowager's dying wish, I would give it a try.

Chapter Six

Until I gave myself the mission, I had no idea how dearly I wished to pay back the dowager's kindness in some way. The Bellingham estate revolved around the dowager countess. Her cheerfulness and generosity over the years had improved countless lives while making the nearby village prosperous due to her great care for its residents. Furthermore, the gratitude I personally felt toward her was immeasurable. She'd given me more than I could ever have imagined: more love, education, and opportunities than anyone like me had any right to expect.

In the early-morning light, I adopted Aunt Anabelle's lady's maid as my companion to venture out into Town. My destination was clear: Mr. Stenton's town house. I knew Andrew would help, if anyone would. Against my better judgment, we walked, but as soon as we closed the door behind us, I regretted the decision. The wind blew straight through my cloak and many layers underneath. My mittens were useless, and my fingers froze almost immediately.

I felt relief only when I stood before the impressive fireplace in Mr. Stenton's home. My fingers burned as they thawed.

"What brings you here this early, Miss Harris?" Mr. Stenton asked. His eyes held mine in their steady sureness.

"I needed to speak with Andrew about something important that could not wait."

Mr. Stenton nodded. "I will have someone fetch him for you. I do not believe he has awoken yet." He stepped out to ask a servant to wake Andrew.

I relished the warmth of the fire, and when Andrew came in, he joined me at the hearth, leaning with his elbow on the mantel, his head resting against his fisted hand. "What is the meaning of your waking me up so early, Miss Harris? I was having a rather pleasant dream."

For some reason, I couldn't help but marvel at every movement he made. The way his jaw flexed as he yawned, the way his long eyelashes touched his cheeks as he blinked slowly, the way his soft hair fell over his brow. He hadn't combed his hair, and it showed; it was still ruffled with sleep. And when his heavy-lidded, chocolate-brown eyes looked into mine, my stomach flipped.

Suddenly the room felt too small. And Andrew was much too near. I glanced around us. Where had the lady's maid gone? I should have retained her as chaperone.

I met Andrew's eyes again, and my heart stuttered in my chest. That expression was something new and did not coincide with the Andrew I knew. I wondered where he'd learned such a serious gaze, one that would turn any unsuspecting young lady into a puddle of romantic sentiment. Perhaps he'd practiced it on someone before.

My eyebrows bunched together, and I stepped back more quickly than necessary.

"Why do you seem so different?" I asked. My voice sounded shaky in my ears; I could only imagine what he heard.

"I wondered when you'd comment on how I've changed. I'm taller, aren't I?" He grinned proudly, which made him look more like the old Andrew. It put me more at ease.

"You are perhaps a bit taller." I tilted my head. "And what of my changes? Do I not seem more of a woman since you left?" I held my arms out, as if to present myself to him. When I realized the connotation of my comment, I let my arms drop and colored. "I mean . . . I . . . it's been a year, so we both must look older."

I peeked up at him after lowering my chin. His smile was gentle and not mocking. I relaxed. "Anyway, this topic has nothing to do with the reason I sought you out. In fact, we need not touch on this subject again. If you don't mind."

He nodded once.

"I have a favor to ask."

"Go on."

"I thought about this all night. In truth, I thought of it well before the events at the ball. After seeing the dowager like that . . . Something must be done. She needs to reunite with her estranged son." I searched his face for his opinion before he spoke.

He looked away and shifted his weight, a sign that made me think he may not agree to help. So I continued reasoning with him. "You know of the dowager's illness. We may only have a few more years with her. Surely we should do all we can for her in the time we have left. She's given us so much."

Andrew rubbed at his chin. "I don't know, Esther. It is a very sensitive topic for everyone at Bellingham. You know that Annie was involved in whatever made Mr. Alexander leave. Her feelings are important to me." He met my eyes again. "I care for the dowager, and I want to heal the rift for her sake, but I don't think it's our place to step in."

I pressed my lips together. I waited for him to reconsider. We watched each other for a few moments, gauging the other's sincerity. I could almost have a full conversation with him simply by reading the changes in his expression.

I do not want to make things worse, he seemed to say.

I cannot sit back and do nothing, I tried to communicate. I raised my eyebrows in supplication. *Please, Andrew. Please help me.*

His sigh made me smile. "All right," he said. "You win. What do you need me to do?"

I took his hand in my eagerness. "Thank you!"

His fingers wrapped around mine, and he sent me a sad smile, nodding. "Let's hope we don't regret this."

I pulled my hand gently from his, then took out a piece of paper from my reticule and unfolded it. "I wrote down a few ways we could move forward." I cleared my throat and read them aloud. "First, we could pen a letter in the dowager's writing asking him to come to Bellingham Hall." I looked at Andrew. "She has me write her correspondence occasionally. I have practiced her penmanship and have been able to successfully copy it."

He nodded. "Let's hear the rest."

"Right." I returned to my notes. "Second, we could meet with him in person and tell him the dowager wishes to see him. Third, we take the dowager with us when we go see him, keeping the details secret beforehand so she can't reject the idea."

I waited for him to mull it over.

He replied thoughtfully, "Meeting him ourselves seems like the most prudent and honest choice."

I nodded. "I agree. Is there a way for us to find his residence?"

"I can ask Stenton's friend who hosted the party. He must know something."

I folded the parchment and put it back in my reticule. "Excellent. I'll return to the town house for breakfast. When you find him, come get me, and we will meet him together."

Our plan was set. The only thing to do now, for my part, was wait and think over how to speak to Mr. Alexander. Surely he, too, wished to mend his relationship with his family . . . even if he did run away at the ball. The polite and sad way he'd bowed to his mother had convinced me well enough that he'd be open to reconciliation. I made my way to the door.

Before I managed to leave, Andrew tugged on my hand. I turned to him, puzzled.

"I missed you. Did you know?" The seriousness in his eyes echoed in his voice, and the quiet way he spoke felt so intimate that warmth spread over my body.

I swallowed hard as my heart sped up.

I did not respond with words, nor did I feel I could. I nodded slowly. A tug that began somewhere in my chest pulled me closer to him, and I turned to face him directly. He hadn't let go of my hand but held it more firmly. What was happening between us made me lightheaded. Surely this wasn't . . . could it be that we felt something deeper for each other than mere friendship?

"Are you coming to breakfast, Mr. Lawrence?" a sweet, melodic voice sounded from the doorway. Miss Beaumont batted her long eyelashes at Andrew before he hastily dropped my hand.

"Ah yes, of course, Miss Beaumont. I will be there straightaway."

I couldn't look at Andrew; I was much too embarrassed. When he turned toward me again, I curtsied and fled with only a quick, "I'll see you soon."

I found the lady's maid in the corridor and practically dragged her with me out into the cold morning. This time I barely felt the chill.

* * *

"You went out awfully early this morning, Esther." The dowager leaned forward, waiting for my response.

"I . . . went to visit Andrew." I had no reason to lie about whom I'd seen. No one would guess the topic of conversation.

Mrs. Lawrence set down her fork. Aunt Anabelle sat back in her chair and wiped her mouth with her napkin. Mrs. Alexander swallowed her drink and held her teacup in the air. Lord Bellingham folded his newspaper down to look at me over the top of it. The admiral would have reacted in a similar fashion, I imagined, had he been present. I did not know what else to say—or why they'd reacted with such interest.

Mrs. Lawrence was the first to ask for details. "Why so early?"

"I . . . it has been such a long time since we've spent any time together. When I awoke, I thought of him and decided to visit." I shrugged to show how normal it was for me to do such a thing. I added, "It is not as if I went alone. I brought Aunt Anabelle's maid along."

Glances were exchanged, but they all seemed to accept my explanation and continued with their breakfast without further comment—until the dowager said, "I am glad the two of you are still close after a year apart. I do recall that you were practically inseparable before he left. Isn't that right, Mrs. Lawrence?"

Andrew's mother nodded. "I have long felt that Esther is like a daughter to me." She leaned toward me. "If I may be so presumptuous, dear Esther."

In the back of my mind, I wondered if she was implying there was an understanding between me and Andrew. I sent her a warm, innocent smile. "I'm glad you think so highly of me, Mrs. Lawrence."

A few more glances went around the table as I tried to ignore them, and then the dowager let out a chuckle and the topic changed. Surely it was not *so* strange that I visited my best friend just after dawn. I frowned, considering how my eagerness to speak with him about Mr. Alexander could have been misconstrued and eventually lead to the truth being revealed. I would have preferred them to know the truth than imagine anything of a romantic nature happening between Andrew and me . . . wouldn't I?

"While we're in London, I want to get a few Christmas presents for Lucy and Robert," Aunt Anabelle said.

"Should I come along to help choose something for Robert?" Lord Bellingham asked his wife.

"I would love that," she replied, standing to kiss his cheek. She laid a hand on his shoulder and stayed by his side, looking down at him affectionately.

He looked up at her and matched her expression. After a few seconds, he drained his teacup and followed Lady Bellingham out of the room. Everyone continued eating in their absence.

"What do you have planned today, Mrs. Alexander?" I asked after taking my last bite. I wiped my mouth and put the napkin on the table.

I caught her in the middle of chewing, so she covered her mouth with a hand before responding. "I will go with Anabelle. You may join us, if you desire."

"I will consider it." I turned to the dowager. "What about you, Dowager Countess?"

"There are several families I have in mind to visit. I doubt you will wish to accompany me, though you are welcome to."

I wondered about her health. Before I could inquire about it, Mrs. Lawrence said she would attend the dowager on her visits. Those worries were settled, then. I stood. "If you all don't mind, I think I'll spend some time in the music room. I am still working on the music for the Christmas party."

Mrs. Alexander also stood. "Are you sure, Esther? You might want to enjoy the splendors of London while you're here. I know you don't visit often."

That was putting it lightly since this was the second time in twenty-one years that I'd come to London. "I'm sure. I think I shall prefer to stay near a fire." I shivered for effect. Then I smiled, curtsied to everyone, and left the room.

Now I would have to find a reason to leave with Andrew when he came to get me. I would have to construct a believable falsehood. I went to the music room, and just as I'd told everyone, I worked out an itinerary for the musical portion of the evening. Then I sat at the pianoforte and played a favorite piece of mine by Mozart.

As I played the final note, I heard applause behind me. I turned to find Andrew smiling.

"You *have* been studying music, I see." His face bore remnants of admiration, but his smile communicated his teasing.

I turned back to the pianoforte and sighed. "You never believe my claims. Now you have proof I did not exaggerate my skills. Are you so surprised? It's not as if I didn't play well before you left."

I felt his body line up next to me on the bench, making my back straighten in surprise. He was facing the door behind me, and we were connected by our hips and shoulders. I stole a sidelong glance at him and found him watching me. His face was too close. Apparently he had learned nothing, or felt nothing, during our last encounter earlier that morning. If he had, he wouldn't have ventured to sit so close to me. As it was, my heart raced and my cheeks flamed with an unfamiliar bashfulness.

He leaned even closer, only inches from my ear. I held back a shiver but felt it just the same. He whispered. "I found his residence."

I hadn't forgotten our mission, per se, but it was not at the forefront of my mind at that moment. I had to push out a breath to calm my heart before speaking. "How far away?" I asked.

He looked away and read something in his hands. "On the other side of Town. He isn't living in luxury, it seems." I heard the sound of paper crinkling and saw him in my periphery, placing it in his jacket pocket. "When shall we leave?"

I didn't answer right away but stared over the grand pianoforte, considering. "Do you have an excuse for when they ask where we are off to?" I asked.

"As a matter of fact, I do have an alibi, in my friends. They have gone to a gathering just outside of London. Stenton's family is hosting it, and I had planned to attend, but this is much more important." I met his eyes and found him waiting for me. He leaned closer again as he emphasized his next words with raised eyebrows. "I know you would have gone traipsing around London on your own if I didn't accompany you." He didn't pull back but instead looked down at my mouth.

My entire body froze, and yet my insides were whirling and flipping as if caught in the undertow of an immense wave. My lips parted as I looked at his. What would they feel like against mine? Did I dare to find out?

Our eyes met again, and then he cleared his throat and looked away once more. "Should we leave now? I think we should before we change our minds." His retreat to the door seemed swift; perhaps he had also felt the shift between us and didn't want to call attention to it.

I followed him after taking several deep breaths.

Chapter Seven

Andrew and I mostly avoided eye contact during the ride to Mr. Alexander's home. Occasionally we would speak regarding our strategy for convincing him to make an effort toward a reconciliation. Finally we arrived, sharing a look of uncertainty before exiting the carriage.

"This is the right thing to do, isn't it?" I confirmed.

"It was your idea."

I blew out a breath and my lips vibrated. Andrew laughed at me before descending from the carriage. When I stepped down, I took hold of his offered hand and didn't let go immediately. He squeezed, and I responded in kind. Then, after nodding to each other, we approached the door and knocked.

An elderly woman opened the door. "Who's this, then?" she asked, looking us over.

I cleared my throat. "I'm Esther Harris. This is Andrew Lawrence. We're hoping to speak with Mr. Nathan Alexander. He may recognize our names. We hail from Northamptonshire."

She nodded and held the door open farther, allowing our entry. We went inside and were led into the small room to the right of the entry. She left us there, and I soon heard muffled voices from a nearby room. After a few moments, footsteps came toward us. Andrew and I faced the person entering the room.

It was Mr. Alexander. Being this close to him, it was difficult *not* to see the resemblance between him and his family. Somehow it made the whole situation more tragic; no matter how completely the Alexanders cut him off, he would still be reminded of who he truly was each day as he peered into a looking glass.

"So you are Mr. Lawrence's son," Mr. Alexander stated.

Andrew stepped forward and put forth his hand for a greeting. Mr. Alexander took it, and they shook. "I am," Andrew said. "Thank you for seeing us."

Mr. Alexander nodded and, after gesturing for us to sit, squinted at me. "I admit to not recognizing your name, Miss Harris."

"I did not expect you to, truthfully. My connection to the Alexander family is meager. My sister, Lucy, married Robert Alexander ten years ago." For some reason, I added, "She used to be a maid at Bellingham Hall."

He nodded as recognition spread across his features. "That's right. I heard about Robert's unique marriage." The ghost of a smile disappeared as quickly as it had appeared, as if he was amused by some private joke. "To think I worried about the niece of the steward becoming a countess." He met Andrew's and my eyes briefly before dropping his gaze. "I apologize. You must know at least part of my despicable past, if you have come to visit me. I had many misconceptions regarding social disparity. I was . . . reprehensible toward your cousin, Mr. Lawrence."

"Admitting to such a mistake cannot be easy," Andrew replied. He glanced at me.

I shifted in my seat, then addressed Mr. Alexander. "Admittedly neither of us has heard the full story." Taking a deep breath, I went into my rehearsed speech. "Regardless of what has transpired between you and your family, I needed to speak with you about considering a reconciliation with your mother, at least. She misses you dearly, and . . . her health is not robust. No one would know it to look at her, but we all live in fear of losing her. The doctor does not have high hopes of her living longer than a few more years."

Mr. Alexander leaned toward us desperately, his eyes moistening. I had never seen such a tortured expression on anyone's face. "My mother is ill? How long has she been ill? What was the doctor's diagnosis?"

I took a breath to explain, but Andrew placed a hand lightly on mine as he responded. "Does knowing that increase the likelihood of a meeting with her?"

Mr. Alexander blinked at his unshed tears and looked down at his hands before speaking slowly. "Of course it does. I know I have no right to attempt a reconciliation. Who could forgive such a thing? I cannot apologize enough to make up for what I've done." I could feel his regret from across the small space between us. When he lifted his eyes, it was clear he was in agony. "But if my mother were to leave this world before I speak with her, as my father did, I do not think I could live from the regret."

"I thought it to be so," I said. I hoped my soft smile would convey my sincere pity for him. "Shall we set a meeting between the two of you?"

I thought he would immediately agree after his earnest admission, but he paused, nibbling on his bottom lip. He stood, pacing as we followed him with our eyes. "What has Peter said?"

Andrew and I exchanged a look. "Lord Bellingham doesn't know we are here," Andrew admitted.

Mr. Alexander raked a hand through his hair, then shook his head. "It is not for me to initiate a reconciliation. I cannot even in good conscience ask my mother to come here." He shook his head again. "No, it's best to leave it. But . . . if you could bring a letter to my mother . . ." His eyes pleaded and then dropped. "Perhaps not."

I stood. "I think that's a wonderful idea. And it might just be the first step toward forgiveness, Mr. Alexander." Though it was presumptuous of me, I took it upon myself to walk over to the writing desk and pull out the chair. I held out a hand to the chair. "Please, sit and write what's in your heart. We'll wait here and take the letter to the dowager ourselves."

Andrew caught my eye and nodded once in agreement. Mr. Alexander seemed to weigh his options, but after a few moments, he took a seat and began scribbling. I sat next to Andrew again, and we decided not to watch Mr. Alexander write his letter. We sat in silence and listened to the quill against paper.

A woman came into the room, someone different from the one who'd answered the door. She was petite and freckled and had hair the color of honey. On her hip she held a baby who could not have been more than six months old. She smiled at us with a curtsy before glancing at Mr. Alexader with curiosity. He looked up and gave her a tight smile before standing to introduce us.

"Miss Esther Harris, Mr. Andrew Lawrence, this is my wife, Sarah. This is our daughter, Amelia."

My mouth fell open, and I could not help a sad "Oh" from escaping. They had named their daughter after the dowager countess. My surprise turned into a sympathetic smile. So he had always kept his family in his heart, regardless of his past wrongs. I suddenly felt how much he must truly regret his choices that had brought him so far from home. Mr. Alexander met my eyes as I communicated my understanding of his pain. He gave me a small smile before returning to the writing desk.

"How old is she?" I asked Mrs. Alexander.

"Five months." She smiled proudly.

"She is exceptionally pretty," I said.

"Thank you. We think so too." She grinned and then sat facing us. "I believe Nathan knows you two from Bellingham?" the woman said tentatively.

Andrew spoke first. "I was very young and didn't have many interactions with Mr. Alexander. I am Lady Bellingham's cousin, Andrew Lawerence." He gestured to me. "Esther is the younger sister of Lucy Alexander, who has married Robert, the youngest son of the late earl." He paused. "That is . . . Mr. Alexander's youngest brother."

The woman looked me over, but not unkindly. She simply seemed curious. "So you are, in a way, my husband's sister-in-law?"

"I suppose that's true," I responded. I had never thought of it in that way. Relationships in Bellingham certainly were complex. "We have come to help Mr. Alexander heal the rift between him and his family."

Mrs. Alexander nodded slowly. I could sense hesitation in her posture and in her eyes. She lowered her brows and then caught her husband's attention. "Have you finally decided to try?" Her tone was gentle but pressing.

He looked up at her and frowned. "My mother is ill. I should try something, if only to speak with her once more. If only to introduce her granddaughter."

Sympathy for her husband was etched in Mrs. Alexander's expression, she said, "I am sorry to hear about your mother, my dear. Perhaps this is your opportunity to finally seek the reconciliation you've always wished for and find peace." She turned to us again. "My husband has gone through much heartache, and I had a difficult time convincing him that he deserved love so that he'd marry me." She smiled softly. "He has done nothing since I've known him but repent of his past sins." She focused on her daughter for a moment, wiping drool and snuggling her closer. "He has done so much for his parish and his congregation. I believe his past mistakes have made him much more empathetic to those he oversees as clergy. But I wish for him to live with a lighter heart."

As I watched Mrs. Alexander and her baby, I could not help the thought creeping in about what he had done all those years ago. If it was so terrible, could he even make amends? My stomach gnawed on the thought that what we had done was crossing a line we could not uncross. I fidgeted with my reticule and nearly jumped at Andrew's light touch on my hand. I looked into his eyes. He must have read my mind, because the look in his eyes said, *We're doing the right thing.*

Mr. Alexander stood after folding his letter and came to sit next to his wife. "If I have but one wish, it is that my mother could meet my daughter." Looking down at the letter, he took a shaky breath. "If I give this to you, will you promise to put it directly into my mother's hands?" He met my eyes, apparently entrusting this to me, specifically.

I nodded with assurance. "Of course."

He handed the letter to me, then looked at his wife. "Sarah, I hope you are pleased. You have asked me to do at least this much for years."

"I am. I truly hope you are able to see your mother once more." She met my eyes. "Please communicate our sincerity; we do not want anything other than to repair the relationships which have been severed. To heal the pain we've all been through these many years."

Andrew answered this time. "That is all we wished for when we came to visit you."

We took our leave. As soon as we sat in the carriage, I let out a long breath. I closed my eyes. "Please, Lord, let this become a Christmas miracle and not a horrible mistake."

My eyes opened when Andrew placed his hand on mine once more. His eyes searched mine, and we both smiled with hopefulness. "If this is your idea of a Christmas gift, you should prepare yourself for it to be rejected." He squeezed my hand. Warmth spread up my arm and comforted me. "Whatever happens, I will be here. You will not take all of the reproof alone," he assured me.

Thank goodness Andrew had returned. In that moment I felt his importance fully—his importance in my life, in my comfort, and in my heart.

* * *

Mr. Alexander's letter felt much heavier than a mere letter should. Part of me knew what a violation of Aunt Anabelle's trust it had been to meet with the second son of the dowager countess. Another part of me—the part that had pushed me to this decision in the first place—knew that fifteen years was much too long to hold a grudge. Bad feelings festered if left alone for too long. I knew that well enough; my father and brother had been holding on to their bitterness toward high Society since Lucy's marriage, and it had only brought about hurt feelings and misunderstandings.

After dinner that evening, I steeled my courage to bring the letter to the dowager.

I made my way to her bedchamber and knocked. She opened the door in her dressing gown and robe. Her hair was down in a long braid. "Esther, what a surprise. Is there something you need?"

I nodded. "May I come in?"

She held the door open for me, and we sat in front of her fireplace. I hesitated before pulling the letter out of my pocket and handing it to her. She took it slowly, meeting my gaze with curiosity.

"I hope you will forgive me for interfering in a matter I have no right to."

She opened it quickly and gasped. "Oh, Esther," she said with wide eyes. "How did you . . . ?" Her chin quivered, and there was no hint of anger or betrayal in her teary eyes. I would almost say she seemed relieved, even thankful. She wiped at her tears, and without another word she read through the letter. Her fingers traced the words tenderly. "My boy," she whispered.

When she met my eyes again, she had questions. "How did he seem? Did you meet his wife and daughter? Where is he living, and in what condition is his living? Does his wife seem kind?"

I smiled softly at her questions and answered each one. "He seems to have a heavy burden of guilt, and his wife seemed worried about him. She was kind and gentle. He lives across Town in a modest home with what looked like one servant. I think he's doing well, despite the heaviness of his heart." I paused, letting her take in the information. "They wanted to be certain I passed their sincerity on to you and explain that they don't expect anything; they simply want to repair what has been broken."

The dowager covered her face and shook with sobs. I came to kneel in front of her, handing her a handkerchief and offering a few words of comfort. "He wishes for you to meet his daughter. He's named her Amelia." She nodded, as if she'd already known. I assumed he must've written as much in his letter.

When she calmed, I took her hands in mine. "I hope you can forgive me, Dowager. There isn't much I can do for you but this. You have been so kind to me, and I wanted to do something to repay you. And after the ball, I knew how desperately you wished to meet with him again."

She sniffed and squeezed my hands. "You did well, Esther. It was brave, if not a bit . . . naive." She nodded. "I cannot deny how relieved I am that you made such a step in my place. However, regardless of how much I wish to meet my granddaughter, I cannot go against Peter or Anabelle. They were the ones most wronged by Nathan, not I."

It was the first I'd heard from the dowager anything close to details about the rift. I waited for her to continue, to explain more.

"If I went to meet him, it would be insensitive to their pain." She reached a hand out to graze my cheek. "But thank you, dear, for your thoughtfulness toward me. Let us not speak of this again."

Disappointment grasped my heart, but I nodded in understanding. I had overstepped, even if the dowager was glad of it. And yet . . . now that I'd met the man who haunted Bellingham, I couldn't help but desire the truth more than ever.

"Will you not tell me the details of his wrongdoing? It will help me understand why I should go no further."

She looked down and shook her head. "It is not my injury, not my story. All I can say is that Peter and Anabelle have every right to continue their lives without paying any heed to Nathan's existence. Some wounds cannot be healed with time."

I thought her response would be thus. Since I would get no answers, I knew my intrusion on her privacy had come to an end. She must be wishing for time alone but was too kind to ask me to leave.

"I will go to bed, then. Sleep well, Dowager."

After closing the door, I placed a hand over my heart. Seeing the dowager's reaction to the letter and hearing my words had filled and broken her heart all at once. Surely this was not all I could do. I shook my head. No, this was the end. It had worked out as well as it could, considering the past that I didn't understand.

* * *

"How did it go?" Andrew whispered to me the next day in the corridor when he brought his belongings to join us as we left London. The dowager had invited his friends to attend the Christmas party in Bellingham, but they had plans already, so Andrew would be coming with us.

"Shhh!" I urged before tugging on his arm to pull him into an empty room.

Everyone in the town house was bustling around as they readied themselves for the journey back to Bellingham, so I chose a room where I knew we would be left alone.

The space was surprisingly dark. With the drapes closed and candles snuffed out, it seemed as if it were the middle of the night rather than daytime.

Though my eyes hadn't adjusted to the dim lighting, I could feel how close Andrew and I were to each other. Moving away wasn't an option for me, as my back was pressed against the wall. Andrew, however, could've moved ten feet and still had plenty of room, yet he didn't put any space between us. I felt the heat of his body, as if he were touching my skin directly and not through layers of clothing.

When my sight adjusted to the darkness, I saw him watching something outside the open door. I grasped the folds of my dress between my thumb and forefinger in an attempt to contain the sudden emotions coursing through me. It took effort to stop looking at him, and my success was brief. When Andrew met my eyes, all the air in the room seemed to disappear.

He spoke as though he did not feel anything new or different between us. "Why must we hide to speak of this?" His whispered words smelled like honeyed lemon tea, his favorite drink.

My speechlessness continued as I noticed he was taking in every detail of my face. He placed a hand on the wall next to my ear, leaning in. A glint shone in his eyes. "You are acting suspiciously, you know."

He glanced again toward the door, and I took the opportunity to gather my wits. I succeeded enough to laugh lightly and keep my voice steady. "*I'm* acting suspicious? Your loud whispering would have captured the attention of anyone who happened to walk by!"

His eyes returned to my face. "Well, did you give her the letter? What did she say?"

I pulled up one shoulder. "She was as determined not to go against Lord Bellingham as Mr. Alexander was. I have decided to be finished with it. Delivering the letter is as far as I dare go."

Andrew nodded, glancing out the door again. His body was so close to mine that I could almost feel him breathing. His hand remained on the wall, making nerves rustle in my stomach. Our situation was rife with the potential of romance. If it had been anyone but Andrew, I would have expected— But his eyes met mine, and all thoughts of him being *just* a friend fled my mind. This was the moment, was it not? The moment our lips would meet. Finally.

What was I thinking? *Finally?* A laugh escaped me, and I could see Andrew's brow crease.

"What are you laughing at?" he asked.

"This position we're in. One might think you are in a dark room with me in order to steal my innocence." My laugh began shaking my shoulders. I reluctantly pushed him back.

When he dropped his arms to his sides, I ignored my disappointment, even if I had been the one to push him away first. His scoff told me I'd been right to laugh at any potential intimacy between us. He meant nothing by his long looks and close proximity.

He reached a hand awkwardly to the back of his head. "What thoughts are you entertaining in that head of yours?" I saw his gaze wander over me briefly before he walked out the door.

"What were the two of you doing in there?" Aunt Anabelle said when we emerged. Andrew and I both jumped. What could we possibly say in response?

I let out a laugh, but Andrew had an actual answer. "Esther showed me one of the new landscape paintings."

Aunt Anabelle narrowed her eyes. "In the dark?"

It wasn't a very good answer, granted.

My turn. "Of course not. We opened the drapes but closed them as we left."

She seemed to accept it. "We're almost ready, Esther. Make sure you have everything you need."

"I already have. I'm ready."

She left us in the corridor after pinching Andrew's cheek affectionately. He rubbed it and watched her walk away. There was a red spot where she'd pinched. I laughed at it. "Don't you hate it when they treat us like children?" I said.

"Not really. The longer they see us as children, the less they'll expect of us." He wriggled his eyebrows in a conspiratorial way. "And they'll never suspect us."

We were still laughing when Lord Bellingham appeared on the stairs with his mother following closely behind. "Let us depart!" he called.

Chapter Eight

The seating arrangements for the drive to Bellingham had been decided before I had a say. As Andrew would be traveling with us, he and I were assigned to the carriage with the dowager and Mrs. Lawrence. The admiral and his wife and Lord Bellingham and Aunt Anabelle shared the admiral's carriage.

"What did you think of London, dear Esther?" the dowager asked me. "Quite the spectacle, is it not?"

"It was lovely. I'd love to spend more time there in the future."

"You deserve a Season, my dear. It would be wonderful to see all the eligible young men vie for your hand." She giggled.

Before I responded, I felt a kick from across the carriage. I hissed and bent to rub my ankle, glaring at Andrew. "What was that for?"

"Sorry." His innocent look only reinforced his guilt in my eyes. "I was just trying to stretch my legs."

"You stretch most violently. Do try to keep your feet to yourself, Mr. Lawrence."

"Certainly, Miss Harris."

I turned back to the dowager, laughing lightly. "I would be very interested to see that as well."

The dowager continued as if our bickering was no interruption at all. "It is a pity your friends won't be joining us, Andrew. I think Mr. Stenton was quite taken with our Esther." The dowager waggled her eyebrows at me. I could only laugh at the absurdity of the idea of Mr. Stenton being interested in me. Not after all the undoubtedly embarrassing things Andrew had said of me.

"He was very kind," I responded. "And a great conversationalist."

Another kick. "Ouch!" I ripped off one of my mittens and threw it at Andrew, hitting him squarely in the face.

He let it drop into his hands with a laugh. "I apologize, Miss Harris. I did not see you there."

I huffed. "Do not be so ridiculous. Don't you see I'm trying to have a conversation?"

"Yes, yes. I do see. I see very well."

"You just said you did *not* see me. So which is it?"

He squirmed in his seat, but his mischievous smile only spread wider. "Well, I do see you, but sometimes I see you *so* well that I think perhaps I do not see you at all."

My eyebrows pinched together briefly before a smile broke through, and I looked out the window to hide it. When I glanced back at him, it was clear he'd seen my smile, and he sent me one in return.

The remainder of the ride was quiet as the dowager dozed.

After passing through the charming village of Lynsfield, we approached the long driveway to Bellingham Hall, lined with tall trees and ferns. As we drew nearer to the manor, the gardens appeared; they were all draped in pure white snow. It shimmered and glittered as if greeting us, making amends for the lack of blossoms, which were always pruned with such care.

We stopped at the entrance of the manor house and disembarked. The dowager was the last to descend, taking Andrew's hand. I turned away and then heard a sharp intake of breath. When I turned back to the carriage, I saw the dowager almost fall to the ground. Thankfully, Andrew was able to catch her before she fainted. I rushed to her, along with everyone else, calling to her. She came around immediately, telling everyone she was very well and not to worry.

Aunt Anabelle placed a shawl around the dowager and took her hand, smoothing it with her own. "Nonsense. Of course we will worry."

Mrs. Alexander motioned for a servant. "Send for a doctor!"

Lord Bellingham seemed the most shaken. Andrew stepped aside as Lord Bellingham took his mother carefully by the shoulders and held her close. He looked at her with great concern, but she waved a hand at him.

"Calm yourself, Peter. It was just a moment of dizziness."

The admiral had been elsewhere, and he jogged up to her. "Mother, are you unwell? What happened?"

Mrs. Alexander came to take his arm. "She nearly fainted when she stepped down from the carriage."

The dowager repeated herself to Admiral Alexander, but he did not believe her insistence that she was well. He, too, revolved around her and fussed over her as they all went inside the manor house together.

Mrs. Lawrence, Andrew, and I stayed outside watching the Alexanders take care of the dowager. I took Mrs. Lawrence's arm when I noticed her chin quivering. She looked at me. "Oh, what will we do if we lose her?"

I patted her hand. "I am certain it is not yet her time. There's still much for her to accomplish. And still more that we can do for her. It could have simply been the strain of the long journey. With rest, she will surely get better."

Andrew met my eyes with worry as he helped his mother walk toward the house. He must have felt it, too, the fear that we'd lose her. I watched them for a moment before following.

We sat in the drawing room while the Alexanders stayed by their mother's side. Andrew, Mrs. Lawrence, and I sat heavily on the overly comfortable chairs that surrounded the hearth, each of us no doubt thinking the same thing: to lose the dowager countess would cause everyone to mourn greatly. Beyond that, however, thoughts of Mr. Nathan Alexander and the dowager's sobs at seeing him again and then reading his letter came to the forefront of my mind. Mr. Alexander's sentiments echoed there as well; he wished for nothing more than his mother to meet his daughter just once before she passed.

This wouldn't do. To leave this matter as it was didn't sit well with me. I knew the dowager wished to see her son before she died. And while she might live a few years more, we might lose her before we expected. Death was unpredictable.

I looked at Andrew and took note of his worried frown and bent head. I watched Mrs. Lawrence wipe away errant tears that she was trying to suppress. Each Alexander ran through my mind. And my own family and our most recent conversation tugged at my conscience. If my father were ailing so much that his death was feared, nay expected, I knew that whatever our disagreement, we would quickly reconcile. Surely everyone at Bellingham would feel the same, even if the reason for the estrangement differed.

Amidst the fear and heartache of losing one of the most prolific and kind-hearted women I'd ever known, I inwardly debated my next steps. Dare I take this as a sign that my mission was incomplete? I had decided to close that door, to lock it. Yet here was a key, a compelling reason to revisit the idea. Debate over, I mentally grabbed the key, and the door unlocked and reopened. This time I would not give up, even if it meant going against the earl and his countess.

Mr. Alexander was going to receive an invitation to the Bellingham Christmas party.

Chapter Nine

The laughter coming from the dowager countess's chambers was unsurprising. It urged a smile onto my lips before I even opened the door. Upon my entering, she looked up at me with her usual welcoming smile. A bowl had been placed before her, its contents steaming. Next to the bed, Lord Bellingham sat with a spoon and a napkin. He turned when he saw his mother smile at me.

"Hello, my dear Esther," the dowager said. "Have you come to look upon the poor old woman in here?"

"Yes, of course, Dowager. Where else in the house could I find another like-minded person? Things have been dreadfully boring since we arrived. How could you leave me to my own devices, I ask you?"

Meeting Lord Bellingham's eyes put me quickly in my place. "Forgive me, Lord Bellingham. I only jest."

The dowager cackled. "Don't mind Peter. His face was just made that way. There's nothing to do but ignore it." She took the spoon from her eldest son and set it down on the tray. "I'm sure you have many things to do, son. Don't waste your time fretting over me. You heard the doctor. I will live a bit longer still."

Lord Bellingham nodded before pressing a kiss to the top of her head and leaving the room.

I sat in his vacated seat. "He truly cares for you, Dowager. How well you must have raised your sons for them to love you so."

She nodded, laying her head back against the headboard. "I was blessed with good sons." She let the sentence hang in the air. "It was not all my doing. A mother cannot change her children's hearts; she can only love them and hope for them."

I covered her hand with my own. "How are you feeling?"

"Grateful."

I raised an eyebrow. "I meant your health."

"A grateful heart is a healthy heart."

"I don't need platitudes. I'm asking in earnest. How do you feel?"

Her sigh caused her features to droop slightly, and I could see the heaviness of her heart, her exhaustion, her carefully concealed worries. "Would that I could keep the truth to myself. Alas, you deserve to know that my body feels dreadful. It is inconvenient getting old, but it is worse still to be ill and old, only to find out from the doctor that recovery is unlikely. Oh, perhaps that's not the worst of it yet. My children's faces pain me, and your face, too, makes me believe that I am one step away from falling into my final resting place. Do I truly look so grave that you all must frown at me like that?"

That much honesty from the dowager regarding her health and her feelings was rare. While I wished to help her overcome those feelings, all I could do was barely catch a tear that began slipping onto my cheek. "Indeed, you do not look grave. You're as pretty as a painting. I thought a moment ago that we should perhaps call in a painter to capture you just as you are."

She laughed, and her entire visage blossomed into her usual, cheerful self. "You are a gem, Esther, dear. Now, why don't you go spend time with Andrew. I know you have missed him. I don't want you to waste any more time with me."

"No time with you is a waste, Dowager. But I think I shall go to the music room and play something for you. The pianoforte does echo up here if I leave the door open. Bach? Mozart? Which do you prefer?"

She chuckled. "No matter. I shall be down for dinner, and you can play for me then."

I took her hand and gave her an encouraging smile before leaving. Her confession was everything I'd needed to be more confident in my quest. No one could tell me this wasn't the right thing to do. Instead of going to the music room, I went to the dowager's salon and found an extra invitation to the Christmas ball; we had been sending them to those outside of Bellingham Estate or Lynsfield. I added a personal note in her penmanship. The deception began with *My Dear Nathan* and ended with *Your mother, Amelia Alexander.*

I took her seal and carefully closed the letter with it. I dared not put his address on the front until I took it to post myself. It would not do for even a servant to know what I had done. I tucked the letter inside of my skirt pocket and then escaped to the music room as if nothing had happened at all.

I was halfway through a sonata when Andrew entered the room. I turned toward the door and could not help the smile that tugged at my lips. Seeing him at Bellingham again, so casual and comfortable, brought back all of my fondest memories. His mere presence made this place feel more like home than all the camaraderie I shared with the countesses and all the luxuries that were bestowed upon me.

I waited for him to approach the pianoforte, watching his every movement. His olive-green coat complemented his dark hair and eyes, making him look like a forest personified. All that was missing to complete the imagery was the morning fog that made the woods seem mystical. Rather than that effect, however, Andrew's brown eyes shone with their own kind of light, which filtered through the air and brightened every shadow.

I'd been so lost in my silly fancy of comparing him to a forest that I hardly realized he'd ventured so close to me. I peered up at him, wide-eyed. He bent down, so close, too close, and reached slowly behind me. I could feel his breath on my cheek, and my heart sped wildly. Then he straightened, bringing with him my shawl, which had fallen off one shoulder. He placed it more firmly around me. The smile that played on his lips made me feel as if he mocked me. Had he been making me a fool by his close proximity? Perhaps he had noticed my reaction to him each time he drew near. If he had, there was no doubt he would tease me for it.

"Thank you," I said flatly.

"Any time."

Even turning back to the piano, I could see his grin in my periphery. I could only hope he didn't know the feelings developing within me. Curse my transparency.

He bent over to read the score I'd been playing from. "Beethoven, eh?"

"It isn't my favorite, but I must practice at least one classical piece per day." I shrugged and reached to turn the page, and Andrew's hand caught mine. Whether it was intentional or he had been reaching for the page as well, it didn't matter. The present reality was that now our hands were touching, and I was overwhelmed.

Overwhelmed by how one single touch could make everything in my mind entirely disappear. He touched only my hand, but I felt it everywhere. My arms, my neck, my spine, my stomach, my heart. Each part of my body was awake with new sensations. And simply because our hands met.

I lifted my head for a glimpse of Andrew's face. What I saw in his gaze was everything I felt. Something lingered in the air, a question or a longing that pulsed between us.

"Oh, there you are, Andrew," we heard from the doorway. Our focus shifted so quickly to Aunt Anabelle that whatever tension that had built between us vanished like a bubble being popped.

"Were you looking for me, Annie?" Andrew smiled at his cousin.

"I should've known you were here with Esther." She looked at me. "You played that piece well, by the way. I've been meaning to have a lesson with you about Beethoven, but it seems unnecessary." She placed a hand on the pianoforte. "Would the two of you help me convince Mother to stay in bed a bit longer? We can play a game of charades to entertain her."

Andrew and I jumped at the chance to help the dowager by playing a game, though we would have been willing to help in any way, and followed Aunt Anabelle upstairs.

As we ascended, Andrew's hand bumped against mine, and I could not help but wonder if I had imagined the way he'd looked at me in the music room or if he, too, could feel what I had felt. At times our relationship seemed the same, comfortable and easy, but each time we touched, everything seemed unfamiliar and thrilling.

Chapter Ten

I HATED VENISON, YET AT least once per week, that was on the menu at Bellingham Hall. Normally I'd devour my meal with nothing left on the plate. But on venison nights, I moved my food around the plate until everyone else had finished. I barely even ate the vegetables because they tasted like the meat.

Andrew sat on my left, just as he always had. I finally had a way to rid myself of the gamey food. First, I cut the venison into small pieces, taking my time with it. Then, *slowly*, I passed the meat over to him one piece at a time, plopping it onto his plate.

Leaning toward me, he whispered with a smile in his voice. "What are you doing?"

I grinned at him and added another piece. I did not answer him because he soon understood, or remembered, that I hated venison. We broke into quiet laughter as I continued to surreptitiously hide my discarded meat on his plate.

Finally, he held up a hand and whispered through fits of laughter. "Stop it! I cannot eat this much."

I knew he hated leaving anything on his plate, but that was half the fun. I scooped one more forkful of venison onto his plate and then set my silverware down. "There," I said. "I can manage this much."

He shook his head and, after raising his eyes to the heavens, began eating an obscene amount of venison.

"The earl himself killed this deer just this morning," Aunt Anabelle boasted about her husband next to her. A general agreement on the superiority of its flavor and texture went around the table.

Lord Bellingham cleared his throat. "That will do, everyone. We all know that how it's cooked, not how it's killed, is what truly brings out the flavor well. If you wish to flatter anyone, please send your compliments to Cook."

I tried hard to swallow the last piece of venison, though there had been only three. I met Andrew's eyes with a pained expression before taking a drink of water to wash it down with.

Suddenly I heard Andrew say, "This venison is delicious. However, I wonder if you know that Esther does not like venison."

I nearly choked on my water. I tugged on his sleeve and whispered, "Andrew, what are you—?"

"Truly?" Aunt Anabelle said. "Oh, Esther, I'm sorry. I didn't know! You should have said something. Cook could have made chicken for you instead." She frowned, sincerely sorry that she hadn't known.

"Don't worry. I'm perfectly able to eat whatever is served," I replied.

I met Andrew's eyes and widened mine at him, silently communicating that I wished he would've kept his mouth shut.

"For someone who is always honest about her feelings, you certainly know how to keep a secret, Esther," the dowager added. "I had no idea you didn't like venison."

I laughed awkwardly. "I do not think I'm *very* honest about my feelings."

"Not with your feelings regarding venison, at least," Andrew said.

I sighed. "Yes, thank you, Andrew."

The conversation turned to something else, and I looked at Andrew again. He must've known I was annoyed at him. He grinned at me. "You're welcome. Now you will never have to eat it again."

"I could've taken care of it myself. Were you so put out that I made you eat mine that you had to insert yourself into my business?"

"So you putting food on my plate isn't inserting yourself into *my* business?" He smirked.

"That is different."

"How so?"

"Because . . . it's *you*."

He paused, looking into my eyes. How I'd said *you* made my heart clench. I'd said it with such care, and so deliberately, that he must have felt the whole of my meaning. Our relationship had always been different from the others. We were best friends, true companions, and equals. Growing up, we'd relied on each other for play, for comfort, for answers, and for understanding. We'd both benefited greatly from Bellingham without actually being related to the Alexanders, and with that came more difficulties than one would imagine. But he understood me, and I him. Even if no one else in the world knew how I felt, he did.

He nodded. "Exactly. If it's *you*, I can insert myself wherever I'm needed."

A small smile tugged on my lips, and I looked away. I began listening to the conversation happening at the other side of the table, about the Christmas ball. It was a subject much easier to think about than how Andrew's attention made my heart flutter.

* * *

"Have you spoken to Bethany about whether she will attend the Christmas party?" the dowager countess asked me the next day in the salon.

Everything had returned to normal at Bellingham Hall, with a couple of exceptions: the lack of Lucy and my curious new feelings toward Andrew. I glanced at his casual position near the fireplace, his feet propped up on a stool and his face covered with a newspaper. Why he had to read in this salon was unknown to me, but his presence did not allow me to focus fully. I took a deep breath before diving into the final details for the Bellingham Christmas celebrations. I had nearly finished choosing each song for the music portion of the family dinner party.

Only one day remained before the semiannual Christmas festival held in Lynsfield, followed by the Christmas Eve ball. Then, the next day, Christmas dinner would take place with only the Bellingham family. I looked forward to it this year more than ever because my sister Lucy would finally come home after an eternity away.

"Esther?" I heard the dowager say. I realized I'd never given her an answer.

"I have not spoken with them about the party since before we left for London. At that time, they were . . . unwilling to join us." I frowned. "I'll ask again, I suppose." I sighed heavily.

If Bethany, Father, and Sam came, it would complete the celebration. Though, admittedly, having them at Bellingham was never a *completely* pleasant affair. With Lucy as mediator, things went more smoothly. But since she had left, things had grown tense. The fault rested mainly on my shoulders, I knew. My temper did not help the matter. With Lucy's return, however, things would surely mend.

Andrew set his feet down from the footstool, then folded the newspaper as he joined the conversation. He had clearly been listening to it all. "Would it help if I asked?"

I tilted my head at him. "Do you believe that will make a difference?"

He grinned. "I've been told I have a face that can easily convince anyone of anything."

My thoughts immediately went to Miss Beaumont, and I found I could not look at him as jealousy took hold. "Is that so? And did you use that face during your time on the Continent?"

"Possibly."

His answer irked me more than it should have, considering I had no notion of the nature of his relationship with Miss Beaumont. "Why are you here?" I asked. "Have you nothing else to occupy your time?"

When I finally looked at him, he furrowed his brow as if I'd asked a ridiculous question. "I'm waiting for you to finish what you are doing so you can play with me." A phrase he used to use nearly every day during our childhood.

I laughed. "It has been a long time since I've 'played' with anyone."

I glanced at the dowager, and she shrugged. "Don't mind me, dear. I have everything nearly settled here," she said.

I nodded at her. "Very well." I turned fully toward Andrew and pulled a face, though I was intrigued. "What do you want to do, fence?"

He nodded and stood, beckoning for me to follow. My intention to visit Satchell Cottage fell by the wayside. Fencing sounded like much more fun. I made a show of it for Andrew's benefit, however.

I groaned. "I will have to change." I stood. "I will have to move." I walked toward him. "I will have to . . . race you!" I got out the door faster than he and ran unladylike through the corridors to the fencing room, practically falling through the doorway. "I win!"

He came in right behind me, panting. "How . . . have you . . . become . . . so fast?"

Grinning in triumph, I took a foil from its place and began swishing it through the air. "How have you become so slow?" I countered. "Did you take a coach everywhere you went on the European continent? You should've walked, my friend." I tsked and pointed my foil at him. "I do not intend to don the attire, so no touching lest your foil tear my dress."

"I thought you were going to change your clothes." He and walked over to take a foil from the rack.

"I lied."

"Are you sure you can fence in that?" He looked skeptically at my blue day dress, which was perhaps more intricately embroidered than most of its kind, and the matching ribbon holding my hair up.

"If I can't, you will have a better chance at besting me," I taunted.

He laughed and then without warning lunged forward to hit my foil. The battle began. We had been fencing together for years. The competition had not been fierce as children, but the older we became, the more we wished to win over the other. We'd both studied fencing and learned the art as well as any amateur could. My skills were rusty, as I'd had no one to fence with in over a year. Andrew, on the other hand, must have practiced swordplay on his Tour. He had improved dramatically, and I could barely keep up.

He laughed. "How do we know who wins if I cannot touch you?"

It was a struggle indeed, but we both knew he would have touched me more than once at this point. We began twirling around each other and foregoing the strict rules of the game. It became more like a dance. It abruptly ended, however, when Andrew slipped on my ribbon, which had fallen out of my hair without my realizing, and landed right on his backside.

I dropped my foil and ran over to him, kneeling to check his condition. "Oh, I'm so sorry! Are you all right?"

He let out a breath through his teeth while holding his lower back. "Ow." I suspected it was not his back that was injured, but his tailbone.

"Shall I call for someone?"

He hissed. "No, no. I think I'm all right. Just . . . give me a minute." He pinched his eyes closed. "That was a particularly devious way to win, Miss Harris," he said before laughing through his pain.

I frowned with mock sympathy. "Oh, you poor thing. It seems you need to blame your lack of agility on me." I put a hand on top of his head. "Did you hurt your brain as well?"

He arched an eyebrow. "Was this your true intention in dropping your ribbon? To have the opportunity to touch me?" Andrew's cheerful eyes turned smoldering.

Shocked, I pulled back my hand.

With very little effort, he pushed himself off the ground and gave me an opportunity to appreciate the length of his legs and breadth of his shoulders as he stood over me. He held out a hand to help me off the floor. "If you wish to touch me that badly, you need only hold out your hand." I could only stare up at him. His alluring eyes did not leave mine for a second.

Hesitantly, I slid my hand into his and allowed him to pull me up. He pulled me too close, though, and when our eyes met, there was no denying the spark that ignited in my chest. Suddenly every hint of humor disappeared from his face. The air around us crackled with tension. The feel of his chest rising and falling so close to mine caused my heartbeat to quicken. When his chocolate-colored eyes dropped to my lips, his hand tightened on mine. Then his unoccupied hand slid around my side and pressed my back lightly, urging me even closer so that our stomachs met. The contact made my breathing hitch and induced a pleasant warmth to run up my spine, growing warmer until eventually spreading a red-hot blush across my cheeks.

"Esther." My name came out like a breath that Andrew had been waiting to exhale.

"Hmm?" I answered, completely absorbed by the anticipation of what was about to happen, what I knew would happen. My attention was on his lips, waiting. Patiently waiting.

"Are you even aware?" he whispered.

I made an effort to look into his eyes and saw the same tortured hunger there that I felt. "What do you mean?" I barely got the question out.

His hand that had been holding mine came up and brushed against my cheek. Somehow it made me more breathless.

"How pretty you are?" His husky voice sounded as if he'd been screaming for hours.

Without waiting a second for me to respond, he kissed me. I instinctively closed my eyes and grabbed his shirt to keep myself upright. My insides were rolling and dancing while my brain became fuzzy. I let out a sound of surprise when Andrew brought his hands to my head and threaded his fingers into my undone hair. My hair, which had been tied up with a ribbon . . . which had fallen to the floor. What an absolutely wicked piece of cloth, to be the cause of this unexpected yet long-awaited and fateful moment. I would never have guessed that tying my hair carefully with a silky ribbon would result in a breathtaking kiss from Andrew Lawrence.

We pulled apart long enough to gauge each other's reaction. Then, both seeing that the event was greatly enjoyed by those involved, we closed our eyes and somehow found ourselves next to a wall that was kind enough to support me while the spark that ignited became a rather unfettered fire. We took turns leading each other through each touch of our lips, and I eagerly discovered a new side to Andrew that was beyond my imagining.

I had no idea these feelings existed. While I should have been surprised that Andrew was the one to bring them out of my naive heart, I wasn't. Who else could love me but him? Who else would I love but him? There had never been anyone else for me. *He* was the reason I'd turned down every eligible suitor.

Footsteps in the corridor alerted us both, and we broke apart. I searched for my ribbon so I did not look as disheveled as I felt. Even if I found it quickly, however, there would not be enough time to tie it neatly. I spotted it under a bench without any hint of remorse for what it had caused. I picked it up and made to at least tie my hair back, but before I could, Andrew snatched it from me and put it into his pocket, saying quietly with a grin, "I'm confiscating this."

I watched him curiously as he casually greeted Admiral Alexander and his wife as they entered.

Mrs. Alexander sent me a smile, glancing at Andrew. "I see you two are whittling away the time with fencing."

I gave a single laugh. "Yes, well . . ." Picking up one of the foils, I placed it back where I'd found it. "If you'll excuse me." I curtsied and left the room in a hurry. One glance at Andrew, and I knew I would not be able to focus on a conversation with anyone.

When I closed my bedroom door, I leaned against it and took several deep breaths. When had Andrew become so devastatingly passionate?

Chapter Eleven

In such a large home, one would imagine that being alone with someone would come easily. Since our fencing adventure the day before, however, Andrew and I had had no opportunities to speak about what happened. In a way, the thrill of an unspoken affection elated me, but my curiosity as to what exactly he was thinking made me feel as if I were going mad. He was occupied by Aunt Anabelle until dinnertime. Then we were not given a moment during cards, and by the time everyone went up to bed, Andrew had to immediately leave with his mother and father to return to the cottage. He held my gaze until the door closed behind them. I sighed and retreated to my room.

The next day was a whirlwind of activities. I aided the dowager in organizing the festival in Lynsfield, which meant communicating with each vendor and performer and explaining things to the villagers. When Andrew arrived, he had with him Aunt Anabelle's two eldest children—Phillip and Rene. He waved me over to join him.

"It was kind of you to bring the children," I said to Andrew while he purchased candy for them.

"I would never say no to Cousin Anabelle."

I knew that very well. "Why is it that you never deny her anything?"

He gave the candy to the children, and we began walking down the street. His hand fell to his side and brushed against mine. His forefinger teased the back of my hand as he glanced at me. "Because without her, you never would have come to Bellingham."

Butterflies tickled my stomach, bringing an uncontrollable smile. I pinched my lips together and looked away from him. Then his fingers found mine and lightly held them only to quickly let go again. I met his eyes. In them, I found an answer to my question. As much as I wanted to hear his thoughts, I admitted that we did not really *need* words. The way I made him feel was clear on his face, and I knew my face was the same. So we happily went through the festival together and played with the children until we all made our way back to the manor house to ready ourselves for the ball.

As soon as we entered Bellingham Hall, I was accosted. All I saw before arms were wrapped around my neck was a blur of blonde hair. My arms hung at my sides for a moment before I realized who this attacker was.

"Lucy!" I hugged her tightly. "How I've missed you!"

She pulled back and grinned at me. "And how I've missed you, little sister." Her face grew unexpectedly serious as she studied me. "Have you grown taller than me in just eighteen months?"

I let out a single laugh. "I have been taller than you for at least three years, Lucy."

My brother-in-law stepped in. "I'm certain that isn't true. Surely you were here when we left for the South." He held out his hand to Lucy's temple. "I specifically remember that your sister looked down on you before we departed."

Lucy gave him a light shove. "Don't play with words, Robert."

"She has always looked down on me, hasn't she?" I responded with a pitiful pout.

Lucy clearly disliked the way Robert and I teamed up against her. She scoffed and gave both of us withering glares. "You"—she pointed at Robert—"stay out of our conversation. And you"—she pointed at me—"tell me everything." Her lips curved upward, as if she'd never been irritated by either of us. Her blue eyes twinkled with joy. She pulled me by the arm up the stairs to my bedchamber.

We sat on the bed together, and I went over a few things that had occurred in Bellingham before she took my hand and placed it in her lap. She leveled her gaze at me seriously. "I admit I have already been to Satchel Cottage. I arrived while you were at the festival. I know about your disagreement with Father, Sam, and Bethany."

I sighed heavily. "Yes, well . . . then you know how much they hate me."

She tsked. "Nonsense. They love you, no matter your misunderstandings. What has kept you from visiting them since you arrived from London? You haven't given up on them, have you?"

"I've been . . . distracted. Besides, my pride prevents me from reconciling." The last word left an echo in my mind, reminding me of the letter I'd sent, but I didn't dwell on it as Lucy spoke again.

"Do you hear that, Bethie?" Lucy turned her head to speak to the wardrobe.

Slowly the door opened, and out stepped Bethany. She held her hands in front of her and sent me a tense smile. "Sorry, Esther. I didn't have the heart to face you."

I stood and went over to her, bringing her into my arms. I sighed. "You must know how wretched I've felt since you moved out. I hope you can forgive me."

It was only a few seconds before Lucy wrapped her arms around both of us and we all laughed as we swayed together. Lucy would always be the mediator in our family, and how glad I was that she had returned to help me fix the mess I'd gotten into. Of course, fixing things with Father and Sam was another matter. That would take more effort than helping Bethany forgive me.

The dowager entered the room and began issuing orders to her maid, setting up my room as a place for all three Harris sisters to get ready together. "How lovely it is to see you three together again. I'm glad you are back in the house, Bethany. I have your dress. Hopefully it fits. You never did try it on before you left."

Bethany bit her lip and curtsied, her head bowed. "Please forgive me, Dowager. I should not have left without telling you."

The dowager pulled her into a tight embrace. "Never you mind, dear. Let's get ready for the ball and have you dance a bit. Seeing you enjoy the ball will be apology enough."

Lucy and I glanced at each other with a laugh behind our lips. We both knew Bethany would refuse to dance. It didn't matter though. We were simply glad to be together again. And I was looking forward to dancing with Andrew. Above all else, I looked forward to that.

Chapter Twelve

My descent down the stairs was calculated. I made sure Andrew was waiting at the bottom before slowly following my sisters. I locked eyes with him, barely seeing anyone else. I smiled and then dropped my lids slightly. I could tell he was admiring me, and I silently thanked the dowager again for the dress, which fit me exactly as I'd hoped. His attention was fully fixed on me, never wavering for a second.

"Andrew! You look dashing!" Lucy remarked, taking our attention from each other.

He grinned at her. "I'm pleased you think so. And you look lovely, as usual, Mrs. Alexander. And, Miss Bethany, you have grown into a lovely young woman."

Bethany didn't answer, but she smiled shyly.

Robert came to the bottom of the stairs with an expression of awe for Lucy. He glanced at Andrew. "You were quick to leave our conversation. Was this your destination?" When he looked at me, his eyes crinkled in a good-natured smile. "You look lovely, Esther. And you, Bethany. A sight to behold, both of you." He then placed his undivided attention on his wife once more. "But no one can outdo your beauty, my love."

Lucy giggled as he swept her away. She took Bethany with her, and I knew she would take care of our little sister for the evening.

Andrew seemed pleased by their departure as he took my hand to pull me toward the dance floor. The ball had already begun, and the musicians were in the second set of the evening. Thousands of candles cast the room in a magical golden glow. Wreaths of evergreen were hung in each window, and boughs were wrapped around every candelabra and balustrade. Holly graced every doorway, and poinsettias sat on each table. The dowager had been busy with all these details since our return from London, directing servants to place the decorations in precise locations.

"Finally," Andrew said, standing across from me as we waited for the music to begin. "We are alone."

I gave him a confused smile. "How do you consider this alone?"

"If there are too many people around, it is like we are the only ones in the room. And no one will be privy to a conversation held in such a crush." He looked around us as if to prove his point. He was right; not a single person nearby had any interest in us. Everyone was completely focused on their partners or those they were soon to be dancing with.

The music began and I followed Andrew's lead. He took me down the line of couples, turned, and spun me until I nearly felt dizzy. We turned and went the opposite direction, returning to our original spots. We stood facing each other, smiling widely. He laughed after I looked down and colored.

"Please, tell me what you are thinking."

I hid my smile poorly as I replied, "You first."

We were soon grinning and laughing so much from the excitement of being near each other that we were startled when the dance was cut short with a few off-key shrieks from the violins. The sea of people around us parted to allow for a scene of some urgency to play out, and the words we both wished to speak were set aside. The familiarity of it hit me immediately. A similar scene had occurred during our recent trip to London, but I hoped it would turn out differently this time. My relationship with Andrew had completely distracted me from the invitation I'd sent to Mr. Alexander.

He had come to the ball. He stood there, hands to his sides, casting his eyes all around before settling back on Lord Bellingham. It seemed he'd come alone, as I did not see his wife behind him. I held my breath and watched Lord Bellingham stare at him, speechless.

"He actually came," I whispered so only Andrew could hear.

"What do you . . . ?" His eyes widened. "Esther? You didn't . . ."

I grimaced. "I did."

"What do you think you're doing here?" Lord Bellingham said with a stormy glare. With such silence in the ballroom, his low voice carried. My heart lurched as I realized what I'd done so rashly. I may be turned out of the house after this. A pit formed in my stomach, and then guilt filled it.

Mr. Alexander held up a hand, his eyes gently pleading with his brother. "I did not come to fight with you, Peter. Please, I wish to make amends . . . though it is far overdue."

"How dare you come at all! You don't have any right to stand before me." Lord Bellingham threw his hand out and pointed toward the exit. "Leave. Immediately."

The dowager stepped out from the crowd. I watched as her chin quivered. Her mouth formed the word "Nathan."

I could not allow him to leave without speaking with his mother. I had begun this; I would see it through to the end. I went to the dowager and took her hand, pulling her toward her son. She gave a sound of refusal but relented nonetheless.

"Mother," Mr. Alexander said softly.

Lord Bellingham stepped between them, as if trying to protect her from Mr. Alexander. Did he hate his brother so much that he didn't trust him with their mother?

"Dear, perhaps we should take this elsewhere," Aunt Anabelle said as she approached the scene and touched Lord Bellingham's arm. She barely glanced toward Mr. Alexander, and I could sense an uneasiness behind her every movement. Lord Bellingham took her hand and looked around, only to realize what a commotion he had caused.

He growled at his brother, "Follow me."

I still held on to the dowager's hand and went with her as she followed her sons and Aunt Anabelle toward the portrait room. She squeezed my arm. "Stay with me, Esther."

"Of course, Dowager," I responded.

The tense conversation continued as soon as we were out of everyone's sight. Lord Bellingham glared, and his words seemed to be supported by the portraits of their ancestors looking down severely on the scene. "What were you thinking coming here? When have we ever allowed you to return? Did you intend to ruin Christmas?"

Mr. Alexander sighed and then looked at the dowager. "Mother wrote and asked me to come." I glanced at the dowager, but she had her full attention on Mr. Alexander and did not seem surprised by his words. "She said to bring my family, for she wished to meet them before she reached the end of her life." He stepped toward her. "Are you very ill, Mother?"

Lord Bellingham looked between them with hurt confusion. I could only imagine what was going through his mind. Perhaps he felt regret at keeping them apart for so long. Surely he could see the pain they both felt at their separation.

I would have expected Mr. Alexander's tone to be antagonizing, but his sincere concern for their mother was emphasized in every word. "Why have you been keeping this from me, Peter? Our mother is ill, and you didn't think she may want to see me before she leaves us?"

"You are not a part of this family any longer, Nathan. You haven't been for fifteen years."

The dowager sniffed beside me. Everyone turned to her. Tears were rolling down her cheeks. Lord Bellingham stepped toward her. "Mother, please don't cry," he said gently.

"P-Peter, please," she said quietly.

He studied her face, and I saw an internal struggle. He looked back at his brother, then at his wife—who had hung back behind the dowager and me—before returning his gaze to his mother. He sighed, dragged a hand over his forehead, and then nodded. The dowager let go of my hand and rushed to her second son. She reached up to touch his face.

"Oh, Nathan. You have aged so much."

His eyes filled with tears, and he held one of her hands on his cheek. He laughed lightly. "Have I? I didn't even notice. You look exactly the same," he said.

"I have missed you."

"And I you."

They stared at each other for a few minutes while Lord Bellingham stood watching with his arms crossed tightly. He seemed as if he would jump in at any moment to fight Mr. Alexander. Aunt Anabelle stood quietly behind us all, and I wondered what she was feeling. As far as I'd been told, she had been hurt the most by Mr. Alexander. I was unsure what to think. When I looked at the dowager, I could assure myself I'd done the right thing. But Aunt Anabelle's skittish actions made me regret it. I glanced at Lord Bellingham. His glare could have turned his brother to ash. What had happened for so much anger and resentment to build up between the brothers?

The dowager began asking questions about Mr. Alexander's life, and they spoke of his wife and daughter. "Did you truly name your daughter Amelia?"

"I did."

The dowager's tears mixed with her pleased smile. She turned to Lord Bellingham. "Did you hear that, Peter?" She wiped at her tears. "Nathan named his daughter after me."

"While I am glad that you have a namesake, I admit I am not pleased that Nathan believes he has the right to use your name." Lord Bellingham's posture didn't change in the slightest, still as rigid and angry as ever. After a few moments, I heard him sigh. "I don't understand why you sent the letter without a word to me."

The dowager looked from Mr. Alexander to Lord Bellingham and then to me. "I didn't send the letter."

Lord Bellingham and Mr. Alexander also turned their attention to me. I could almost feel Aunt Anabelle's eyes on me as she stood at the door behind us. The room suddenly felt too small.

Now was the moment I'd dreaded. I stepped forward with my head bowed and hands clasped in front of me. "I sent it," I admitted. "I apologize for going behind your back. I had no right to do such a thing when I didn't understand the situation. But . . ." I glanced up at the dowager. "I knew the dowager wished to see her son. And after meeting with Mr. Alexander"—I bit my lip as I saw the look of betrayal in Lord Bellingham's eyes and heard the intake of breath from Aunt Anabelle—"I saw that he truly felt remorse and wished to repair this rift." I took a breath. "Please forgive my intervention. However, I cannot deny that there is a part of me that is not sorry. Fifteen years is far too long to continue in such a manner. Especially when the offender clearly regrets his mistakes. Might you give him a chance?"

Silence stretched out for an immeasurable amount of time. I swallowed, but my throat felt painfully dry.

Lord Bellingham shook his head at me. "Leave. The damage has been done. Just . . . leave."

I curtsied and left without another word. Tears pricked at my eyes. My stomach had dropped so far, my core felt empty.

Lucy stood just outside the door with an expression of shock and disapproval, and I knew she'd overheard the conversation. "Esther, what have you done?"

Chapter Thirteen

Lucy did not stand there alone. Bethany, Robert, and Andrew also waited to hear my answer. Each of them had some form of curiosity in their expressions, but their secondary emotions were vastly different.

Lucy clearly wished to reprimand me. Robert was aghast, disbelieving. Bethany's doe eyes showed signs of pity. Andrew sent me a small smile of encouragement. I took a deep breath. "I . . . wrote a letter to Mr. Alexander in the dowager's hand, asking him to come to the ball for a reconciliation."

I bit my lip in anticipation of their reactions. Lucy covered her mouth with a hand in near horror. Robert whispered my name to admonish me. Bethany whimpered. Andrew came to stand next to me, taking my hand and pulling me close to him. "Should we sit somewhere quiet and talk about this?" he suggested.

We entered the nearest salon not in use. I sat heavily on the settee next to Lucy. "Please say something," I probed.

Her eyes held mine with something like pity. "Oh, Esther. What a thing for you to do. You, who have no idea what happened fifteen years ago. How could you?"

I did not say anything in response. She must have known why I did it. Her question was rhetorical.

Then Bethany asked the question I had always wished to know the answer to. "What *did* happen?"

"Don't we deserve to understand why my actions were so horrendous? No one has ever explained anything."

Lucy and Robert exchanged glances. "Still, for you to act alone like this . . ."

"She did not do this alone," Andrew admitted. Everyone focused on him now, surprise in all their features. "I went with her to see him in London."

He failed to mention that we'd given up the scheme after meeting with Mr. Alexander.

Silence fell, and we all watched each other. Then Robert spoke. "Nathan tried to ruin Anabelle."

I gasped. "Why would he do such a thing?" I felt Andrew's hand on my shoulder and a squeeze communicating his shock and worry. I touched his hand.

"He was jealous of Peter," Robert said. "Always has been. For years, he envied Peter's betrothal to a woman he loved, and when she died, he blamed Peter for somehow stealing a happiness that had never been his to begin with. When Anabelle came to Bellingham, Nathan harassed her from the start, spreading rumors about their relationship, belittling her station, and in the end, accosting her while drunk. Had Peter not confronted him, who knows what might have happened. When the issue came to light, Father disowned Nathan at once."

Lucy spoke quietly. "It was a terrible time at Bellingham. Now do you understand, Esther?"

I nodded slowly. "I know it was not my place to meddle."

"We will just have to wait to see how things unfold from here," Lucy said. "I should punish you for such a misguided action, Esther. Since you were naive enough to do this without understanding everything, however, I believe your guilt and regret will be your punishment." She stood, taking Robert's hand, and they left the room together.

Bethany left as well, leaving Andrew and me alone.

I put my face in my hands. "What have I done?" I lamented.

Andrew sat next to me and placed a warm hand on my back. "The only thing you could do at the time." I heard him sigh. "Your heart was in the right place, Esther. We were both in the wrong. However, I have a feeling that things will work out. You saw how sincerely sorry he was for the past. I think everyone will be able to see the truth and find a way to forgive him. At the very least, you have given the dowager a chance. Lord Bellingham and Cousin Annie may resent you for a while, but in the end, they will be glad the dowager had time with Mr. Alexander."

I looked into his eyes. They steadied me. "You truly believe that?"

"I do."

Without thinking, I laid my head on his shoulder. "Thank you. Although I don't deserve to be comforted, you have done so."

I felt him laugh, his chest rising and falling quickly under my head. "I will continue to do so for my whole life." An arm came around me and I snuggled into him. "Esther, I love you. I love your stubbornness; I love your naivety; I love your compassion, your humor, your beauty, and most of all your poor decisions. Like kissing me, for instance."

My heart hung on to every syllable he spoke and seemed to swell with each utterance of love. I laughed and lifted my head to look into his eyes. "Why would you bring that up at a time like this?" I pulled up a corner of my mouth. I was certain my eyes were sparkling with glee.

"Are you not going to respond to my confession of love?"

I shook my head. "I am curious about something."

He raised an eyebrow. "Oh?"

"How long have you loved me?"

He looked away with a grin. "Does it matter?"

"It does to me."

"Well, I can't answer that. Next question." His arm now rested on the back of our seat instead of around my shoulders.

"Very well. Don't answer. Then, I won't tell you either."

He sat straighter. "Is that how it is?"

I stuck out my tongue at him. "I will not give away my secrets to someone unwilling to share his."

"Very well, Miss Harris. We will both go on without knowing when one fell for the other. The future is much more important anyway."

I lifted my brows in anticipation.

In one fluid motion that seemed slow, Andrew knelt before me. He took my hands. Tenderly, he said, "You will marry me, won't you?"

A laugh burst from me, as if my heart were too full and could not contain all my happiness. I pressed my lips to his. When I pulled back, he followed me with his mouth and sat next to me again. I placed a hand on his cheek, brushing a thumb against his lips. "I don't think I have any other choice."

His grin flashed just before he kissed me again. "Now, before you think I've asked for your hand on a whim, I will explain my situation." He cleared his throat and spoke without letting go of my hands. "I have enlisted in the army and plan to purchase a commission next year after I acclimate to the profession. Once I have a commission, I will go where they tell me to go and do my best to serve His Majesty, the King. My wife, I hope, will accompany me in my travels and never leave my side unless I am at war."

I frowned. "Must you go to war?"

"I will not if I can help it. I would much rather stay with you." His eyes were warm.

"Very well, Mr. Lawrence. I suppose your future sounds acceptable. Let's marry as soon as possible." My face fell. "Oh. What are we even talking about when so many things are happening? We are speaking of our felicity when Aunt Anabelle is perhaps struggling most terribly."

Andrew let out a breath. "I know. It is just that there isn't much we can do at this point. And since we are alone, I wanted to make sure we had an understanding. Is that so wrong?"

I kissed his cheek. "I suppose not. But we should go out and see if we can help somehow."

His hand held me back. I looked at him and saw a longing there that I wished to fulfill. But I could not allow myself to kiss him again when so much guilt plagued me. I wished to have such moments only when I deserved them. I could barely contain my joy in being engaged to Andrew as it was. If I gave in now, I thought I would come undone. I squeezed his hand, shook my head, and led him out of the room.

The ball seemed to be ending. The atmosphere did not seem cheerful, and I knew it had been my fault. I'd ruined Christmas for everyone—for the Alexander family and the entire village. Before I could find Lucy, she ran up to me.

"Have you seen Anabelle?" she asked in a panic.

My heart seized. "Has she gone missing?" I exchanged a wide-eyed glance with Andrew. "When?"

Lucy looked around before returning her attention to me. "Just after you left the portrait room, I think. The dowager went to Mr. Alexander's inn to meet his family, and Lord Bellingham has been searching for Anabelle ever since."

I went into action. "Let's split up. Lucy, you go through the ballroom. Send Bethany upstairs. Andrew and I will go to the gardens. Have Robert check the stables."

Lucy nodded. "Let's meet back here in half an hour if we haven't found her. If someone does not return, we will assume they've found her."

Andrew and I went outside and rushed through the garden mazes. It was dark out, but the moon reflected off the snow and made it easy to see everything before us. We were out of breath after we checked the whole of the gardens. "Where could she have gone?" I asked him.

After a moment of thought he snapped his fingers. He turned to me with wide eyes. "Bellingham Cottage. She could have gone there to be alone. Come on." He took my hand, and we hurried to his home.

When we arrived, the wooden gate was open and a candle flickered in the upstairs window. "She must be here," he said.

We entered the cottage and found the maid, Betsy, coming down the stairs. She confirmed that Aunt Anabelle was in her old bedroom. Andrew asked her to inform Lord Bellingham that his wife had been found. We went upstairs and found Aunt Anabelle sitting quietly on a bed draped with a worn quilt. The candle danced on the night table, casting shadows on the walls. She looked up at us when we entered.

Andrew rushed to her, but I stayed back. I felt ashamed to be in the same room as her. She, who was hurt most by Mr. Alexander's actions. She, who no doubt had been tortured these many years because of her memories of Mr. Alexander. Her eyes met mine briefly before focusing on Andrew.

"Annie, why on earth are you here? Your husband is frantic, searching for you," Andrew said.

Aunt Anabelle's mouth opened in an O. She took Andrew's hand. "I didn't think . . . should we send someone to tell him where I am?"

"We already did," I assured her. "Betsy went to tell everyone not to worry. I am certain Lord Bellingham will be here soon." I almost regretted speaking, but after Aunt Anabelle watched me for a moment, I decided to broach the expanse between us. "Aunt Anabelle, I cannot tell you how sorry I am for inviting Mr. Alexander to the ball. If I had but known of the true situation, I would not have ventured to do it without speaking to you. My actions cannot be excused, but my ignorance and naivety are the only excuses I have. I do not expect your forgiveness right away—"

"You have it," she said quickly.

"You . . . forgive me?" I could not believe what I'd heard.

"Are you surprised? You must think I hold on to grudges, considering how long I've kept Nathan from Bellingham." Her tone seemed regretful. "I know your intentions were innocent and kind, Esther. Don't think I don't know you after all these years. You never do anything intentionally devious." Her small smile relieved most of my tension.

"Thank you," I said simply.

She nodded. "It is not as if I have not thought about reconciling. It has been so long that I'd gotten used to Nathan not being a part of our lives. Now that he's here . . . well, I suppose we'll see."

She sniffed, and Andrew handed her a handkerchief. "You are surely the most generous countess who ever lived," he teased.

She pushed his shoulder. "Oh, be quiet, you."

A loud noise came from downstairs. "Anabelle!" a male voice said. I heard footsteps pounding up the narrow staircase. Lord Bellingham appeared in a sweaty panic. His jacket had been discarded, his shirtsleeves had been rolled up, his cravat had been removed. "There you are," he breathed. He had eyes for no one but her. He sat on the bed next to her and pulled her into an embrace.

Andrew and I looked at each other and backed out of the way. I considered leaving, but one apology wasn't enough. I decided to find a moment to ask for forgiveness from Lord Bellingham as well.

"Have you been crying?" Lord Bellingham asked.

Aunt Anabelle sniffed. "I'm sorry to worry you."

"I'm not worried. I'm angry." A light laugh told me he did not mean it.

"I know, I know. I'm not supposed to cry without you."

Andrew and I shared a glance at their exchange; the way they spoke to each other could be comical at times, but it was clear they communicated well.

"Why did you disappear without a word? Did his reappearance shake you so badly?" Lord Bellingham asked.

She shook her head. "Actually, my heart aches for another reason." She took a breath before continuing. "I feel guilty for keeping him from his mother for so long. And . . ."

"You think he deserves our forgiveness?"

A moment of silence stretched, and I wondered again if I should leave. Andrew and I stood still, however, trying to be invisible.

"I think perhaps we are at fault for not giving him a chance to make amends sooner. Fifteen years is a long time, Peter. Have we been so cruel as to discount his suffering?"

He looked down and shook his head. "Anabelle, I don't know if I can forgive him."

She took his hands in hers, and he lifted his eyes to meet hers. She smiled softly at her husband. "Shall we try? Together?"

He nodded slowly. "If you think it's possible, we shall try." He turned his head and seemed to finally see Andrew and me standing there. "Thank you for finding Anabelle for me." He met my eyes, and I knew it was the time to speak. I stepped forward and looked at the floor.

"Lord Bellingham, I want to apologize for inviting Mr. Alexander without understanding the situation. I have caused pain for you and Aunt Anabelle. It was never my intention to bring back painful memories. I'm truly sorry." I kept my eyes down and pressed my lips together as I waited for his reply.

"Esther, look at me," Lord Bellingham said. I lifted my gaze to his. He regarded me with calm sincerity. "Your choice to bring him here was a little naive. But we all agree that you meant well. I am not angry with you. Why don't you and Andrew return to the house now. We'll stay here a while longer."

I dipped into a quick curtsy. "Thank you, Lord Bellingham. We'll leave you two alone. Come on, Andrew."

As the door closed behind us, I heard them begin to pray, and I motioned to Andrew to head down the stairs.

We walked in silence outside before he grabbed my hand. I turned my head to find he was watching me. I smiled slowly. "What?"

"I think this is the first time I've been this aware of how beautiful you look in the moonlight."

My smile would not be hidden, so I turned my face away. "You have not been looking at me in that way for very long," I teased.

Was he truly not going to comment on that? I looked at him again. He faced forward, a smile on his lips. How long *had* he been in love with me? I tugged on his arm. "Will you not tell me how long?" I asked.

He shook his head, grinning. "Let's get back and help with the end of the ball."

So we returned to the manor house and assisted Katherine and the admiral with tidying things up and saying farewell to the last few guests. It had been a tiring day. Once everything was in hand with the servants, Andrew made sure I retired to my room before he left with his parents to return home.

I fell asleep as soon as my head hit the pillow and dreamed about what tomorrow might bring.

Chapter Fourteen

Christmas morning began with my door bursting open. Philip and Rene came in and jumped onto my bed, waking me up quite effectively.

"Happy Christmas," I said, smiling. They were too darling to resent.

"Uncle Nathan is coming! Uncle Nathan is coming!" They sang together.

"Truly?"

"Papa and Mama went to get him. They want him to come to breakfast," Philip said.

My heart soared. They had already begun repairing their relationship. Aunt Anabelle truly was generous. I did not flatter myself that it was my doing; her choice to forgive was due to her own charitable heart. This was a breakfast I did not want to miss.

I shooed the children out of my room so that I could dress for the day. When I entered the dining hall, I greeted its occupants as a whole and then took my usual seat next to Andrew. He grabbed my hand easily and held it underneath the table, as if we'd always been so affectionate and intimate. It felt perfectly natural, even if it did make butterflies take flight in my stomach.

Besides Bethany, who had returned to Satchell Cottage last night, we were only missing Lord Bellingham, Aunt Anabelle, and the dowager. All was quiet while we waited, until the entry door opened and voices echoed in the corridor. The remaining members of the Alexander family—and two new members, one of which was a lovely baby girl—entered the dining hall and were greeted warmly. After Lord Bellingham helped his mother and his wife sit to his right, he directed Mr. Alexander and his wife to take seats to his left. This was all done in stiff formality, and it felt rather awkward. But such was understandable in repairing a long-standing rift, I supposed. A servant came to take baby Amelia so that Mrs. Sarah Alexander could eat her breakfast more easily, but before she was taken away, the dowager offered to take the baby instead.

"Oh no, Dowager, you mustn't worry yourself," Mrs. Sarah Alexander said with sincerity.

"I wish to hold my namesake, Sarah. Do enjoy your breakfast while I enjoy spending time with her." She smiled fully at her daughter-in-law. "I am so pleased to have you here. Nathan seems to have been blessed with a kind woman."

Mr. Alexander took hold of his wife's hand, looking at her tenderly. "I have been blessed with much more than I deserve."

"It is simply because of the gifts you have given him," Mrs. Sarah Alexander said to her mother-in-law.

The dowager looked puzzled. "Oh? What gifts might those be?"

Mrs. Sarah Alexander looked at her husband and held out a hand to his face, as if to present him. "His impressively handsome visage."

A rumble of laughter filled the hall. I suddenly had a high respect for Mrs. Sarah Alexander. She not only seemed genuinely kind, but she knew just how to bring warmth to a room. From then on, things went much more smoothly. Before church, we spent time together in the drawing room. Baby Amelia was passed around the room so everyone had a chance to hold her. After my turn, I handed her back to her father while Mrs. Sarah Alexander told us about the Christmas traditions in their small London neighborhood.

"Nathan has created the tradition of reverse wassail, in which the vicar and local magistrate visit the home of the less fortunate and drink to their health. We give them a few pence each and sing carols." She grinned at her husband. "It was just one of the reasons I fell in love with him."

It seemed his time growing up in Bellingham had had a great effect on his leadership abilities.

The dowager pushed for more details about their courtship only to find that Mr. Alexander had waited years before accepting his wife's feelings for him. He had been so guilt-ridden that he had planned not to allow himself to marry. Eventually she had worn him down and helped him see that redemption was for everyone. During this story, Mr. Alexander didn't speak. Instead, he held and rocked his daughter and smiled at his wife when she met his eyes. I observed Lord Bellingham and Aunt Anabelle carefully and saw their reactions to Mr. Alexander change. Lord Bellingham's shoulders relaxed, and Aunt Anabelle's smile seemed less nervous. It was as if I were watching them forgive without words.

The walk to the chapel was familiar and comforting, and with Andrew by my side, it was as if nothing had changed. But I was ever so glad that everything had changed. The chill of the morning had little effect on us, due to the thawing of hearts.

When I entered the chapel behind the Alexanders, I heard much whispering and saw many wide eyes among the parishioners, but with Lord Bellingham by his side, it seemed no one questioned his brother's return too harshly.

I caught Sam's eye from his usual seat next to our father and Bethany. His expression hadn't changed since I'd last seen him. He was still angry at me, no doubt. I cast my eyes down. After all the hard feelings softening at Bellingham Hall, one would think it would be simple to repair the rift in my own family, but it wasn't. That only reinforced the realization of my own naivety at having believed I'd had the right to send that invite to Mr. Alexander.

When I looked at Sam again, I also caught my father's gaze and frowned. I hoped to convey an apology, but I knew it would not be enough. They both deserved a proper apology and heartfelt invitation to Christmas dinner.

At the end of the sermon, I touched Andrew's arm and told him I would go with my family to Satchell Cottage. He nodded. I said the same thing to Lucy, and she followed me. Having her with me would make this reconciliation much more possible.

Lord Bellingham and Aunt Anabelle, the dowager, and Mr. Alexander and his wife stood outside the chapel doors to greet everyone and wish them a happy Christmas. They returned with Andrew's family to Bellingham Hall to begin the Christmas festivities. I knew they would play snapdragon and make mistletoe boughs, as they did every year.

My family arrived at Satchell Cottage together, no one speaking a word. I stood outside as they all entered, cloaking myself in an impenetrable shield that would keep me from saying anything offensive or childish to Sam, and then followed.

We took our seats in the small room, and Lucy began speaking. "I have missed you all so very much." She took hold of my hand and Bethany's while smiling at our brother and father. "Is it not wonderful to be together again?"

Sam and Father made identical grunting noises. I almost laughed at how much they resembled each other, but the weight of my regret held me back.

I sighed. There was no need to delay. After everything that had happened with Mr. Alexander, I knew waiting would only make the divide between me and my own family members widen. Everyone gave me their attention. I met my brother's and father's eyes briefly.

"I know my behavior of late has not been acceptable. I never wished to disappoint either of you, and I did not want to make Bethany feel uncomfortable by forcing her to move into the manor house. I simply wanted to link my two lives."

"Then, you should have considered our feelings before making your choice," Sam responded harshly. I saw him glance at Lucy, so I looked at her too.

Our eldest sister pressed her lips together in disapproval. She didn't need to say a word for Sam to understand her reprimand.

He squirmed in his seat, not looking directly at me. He let out a breath. "I should not have pushed suitors onto you. You can find yourself a husband if you wish it."

"You don't need to worry on that account. I will certainly find my own husband." My smile grew too large, probably. Confused expressions crossed everyone's faces. "Thank you for saying that. I can understand you if you can understand me. We do not have to see eye-to-eye on everything to get along well." I met my father's gaze. "Papa, I hope you can forgive me for being disrespectful. When we last spoke, I made it sound as if I did not want you to come to Christmas dinner, which isn't true. I want all of us together on Christmas. The Alexanders want you there as well. Please, will you come?"

My father hesitated before speaking. "I am sorry as well. And we will come to dinner. I am sure there is a way to fix things with the villagers without separating ourselves from the Alexanders. Everyone knows they are generous people. I didn't mean to accuse them of anything."

Not for the first or second time that day, my heart swelled. Perhaps it was the season, but the amount of forgiveness and acceptance that was happening at Bellingham seemed nothing short of a miracle. We stood, and one by one, we hugged each other. Things would come between us and we would continue to have disagreements, but as long as we pushed aside our pride and attempted to understand and accept one another, every rift was reparable. That was the essence of family, a lesson I'd finally learned after seeing the Alexanders forgive each other. It took humility, but it was worth the inner struggle to create a more harmonious family.

Chapter Fifteen

At last, the final members of the Bellingham Christmas dinner party arrived, and we gathered in the dining hall. I looked around the table in awe. There were so many people; I couldn't believe we all fit. Whatever disagreements existed between anyone didn't affect the joy of the party.

After dinner we gathered in the music room. I'd assigned a few songs to Aunt Anabelle and Lord Bellingham—they loved singing duets together—and the dowager, too, played a Christmas song on the pianoforte. Then it was my turn to entertain. I played the violin and the lute, then a final song on the pianoforte that encouraged all to sing along. The children clapped and sang while running around together, making everyone laugh.

After the musical concert had commenced, we retired to the drawing room. A roaring fire had been built in the hearth, and we all gathered to tell stories. Before the first story could be told, however, Andrew entered the room with a large package. "I hope you can all forgive me, but I have a surprise for Esther."

Every head turned to watch my reaction. Surprise and pleasure and something like embarrassment were probably evident on my face, because laughter rippled through the room. Lord Bellingham allowed it with a wave of his hand, smiling.

"Is this the aforementioned *perfect* Christmas gift?" I asked, laughing.

Andrew grinned and kneeled in front of me, placing the poorly wrapped gift in my lap. I sent him a curious look before tearing it open.

I gasped. "Oh, Andrew. It's beautiful!"

It was a French mandolin—a beautifully painted one. I traced the colors on the face of it. Blue and white flowers were painted around the sound hole, and green vines with leaves encircled them, trailing around the neck. "I love it." He truly knew me.

He straightened his shoulders to boast, "I painted it myself."

I laughed and pushed at his shoulder. "Liar."

Andrew laughed and held out his hand to take the mandolin from me. "Maybe I didn't paint it, but I did write a song for you."

I let it slip from my fingers into his. The idea that he'd written a song for me left me speechless, and I could do nothing but stare at him open-mouthed.

When he began playing clumsily, it was only the two of us in the room, as if everyone else faded from view. Andrew could not look at me for very long before he had to focus on the strings, but when he did meet my eyes, my stomach flipped with pleasure. He began to sing, and the words had me falling in love with him all over again.

You never knew, did you?
You hadn't a clue.
My heart has been yours all along,
So I have to declare it using this song.

Esther, I love you.
Esther, I do.
The time for us has come,
Now that I am home.

Will you give me your hand?
Will you make my life grand?
Will you give your heart to me?
Will you spend your life with me?

His eyes glistened with tears, and despite—or because of—his amateur lyrics, it was the most beautiful song I'd ever heard. His pure, honest feelings were laid bare for everyone to see. I pressed one hand over my heart, and the other touched my mouth to hide my enormous smile. He finished and stood, holding out a hand to me. I took it, standing, and when he placed his hand around my waist to pull me closer, he turned to the room and announced our engagement.

I laughed, everyone cheered, and I allowed Andrew to kiss me chastely in celebration.

* * *

"So you have loved me all along?" I asked him later, after most of the others had gone to their respective homes and rooms. We were sitting close together in front of the fire. His arm was securely around my shoulders, and he pulled me in to kiss the top of my head.

"I have loved you from the very moment I understood what love was."

His answer had me staring up at him with puzzlement. "How long ago was that?"

He looked up in thought. "Do you remember the fishing book I gave you for Christmas that one year?"

I nodded.

"Well, there was a purple flower—"

"Pressed into the pages." I sat up straighter and turned toward him. "We were only seventeen."

He shrugged and avoided my gaze shyly.

"You . . . you've loved me since we were seventeen?" I laughed. "You are playing me for a fool again."

His laughter came out nervously. "If only."

"It doesn't make sense. You are not one to hold back your feelings. Why did you wait so long to confess?"

"I may be careless with everything else, but I loved you enough to wait until you saw me the same way. Not to mention I needed to wait until we were at an age that we could consider marriage. I knew we would be separated for some years due to schooling and training and my Tour. There were many things holding me back from telling you sooner."

"How careful and mature you are about matters of the heart." I held his hand. "And how disappointed you must be that I did not love you until I saw you again in London a few days ago."

He laughed loudly, breaking the peace of the room. "If you think back, you will realize you've loved me much longer than that."

"Hmm. I'm not so sure." I laid my head on his shoulder again, enjoying our closeness and the knowledge that he had loved me for years.

I had so much affection to share with him, and I hoped to have enough time to show him just how much I loved him before he left for training after Twelfth Night in one week.

I pulled him into a dimly lit salon and wrapped my arms around his middle. He held me as well, first resting his chin on my head, then burying his face in my neck. We breathed each other in, and before I knew it, we were kissing. This time we began learning every facet of each other's desire. He enjoyed it when I wrapped my arms around his neck, and I loved when he held my face in his hands. He sighed when I touched chest, and my breath caught when he kissed my jawline. It was time to see him out to return to Bellingham Cottage, but that we would be able to enjoy this closeness for the rest of our lives brought every pleasant emotion swirling through my body and mind. This was perfect happiness; this was pure joy.

This had been the most beautiful Christmas Bellingham had ever seen. Of that, I was certain.

The End

About the Author

Katie Stewart Stone is an Austen enthusiast, a blogger, a journal writer, and a wife and mother. With her debut work, *Coming Home to Bellingham*, Katie achieved a lifelong goal of finishing and publishing a novel. She writes what she wants to read and rarely reads anything without a good romance. Katie graduated from Brigham Young University in 2012 with a bachelors in therapeutic recreation and spent six years working in the nonprofit world while writing on the side. When her beautiful boy was born, she quit her day job and committed to finishing her first Regency novel. Now she is a stay-at-home mother with two remarkable children—both named after Austen characters—and is continuously working to become a better writer.

Learn more about Katie at absolutelyausten.com and follow her on social media.

Facebook: Katie Stewart Stone

Instagram: @katiestewartstone_author

OTHER COVENANT BOOKS AND AUDIOBOOKS
BY ANNEKA R. WALKER

Standalone Regency Romance

Love in Disguise

Refining the Debutante

Contemporary Christian Romance

Brides & Brothers

Matchmaking Mamas Series

Bargaining for the Barrister

An Unwitting Alliance

A Gentleman's Confession

Rules of Matrimony

Enchanted Regency Romance Series

The Masked Baron

The Dreaming Beauty

The Lady Glass

Novellas

"Lord Blakely's Gift" in *A Hopeful Christmas*

"Healing Hearts for the Holidays" in *Meet Me under the Kissing Bough*

"A Season to Love" in *The Holly and the Ivy*

"Christmas in Amorwich" in *A Christmas Serenade*

Christmas in Amorwich

ANNEKA R. WALKER

Chapter One

December 1814
Amorwich, Northamptonshire, England

Amelia Park was the only member of her family who did not associate Christmas with romance. Such a silly belief had been expunged from her mind after the previous Twelfthtide season, but she wagered her dear sisters-in-law and their sister Alice would attempt to convince her otherwise over a steaming cup of tea. Why else had they cornered her in the morning room on the first of December like giddy schoolgirls initiating her into their secret club?

Ivy had had a footman drag one of the stately mahogany elbow chairs from beside the fireplace right up to the tea table. She was the obvious ringleader, a true baroness, but Julia and Alice, in their inconspicuous places on the sofa to the side of her, were guilty nonetheless. Amelia saw right through their sidelong glances and knowing smiles.

"More tea, Amelia?" Ivy hovered with the blue floral teapot—Amelia's mother's favorite. Two cherry-auburn ringlets fell onto her cheeks, framing her calculating eyes.

Amelia's brow furrowed. "Why do I have the feeling I should say no? I've seen that look before. What are you scheming, Ivy?" Ivy had single-handedly reformed Amelia's grumpy older brother Curtis into a generous baron, and she never passed up a project. If Amelia was not careful, she would be Ivy's next undertaking.

"I don't know what you could mean." Ivy went ahead and refilled Amelia's teacup. "We only desired a morning with just us ladies. Isn't that right?" Ivy looked at her sisters, Julia and Alice. The three redheads exchanged more secretive glances.

Very well. If Ivy wouldn't tell her, Julia would—she was honest to a fault. "Tell me plainly, Julia. What is this about? Why is Ivy looking at me like she wants to fix me?"

"She doesn't want to fix you," Julia hedged, her hand absently going to her much darker auburn curls while she attempted but failed in her dishonesty. "Not *exactly*."

Alice snorted. All eyes turned to the youngest Hunt sister—the only woman in the room Amelia was not related to since Amelia had run out of brothers for her to marry. Alice's hair was the boldest red of the three sisters', but that was not the only reason Alice stood out. She had the best of intentions but a rather unique way of going about life.

"Alice?" Amelia prompted. "Please, tell us what you find so humorous."

"Don't say a thing," Ivy warned.

Alice grinned at her sister. "Amelia is an intelligent woman. I don't have to say anything for her to be suspicious."

Amelia cast her gaze to the ceiling. So much for hoping for a direct answer. "This had better not be another lecture on your mad ideas about love and Christmas miracles. You know I don't believe in such nonsense."

Not anymore, at least.

Not after her last holiday with the Brookses, when Noah had led her to believe he felt more for her than he really did.

"It isn't nonsense." Alice pointed a biscuit at her. "Three impossible marriages three years in a row, and all at Christmas. They were genuine Amorwich Christmas miracles. It's liable to be your turn next."

Amelia ignored her passionate friend and looked at Ivy, the instigator. "You cannot mean to try to persuade me again. If it hasn't happened yet, it never will." She had loved Noah since they were children, having fallen for him over their many summer visits to each other's homes. But no longer. She had given up on unrequited love. Especially since he was now in love with someone else.

"You're right," Ivy said, running her hand along the edge of the red seat cushion. "I have far too much on my schedule to convince you to believe three *very* true stories. However, I do have time to talk about a more pressing matter. I wondered if you might tell us what transpired last year at the Brookses' estate that sent you home upset."

How had Ivy read her thoughts? "I don't know what you could mean."

"You chose to forgo your mother's elaborate Christmas ball two years in a row so you could be with the Brookses. Only, this year, there was no petition made for you to leave. Something happened that you will not breathe a word of; I am certain of it. And since you haven't been home with us for the holidays for some time, we do not want to repeat anything that might upset you."

While Ivy loved a project, Amelia hated being one. She was managing very well without dredging up bitter memories. "Last Christmas?" She tapped her pursed mouth and tried to appear as if she were recalling a lost memory. "I fear I can barely remember the holiday. So much has happened since then. My mind is all but consumed with thoughts of—"

"Of Mr. Wilson, we know," Alice interrupted. "You long for January when you might return to London, where he is sure to propose marriage."

"Exactly," she said. Mr. Wilson was a safe, unexcitable, steady choice—unlike another gentleman she knew.

"Alice," Julia censured. "Be nice."

"How is it that no one will say what is meant to be said?" Alice retorted.

Amelia pointed at Alice. "Indeed. What is it that no one will say, Alice?"

"Nothing about Mr. Wilson," Ivy said quickly. She motioned to Alice's plate. "Eat another biscuit, Alice." When Ivy met Amelia's gaze again, it took a moment for her to school the annoyance from her features. "We know you cannot have forgotten the holiday last year completely, but we understand if you do not *trust* us enough to confide in us."

"What she means," Julia rushed, her tone soothing, "is that you don't have to tell us, but we are ready to listen when you are ready to speak. We were merely surprised when you announced you would not be joining the Brookses for Christmas this year. You have always loved being at Lord Gladford's home."

Amelia took a long drink from her teacup to hide the sudden swell of feelings flooding over her. So much had changed because she had given herself false hope, and the damage could never be undone. After all these months, the ache was still too familiar, too raw.

Ivy raised a curious brow. Drat her observant manner. "In Lady Gladford's last letter, she mentioned they would be hosting Rachel and her new husband this year." Clever Ivy. She was watching for Amelia's reaction.

But Alice was right. Amelia was on to Ivy, and she kept her face impassive this time. "Indeed, I heard the same from Rachel. The household is sure to be as merry as ever with a pair of newlyweds." Rachel was Lord and Lady Gladford's daughter and Amelia's dearest friend in the world. Amelia was sorry to miss seeing her, but it was extremely necessary to avoid seeing Rachel's brother. Another long drink and her teacup was empty all too soon.

Ivy did not appear satisfied. "Rachel's *brother* will be at home too, of course. Lady Gladford also mentioned in her letter that Mr. Noah Brooks is as unattached as ever."

"Oh?" Amelia feigned disinterest but mumbled under her breath, "Not for long."

Ivy didn't hear her. "Rumor has it Mr. Brooks will not remain a bachelor for long. She said the entire female population of Lincolnshire rejoiced when he did not go to London in the spring, anxious as they were to keep him for themselves. But that isn't the best part. Lady Gladford writes that Mr. Brooks is determined to marry *very* soon. I wonder who will catch his fancy."

Her words poured like salt over a festering wound. Hearing that Noah was surrounded by flirtatious young ladies with the ambition to marry did not surprise Amelia. He was driven, smart, and more handsome than was decent. What woman wouldn't be drawn to him? But the mention of his determination to marry felt like his affections were irreversibly final. He would marry, and Amelia would not be his bride. Her heart twisted inside her, stripping back her calm facade. She bit back her sadness, replacing it with anger. Anger at wasting years of her life pining for a man who would never ask for her.

She set her teacup down, clinking it against the tray, and stood, her nerves simmering. "I don't care one whit what Lady Gladford has to say about her son. He can be the favorite of the country, but he will *never* be a favorite of mine. Good riddance to him, I say."

A knock rapped on the open door behind her, and all eyes, including her own, whirled in the direction of the sound.

Amelia gasped.

Her brother Esmond had his usual knowing grin on his face, but it wasn't him who drew her eyes. It was the man beside him. Noah Brooks folded his arms across his broad chest, his athletic legs taking a defensive stance. His sandy hair was thick and finger-combed, like he had just removed his hat. His skin was much too golden for this time of year, and his jaw too firm for his usual demeanor. But it was his eyes that arrested her own. Those intelligent, keen eyes that absorbed life like a textbook. Under his raised brow, that ocean-blue gaze, filled with confusion and hurt, met hers from across the room. He looked as if she had slapped him.

"Surprise," Esmond said, incapable of sensing the mood hovering around him.

Amelia swallowed and gave a quick curtsy. Her weak heart had secretly longed to see Noah again, but her rational mind dreaded it above all else.

Regardless of what was wise or not, he was standing in front of her. "W-What are you doing here?"

"Curtis and I invited Noah to stay for the holidays." Esmond spread his arm around Noah's shoulders. "It's dashed hard to get away anymore, so it was necessary to bring him to us."

Amelia's fists tightened as she fought against the heat scorching her cheeks. An entire month stuck in a house together? Once, such an arrangement would have thrilled her to no end. Now it sounded like a nightmare. "No one thought to mention it to me?"

"I can see why," Noah said. "Since I am no favorite of yours." Any jest in his tone fell flat.

Drat! He had heard everything she had said. Why had she not managed her feelings better? For an entire year, she had kept her heartache bottled inside, refusing to admit she had ever thought of Noah as anything other than a dear family friend. That she had ever thought herself capable of attracting his attention was laughable now. But he *had* led her to believe otherwise.

She hid her fists in the fold of her skirt. "You mistake me," she stammered. "I merely meant I do not have any interest in whatever courtships you have embarked on, as it is none of my business." She cleared her throat, stalling for words. "Of course you are always welcome here. You are practically family." She finished the most awkward speech of her life with a tremulous smile, but one corner of her mouth refused to lift properly, giving her away.

Ivy came to her rescue, jumping to her feet. "Mr. Brooks. You have arrived several days earlier than expected."

"Lady Blakely." Noah seemed to see Ivy for the first time. His features softened into a smile—one far steadier than Amelia's—and dipped into a bow. He had always had excellent manners. "I pray you will forgive the inconvenience. My father did not have any business left for me to complete, so I thought to extend my time here."

"It is Ivy, if you please. If we are going to spend three weeks together, I cannot be called the same name as my mother-in-law from morning until night. It is entirely too confusing in company as it is. And we would never regret a few extra days of your company, Mr. Brooks."

"I thank you. If we are dropping formalities, please call me Noah."

Ivy nodded. "Come. We will get your room ready for you in a trice." She gave Julia a pointed look before ushering Noah into the corridor. He took one last look at Amelia before disappearing.

She could have sworn he looked regretful, but she doubted it was because of any of his own behavior. He was hurt that she, his longtime friend, had said such terrible things about him. She could see it in his eyes. Well, no one was sorrier than Amelia. She wasn't usually a spiteful person. Just recently. And just when it came to him.

Julia sent Esmond, who had lingered behind, a scolding look for his part. An immediate expression of contrition followed on his face. If only Amelia had the same effect on her rascal of a brother as his wife did. Her own glare was far more extreme with significantly inferior results. Julia shoved Esmond out the door and shut it behind him before turning to face Amelia. "I am so sorry, Amelia. We had thought to warn you over tea. You were supposed to have a few days to warm to the idea."

A shaky breath pulled from Amelia's chest. "Then, you guessed what happened last year? Is that why no one wanted to tell me earlier of his coming?"

Julia bit her lip and gave a slow nod.

"We weren't positive," Alice explained. "Ivy said you were excessively happy before you left last December but that you arrived in London at the beginning of the year quite despondent. She said that after spending a few months acting rather heartbroken, you threw yourself into the Season with reckless abandon, flirting with every man who smiled at you."

"Alice!" Julia chided. "Must you be so frank? Forgive her, Amelia. She means well; I promise."

Amelia let the truth sink in. Ivy was right. Alice was right. They all were right. But not one of these three sisters was going to make a project out of her. She cleared her throat. "Fortunately, I met Mr. Wilson. He helped me root myself once more. I daresay we will be wed by spring." The words came out stilted, and neither Julia nor Alice appeared to believe her.

She believed it though.

She had to.

Otherwise, she was doomed to have the worst Christmas in history.

Chapter Two

Noah's mind reeled. Not in a million years had he expected to hear Amelia slander his name. Her brothers might have invited him here, but he had come all this way to see her. She was the woman he intended to marry. How had he misjudged their relationship so completely? Or perhaps he should say friendship, for he had not won her heart yet—that much was painfully obvious.

He followed Esmond mechanically into the billiards room.

"I know that look." Esmond handed him a cue. "Your early arrival isn't putting us out. When Curtis returns from his ride to town, you will see he agrees."

Noah grabbed a piece of chalk and rubbed it on the end of his cue. "Not everyone is pleased."

"You mean Amelia? She didn't mean anything by what she said. The women had her cornered again. I love the Hunts, especially my wife, but they haven't let Amelia breathe these last few weeks." Esmond smoothed his hair, but the persistent cowlick above his forehead kept his dark hair pressed up in front.

Noah couldn't believe Amelia had blurted those words only to defend herself. They had been delivered with far too much passion. He wanted to hear out Esmond anyway, in hopes that there was an explanation. "What is their intention with her?"

"It's Christmastide. What else?" Esmond took the first shot, sending a ball flying into the pocket.

"I don't take your meaning."

Esmond froze, still bent over the table. "You're fooling, right? You mean Amelia has never told you about the Legend of Amorwich?"

Noah shook his head. Was this legend particularly meaningful to Amelia? He'd thought he'd known everything about her, but he was beginning to think he didn't know her at all.

Esmond straightened. "It will be my honor to educate you, then. I thought it was a coincidence when Julia and I fell in love over Christmas exactly a year after Curtis and Ivy did. But after the vicar and my sister-in-law Alice fell in love at Christmas too, I began to agree with the Hunt sisters that something strange was happening here. They kept calling it another Christmas miracle. All of us began asking around and learned there is a legend behind the town's name."

"A Christmas legend?" Noah preferred facts to fiction and couldn't wrap his head around it.

"It's as true as I am standing here," Esmond said. "I have only learned bits and pieces. The gist of it is that if a worthy couple can find each other in Amorwich during the holiday, true love will blossom between them, and their union will prosper forevermore."

Noah squinted at the table. "And you think Amelia is next?"

"Curtis and I have our own reasons for wanting you here, but I imagine our wives have a different scheme entirely." Esmond wagged his brows, letting Noah's imagination fill in the gaps.

A Christmas legend wasn't going to solve his problems. "It's a nice story, but hardly believable."

"I believe it." Curtis entered the room and put his arm around Noah, slapping him on the back. "When did you get here? I did not expect you until next week."

Noah grinned, relieved to see that at least the men were glad to see him. "Not a half hour ago." They were all tall, but somehow the easiness between them made him feel like they were small boys again, excited to spend the holiday together.

"Do you have a room yet?" This was the Curtis he knew, all business.

"Your wife set the housekeeper to it already. I am to be in the first room in the west wing."

"Excellent. Has Amelia seen you? We thought to surprise her."

"Oh, she was surprised, all right." Esmond's angular jaw tightened, as if to hold back a laugh. "Sorry, Noah. It's not at all funny. But I never thought to see the day when Amelia would be angry with you. She's always had a bit of hero worship where you are concerned."

Noah glowered. "Your words aren't comforting."

Curtis's brow peaked in the middle. "Ivy was most particular about surprising her, but I did not guess Amelia would be upset."

Noah sighed. "I am trying to decipher her reaction myself. Somehow I managed to offend her. By the sound of it, she was angry with me before I even arrived. I am lucky she did not insist I stay in the nursery with your boys."

Curtis leaned against the billiards table. "If you did not see her the entire year, how did you manage such a feat?" When Noah didn't answer, Curtis looked to Esmond.

Esmond only shrugged. "I haven't the faintest notion. Noah, do you recall anything?"

Noah went back to chalking his cue, though it was chalked enough. "I thought we parted on amiable terms on New Year's Day. Perhaps she was a mite subdued, but it had been a month of late nights and parties." He had wanted to propose marriage the evening before she departed, but he hadn't been certain Amelia was ready.

They'd attended a ball together last December, and Amelia had smiled and laughed with every gentleman who spoke to her. It was true, she had always been a bit of a flirt and had been quite popular amongst the *ton*. He was a witness to the many admirers she constantly drew and knew from Rachel that they meant nothing to her and that she'd later refused their offers of courtship. He didn't want to be another man she rejected. At the same time as he had been contemplating proposing, Father had been begging for help with a pressing matter of state. Noah had hoped that if he gave his father his focus for a year, Amelia would grow tired of such games and know her own heart.

He stared at the tip of his cue while Esmond took his turn. It had been the longest year of Noah's life. He did not regret helping his father, but his ache to be with Amelia had grown with every passing day. Now his only goal was to convince her to love him and him alone. Never had he expected to arrive and find she despised him. Had he mistakenly said or done something before she left? He didn't like thinking he had upset her in any way.

Or could it be the influence Mr. Wilson had on her? Noah couldn't claim a great acquaintance with the man, for he was far too dull-witted for his taste. He had not believed Rachel when she told him of Amelia's impending engagement. The notion was so completely ridiculous—their personalities so incongruous—that Noah had been more than a little upset.

There was only one match for Amelia, and it was him.

"Stop scowling," Curtis said, breaking through Noah's tremulous thoughts. "Amelia is a forgiving person and isn't one to hold a grudge. After a few days, everything will be set to rights."

"I hope so. I don't intend to be a burden while I am here."

"Not possible," Esmond said. "She adores you almost as much as she does your sister."

Had Esmond forgotten the anger in Amelia's voice? There was nothing adoring about it. Noah's plans to propose were once more on hold. He couldn't force her to care for him, but neither would he ever stop hoping. Christmas legend or not, he loved her.

Chapter Three

Amelia stepped away from the window where she'd been reading her letter in the early-morning light and set the folded parchment down on her dressing table with a groan. Rachel had kindly written to inform her of Noah's impending visit, only her letter had arrived a day too late. Amelia pushed aside her perfumes and hairpins and pulled out her writing box to pen a reply. Spreading a fresh paper down, she dipped her pen into the inkwell and vented all her feelings to her best friend.

Only you thought to warn me about your brother's visit. I am put out with my entire family. Of course, I cannot blame them completely for supposing I should be overjoyed to see a favorite family friend, especially when I did not take the opportunity to explain to them the events that transpired last Christmas. But neither can I humble myself to tell them the whole of it. Only you knew I had hoped Noah would form an attachment to me and how bitterly disappointed I was to leave without any promise from him.

I know you two have never been great confidants, but thank heavens you warned me that he might have feelings for another. Poor Miss Hampton. To think he went and stayed with her family again this spring and still no proposal was made. I have news that might surprise you to that end. Your mother writes that Noah is finally determined to wed. Perhaps Miss Hampton will become your sister yet. Having witnessed my humiliation last December, you understand why this holiday is doomed to be most uncomfortable. I wish he had not come. My heart still bears an aching hole I fear will not be filled until I am wed to another.

But never mind my woes. I want to hear all about married life.

Amelia penned a few more paragraphs before signing her name and blowing the wet ink dry. After folding the paper carefully and sealing it with a wafer, she went in search of a footman who could post it for her. She peeked around her bedchamber door to make certain Noah was nowhere in sight. Not the tiniest part of her desired to speak with him after her rude outburst yesterday. Her embarrassment was second only to the bitter frustration of being utterly undone by his presence. A year's separation from him had not been long enough.

The corridor was as silent as a tomb. She tiptoed past the family rooms, not caring to wake her mother or Curtis and Ivy if they were still in bed. Putting her back to the wall, she turned slowly onto the staircase.

"Ah!" she screeched, nearly colliding with Noah. She stumbled back, putting space between them. What were the odds that he would happen to be ascending the top stair the very same second as she was turning the corner?

Noah gave her a half smile, but wariness hovered about him. With only a foot between them, she could smell his familiar shaving soap—lemon mixed with sandalwood. Her eyes went naturally to his smooth, lean jawline.

"Forgive me, Mel," he said. "I did not mean to startle you."

Mel. No one but he called her Mel. In her vulnerable state, just hearing it did strange things to her. "You didn't startle me," she said, smoothing her skirts as if the motion would also smooth her nerves.

"Oh? Do you scream when you greet your other friends?"

She had made a sharp noise, hadn't she? "It depends on how you define scream. I would say it was more of an eek. I wasn't expecting to see you—er, anyone—on the stairs." She paused. "Not *never* see someone on the stairs, just not this second. You know, at the same time I was rounding the corner." She was blushing; she could tell. And rambling like a raving, mad baboon from the circus.

She had practically thrown herself at him twelve months previously, which had likely been a source of entertainment to him. It was shameful to be acting like a bashful schoolgirl. No wonder he had no interest in her.

"I have always preferred eeks to screams," Noah said. "I think this a very original place to meet, and the perfect place for a friendly little chat."

"Chat?" The two of them? *Alone?*

He gave a deep, exaggerated nod.

"No, thank you. I don't care to talk this morning." She pointed to her throat. "I am feeling a little parched. Dry throat." She tried to move around him.

Noah stepped directly in front of her. "I will accompany you to the kitchen for some water." A confident smile curled across his lips. "In case your dry throat prevents you from being able to ask for it yourself."

She glared at him. "I think I can manage on my own. Perhaps Esmond will speak to you. I thought I saw him ride over this morning, out my window."

Noah's hand rested on the newel cap at the top of the stair. "I've just come from speaking with Esmond, actually. He had obligations at Ravencross he had to return to, but he will come again tomorrow with Julia. I am free to speak with you at your leisure." Noah was a peacemaker, not unlike Julia, but he seemed determined to confront Amelia about yesterday. She could read his unwavering gaze even better than she could Ivy's.

"But I am not at leisure to speak just now." She held up the folded missive. "Forgive me, but I was just rushing off to post a letter. It's to Gwenyth Wilson. She is the sister to the man who has been courting me. Perhaps you know him. Mr. Harold Wilson III?"

Noah's jaw hardened.

It gave her an odd sense of satisfaction knowing she had caused a reaction in him. It wasn't much, unfortunately. Not enough to prove he was jealous.

He took one glance at her missive. "I don't know the Wilsons well, but it is quite clear this letter is addressed to *my* sister, Rachel."

She glanced at the address facing him and gave a sheepish laugh before tucking it behind her back. "Oh, I must have left the other letter . . . somewhere. Excuse me." She finally managed to get around him. "Let's finish this little chat another time, shall we?" Her voice held no sincerity, for she truly hoped that they would manage the entire month with a vow of silence between them. Was that too much to ask for?

With careful planning, Amelia managed to escape Noah all afternoon. Avoiding Ivy, however, had been a different story. She took her role as the new baroness of Fairmore very seriously and flitted about the house constantly, directing one task or another. Not even the nursery was safe.

"Are you hiding in here?" Ivy asked, lifting her toddler son onto her hip and kissing little Lewis on the cheek. Amelia already had her arms around baby Jonah and wasn't planning on sharing.

"I'm not hiding," she said defensively, although that was exactly what she was doing.

Ivy raised a knowing brow. "You cannot avoid Noah for long. Whatever happened between you two should be resolved. Curtis says that, despite the distance between your homes, your two families grew up quite close. You don't want to lose a relationship so precious to you."

It had been Amelia's most treasured connection in the entire world—even more so when Noah had begun making all sorts of excuses to be near her last December, wanting to spend his every second by her side. But it had only been a passing fancy, and now her unrequited love would taint their friendship with awkwardness. To think she had naively waited for him to come to London and propose to her. It was so humiliating; it infuriated her. How could he have taken advantage of her feelings? What did Miss Hampton possess that she didn't? Never mind. She didn't care to know.

She stared at baby Jonah's soft, sleeping features and sighed. "I'm still adjusting to the shock of his presence here. You should have told me sooner."

Ivy's brow softened. "You would have refused to let us invite him, and your brothers were quite set on it. I hope you will come to forgive me, for I did not mean to hurt you."

"I do forgive you. It would be selfish of me to keep the others from his company. But please, let me take this at my own pace."

Ivy smiled. "Of course. But if you need me, please let me know."

They spoke for a few more minutes, and Amelia steered the conversation to safer ground. She had become quite good at evading Ivy's prying questions over the last year, even if she was beginning to crack. Feigning indifference toward Noah would be her greatest challenge yet.

When dinner came, Amelia prepared to face her first task: surviving a meal in Noah's presence. By the time the family had gathered in the drawing room, she felt herself folding. One look at Noah dressed in his evening jacket and she was positively palpitating with nerves. Her hands were sweating, and her face flushed with heat. She was certain the entire room could see how he affected her.

At the announcement of dinner, Noah crossed to her and stuck his arm out to escort her into the dining room. The action was so natural, as if he had been leading her to dinner every night for months on end, though he hadn't been anywhere near her in a year. He had been by Miss Hampton's side instead. Amelia stared at his arm. Mere feet separated them from where they stood and the next room. Must she touch him to get there?

He raised a brow, challenging her.

She was afraid. Very afraid. But she hadn't been raised with two older brothers without consequence. A competitive spirit was trained into her, and a decent dose of pride. She took his arm and willed herself to survive the bodily response it inevitability brought. Internal butterflies had yet to kill a person—she set her free hand over her chest and swallowed—even if they did produce havoc on the heart.

Noah bent his head low by her ear, his whisper tickling her neck. "We need to talk, Mel."

Not this again. "Dinner is always informal. You may speak to me while we eat."

He gave a single shake of his head. "Privately."

She got lost in his intense stare for a moment, tripping over her feet. She'd thought she had recovered, until his hand covered hers on his arm to steady her. It worked for her suddenly awkward limbs but did the opposite to her mind. "I . . . I could speak with you in the l-library." Drat! Why had she said that?

"When?" He paused on the threshold of the dining room, waiting for her answer.

She thought quickly. She could sneak away from the family tonight and meet him there, but the idea of it vaguely resembled a romantic tryst, and she did not want her imagination to run wild. "How about before breakfast tomorrow, say seven? Curtis usually rides early, and Ivy goes directly to the nursery."

"And your mother?"

"She sleeps late and retires early. Since my father passed, she wakes often in the night, so it can be depended upon."

He gave a firm nod and led her to the dining table.

Amelia's appetite was ruined. How could she enjoy a meal when she had a meeting with Noah on the morrow? What on earth would he say to her? Whatever it was, she would never again let her imagination believe there was anything between them.

Chapter Four

Noah did not call his valet to dress him. He needed a task to keep him busy during the early hours of the morning until he could meet with Amelia. It took him four attempts to produce a limp cravat that wasn't crooked, so it might not have been the wisest decision. After dressing, he took up pacing until his small timepiece read the seventh hour. Silently closing his bedchamber door behind him, he made his way down the corridor, not expecting to meet anyone. His mood soared at the sight before him.

Amelia stood on the upper landing of the staircase again, unaware of his approaching steps. This time they were going the same direction. The symbolism did not escape him, and he would take it as a good sign. "Good morning, Mel."

Her eyes jumped from the carpet she'd been studying to meet his gaze, and her body went rigid. While he waited for her to decide whether she would greet him or flee back to her bedchamber, he soaked in her appearance. He'd always loved to look at Amelia, and today was no exception.

She wore a becoming lavender morning gown dotted with almost indiscernible white flowers. Her fine brown hair was pulled back at the nape of her neck in a simple knot, with two small tendrils curled in front to frame her slender face. There was a youthfulness to her petite features and build, but she had more intelligence than many mature members of Parliament. Some might overlook her, but Noah thought her the most beautiful woman of his acquaintance. Heavens, he had missed her. Missed speaking with her. Missed their adventures. Missed it all.

"Good morning," she finally eked out.

He smiled when she ducked her head, and he noted the sleep line tracing up her cheek and to the side of one eye. It was adorable. "Did you sleep well?"

"Mmm." She lifted her head, though her eyes did not focus on him again. "Is your room comfortable enough?"

He didn't nod right away, not that she would have noticed. She seemed caught up in her mind about something. The Amelia he knew did not waste time carefully exchanging pleasantries if she could help it. She jumped into life, ready to take on the world. What had he done to upset her this much? When had she ever been uneasy in his company? She seemed intent on placing her attention anywhere but on him. He tested his theory. "I've been eaten alive by bedbugs, and my fireplace pours smoke into my room."

"I am pleased to hear it." Her voice waned as her gaze wandered down the stairs. "Wait, what did you say?"

He chuckled. "My room is excellent."

"Oh. Wonderful." She played with the sleeve of her dress, quite obviously dreading their private conversation.

It made him all the more eager to have it.

He motioned with his head. "Shall we?"

She gave a short nod and accepted his proffered arm. Neither said anything until they reached the library door. It was cracked open, and voices came from inside—one male and one female.

He pulled up short, not wanting to intrude if Curtis and Ivy were speaking together inside.

"Wendy, why are you pushing me away? We love each other."

Wendy? Noah hadn't meant to overhear, but he had no idea who Wendy was. He did, however, recognize the deep tones of his valet. When had Lawry fallen in love? They'd been here for *one* day.

Amelia tightened her grip on Noah's arm just as he tried to step back. He looked down to see her eyes wide. She mouthed three words: *My lady's maid.*

His own eyes widened in response. The two servants must have fallen in love during Amelia's visits to his home.

"Wendy, speak to me," Lawry pled again.

"We cannot be together, Lawry. We lead two very different lives."

"I can find work here, or you can come to live with me. I don't want to be apart anymore."

Wendy was silent again, but finally she responded. "I don't rightly know what to think. I'm not sure love is enough."

There was a rustle of movement from inside the library, and Amelia tugged on Noah's arm. They retreated quickly down the corridor, slipping inside the breakfast room, which was empty of family or servants. The savory smells of ham and eggs wafted from the sideboard toward them.

"Who is Lawry?" Amelia blurted.

This was the open, talkative Amelia that Noah was used to. "My valet. I suppose I did him a favor by not calling him to help me dress this morning."

"I did not wake Wendy either. She was not herself last night, and I thought she might be taking ill. It was a miracle I found a dress I could manage on my own. But never mind that. What do you make of this?"

"I think it's sweet."

"It could be . . ." Amelia raised one delicate brow. "But it doesn't sound like it's going smoothly."

"No." Noah sighed wistfully. "Love is fraught with hardship."

"I must agree. I adore Wendy, and I do not want to see her hurt." Amelia slipped past him to the sideboard and selected a plate. "I am surprised to hear you philosophizing about love though."

Her profile colored, and he knew the words were a slip of the tongue. "I think even I know a little of the subject," Noah said. He took up a plate of his own to keep his eyes from following Amelia's every movement. Admittedly his reading had never covered the topic of romance, but he had devoted time to learning about *her*. And studying Amelia had become his favorite kind of research. "Lawry is a good man. He deserves someone in his life."

"What about Wendy?" Amelia said, dropping a scone onto her plate. "If anyone deserves a secure and happy union, it is her. We are devoted to each other. No servant is more loyal or works harder."

"Oh? Are you that needy of a mistress?"

Amelia attempted to poke him with her serving utensil. She must have remembered she hated him, because she quickly withdrew the playful gesture. He could see the exact moment flash in her eyes.

She cleared her throat. "I am not so demanding as you might think. But Wendy is still every bit as good as your valet."

When they finished serving themselves, they sat across from each other at the table. He regretted not taking the seat beside her, but at least he could watch her better this way.

How he loved to watch her. The way her nose wrinkled when she laughed. The way her graceful movements were like a dance. Even the way she ate enthralled him. When he walked into a room, he swore her eyes brightened. Had he only imagined it? He'd spent eleven months wondering exactly that.

He wanted to talk to her about *them* and get to the bottom of her hard feelings—to learn whether she really did care for him. But she had to like him before she could love him. He needed her to warm to him again. "So what are we going to do about it?"

She blinked and swallowed her bite. "About what?"

"About us playing matchmaker."

She seemed to think on it. "I do wish for Wendy to find someone to take care of her for a change." She shook her head. "But she doesn't tolerate any nonsense. If the arrangement is not practical, she will not be interested."

Noah scoffed. "The Mel I know would have championed a love match." He was the one who would have hesitated, but it seemed their roles had reversed.

Amelia ducked her head, speaking to her scone and eggs instead of to him. "Love isn't always meant to be."

He leaned back in his seat, his own food forgotten. What had happened to give his bright, optimistic Amelia such a bitter mindset on love? Was that why she was settling for the likes of Mr. Wilson? Certainly the man had money and was a decent human being, but that was the summation of all he had to recommend him.

Noah lifted the pitcher of water on the table and poured them both a glassful. After taking a long swallow, he had an idea. "What about the Legend of Amorwich?"

Amelia scowled, but at least she was looking at him again. "Don't tell me my family has convinced you to believe a mere fable. I thought you had more sense than that."

They hadn't convinced him of anything, but he wouldn't admit it. For some reason, it suddenly seemed imperative that Amelia believe in the legend. If he ever hoped of having a second chance to win her over, he needed to prove to her that love existed—*their* love existed—and it was worth investing in. Even Parliament took the right kind of persuading before they ever passed a bill. This might be the only way to convince Amelia to be with him over Mr. Wilson. "How do you know the legend isn't true?"

"Because . . . because it's impossible."

"Come now, Mel. Wasn't it you who told me that no amount of book learning could teach me about the real world?"

She paused, her fork suspended in the air. "You remember that?"

"Quite clearly. I was poring through law books for a bill my father and I were writing. You said I was missing the most obvious part. You told me if I wanted to help my father, I needed to—"

"To get to know the people he was making the laws for," Amelia finished. She smiled—the first real smile he had seen since he'd arrived. His own lips tugged at the corners. She had a way of making him stupidly happy with one single grin.

"I think we ought to take a note out of your collection of personal philosophies and dig out the truth behind the legend." He held his breath, hoping she would take the bait.

Amelia's mouth morphed into a line of curiosity. "How? It's only a story passed down by word of mouth."

He thought for a moment. If he were to treat this as any other research project, it shouldn't be too hard. "Let's start with your brother Esmond."

Amelia snorted. "Esmond? Really?"

"No one knows his neighbors like a man who manages and farms his own land. Men like that need a different sort of connection from their neighbors—one more personal than that of an owner to a tenant."

"And you know this because . . . ?"

"Because I know Esmond likes to talk, unlike his sister."

Amelia slowly pushed aside her plate. "I suppose you've been waiting to speak to me about my rudeness when you arrived."

Noah nodded. "I think tomorrow should be soon enough."

"Really?" Her face brightened marginally. "How generous of you."

He shrugged. "I'm having a good day. The food is good—the company even better."

She shook her head, her smile peeking out. "Very well. Tomorrow when Esmond comes, we will ask him about the legend. But only because Wendy's happiness is my priority."

"Thank you." Playing his cards carefully was working. Today he would celebrate the small triumph that she had agreed to a project with him. Hopefully, searching for the legend would soften her toward him once more. He didn't want to wait another year to convince her to marry him.

Chapter Five

Amelia chewed on her lip while Wendy administered to her toilet the next morning, completely ignorant to the fact that Amelia knew about her secret love. Dare she admit what she had overheard? With hair the color of dried wheat and eyes as pale as a clear sky, Wendy was quite pretty. No wonder Noah's valet had noticed her. In the several years Wendy had been assigned to her as a lady's maid, Amelia had appreciated how efficient and caring she was, and they had become good friends. Selfishly, she didn't want to give up Wendy, let alone subject her to the risk of heartbreak. But even with Amelia's current hard heart, she could carve a slice of hope on Wendy's behalf—a hope that her maid might have a chance to experience a happily married life.

"Is something the matter, miss?" Wendy asked. "Can I get you anything?"

Amelia caught her own deep frown in the mirror, her bottom lip red from how she had abused it as she worried over Wendy's troubles. She immediately softened it into a smile. "Not at all." She only now noticed the light-pink ribbon Wendy had placed around Amelia's head to match her dress. "You have excellent taste, as always. Thank you." She paused, an idea coming to her. "Wendy," she hedged. "How is your family? I haven't heard you speak of them lately."

"Fraught with chaos, as always." Wendy clicked her tongue and added another hairpin to Amelia's coiffure.

The Clark family *was* a bit chaotic. And they exceeded the entire neighborhood in numbers. "How is your new little sister?"

"Plump and happy, that one." Wendy's gaze drifted, and she gave a hint of a smile.

"I cannot imagine having ten children." However did Mrs. Clark manage?

"'Tis a challenge. I am grateful your mother took me in when I was but a girl myself. I know the coin I send every week helps."

"No one is happier than I am. I love having you here." Wendy's response did make Amelia wonder though. Were Wendy's family obligations the reason she would not let herself marry Lawry?

Later that morning, she was still pondering about Wendy when she faced Noah again. Everyone had gathered in the drawing room for an impromptu invitation-writing party for her mother's Christmas ball. Mother never hired anyone to do her invitations, preferring to have her family do it instead. Amelia fingered the knot of the ribbon tied around her hair, suddenly thankful she had a pretty embellishment to aid her waning confidence. But even with the ribbon, it proved difficult to keep her feelings from showing with Noah so near.

Amelia approached Noah, Esmond, and Julia, who were crowded around a table that the footmen had brought in that was usually reserved for card games.

"Where are Curtis and Ivy?" Amelia took a seat at the table, purposefully leaving a chair open between her and Noah.

Amelia's mother took the open seat she'd avoided. "Curtis is occupied with estate business, and Ivy insisted on helping in the nursery, as little Lewis has come down with a cold."

"Poor Lewis." But how fortunate that they had excuses to be absent. She didn't dare say as much out loud and upset Mama. Not when she appeared more radiant today than usual. Her rich, dark hair had a shine to it, and despite the subtle dark circles beneath her eyes from many sleepless nights, her gaze was bright. Mama was noticeably happier tasked in her element instructing them all, particularly Noah, on the art of invitation writing. Amelia was glad to see her enjoying herself.

Mama leaned over Noah's card. "Oh dear. You're not improving. Perhaps penmanship is not your strongest suit. How about the women copy the invitations and the men seal and address them?"

Amelia tried not to laugh. She took up her pen and began copying the example her mother had made, using careful strokes, per Mama's specific guidelines, hoping no one would speak to her.

It worked, for a time.

Which meant she was bored and anxious. Sunlight poured through the large bay window, and she forced her gaze there instead of toward Noah. The image gave a deceptive picture of warmth when in truth the weather was cold enough to freeze the river down the lane and frost the tree limbs. It was a little like her own game of pretend, trying to smile and feign that her heart wasn't frozen over from the previous winter. Inevitably, her cursed gaze drew back to Noah when her mother posed a question to him about his family.

"Were your parents sorry to see you slip away for the holidays?"

Amelia pretended excessive interest on the paper in front of her again, but Noah's smooth voice had her complete attention.

"My family has Mr. Iverson, my sister's new husband, to distract them this year. I fear I would have been quite overlooked had I stayed. I am much better off here."

This made Amelia's smile slip out. Noah was not one to seek attention; his sister, Rachel, was the one who required doting. Still, his family depended on him more than he likely realized.

When she sneaked another glance up, her mother was grinning. "Well, we will not shirk our duty to you. Christmastide is very special at Fairmore Manor. You will not regret joining us."

Noah thanked her. "I have heard much about the magic of Amorwich at Christmas. In fact, Esmond told me the day I arrived about a holiday legend."

Her mother nodded, beginning another invitation. "I heard it a few times myself growing up, but not many believe in it these days. Though, I see my children are doing their utter best to resurrect it."

"Not trying," Esmond said, blotting some ink for his wife. "We are living proof of its existence." He reached over and captured Julia's free hand, planting a kiss on it. They shared a sweet, intimate smile.

"I would love to know more." Noah's gaze met Amelia's in a way that seemed just as intimate to her as her brother and his wife's touch. She willed the flutters in her stomach to still. Noah didn't mean anything by it. She had to resist whatever silly pull she felt between them, as it was entirely one-sided.

Mama blew on her ink. "I wish I remembered more of the story. Something about when the town was created."

"When was that?" Amelia asked, forgetting her decision not to join in the conversation. "Surely hundreds of years ago?"

"I regret I know more of England's history than Amorwich's." Her mother gave a sheepish shrug.

"I would imagine it is the same for most people." Noah stamped the official waxed seal of Lord Blakely—an elegant crest wreathed in holly—onto a finished invitation. "Someone in this town must know more about the legend."

"Esmond asked my grandmother at Ravencross about the legend just the other day," Julia said. "She said there have been plenty of accounts over the years of couples here finding love at Christmas. Grandfather once told her a saint passed through on Christmas Eve and gave a special blessing on the town."

"This gets more intriguing by the moment." Noah's eyes were alight. He loved learning, and his whole person became visibly excited when he discovered something new. Although, it usually related to history or Parliament, not silly legends. "Julia's grandmother cannot be the only elderly expert about the town." He rested his arms on the table and leaned over them. "Who else might we ask?"

"What about Mrs. Golightly?" Julia asked.

"She is old, but she did not grow up here," Mama said. "She moved here to live with her daughter after her children were all married."

"If we want someone older, what about Mr. Reed?" Amelia asked, tucking a curl behind her ear. "He is a knowledgeable man."

Her mother shook her head. "He *was* a knowledgeable man."

"Oh dear." Amelia covered her mouth. "I did not know he died."

Her mother gave a sad nod. "It's been two years now."

Amelia grimaced, and she noticed Noah attempting to hide his smile.

Esmond snapped his fingers. "What about Mr. Cunningham?"

"Oh no." Amelia groaned. She could already picture them asking the old codger about the legend and him responding by throwing them off his property. "He is a hermit who refuses all company. I would rather search the town records."

"Why not do both?" Noah asked. There was a twinkle of mischief in his eyes that she didn't trust. It was one thing to do research, as he was quite good at that, but Noah didn't know Mr. Cunningham like the rest of them did.

She shook her head. "Mama, you must forbid him. He has never been hit by an apple that Mr. Cunningham threw."

Noah held a question in his eyes, but she didn't plan on giving him yet another childhood story to tease her about. He would never understand how difficult it was for a girl to keep up with her brothers.

"That was a decade ago," Mama said. "But I must agree he isn't the most personable town resident."

Esmond nodded. "It might take some persistence, but if anyone knows anything about the legend, it'll be him. His memory is as sharp as the end of Grandmother Hunt's walking stick."

Amelia could only imagine how Esmond had been on the receiving end of that nice old woman's cane. There could be no doubt she and her brother were related. "Won't it be dangerous to be persistent where Mr. Cunningham is concerned?" She blew on another finished invitation. She wasn't scared of the old man, only duly wary of his temperament.

Esmond leaned back into his chair. "I've only spoken to him a few times, and he might have growled, but he didn't throw anything at me."

"He wasn't always so surly," Mama said, tapping the corner of her mouth with the end of her quill. "When his wife was alive, why, they used to throw the most delightful Twelfth Night party every year. He was a much softer man then. Now even I am a little intimidated by him."

"I can handle a little surliness." Noah straightened, appearing quite certain of himself. "Let's pay him a visit this very afternoon."

Julia frowned. "It does sound intriguing, but I must get back to my baby."

Esmond looked even sorrier. "And I promised to ride out with Curtis to check on the gamekeeper's roof."

"I cannot possibly leave until the invitations are finished," Mama said. "Amelia is free, however. Take Wendy with you as a chaperone. It isn't far, and I doubt the visit will be of a long nature."

Mother had mentioned time and again after Julia's wedding that a maid was not a proper chaperone. Amelia opened her mouth to remind her but stopped herself. The idea of a little adventure appealed far more than painstakingly copying cards—even if it involved the odious Mr. Cunningham. And surely a year of suffering had taught her not to bend to any senseless emotions after a short window of time in Noah's company. "I suppose I could spare an hour."

"Then, it is settled," Noah said, clapping his hands together. "I cannot wait to meet this intriguing man and satisfy my burning curiosity about this legend."

His eyes rested on Amelia, but it wasn't her curiosity that was burning. Under his steady gaze, there was no need for any fireplace. But she could do this. She could handle a simple visit with Noah. With a little safeguarding and carefulness, she could protect her heart.

Chapter Six

As the afternoon arrived, Noah eagerly prepared to immerse himself in the renowned Legend of Amorwich. He placed his hopes on the outcome, having arranged the carriage, warmed bricks for their feet, and even extended an invitation to Lawry to accompany them. He couldn't decide who was more surprised by his efforts: Amelia or Wendy.

He greeted the women before setting a casual hand on Lawry's shoulder. "Lawry is acting as a groomsman for our errand. Don't mind him."

Amelia speared him with a disapproving glare. When he assisted her into the carriage, she whispered, "You're being too obvious."

He couldn't help whispering back, "That's the plan."

Her glare melted into curiosity, but there was no privacy to continue their conversation again until they arrived at Mr. Cunningham's estate.

If a person could call it an estate.

The crumbling house was covered in slumbering ivy, its brown twigs like a suffocating blanket. A thin layer of crusted snow from the week before took away any chance of color, leaving the whole picture dreary and uninviting.

"I can't wait to go inside," Noah said, masking his misgivings with the overstatement.

Amelia saw right through him and chuckled. "All right, Mr. Researcher. Let's do our homework and get this over with."

He helped her down from the carriage but regretted when she pulled away quickly. "What is it? The apples aren't even in season. If Mr. Cunningham, kind man that he probably is, dares to throw anything at you, I vow to protect you." He crossed his heart with his hand. "On my honor."

"It is you I am worried about." She stalked toward the house, turning to say over her shoulder, "I hear that with every legend comes a curse. If the worthy find love, then the unworthy find heartache. I just hope you are prepared."

He hurried to catch up with her, leaving Wendy in Lawry's all too capable hands. "Such cynicism isn't like you."

She shrugged. "I was jesting."

"Were you?"

"Of course. If you did not notice, I am not exactly thrilled with this outing."

"It's not the outing, I wager, but the company. Amelia, you have been angry with me since I arrived. Now you are wishing me cursed?" Maybe he *should* have studied a few books on romance. He was clearly inept.

"I said it was a jest."

They stopped on the landing in front of Mr. Cunningham's front door. "Have I offended you?"

She looked ready to deny it again but paused, her expression turning serious. "No. You disappointed me."

Her statement made him trace back through time to the moment he'd thought he was going to propose, right after their midnight dance. A sudden thought struck him. Had she expected it? The idea shook him to the core. Her expression had always said how she felt before she ever opened her mouth. But this time it was hard to read her down-turned hazel eyes.

If she had expected a proposal, would she have said yes?

He sighed. Those walls she had erected like a fortress around her had at least lowered enough for her to admit this much. It was progress, even if it gutted him. If she thought he had toyed with her affections, he wouldn't forgive himself.

His worries were cut off when the door swung open in a rush of cool air. A man stepped forward. His gray hair was a half wreath around his head and bare on top. His clothes were ill-fitted and wrinkled, much like his rippled skin. His eyes were alert with intelligence.

"Mr. Cunningham?" Amelia gasped.

"What? You think I need a butler or some puny footman to open my door? No? Then you expect me to wait by the window until you knock?"

Amelia's mouth fell open. "Um . . ."

Noah stepped in. "Since Miss Park has been rendered speechless, I will introduce myself. I am Mr. Brooks, and you are Mr. Cunningham, I presume? I wonder if we might have a moment to trespass on your time."

"I don't care for trespassers." Mr. Cunningham started to close the door.

"Wait." Noah set his arm on the weathered wood. "It's about the Legend of Amorwich."

Mr. Cunningham paused only to shake his head. "Utter rubbish." He pushed the door closed again, but on impulse, Noah stuck out his boot and caught it. He couldn't risk ending this now. Not when he thought he finally knew what was bothering Amelia. This might be the surest way to win her back.

"Noah," Amelia begged from beside him, catching his sleeve in her hand and tugging at it.

"Of all the impertinent upstarts," Mr. Cunningham growled. "Remove your foot and be gone."

"Forgive me," Noah said. "I am in the middle of a very important project, and I must speak to you." When Mr. Cunningham moved the door tighter over his boot, Noah winced and added, "I will do you a favor in exchange for information."

"A favor?" Mr. Cunningham grumbled, releasing the door just an inch. "What kind of favor?"

"Surely there is something you need assistance with that a strapping young man and a particularly intelligent woman can be of help with." He glanced at Amelia and caught the beginning of her charming blush.

Mr. Cunningham studied them with a scowl before finally letting the door swing open again. "I suppose I have a minute. But just one."

Noah exchanged a startled expression with Amelia. Amelia waved Wendy to follow them in, leaving Lawry to help tend to the horses, and they let Mr. Cunningham lead them through his tomblike house. The corridors were dim from very few candles, and when they entered the drawing room, they discovered it chilled. Where were the servants to stir the fire?

Mr. Cunningham must have been thinking along similar lines. He pointed to Noah with a bony, crooked finger. "You there, Mr. Brown—"

"Brooks," Noah corrected.

"Brooks, then, tend to the fire. And, Miss Park, there is an old rag beside the box of tinder. Give the room a thorough dusting."

"Me?" Amelia's eyes darted to Noah.

Noah winked and gave his best nod of encouragement. Her gaze took in the musty room, and her nose wrinkled.

Mr. Cunningham was looking around the room too, but probably for more tasks to force upon them. "I suppose I ought to search out my cook in the kitchen and request some tea." With that, he exited the room.

Wendy busied herself with stacking a haphazard pile of books on a shelf.

Noah reached for some wood, but the box was empty. He would have to go in search of some outside. He did see the old rag, though, and picked it up. Amelia came up beside him, and he tossed it to her. She caught the filthy thing but quickly uncurled her hand and pinched it with two fingers instead.

He winked again, making her scowl deepen.

"This won't work," she whispered.

"It's worth a try."

"But I know Wendy's reasons," she hissed, loud enough for only him to hear, "and Mr. Cunningham won't tell us a thing that will help."

"Later," Noah promised, walking around her. He needed to find some wood, and he didn't want her to talk him out of staying. He had some walls to break down, and Mr. Cunningham was going to help.

There was no neatly stacked wood pile outside, but there were a few logs and an ax. He went straight to work, motivated by the chill in the air, and replenished the pile. Even though he moved quickly, he worried he had stayed outside for too long. How was Amelia faring? Surely Wendy's presence was enough if Mr. Cunningham returned before Noah did.

Once his arms were full of wood, he made his way back inside. The drapes were pulled back, and Amelia was dusting the top of a small portrait frame on the wall while Wendy swept a little brush across the hearth. Mr. Cunningham was dozing on a mottled brown sofa, a teacup balanced precariously on his stomach.

"Where have you been?" Amelia hissed.

Noah placed the wood carefully in the box and selected a few logs for the fire. "Forgive me. I tried to hurry. Did you get anything out of him?"

She grimaced. "Yes, he ordered me around like a servant."

It took only a moment to get the fire started. Noah poked at it a few times until more of the tinder caught into a bigger flame. "I meant about the legend." As soon as he asked the question, the growing light illuminated a framed portrait of a young lady hung just above the mantel. The subject portrayed was a mature woman, likely in the middle of her life, with large brown eyes. By the style of her dress, Noah could tell the portrait had been painted at least twenty or thirty years previously.

Amelia's answer distracted him from his curiosity about the portrait. "He wasn't going to answer anything about the legend until the *favor* you offered was complete." She glanced at Mr. Cunningham, who remained fast asleep. "We might not get any answers from him at all."

"Why is that?"

Amelia's face softened into one of remorse. "While Mr. Cunningham was drinking his tea and directing me about, his maid whispered to Wendy that Mr. Cunningham let go of all the staff except her and the cook six months ago. He told them he planned to die soon and to find other employment. The whole house has fallen into disrepair since. He rarely lights a fire in any room and hardly eats his meals. I am not certain he will tell us anything when he so clearly wants to done with this world."

Noah didn't know the man, but he felt sorry for him. No matter how hard life was, no one should have to feel compelled to purposely cut theirs short. With Mr. Cunningham's cantankerous moods, he doubted the man had many friends either. Noah would have to think of how they could help him. He sighed. "Well, he is not going to die today. Not when we haven't had our chat yet."

He took the rag from Amelia's hand and motioned for her to sit on the sofa opposite the one Mr. Cunningham occupied. Then he put the dirty thing back where he had found it. "You sit too, Wendy," he instructed.

He made his way to Mr. Cunningham and removed the teacup before nudging him with his foot.

Mr. Cunningham snorted, and his eyes flew open. "W-What is going on? Who are you?"

"Mr. Brooks, if you recall. It is time for the little chat you promised us."

"Oh yes. The intruders." Mr. Cunningham looked around his drawing room, scrutinizing their efforts. "Very well. What is it you want to know?"

"What can you tell us about the Christmas Legend of Amorwich?"

"I don't know why you want to know about that," he grumbled.

Noah took a seat beside him. "We want to know every detail."

"It's been a while since I have thought about the story. The womenfolk liked it best, you know." Mr. Cunningham scratched his face. "It all started with the Morgans the first Christmas after the town was formed. I'd say it's been nearly two centuries since the Morgans ran away from their homes. Neither of their parents blessed their union, and they eloped to Scotland. It shamed their families, so they came here and built a home with few neighbors to call their own. But they rallied together to form a town and support each other. The Morgans were in love. They always are in the beginning. But the rash ones always pay for being impulsive."

"What do you mean?" Amelia interjected.

The man raised his brow. "Exactly what I said. After putting their funds into their home, the Morgans were as poor as orphans in a workhouse. But I suppose they were happy, ignorant as they were, because they had each other. Their first Christmas was destined to be a miserable one, with hardly enough money to put bread on the table. On Christmas Eve, a missionary passed through and asked for a place to lay his head for the night." Mr. Cunningham paused. "Well, that is all there is to it. The rest is history, as they say."

"What happened with the missionary? Did they let him stay?" Noah tilted his head, waiting for the answer.

"I never agreed to tell you every monotonous detail. I have things to do." Mr. Cunningham pushed to the edge of the sofa and with some effort made it to his feet. "You two go on home now and let a man take a proper afternoon nap."

"Mr. Cunningham," Noah argued. "We did as you asked in agreement for your cooperation."

Mr. Cunningham lowered his shrewd eyes. "Are you offering another favor, young man?" He shook his head. "I suppose you can come back tomorrow, and I will consider a trade again."

Noah met Amelia's incredulous eyes. She shook her head, begging him with her eyes to say no.

"We'll do it." Noah hoped he was doing the right thing. Two couples depended upon him. If he could convince Amelia to love him, then the road would be far simpler for Lawry and Wendy. Now he had to convince Amelia to do her part. By the fire in her eyes, it was going to take a lot of persuading. Strange, since it was generally *her* convincing *him* to do something new and exciting. But he could be resourceful when he wanted to be. And there was no better motivation than the lovely Amelia Park.

Chapter Seven

Amelia woke the next morning and immediately scowled. "How dare he!" She pushed the side of her face into her pillow. Why was Noah chasing information on this silly legend and roping her into spending more time with him in the process? She doubted the latter was intentional, but it was happening all the same.

She rolled out of bed and groaned, yanking on the bell pull for Wendy. So this was what an unjust prison sentence felt like. Did torturers ever try confining a heartbroken person with their unrequited love? They really ought to. It was the worst sort of punishment. And the dolt who had voluntarily imprisoned himself with her had no idea what he had gotten himself into.

Well, it was decided. She would decline joining him this time. He could clean Mr. Cunningham's house himself. She scratched the back of her neck, thinking of the odious old man and his musty house, only she could not conjure the same distasteful feelings as before for Mr. Cunningham. As the daughter of a baron, Amelia *had* been a bit spoiled growing up, and her view of him might be a tad colored. Her London Seasons had demonstrated her obviously sheltered youth and ignorance. Indeed, she had assumed Mr. Cunningham to be of decent means. His humble house had startled her.

He could barely take care of himself. And while she was put out with Noah and being forced to be with him, she did feel sorry for Mr. Cunningham. The rooms in his house had been so cold. Did he have enough to eat?

She poured water into the basin on her wash table and splashed away her thoughts with a good dousing in the face. Mr. Cunningham needed aid, but Amelia couldn't submit to her empathetic ways. It couldn't be her coming to someone's aid, not if it meant being in Noah's company again and again. Even if the tale of a runaway couple intrigued her, who knew how long Mr. Cunningham would string out his story and keep them tending to him?

Sliding into her chair at her dressing table, she brushed out her tangled hair, pulling the brush all the way to the curled ends at her waist.

Wendy came in a moment later with a muted, "Good morning."

Amelia glanced up at the uncharacteristic tone of her maid's greeting, startled to see the whites of Wendy's eyes red and the skin around them swollen. "What has happened? You've been crying."

"I did not sleep well is all." Wendy's expression pinched. She reached for Amelia's hair and began braiding it.

"It is plain there is more to it than a poor night's sleep. Is it your family? Your baby sister?"

Wendy shook her head, not giving an inch. "They are well enough."

Without asking more, Amelia knew Lawry was the culprit. She bit her tongue, forcing herself not to pry any further. Wendy could be frank, but she could also be private. She tried very hard to keep a proper line between mistress and servant, which Amelia did not always understand. More evidence of her small-town life.

By the time Wendy pinned the braid into a coil on Amelia's head, Amelia was ready to do anything to cheer her up. No one was more resilient than Wendy, and she was rarely upset. Amelia would even . . . even go as far as to meet with Mr. Cunningham again if it helped.

When she found Noah later that morning, he was resting on the edge of a ladder rung in the two-story library, flipping through a book. He looked comfortable despite the awkward seat he had chosen. She paused at the door. Her determination to refuse him had faded completely thanks to Wendy, and she mentally kicked herself all the way over to his side.

Noah looked up when he noticed her approach and grinned too warmly for someone who supposedly did not care enough to marry her. "In the mood for reading?"

She shook her head. "We need to talk."

His brow rose, and he snapped his book shut. "Really?"

"About Lawry and Wendy."

He sucked in his lips and nodded. "Certainly, if we can also talk about us."

"Us?" Why did the word set her heart pounding?

"We make a good team, you and I."

What was that mischievous glint in his eyes? She dared not read into it. "Team?"

His gaze turned studious, like it did when he was going over his father's parliamentary papers. "Remember the time when you convinced Rachel, Esmond, and I to search for treasure in Widow Walbridge's attic? You had the brilliant idea but a terrible plan that would have cause my poor neighbor to send the constable after us."

Amelia cringed. "Thankfully, you came up with the idea to sneak into her parlor window while she was out for calling hours."

"Exactly—your idea and my execution. Wouldn't you call that teamwork?" He stood and stretched his broad shoulders, putting himself much too close to her.

"One situation hardly qualifies us as such." She wouldn't be his favorite friend to have adventures with anymore. It would only make things harder.

He set the book down on the shelf next to him. "It wasn't just one time, Amelia. You helped me look outside myself. This year I was able to do better research for my father because of your advice. You heard he is in Belgium for a time, doing peace negotiations with the Americans? I spent time at the ports, Amelia. I spoke directly to our captains and heard their opinions of our wasted time, money, and valued men because of our interference with America. I believe my correspondence to my father has been of some help. We are so close to signing a treaty and having peace again."

Her eyes widened, and she briefly forgot what they were originally speaking about. "That's wonderful. I am so proud of you."

"I couldn't have done it without your guidance, Mel."

Amelia shrugged. "You had it in you all along."

He shook his head. "You inspired me, and lives will be saved because of it. And look at us now, trying to help Lawry and Wendy. Admit it. We are good together."

She swallowed. "I suppose."

He grinned, wide and full, his eyes arresting. "Good. I am glad we are on the same page."

They weren't on the same page at all. She had inspired his work but not his heart. But his smile weakened her knees and turned her insides to gooey porridge, preventing her from arguing.

"What was it you wanted to say about Lawry and Wendy?" he prompted.

Amelia struggled to find her voice. "Wendy comes from a large family. They depend upon their older children's incomes to supplement her father's. I fear Wendy will not accept Lawry on account of the duty she feels to her parents."

Noah rubbed his jaw.

Amelia had touched his jaw once before, and she could almost feel the prickles under her fingertips. Rachel had interrupted their near-kiss shortly after. Her head tilted as it had that night in the middle of an empty ballroom, Noah's closeness and that smile all too familiar.

"What are you thinking about?"

Amelia blinked and straightened her head. "Me? N-Nothing."

"You were looking at me like . . ." He dropped his voice and lowered his head. "Like you wanted to know just how good a team we make."

Her eyes widened with alarm, and her hands came up to his chest to push him away.

He caught them, holding them to his green satin waistcoat and temporarily paralyzing her. "Woah there. I can take a hint. You cannot fault me for hoping though."

"I wasn't hinting anything." She tried to pull back while she still had some sense.

He held tight. "If not a hint, how about an explanation? I wouldn't mind you telling me why I disappointed you. I have never wanted to hurt you."

"Well, you did."

"Amelia, I swear it. I care about you. Tell me what I have done so I might make amends."

Care? If he cared, then he would want more than flirtations between them. He had proven himself by not proposing. "I don't want to play games, Noah."

"Who said anything about games?"

He didn't have to say anything. She knew perfectly well that he had all the debutantes in Lincolnshire to choose from. She yanked her hands free and stepped back. "If you cared about me, why didn't you come to London to see me?"

He frowned. "I had a duty to my father and to our country."

And a duty to see Miss Hampton, she added silently.

He finally shrugged his shoulders. "I wanted to see you, but I thought some time away would help."

"Help what?"

"Help you learn your heart."

She stared at him, not knowing what to think or how to answer. "You *wanted* me to be courted by other men?" To fall out of love with him, no doubt. She shook her head. This conversation was only making things worse.

"Not at all. Why would I want that? I'm speaking of your tendency to flirt." Noah folded his arms, tightening the fabric on his jacket and making him look like a man not to be crossed.

But it had always been her specialty to cross him as a child, and this was not going to be the day she backed down—especially against an unfounded accusation. "Flirt? You mean, when I am nice to my dance partners and they interpret it as meaning I like them?"

"Yes! Maybe." He shook his head. "I didn't see it that way. I suppose that could be all it was."

The last thing she had ever wanted was to imply she had feelings for someone else when her heart had always been unequivocally Noah's. "Your brilliant logic fails to impress me."

He scoffed. "Well, it certainly wasn't to send you running to the likes of Mr. Wilson."

She folded her arms too. "I happen to like Mr. Wilson. He knows how to commit to a woman."

"Oh?" Noah's brow lowered. "Then, why hasn't he proposed?"

Amelia fumbled for an answer, but she didn't have one. Not a good one. Everyone knew he would propose when they returned to London. Curtis had said that several men had good money on it in their club books. It was a sure win. A guaranteed thing.

"Perhaps we should focus on Wendy and Lawry," Noah said rustling his hair and dropping his hands in defeat. "I never should have said anything about Mr. Wilson. I don't want to fight with you."

Her own ire softened at his contrite tone. "I think that would be best."

Noah blew out a breath, clearly frustrated. "Would you like me to speak to Lawry? To explain about Wendy's family?"

"I have already betrayed her confidence to you. There has to be another way."

"We can try Mr. Cunningham again. I am free for the afternoon."

Amelia had less faith in the legend than she did in her abilities to resist Noah, but she didn't like feeling so spiteful inside. "At least it's something."

Noah nodded. "In the meantime, we can keep thinking of other ideas. I'll call for a carriage."

Watching him leave the room deflated Amelia. Would that they could keep arguing until he admitted that he had used her ill. And then, of course, he would beg for her forgiveness, confess his love, and plead for her hand in marriage.

Her shoulders slumped farther. Such a conclusion would take a Christmas miracle. Could the Legend of Amorwich work for two couples this time? She almost wished Mr. Cunningham would tell her.

Chapter Eight

Noah had hoped Mr. Cunningham would pick up his story from where they had left off, especially after the way he had consumed the gingerbread they'd brought him. But the man's many years had clearly taught him to be cunning, if not manipulative. Which was how Noah found himself holding a stocking with holes in one hand and a needle in the other, a victim of free labor.

Wendy sat in a chair by the fire—a fire that was actually burning before they'd arrived—and Amelia on the sofa beside him. Both held shirts they were mending. He glanced from them to his stocking. No one had ever taught him to sew—it wasn't exactly a man's pastime—but how hard could it be?

He wasn't about to ask Amelia for help. He was feeling a little petty after their argument. If only he could get the thread through the needle, he was certain he could figure out the rest. Mr. Cunningham, of course, would be no help. Seated across from them, alone on the other sofa, the aging man was napping again with his hands over his stomach.

Noah glanced over to see if Amelia had threaded her needle yet.

She not only had it threaded, but she was nearly finished closing a small tear in the sleeve of the white linen shirt she was working on. She glanced up and sighed with heavy exaggeration. Taking mercy on Noah, she took the needle from his hand and slid the thread through the minuscule hole with ease. He accepted it with a gracious smile, but she glanced away before she could see it.

He stabbed the sharp point through the stocking and mimicked the ladies' back-and-forth motions. If he couldn't hear more of Mr. Cunningham's story, he could at least make the most of the opportunity to speak with Amelia.

"You know," he said, "I cannot remember a better Christmas than last year."

"Oh?" Her monosyllabic answer held no enthusiasm.

"Maybe it was because you were there." He waited for her to look at him. He had to know if she had expected his proposal. If she had wanted it.

He watched Amelia's creamy throat as she swallowed, her eyes intent on the shirt in her hands. "It cannot be that. I joined your family for the previous Christmas, and that one was not your favorite."

She was right about that. It had been a few years since Noah had first noted her as a woman. She had grown from the girl he'd teased with her brothers into a woman who was beautiful inside and out. Still, she was his sister's particular friend, and Rachel had made it clear for years that she did not want him butting into their time. It was not until last Christmas that he had acted on his attraction, unable to resist being near Amelia. She drew him to her with her bright smiles, engaging personality, and warm looks. His family already adored her, carving a place for her with them before he had even realized his desire to make it permanent.

"I suppose the other times we were together were enjoyable enough, but last year was special. Wouldn't you agree?"

One shoulder came up. "I didn't notice a particular difference."

He shifted closer, her vanilla and lavender scent teasing his senses. "We spent a great deal of time together. Remember how easily I guessed you in blindman's buff?" It had been this very scent that had given her away.

"I would not call that success overly memorable." She knotted her thread and snipped the remains from the shirt.

"Your work is impressive," he noted.

"Thank you."

"Just like your dancing."

"My dancing?" Finally, she looked at him. Those wide blue eyes were far from innocent. She knew exactly what he was talking about.

"You recall our private dance last year."

Her eyes flickered to her maid, who was doing her best to pretend she did not hear them.

"I . . . I . . . don't remember." Her lie was as apparent as the blush stealing across her cheeks.

"Then, shall I remind you?"

She reached for some thread and a pair of breeches, succinctly ignoring him.

But he had to know, so he pressed on, his voice soft so only she would hear. "Neither of us could sleep. We bumped into each other in the corridor by accident, but when we heard footsteps, we ducked into the ballroom for cover." He could still hear her subdued laughter from that night. "Once the house was silent, you had the grand idea of a dance."

"It wasn't my idea," she whispered, almost to herself.

He chuckled, turning his body toward her on the sofa and propping his elbow on the back of it. He could watch her better this way. "Oh, I mistake. It was my idea, wasn't it?"

She gave a quick nod, threading her needle again.

He continued the story. "We took a fast romp around the room, laughing until we could barely breathe."

Her hands fumbled, no longer as steady as they were before.

"But it was our second and final dance that was my favorite. I learned that night that there is nothing as memorable as a midnight waltz." Her hands were still now as she seemed to listen with the same intensity with which he watched her.

"Moonlight streamed through the windows, falling upon your braided golden hair, making your white nightgown and matching robe glow and your skin gleam iridescent." How he wished to touch her skin even now—her soft, rosy cheeks, the curl just over her ear, and the hollow of her slender neck. He had started the story with the intention to make her react, but it was he who was falling under her spell.

He found his voice again. "Amelia," he breathed. "I regret not—"

"Mr. Cunningham!" Amelia shrieked, bouncing to the edge of her seat.

Noah pulled back, startled. At the fireplace, Wendy jumped in her seat. Mr. Cunningham choked on his snore as his head whipped forward.

"What is it? What happened?" Mr. Cunningham blustered.

Amelia held the shirt out in her hand. "We have nearly finished here. Tell us your story so we might leave."

Noah stared, still processing what had happened. She had reacted to his story, but the reason alluded him. Did the memory of their dance disturb her now? Or did she cherish it like he did and fear what he would say next? It had taken every ounce of his self-control to walk away that night. The only reason he had was because he had wanted to treat her as a gentleman would. One night was nothing to the hope of a lifetime together.

Now he didn't plan to spend another day without her.

Mr. Cunningham scrubbed a hand over his face. "Very well, Miss Park. I haven't had a hollering female in my house for years. I forgot how demanding they can be."

Noah felt bad for him. The hollering demands of a woman, as Mr. Cunningham called them, were far better than being alone. How many years had Mr. Cunningham been on his own? Had his wife passed long ago or recently? Maybe Noah would ask Lady Blakely if she knew more of Mr. Cunningham's life. Until then, he had to backtrack to fix the uncomfortable tension between him and Amelia. He straightened, shifting away so she would relax. "Mr. Cunningham, you left off with the missionary."

Mr. Cunningham sat up a little, his eyes still laced with fatigue. "Right. The missionary. Some said he was a saint or an angel disguised in a poor man's attire." Despite Mr. Cunningham's gruff voice, Amelia slowly sat back, her rigid shoulders softening marginally.

Mr. Cunningham, oblivious to anything amiss, continued seamlessly. "The missionary came to the Morgans half-starved that night. They had little to offer him, but neither could they in good conscience turn him away on such a cold night. They shared their small portion of Christmas pudding that the missus had been preparing for weeks. After a meager dinner, they sang over the fading fire of the shepherds coming to the Christ child.

"The missionary was deeply touched by their generosity when they had so little and offered to leave a blessing upon their house—one of prosperity and future riches. The Morgans requested something far different. The missionary could hardly believe it when he heard their humble request but could not withhold the blessing they wished for: a Christmas promise that would bring lost souls together in love."

"How does it work?" Amelia's voice was filled with curiosity and eagerness.

Noah wanted to know the answer too.

"It's just a story, you know," Mr. Cunningham said, his eyes going to the painting on the mantel. He stared at the portrait Noah assumed was the man's wife, his expression folding with sadness until it was completely closed off.

"Did the promise mean it would happen every Christmas?" he asked at the same time Amelia blurted, "How were the lost souls selected?"

Mr. Cunningham held up his hand and shook his head. "I have things to do." He fought the sofa, pushing away from it until he was standing again. Noah and Amelia stood too.

"Wait," Noah pled. "We will only take another minute."

Mr. Cunningham didn't look at them. Something was off. He was no longer gruff and overconfident but carried himself like a lost old man. "Ask someone else. Don't come here again." He left them alone in the drawing room, staring after him.

Wendy came to Amelia's side, collecting the mended shirts from her and piling them back into the sewing basket.

"I suppose we will have to find someone else to help us." Noah set a hand on his hip.

Amelia glanced at him and snorted.

His gaze flicked to hers. "What?"

"Nothing." She pulled Wendy, who held a hand over her own mouth, toward the door. Their barely suppressed snickers followed them into the corridor.

He hastened after them, grabbing his hat from a table by the door as he went. "What is so humorous?"

It wasn't until they were in the carriage that he discovered the reason for their laughter. He had sewed Mr. Cunningham's stocking to his breeches. It felt symbolic of his clumsy efforts to win Amelia. Instead of fixing things, he worried he had made them worse. He didn't know how else to get her to open up to him. He could only hope his pressing did not make the gap between them all the wider. By the way Amelia continued to avoid his gaze, there wasn't any fantastical Christmas legend on their side either. He thought of Lawry, just as sorry for his friend as he was for himself. With a tug, he ripped the stocking from his breeches, his pathetic stitches sliding free with little effort. His willpower wouldn't give so easily. He would think of something.

Chapter Nine

A dimness shrouded Amelia's bedchamber, a result of the early hour combined with the heavy cloud cover outside the window. There would likely be snow by the afternoon. Nearly a week had passed since their fruitless visit with Mr. Cunningham. Avoiding more talks with Noah during that time had been Amelia's sole motivation and had been best completed by building up her trousseau for when Mr. Wilson proposed. Her success in evading Noah in her thoughts, however, had not been so successful. Repeatedly she recalled Noah's sultry whispers about their midnight waltz, his deep voice awakening her every sense without his even touching her. She had yearned to lean into him. To let him confuse her. To relive every second of the best Christmas of her life.

She blinked hard to chase away her torturous thoughts, her focus taking in the image behind her in the mirror. Wendy was quietly transforming Amelia's hair from its morning snarls into perfectly coiled curls on the top of her head. She didn't seem sad anymore. Merely resolute.

It hurt Amelia to see her maid closing off all hope, but it also inspired her to do the same. She wanted to marry someone as wonderful as Noah, but she also wanted someone she could trust with her feelings. Someone who wouldn't play with her emotions. For the first time, she was glad Noah had not come to London. Glad she had met Mr. Wilson. And glad that, despite her disobedient imagination, she had not fallen prey to Noah's charms.

Would that she remembered her commitment today since avoiding anyone was out of the question. It was St. Thomas's Day, and Amelia had decided her entire family should participate. They hadn't celebrated the holiday since before her father had died. It was high time they do something for the widows and the poor of their community. It might put her into Noah's path, but it would be just the thing to keep her mind occupied.

When Wendy finished her administrations, Amelia bestowed a glowing compliment and made her way to the kitchens. Warmth from the ovens hit her as soon as she opened the door. A second, different kind of warmth followed. The kind that came from an appreciative look from a man one couldn't help one's attraction to. Noah pushed away from the long table Amelia's entire family was gathered around and crossed the room to greet her.

He had given her space these last few days. Why couldn't he continue?

"Your hair is rather fetching dressed that way." He reached up and fingered a lock by her cheek.

Amelia stilled, swallowing hard. She glanced at the others, but no one noticed. "Thank you."

He dropped his hand, rubbing it on the side of his leg. Together they moved toward the others. "I am looking forward to today's festivities," he said. "My family sends a charity basket or two to the church, but we have never rallied the house to help feed a community."

Curtis looked over as they approached. "We used to do the same until Amelia here thought we could do better."

"You started this?" Noah seemed impressed. "I should have visited your family for the holidays and not the other way around."

Lady Blakely smiled. "She was probably eight or nine when she insisted it was our duty to be more charitable. And it is because of her insistence that we are starting the tradition up again."

Amelia wasn't the sort of woman to take on projects like Ivy did or to nurture everyone as Julia did or even be as creative as Alice was. "It's nothing."

"It's not nothing to those you help," Noah said. "And your notable enthusiasm started a family tradition."

She shouldn't care so much for his opinion, but she did. She felt a smile tugging at her lips, which was as close as she could come to a thank-you. He gave an understanding nod. The small interaction gave her a desire to put aside her trepidation and make the most of the day. "What needs to be done?"

Only Cook and a few servants milled about the room. The others were likely tending to chores about the house and would join them when the townspeople began to arrive.

"Why don't you and Noah make another pound cake," Ivy suggested. "Cook already put several loaves of bread into the oven, and Julia and I are kneading another batch. Alice and Thomas should be here soon with the wassail."

Amelia was not an expert in the kitchen, but pound cakes were as much a part of their St. Thomas's Day as anything else. And she was secretly delighted to have Noah help her since it required a strong arm to beat the ingredients for an hour before the batter was ready for the oven. She held back a snicker. He might not thank her for this tradition when they were through.

Esmond pushed a bowl and wooden spoon toward them, and Lady Blakely brought over a pound of butter.

"I didn't think we would actually help prepare the food," Noah said, unbuttoning the cuff of his sleeves and rolling them up.

Amelia hadn't seen him discard his jacket for some time, and she had to pull her eyes away from his exposed forearms. "Do you think you can bear the burden of menial labor?" she asked. The food preparation was part of the tradition.

Noah grinned. "I will have you know that I helped our cook make biscuits a time or two. I am practically an expert in the kitchen."

"Better than sewing, I hope," she teased. "And since you are an expert, you can beat this butter until it is creamy." She pushed the bowl toward him.

Noah eyed it strangely.

"Stir," she prompted.

"I knew that," he said with a wink.

She shook her head and left him to the butter while she went to gather a dozen eggs. When she returned with a second bowl and the eggs, she found Noah chopping at the butter in cutting motions. The others were too busy with their own tasks to notice. Setting her bowl on the table, she reached for Noah's.

"Let me help you."

He gave her a sideways glance. "I have almost got it."

She stifled another laugh. "I am sure you do, but I can show you a faster method."

When he wouldn't willingly relinquish the bowl to her, she reached out to show him the circular motion. Besides a little exertion, it was a task simple enough for children. But as soon as her hand covered his, she realized that even a child would know how stupid her decision had been.

Never touch an attractive enemy.

Noah's hand stilled, and her own was paralyzed atop his. He met her gaze head on, and she swallowed.

"You, er, do it this way." Her hand caught up with her mind and began to direct his hand around the sides of the bowl. All the while, their eyes remained on each other.

Noah's slow-creeping smile held a mischievous glint.

She immediately dropped his hand. "You already knew how to stir, didn't you?"

His lips pursed. "Remember, I've helped my cook in the kitchen before."

She shoved his shoulder, but Noah was too sturdy and did not even budge. "For that, I plan to make you stir the entire time."

"I think I can handle that." He demonstrated a steady whip of the butter and raised his brow for her approval. "Am I adept enough for you?"

"That depends on what you are referring to." She held back her smirk. He had clearly never stirred for as long as she planned for him to. While those present added the eggs, flour, and sugar to a separate bowl on the other end of the table, Noah regaled her with shared stories about raiding the kitchen as a child and how Cook had put him to work as a consequence. His being a rule follower juxtaposed with his being a boy in a constant state of hunger made for some entertaining tales. Amelia pretended not to relish every word of his shared confidence. With the ingredients together, she instructed Noah to stir again.

"It would be my pleasure." He picked up the bowl again and combined the mixture easily. She blinked. His effortless motions were highly distracting.

After several minutes, he set it down and pronounced it sufficiently mixed.

"Oh no," Lady Blakely said, coming over. "It must be whipped for a solid hour to make it light and airy."

Noah's brow soared high on his forehead. "An entire hour?"

Amelia covered her smile with her hand. "I would help, but you did say you would stir for the entire time."

He growled under his breath and started beating away with the spoon again.

After preparing the pan, she made an exaggerated show of relaxing into a chair and feigning a yawn.

"Sit up straight, Amelia," her mother chided from the far end of the table. "Noah is going to think we haven't any manners at all."

Amelia straightened, her cheeks warming.

"I would never think that, Lady Blakely," Noah said. "In fact, Amelia was just insisting on doing all the stirring. She is a testament to you." He handed the bowl to Amelia with a wry grin.

She glared at him. This was the Noah of her childhood. The one who joined Esmond in riling her. "Thank you, but I couldn't let you miss out on this inspiring experience." She pushed the bowl back to him.

After Mama turned her attention away, Noah said, "I have an idea." He set his hand on the table and leaned toward Amelia.

She glanced up at him, her ill-behaved imagination suddenly envisioning him leaning in to kiss her. She was certifiably mad. "Your ideas make me nervous," she said quickly. She tried to look around him to focus on the others, but he blocked her view of them.

"We could stir together."

She shook her head, convinced he might possibly be madder than she was.

"No? How about we make a game of it?"

Her brow crept up. "What sort of game?"

"Answer a question or take the consequence of stirring for five minutes. We'll take turns."

"I don't care for games while baking. It's distracting." She stuck up her chin, but it only made her feel like she was inviting him to lean in closer, which he did.

She leaned back into her seat. "I'll do it."

He chuckled and gave her a little more breathing room. He was far too comfortable around her family. And had she just agreed to his silly game? At least they were in company. He might give a whispered flirtation, but he wouldn't dare ask any personal questions.

Noah reached for the spoon and tapped it on the edge of the bowl. "I'll go first. How could you give up being with your family for the holidays to visit my home?"

She took in the scene before her: her mother instructing the housekeeper on where to put the guests and how much to serve them, Curtis and Ivy assisting Cook and two kitchen maids in slicing bread—all of them laughing over something Ivy had said—and Esmond smearing a streak of flour across Julia's nose while she tried to push him away so she could concentrate on the bread dough. Her family was likely causing more trouble than they were helping, but she loved that they were doing this again. It had been too long.

She glanced up at Noah. "I could leave because the holidays were hard without Papa. Visiting your home was the perfect distraction. I only now realize that it was selfish. I should have been here supporting my family." She squeezed her hands together in her lap. Instead of trying to gain Noah's favor and giggling night after night with Rachel, she should have been here, where she was most needed.

"Thank you for telling me. I suppose that means these five minutes are mine." He went back to work, not saying anything for a moment. He caught her eye and sighed. "You know your mother wanted you with us, don't you?"

Amelia frowned. "Why would you think that?"

"Remember how my mother loves to read her correspondence out loud over breakfast?"

She groaned. "And sometimes it is quite revealing."

He gave a long nod. "She wanted you to have a happy Christmas. She sent Esmond first, then you."

"Curtis wouldn't come," Amelia said. They both looked at her oldest brother. Next to her mother, he had taken Father's death the hardest.

Noah captured her gaze once more. "It wasn't selfish for your mother to want your happiness, Mel. And it wasn't selfish for you to seek joy either."

She smiled. For a moment their friendship was like it had been last Christmas, a feeling of being seen and heard connecting them in the kind of bond she had treasured between them.

"It's your turn," he said. "Ask me a question."

She studied his strong forearm beating the batter. "You told me why you did not come to London, but may I ask if there was a second reason?" It was the one question that had burned on her lips for more than eleven months. It had slipped out so easily, but she couldn't call it back.

His hand stilled again, and he looked at her. "I think I'll take another five minutes."

She gawked. "You aren't going to answer? That's not fair."

He shrugged and smiled mischievously. "I didn't make up the rules."

She shook her head. "You're impossible."

He went back to stirring. "I could answer, but this isn't exactly the time or place for it."

Amelia looked up to see Ivy watching them at that exact moment. "I can understand your hesitancy . . . if your answer is personal." She waited to see if he would take the bait. Curiosity burned inside her.

"It's extremely personal." There was something in his eyes that she barely caught before he looked away. He wanted her to guess. His family always came for the Season, but he had told her that he had stayed to help his father with his research. Could Noah's personal reason be Miss Hampton? Even after a year of assuming just that, Amelia questioned why he would not be more forthright on the matter.

Alice and her husband, Thomas, came through the kitchen door followed by some footmen carrying large pots of wassail. Her family rushed to help, but Amelia stayed firmly in her seat. "Hand me the bowl."

Noah raised his brow, but she insisted. She reached for it, and he let her take it.

"I cannot watch you do all the work, game or not. It doesn't sit well with me."

He smirked. "I'm still not telling you what you want to know."

"You can tell me later." She scraped the edges of the bowl with the spoon.

With a laugh, he shook his head. "I've always liked your persistent side. You aren't afraid to go after what you want."

She swallowed. "Sometimes my persistence is misplaced."

"Then, by all means, fight only for what is worth attaining." He eyed her long and hard, searing her middle with heat.

She didn't answer, but his words circled in her mind. She knew what she wanted, but was it worth fighting for something she could *never* attain? It was a painful way to live.

With Alice and Thomas joining them, it was soon impossible for any more private conversation. Noah stole the batter back after a few minutes and insisted on finishing the stirring. As the morning progressed, their cake was taken away to bake while they ate a simple breakfast. Someone propped open the kitchen door when it grew too warm in the room, and before long, the first townspeople arrived.

More of the servants filed through the kitchen, bustling about and helping everyone. The Boals—one of Curtis's tenant families—arrived, and each member enjoyed a slice of cake and buttered bread along with a drink of wassail. When they left, they carried a bag of wheat and a small pouch of coins bestowed by Curtis.

A thrill of satisfaction passed through Amelia as more people streamed through their kitchen. Some she knew, but many she didn't.

When the Clark family came in, she noticed Lawry, Noah's valet, give Mrs. Clark special attention. Amelia searched the room for Wendy and found her holding her younger sister on her hip. Wendy's wary eyes watched Lawry's every move. Amelia tried not to be obvious in watching them, but she couldn't help it.

"Why not go stand right beside them so you can eavesdrop too," Noah said over her shoulder.

She looked behind her and scowled. "A lady never eavesdrops."

"Suit yourself," he said, backing away.

An older gentleman came into the kitchen just then, and for a moment Amelia thought it was Mr. Cunningham.

She reached back and grabbed Noah's forearm.

"What is it?" He bent over to pick up a platter of freshly sliced pound cake off the kitchen counter—most likely the one they had made.

"What if we brought some food to Mr. Cunningham?"

He hesitated. "I'm not so sure that is a good idea."

"What does his holiday consist of? He has no children to visit him or relatives nearby. His home was rather cold, and the way he shoveled the gingerbread into his mouth said a great deal." She hated to volunteer to spend more time in Noah's company, but she couldn't put the thought aside. "We have plenty to share. I think Mr. Cunningham might appreciate it."

Noah hesitated. "He told us not to come back."

"I know, and we will respect his request and won't ask about the legend. But couldn't we deliver him some Christmas cheer?"

Noah's pinched brow held for a moment and then quickly smoothed. "I believe it would be just the thing. Everyone deserves to be thought of this time of year."

Just like that, she had convinced him.

This was the man she had fallen in love with. Noah would never intentionally hurt anyone. But the truth was, he *had* hurt her simply by not loving her. She wished she could forgive him.

She took a deep breath. "I would be honored to have your assistance, Noah Brooks."

Her words lit up his eyes. "Is that so?" There wasn't any teasing in his voice. He wanted to know if she meant it.

"It is the Christmas season, is it not?" she asked.

He nodded slowly. "It is."

"Then, let's make it a memorable one."

Chapter Ten

Noah was tired of giving Amelia space. He had already done so for nearly a year. This past week had been twice as hard, even with various trips into town to distract himself. He also didn't want to push something on her that she didn't want, but after their day together in the kitchen, he thought maybe his patience was finally paying off. He was convinced she was softening to him.

He watched her and Cook gather a basket of foodstuff for Mr. Cunningham. Wendy had agreed to accompany them again, and of course, Noah had insisted Lawry assist their driver. Wendy might be as stubborn as Amelia, but Noah wanted to at least provide opportunities for Lawry to win her over. Surely one of the couples would be engaged by the end of the holidays.

"The carriage is ready," he said to Amelia, anxious to get on the road. The weather was turning, and the townspeople were rushing back to their homes.

"The food is ready too," Amelia said. Cook draped a flour cloth over the top of the basket, and before Amelia could pick it up, Noah swooped in and took it.

"Allow me."

"Thank you."

Amelia and Wendy followed him to the carriage and climbed inside. He was the last to sit and took the lone bench in the back.

"Have you learned anything about the legend since our last visit?" Amelia asked.

Had she been waiting all week to ask him this question? How unfortunate that her intent to avoid him had trumped her rather intense curiosity. Still, he would humor her with what he knew. "I rode to town to look over any records, and Amorwich was indeed founded the year the Morgans arrived in 1612. I haven't had any more luck with the legend though. A few have heard of it, but they have no more details than we already know. In fact, Mr. Cunningham's knowledge is by far the most in-depth."

Amelia peered out the window at the snow flurries beginning to descend on the dusk skyline. "It is a shame he will not tell us more about it. Not that I am convinced of its power, but I admit to being enthralled with the story itself."

This was a glimpse of the old Amelia he knew. Curious, romantic, and daring. It took a special kind of person to feed a recluse and hunt after a mysterious legend. The carriage rumbled to a stop, and the footman pulled open the door. It took only a moment to descend, stroll up the walk dotted with clumps of newly fallen snow, and climb the few steps to Mr. Cunningham's home. Noah knocked and took a step back, putting himself directly beside Amelia. "This is a good thing you are doing," he said, shifting the food basket in his hands.

"You mean, it is a good thing *we* are doing." She turned her head to meet his gaze. "I wouldn't have been able to come on my own. I might talk like an adventurer, but the secret is I can only be brave when someone else is by my side."

Noah bit his tongue before he could jump to volunteer for life and scare her away again. When no one came to the door after a few minutes, he reached and knocked a second time. Amelia shivered beside him.

"I wonder what is keeping him." Amelia bounced on her toes. Another knock and nothing. "Could he have gone out?"

"In this weather? I would be surprised." He stepped to the side and peered through a narrow window.

"See anything?" she asked.

"It's too dark."

"Noah, I have a bad feeling about this. What if he died?"

He looked over at her. "That is a rather dire guess for why a man hasn't opened his door."

"I wasn't aware when Mr. Reed died, and he was a similar age to Mr. Cunningham, who we both know has lost his will to live."

Noah set his hand on her back. "We mustn't jump to conclusions. Let's reserve hope while we can."

Amelia gnawed at her lip. "We should do something too."

Noah agreed. "Let's try the kitchen door. His cook can at least take our basket."

Amelia nodded. "And assure us that Mr. Cunningham is indeed alive."

"That too." He winked and offered Amelia his free arm. She clasped on to it, the snow flurries thickening and clinging to their cloaks and hats. He noticed Wendy had her back to the two of them. "You can wait here," he said to her. Noah motioned with his head for Lawry to keep the maid company. "We should only be a moment."

Amelia did not object, and the two of them circled around the cottage until they found the servants' entrance. Noah was the one to knock again. A rustle sounded behind the door before it creaked open. An older woman with white hair and aged, sunken cheeks greeted them with a single nod.

"Good evening," Noah said. "We received no answer at the front door. Is Mr. Cunningham not at home?"

The older woman sniffed. "I don't concern myself with Mr. Cunningham's comings and goings. I just prepare the meals."

Noah glanced at Amelia, whose worried eyes confirmed her concerns were not abated.

"We have an offering from Lord Blakely and his family." Noah handed the older woman the basket. "But we would like to reassure ourselves that Mr. Cunningham is not out in this weather before we return home."

The cook shook her head. "The master prefers his privacy, but I will tell 'is maid about the delivery. I suggest you try again tomorrow."

Noah opened his mouth to say more, but the door swung closed. "They do love to shut the door in people's faces here, don't they?" He backed up and faced Amelia. "At least he will know we are thinking of him."

Amelia brought her gloved finger to her mouth. "Let's do one better and break in through the front door."

Her serious expression was the only thing keeping him from laughing. "What would that accomplish?"

She blinked rapidly. "We would know if he is dead or alive."

"If he is alive, we would be trespassing. Our goodwill would be for naught. If he is dead, he won't mind waiting until the morrow."

Amelia scrunched up her face. "I don't care for your reasoning, but you do have a point."

Noah nodded. "I usually do."

They took a few steps away from the door when Amelia tugged on his arm, halting their progress. "Remember this morning how you said when we were alone, you would tell me the other reason you did not come to London?"

He swallowed. "Is that what I said?"

"Perhaps not exactly, but if I cannot be satisfied where Mr. Cunningham is concerned, the least you can do is indulge me on this other matter."

"Don't you think it's a mite cold out for a heart-to-heart?" He took a step forward, but she did not follow.

"I don't mind the weather at all." She shivered involuntarily, effectively refuting her statement.

He wasn't going to be able to put her off for much longer. He might as well have it out now and let the natural consequence take its course. "I didn't explain myself very well when we spoke about this in the library. I wanted to give you your freedom without me hovering about."

"My freedom? What do you mean by that?"

He remained stock-still, dreading how she would respond. "I didn't want you choosing me because I was the man you grew up with. Because I was familiar and comfortable. I wanted you to dance and be escorted to parties with whomever you fancied and not be hindered by any sense of obligation to me. I wanted you to be able to enjoy your Season and come to know your own mind."

She did not so much as blink. "I know my own mind."

"Of course you do, but you are still young and—"

"Young? I have had four Seasons now. If anything, I am practically on the shelf. Not that you should concern yourself. I would hate for you to feel any *obligation* toward me."

He kept his tone calm, opposite of hers. "You wanted to know my reason, but you do not understand my motivation."

"Then, please tell me. Because I don't think this is about me at all. You did not want to give me the wrong idea about your intentions, so it was necessary to avoid me."

"Mel, it wasn't like that. Not everyone has friendships they've nourished for years like we have. I couldn't throw it all away. I had to be sure."

"Sure of *my* feelings?" She shook her head. "You can set yourself at ease. Our *friendship* is perfectly safe." She threw the words at him and marched away before he could finish explaining himself.

He took a fortifying breath and rushed after her. When they reached the carriage, Wendy was already inside, and Lawry was speaking to the driver, his expression grim. It seemed their trip wasn't the heartwarming experience he had expected. No one was returning very happy.

The carriage brimmed with tension when he climbed inside. Amelia would not even look at him, and he knew she was more hurt than angry, which somehow made it all the worse. As soon as they were out of the carriage, he would send Wendy inside and finish his conversation with Amelia. She needed to hear how he felt about her—to know how much he had missed and loved her.

The carriage jolted to a stop, jarring him far more mentally than physically. It was time to confess his heart and take the greatest risk of his life. He had to prove to Amelia that he couldn't live without her.

Wendy descended first with the help of a footman. Noah hurried to be next so he could be the one to hand down Amelia, but she beat him to the door. With nerves high and his patience waning, he watched the young footman take a hold of Noah's future wife's hand. Or, at least, he hoped it was his future wife's hand.

He practically jumped from the carriage and had to jog to catch up to Amelia's near-sprint up the lane to the front door. "Mel, wait. I need to explain."

She whipped her head from side to side, her bonnet swaying with the motion. "It's been a long day, Noah."

He sidestepped in front of her, putting a hand on each of her shoulders. He said the one thing that might soften her the most. "Amelia, I love you."

The front door swished open behind him, and reflexively, he dropped his hands. He turned instinctively to see who was there. The last person on earth he expected to see stood before him.

Mr. Wilson had come to Amorwich.

Chapter Eleven

Amelia's heart stopped cold in her chest.

Noah loved her?

Her Noah?

The one who had made her feel adored, only to abandon her?

And yet she had never seen him look more sincere.

Mr. Wilson, like a rescuer in the storm, loomed over them from his perch on the steps, ready to offer her a safe abode.

What was she to do?

"Are you ready, miss?" Wendy's voice caught her attention. Amelia pivoted to face her. "We should get you out of this weather."

For a moment, Amelia had no longer noticed the swirling snow contrasting the oncoming night or the brisk wind stinging her cheeks. "You are right. Excuse me, Noah." Her words were breathless and nearly lost in the frigid breeze. She backed around Noah, risking a glance at him. He watched her, his eyes solemn, his mouth pulled tight.

She should have answered him. Said anything. But not with Mr. Wilson watching. And not until she had a moment to be sure *how* to respond.

Wendy, the angel, stayed by her side as she approached Mr. Wilson. He stood like a stoic tower, his brown hair trimmed short, his dress immaculate, and his manners controlled. He motioned her into the house, where Curtis and Ivy spoke with her mother. He allowed them inside before greeting her.

"Good evening, Miss Park." He did not smile when he rose from his bow. He rarely did. But she could guess his mood by the slight fluctuation in his tone. He was happy to see her. Or, at least, she thought he was. "I do hope you did not catch a cold on your charity visit."

Charity visit? She hadn't considered her visit to Mr. Cunningham as charity but one of friendly concern. She curtsied, all the while wondering why his statement bothered her. "Good evening, Mr. Wilson. I am terribly surprised to see you. Forgive me. What has brought you here?" She felt more than heard Noah come up behind her.

"I came on the invitation of your mother to join the household for the duration of the holidays." He looked at her mother. "Did you not receive my acceptance letter?"

"We did, Mr. Wilson," Mama answered. "We thought to surprise Amelia."

Amelia set her hand on her stomach. Another surprise? Did her family wish to kill her? At least Ivy had the heart to appear sorry for it.

"I regret I cannot stay past the twenty-sixth," he said. She would have to take his word for it, for she could not measure his regret, only her mounting nerves. He continued. "I have unavoidable business I must see to."

"At Christmas?" Noah's words made her jump.

Mr. Wilson looked over her head at him. "And you are?"

"This is Mr. Noah Brooks." Amelia moved aside for the men to address each other better.

"We have met before." Noah dipped into a bow.

"Oh yes," Mr. Wilson said. "I am not good with faces. How are you, Mr. Brooks?"

Amelia did not hear Noah's answer. She was moving slowly toward the stairs. As soon as there was a lull in the conversation, she inserted, "I should change for dinner. Excuse me."

Wendy had followed her every step and was right behind her all the way to Amelia's bedchamber. Amelia shut the door behind them, throwing her back against it. "Tell me this isn't real."

"Which part? Where Mr. Brooks confessed or Mr. Wilson came all the way from London to see you?" Wendy was not dull-witted. She knew exactly how horrific this was for Amelia.

"The part where it happened all at the same time!" She needed to sit down. No, she needed to move. "There I am, worried about Mr. Cunningham, and then out of the blue, my life is turned upside down. Again. I cannot entertain both gentlemen. Besides, I am supposed to be angry with Noah, not considering him. And I should be thrilled to see Mr. Wilson, when instead I am confused. What shall I do?"

"Get dressed for dinner?" Wendy gave a sheepish smile.

"That is all the advice you have for me?"

Wendy clucked her tongue and turned toward Amelia's closet in search of a gown. "You know I do not put much stock in love. I've told you that much before."

Amelia sighed. "Then, you think I ought to pursue Mr. Wilson? He is the sensible, reliable choice. Noah has shown interest before, and it came to naught." She couldn't bear the heartache a second time.

"I cannot advise you, miss. No one knows what is best for you as well as you do."

Amelia dropped her chin to her chest and stalked to her bed. She turned and let her back fall against her quilt-covered mattress. "What if I choose wrong? Is it worth a lifetime of regret?"

Silence greeted her. After a moment, she lifted her head to see Wendy frozen in the threshold of her closet. Her maid's hand was suspended in air, inches from one of Amelia's gowns. "Wendy?"

Wendy's hand lowered slowly to her side. "I do know a little of regret." Amelia had seen how sweet Lawry had been with Wendy's younger siblings. She wondered if they were thinking of the same thing. Wendy sighed. "Whatever you do, don't be hasty in your decision. Some decisions cannot be undone."

Amelia briefly forgot her own problems. Was it too late for Wendy and Lawry? She wanted them to be happy—to have a chance to make a life together. Her own struggles combined with those of her friend and maid's and circled round and round in her mind so that, by the dinner hour, she was properly tortured. Somehow Wendy managed to convince her to dress and then urged her out the door.

When she descended the stairs, Mr. Wilson met her at the bottom. Calm, unsuspecting Mr. Wilson. He might not be as charming as Noah, but he was sweet in his own way. He stayed by her side, complimented her gown, and gallantly offered his arm when it was time to walk into the dining room. All while Noah observed from a distance. She knew because she could feel his gaze riveted on her.

After they were seated, Mr. Wilson turned to her. "How are you enjoying being away from the hustle and bustle of London?"

"I always enjoy the peace of the countryside," she said.

"It's too quiet for me," he responded. "I can handle no more than a few weeks at most."

Amelia opened her mouth to argue that he had clearly never stayed in Amorwich before, but the words caught on the edge of her mouth. Noah wasn't the only one observing her; her entire family looked on as well.

She altered her comment. "I am glad you could make time to visit us, then." Did her family note her forced smile, or was she fooling them?

"How could I miss it? Your presence makes the countryside far more appealing." Mr. Wilson was no flirt, so this was indeed a great compliment.

Her smile turned more genuine. "I thank you."

A screech sounded from Noah's seat, his fork dragging against his plate. He cleared his throat. "Pardon me."

She caught his eye, and he raised his brow. Blinking, she dropped her gaze. Mr. Wilson was courting her, so why shouldn't he compliment her?

I love you.

Noah's previous words taunted her, answering her question more succinctly than any other explanation could. She wished he would repeat those three words again and make her believe them. She wanted him to beg for her to come to him. There was only a table between them, but in some ways, it sat like a gray abyss of lost hopes. She had chosen Mr. Wilson already. To un-choose him went against what Society expected.

By the time their meal ended, more than one in their company was caught yawning. With such an early start to their day, all of them were ready to retire. Good nights were said in the drawing room, and they filed toward the stairs.

"I hope you find your room comfortable," Amelia said to Mr. Wilson.

"I have no doubt it will be satisfactory."

Just like their relationship.

Amelia could ask for no more.

She felt a slight tug on the back of her dress. She looked over her shoulder and caught Noah's crooked half smile.

"Let's talk," he mouthed.

Did all that man want to do is talk? "No," she mouthed back, facing forward again.

Another tug at her back. They were almost to the stairs, but her self-control had always been weak where Noah was concerned, and even Mr. Wilson's presence beside her did not fortify her.

She glanced back again.

Noah motioned toward the library.

She had already promised herself not to do anything that resembled a late-night tryst with Noah. He tugged her dress again before she had fully turned away.

"Please," he mouthed.

"Mr. Brooks, is there a reason you keep touching Miss Park's gown?"

Amelia reached for the stair post and willed herself not to laugh. It wasn't funny. Her near intended could not think Noah was sweet on her, for a myriad of obvious reasons.

"I, er . . ."

She wasn't going to help him out of this one. Even if she wanted to, she didn't know how.

"I have a childish habit of communicating with Miss Park this way. We grew up together, so do not be surprised by it."

"I am most surprised. Your continued juvenility is not to your credit."

"Yes, well, do not be shocked if you see Miss Park kick me in the shins at some point. I bring out her worst."

Amelia's brow shot upward. That had been years ago! Before she could defend herself, Noah motioned his head to the library again the moment Mr. Wilson turned away.

"On that note, let's retire to bed." She whipped around and took the stairs at a very unladylike pace, leaving both men to walk up together.

She was going to meet Noah in the library after all. If only so she could remind him of how hard she kicked.

Chapter Twelve

Noah waited in the library, hoping Amelia would risk meeting him. His restless fingers plucked a book off the tea table, his thumb running through the pages. Whether she came or not likely depended upon how angry he had made her. After an entire evening of waiting for her to come to him, he had been forced to act on his own accord.

She was confused, but she had no reason to be. Mr. Wilson wouldn't make her happy. A blind man could see it. No one knew her like Noah did. He needed to explain it to her, lay it out plainly, and then she would fall into his arms.

Heaven willing.

A few more moments ticked by on the small, wooden clock on the mantel. Just as he flopped onto the settee by the glowing fireplace, the library door opened a few inches. His breath hitched for the briefest of seconds. Until Curtis stuck his head into the room, causing Noah to jump to his feet.

Curtis gave a wolfish grin. "Disappointed?"

"Bitterly."

Curtis laughed and opened the door wider, revealing Amelia by his side.

Amelia didn't share her older brother's amused grin. "I thought if you needed to speak to me at such a late hour, we ought to have a chaperone."

Noah grimaced. A chaperone would keep him from kissing Amelia, and he had waited long enough. "If you insist."

"I do," Curtis said, his teasing smirk making him look a little too much like Esmond. "I will just take a book into the far corner, but don't think I won't be listening."

"How very diligent of you," Noah said. His gaze swung to Amelia. "Will you sit?"

She nodded, wariness hugging her entire form. She slid onto the farthest cushion on the settee. He sat down directly beside her. Her hazel eyes widened. He raised his brow in return, defying her to complain.

"Since when have you been afraid of me?" he asked.

"Since three hours ago, when we were outside."

His frustration melted. It was so good to be near her. "I meant what I said."

"Wasn't it a little sudden?"

He chuckled and dropped his voice. "On the contrary, Mel. It was a long time coming."

Her stare darted from his eyes to her lap and back, disbelief stealing her features. "Next you are going to tell me that you fell in love with me last Christmas but withheld your confession because you didn't know the depth of *my* feelings."

He nodded slowly.

She looked at her hands. "What if I told you that I knew my heart quite well and had for some time?" Her whisper sliced through him, giving him all sorts of hope.

"Then, I would gladly admit I am an idiot and insist we must make up for lost time."

Her cheeks colored a beautiful shade of pink. "What do you mean?"

"I mean," he whispered, drawing closer, "that I plan to kiss you until . . . until your brother lands me a facer." He smiled just before he closed the gap between them.

Only, love's triumph was cut bitterly short when Amelia put her hands up to his chest and pushed him back.

"Well done, Amelia," Curtis said from across the room.

Noah glanced over long enough to see Curtis's obnoxious grin just above his book. Noah would never live this down. He swung his gaze back to Amelia, her eyes wide and deerlike again. "Forgive me. I thought—I thought we were of the same mind."

"I am courting Mr. Wilson now. We are soon to be *engaged*." She said it like it was a problem.

And it was. "But you are not engaged, so there is no harm in crying off."

"I have not yet decided—"

"What is there to decide?"

"What if you change your mind by the morning?" She slid to her feet, her chin quivering. "I'm sorry, Noah, but I cannot bear to be hurt by you again."

He didn't stop her when she walked away, leaving him alone in the library with Curtis.

Curtis slapped his book shut and tossed it onto a side table by his chair in the corner. "Well? Am I to congratulate you?"

"On losing?" Noah scoffed.

Curtis frowned. "You mean she said no?"

"I didn't get to ask the question." Noah stared at the library door. "I thought you heard the whole thing."

"You were whispering," Curtis answered. "It was harder to hear than I imagined."

Noah sighed. "Your wife will be disappointed in your poor choice of seat."

Curtis shook his head. "Ivy is too busy fretting over Mr. Wilson's presence. It was her idea to invite you, but it was Mother's idea to invite Mr. Wilson."

"Ah, so I have Lady Blakely to thank for this."

"It sounds like you have yourself to thank. What happened last Christmas, anyway, if you don't mind me asking?"

Curtis wasn't normally the one Noah confided in. Where Esmond pried and prodded, Curtis usually kept to himself. But he trusted Curtis, and he needed a friend.

"I think I was wrong last year. I doubted the sincerity of Amelia's affection. Rumors spoke of her popularity amongst the *ton* during her recent Season, and I was not confident in her favor of me."

"You should have asked us. We've all known for years that Amelia prefers you."

Noah swallowed, an ache gnawing at his middle. "Apparently I was the only one in the dark." He prided himself in being thorough, but he had missed a crucial piece of information.

Silence followed his miserable response.

Curtis stood and walked over to him before sitting on the sturdy tea table. "I know what it's like to miss things going on under my own nose. When your mind is consumed heavily with one matter, it shuts out everything else."

Noah guessed he was speaking of when his father died. "What woke you up?"

"Ivy did." Curtis toed his boot into the purple Persian rug beneath their feet. "You've been busy working for your father these past several years. What matters is not that you missed it then but that you are aware now."

"Is this where you tell me how to fix the mess I made?" He needed Curtis's wisdom. Whatever he said, Noah would do it.

"It's up to Amelia."

That wasn't the answer he had hoped for. "You cannot let her marry Mr. Wilson." Need he list the many reasons the man was utterly wrong for her?

"I *can* let her marry Mr. Wilson, and I will, if that is who she chooses. And you must do the same."

Noah ran a hand over his jaw, scrubbing his rough skin. He would do anything to convince Amelia. But Curtis was right. In the end, she might not choose him. The thought was worse than any facer.

Chapter Thirteen

Creating sugar crystal molds was an old Christmas tradition of the Hunts, although the sisters had not done it for years. Amelia had never heard of it, and neither had her brothers. However, if everyone supported her enthusiasm for St. Thomas's day, surely she could put her heart into it. It would be a worthwhile use for her sad little organ, especially since her heart had no idea where to put its energy these days.

They were all gathered at the long table in the kitchen again, with dozens of wooden molds spread out in front of them and servants scurrying about preparing the ingredients for the sugar paste. Amelia sat near the end of the bench, with Mr. Wilson across from her. Everyone was present—even Alice and Thomas. Everyone, that is, but Noah. A keen disappointment rested on her shoulders, producing all sorts of worries. Had she offended him the night before? She had made him angry many times, but he had never held a grudge before. Would he leave? Had he left already? The more rapidly her wild thoughts came, the less she could bring herself to stay seated.

"Did you sleep well, Miss Park?" Mr. Wilson asked.

"Y-Yes." She had slept well once she had finally fallen asleep. It had been far too short though. "And you?"

A body plopped onto the half a foot left on the bench next to her, knocking into her shoulder. *Noah!*

"I slept well enough," Noah said, answering the question she had posed to Mr. Wilson.

Amelia blinked back her astonishment. "I wasn't speaking to you, and there is not enough room for you here."

"Yes," he said, eyeing their seating arrangement. "I think next year we will have to bring in another table."

Sure enough, there wasn't room anywhere else. "Can't we bring in another chair?" she asked.

Noah shifted toward her, not sparing any air between them and pushing her tighter against Julia on her other side. "I fit well enough."

She wanted to argue, but Mr. Wilson was watching her, and she had not yet learned how to relax or speak her mind in his company.

"Do you hunt or fish, Mr. Wilson?" Noah asked, drawing Mr. Wilson into a conversation that, like a game of shuttlecock, tossed back and forth.

Amelia was fascinated by how easily they could get along. But, then again, Noah's talents were many. He might not be the most observant or even be the first to agree to a social outing, but he could converse with just about anyone.

A few kitchen maids set bowls of sugar paste at various places on the table. Julia selected a fruit-basket shape to make with Esmond, who had always loved to eat the jeweled fruit that Cook would place inside such a mold for their Christmas dinner.

Mr. Wilson selected a mold of an urn. The Greek vases were popular decor, making it a safe and predictable choice. There was comfort in the familiar—comfort in Mr. Wilson.

"What are you making?" Noah asked, and Amelia was reminded of how close he was to her. Not that she had forgotten, but she feared they would both turn their heads at the same time and only the difference in their height would keep them from having an embarrassing collision.

"I thought I would try a cherub."

"A fitting choice."

The way he said it, mixed with his breath on her cheek, sent gooseflesh down her arms. She bit her bottom lip. "What about you?"

"I think I will try for an original design."

He had a glint of something in his eye when he said it, like she would want to pay attention to what he created. Before she could ask any further questions, he started selecting molds, but all seemed to be generic shapes. One was a tart mold; another was almost a drinking-glass shape. The other was a swan. He could be artistic when he wanted to be, but what could he possibly be making?

Her cherub was rather straightforward. She packed the paste into the mold, subtly watching Noah as she did so. He whipped out his tart shape and set it upside down beside him before going for the glass. Soon he had the glass shape on top of the upside-down tart.

Enthralled as she was, she forced herself to pay attention to her own work. Whoever had made the cherub mold had done an exquisite job. Her little angel came out with two delicate wings, a darling little face, two hands clasped together in prayer, and two legs bent back like he was kneeling. She would have it sent over to Mr. Cunningham. She hadn't stopped worrying about the grumpy old man. If she heard from him, perhaps she would be at ease again.

"I thought this would be more challenging," Mr. Wilson said, interrupting her thoughts. She admired his simple urn. It had turned out perfectly.

"Why don't you make a second," Amelia suggested. She wanted to remain at the table long enough to see Noah finish.

"I suppose I will." He grabbed another mold and set to work.

With that, her eyes wandered again to Noah's project.

"No peeking," he whispered.

She straightened, caught in the act. "I was merely curious." He had sugar only in the neck and part of the body of the swan. "Have you done this before?"

"No, but I find I quite enjoy it. It's almost like sculpting mud pies."

They had made their fair share of those growing up, but none of them had been very pretty. "I am sure, whatever it is, that it will be . . . interesting."

"Do you think so? Because I plan to make certain it sits above your plate at Christmas dinner."

She snorted and covered her mouth, hoping Mr. Wilson did not hear her. He was intent on his mold, however, and didn't seem to have heard the unladylike noise over the rumble of conversation around them. "I hope it does not ruin my appetite," she whispered to Noah.

He leaned close—too close in company—his eyes intent on her own. "Prepare to be rendered speechless."

Speechless? She swallowed. She couldn't even breathe.

He pulled back and grinned before turning back to his creation. She did not hide this time that she was watching his hands work. Once he placed the partial swan mold atop his glass mold, he selected a few carving tools amongst the supplies on the table. With a few clean swipes of a little knife, he blended the molds into one. She could finally see his creation taking shape.

A headless woman?

It had an arm extended, and the bottom looked like a dress, especially with the pretty curves from the tart mold. She frowned as he grabbed another mold—her empty cherub. Soon he had the head on and was shaping it by thinning out the face and carving a second arm into the body, giving the woman a waist. It wasn't perfect. The extended arm had no hand, and the cherub head was not terribly feminine, but the overall appearance was entirely unique.

"What do you think?" he asked.

She blinked. "I had no idea you could do anything like this."

"Good."

"Good?"

"You have surprised me a few times on this trip, and I would like to think I can still surprise you."

Did he mean her love for St. Thomas Day traditions or that she had been in love with him too? Her hands fumbled together, and she pointed with a nod of her head to his sugar creation. "She is lovely."

"*She* is you."

Amelia swallowed. "She is?"

"It's you dancing." He paused. "With me."

Amelia forgot about everyone else at the table. That night had meant something to him. She had been sure it had been memorable for her alone. Her heart pounded, aching for her to choose Noah over Mr. Wilson. She wanted the man who thought of her in his arms, described her hair and skin in the moonlight, begged her to consider him, and made sugar molds of her dancing.

Her eyes unwittingly flitted to Mr. Wilson. Could she give up a sureness for her whims? What about Miss Hampton? Did Noah still think of her? He had mentioned love in his confession to Amelia but not marriage. She had to be certain before she surrendered completely. Desire was not a currency for happiness. But love, the absolute kind, could buy her the peace of mind she craved. She must learn which one Noah felt for her, and soon. She had a feeling Mr. Wilson had not come all the way to Amorwich to simply visit. She was quite sure he would not leave without offering a proposal of marriage. That left only three days, assuming he waited until Christmas.

She gulped.

Chapter Fourteen

Noah woke early, his thoughts plaguing him. He hadn't made any progress at getting Amelia alone. After their sugar sculpting and earning a painful ache on his backside from sitting on half a seat for so long, he had hardly even had the chance to speak to her the rest of the day. The day following had been equally futile, as Mr. Wilson had thoroughly dominated Amelia's time, playing chess with her—which Noah knew was a game she hated—sitting by her at dinner, and hovering over the pianoforte as she played for them that evening.

But Noah was determined to outwit the tenacious intruder today. It was Christmas Eve, which meant the entire household would soon be in a flurry of activity decorating the house. A few extra guests had arrived the night before for the ball on the morrow, and everything was sure to be chaotic. If Noah could just get Amelia away from it all for a moment, he might be able to assure her that her worries were unfounded.

She could trust him completely.

But how to sneak her away and get her alone? Once he was ready for the day, he shut his bedchamber door softly so as not to wake anyone, then strolled down the corridor, rubbing his hand on his freshly shaved jaw. He was so deep in thought that he didn't notice Amelia until they were both at the head of the stairs.

Again.

This time she did not seem ready to bolt. In fact, she seemed as pleased to see him as he was to see her.

"We keep meeting here," she said, clasping her hands together in front of her pink muslin gown.

"I think it's fate."

"Ah, a chance staircase encounter?" She smiled. "Even considering we are residing in the same house and use this passage frequently?"

"You cannot argue that the timing is profound."

She snorted under breath. "You don't even believe in fate."

"This might convert me." He took a step nearer. "I have a proposition for you."

Suspicion etched her furrowed brow. "Go ahead."

"I keep thinking about Mr. Cunningham being alone over the holidays."

Her eyes widened. "You too? I cannot keep him from my mind. I had one of our footmen take my sugar mold to him. A maid received it, but there was not a sight of Mr. Cunningham."

He resisted reaching for her hand to comfort her. "That was very kind of you. I thought we ought to bring over some greenery and decorate his drawing room for him."

She grinned. "What a wonderful idea! We will know if he is well, but he will absolutely hate it."

He chuckled. "And secretly he will thank us."

She snapped her fingers. "We can invite him to join us for Christmas dinner and the ball tomorrow too."

Noah leaned into the rail at the top of the stairs. "We will be lucky if he will come for the food." Her laugh did wonders to ease the turmoil he'd felt the last few days.

"You are probably right. I will let Ivy know what we are about so she can tell Mama when she wakes. Let me grab my cloak and a basket, and we can collect some greenery on our way to his house. Oh, and I know my mother has more ribbons and bows than she will use today. We should have plenty to bring over for his small drawing room."

"Splendid."

"Oh dear." Amelia put her nail to her teeth. "What if Mr. Wilson has other plans this morning?"

Noah's shoulders sagged. "Then . . . we go without him."

Amelia shook her head. "I cannot leave him here alone. I'll see if I can convince him to join us." She started backing away toward Curtis and Ivy's rooms. "I'll meet you in the breakfast room?"

This was the Amelia he knew. The take-charge, full-speed-ahead woman he adored. Even if she had to go and invite Mr. Wilson to join them. Noah forced a nod. "I'll grab my cloak and arrange for the carriage." He would also let Lawry know so he could join in their hunt for greenery. If Noah missed Amelia, Lawry must be just as anxious to be with Wendy.

After taking longer than he hoped to complete his tasks, Noah burst into the breakfast room. Disappointment struck hard. Amelia wasn't alone as he had hoped but was sitting across from Mr. Wilson. Noah cleared his throat, attempting to swallow his contempt for the man. "Good morning," he said to the room at large.

Mr. Wilson scowled and gave a curt nod. "Is it you I have to thank for our morning plans?"

Noah glanced at Amelia, who had the decency to grimace.

Noah snatched up a lemon scone. "Mr. Cunningham is an acquired taste, but he grows on a person. You'll be glad you helped."

"Interesting. I thought you would attempt to convince me to stay here."

That was what Noah had wanted to do, but in that moment, he was glad he had suppressed his selfishness.

Mr. Wilson pushed back from his seat. "I will fetch my overcoat and hat."

A footman slipped through the doorway. "Mr. Wilson, a letter has arrived for you."

Mr. Wilson accepted the letter and broke the seal. He read through the contents and frowned. "My solicitor has presented some pressing needs I must respond to." He looked at Amelia. "Forgive me. You will have to excuse me from this morning's frivolities."

"Of course. Your responsibilities are important."

Mr. Wilson gave Noah a shrewd look full of silent warning before he dipped his head and left them alone.

Noah turned back to the sideboard to hide his triumphant smile. It was obvious Mr. Wilson felt threatened by Noah's fixed attention on Amelia, as well he should. Noah picked up a plate and began whistling a festive tune under his breath as he filled it.

"Must you whistle?" Amelia asked.

He bit back a chuckle and brought his food to the table. "Beautiful morning, isn't it?" he said, taking Mr. Wilson's seat.

"I know what you're doing," she said, sitting back in her seat.

"Enjoying my breakfast?"

"Rejoicing that Mr. Wilson cannot come."

How could he deny it? "I hate to hurry you, Mel, but we really should get an early start. Have you gathered those ribbons yet?"

She shook her head, a smile stealing out. "I will go fetch them right now. You can use one of them to wipe that smug smile off your face."

He laughed. It was rather smug, wasn't it? His Christmas Eve was looking more and more promising.

Chapter Fifteen

Amelia adored sleighrides, and to her surprise, Noah had arranged to use a sleigh instead of a carriage. The carpet of snow was thick enough for it, and despite the cloud cover, the temperature was not too bitter. She and Wendy burrowed under their lap blankets, rubbing their mitten-covered hands and warming their feet with the heated bricks while they waited for Noah to join them. They had already stored their baskets of supplies beneath the seats, and she was left anticipating what would come next—an entire morning with Noah. Her pulse raced at the thought.

Beside her, Wendy watched Lawry speaking with the driver. Her longing gaze was tempered only by what could be described as measured carefulness. When she caught Amelia watching her, she whispered sheepishly, "Must Mr. Brooks bring his valet with him everywhere? It is not a common habit among gentlemen."

"It is a bit strange," Amelia answered. Deciding to press this time, she added, "Do you not enjoy his company?"

Wendy looked down at her hands. "It's complicated, miss. Men can be frustrating. He says he understands my devotion to my family, but he doesn't." Wendy drew up her gaze to meet Amelia's. "I suppose it's a similar entanglement of emotions as your situation with Mr. Brooks."

Amelia could well imagine. "Then, let's both take your advice from the other day and not be too hasty this afternoon. There must be a happy compromise between sound judgment and following the heart." She wanted to believe it herself as much as she wanted Wendy to.

"I suppose." Wendy's frown grew into a small smile.

Just then, Noah strolled out through the front door and jogged down the path to join them. He climbed into the sleigh, a wide grin stretching across his face and his blue eyes bright.

"We did it. We escaped before the entire house was awake and festivities erupted in full force." He took his seat on the bench in front of Amelia's and tapped the side of the sleigh with a firm hand. One of the horses whinnied, and the conveyance rocked into motion.

Amelia grinned, feeling the cool breeze brush against her cheeks. She had been entirely too anxious the past fortnight, but this invigorated her. The fresh air made her want to forget about her life decisions for a few hours and enjoy the moment.

She watched the winter-laced countryside pass by and wondered again how Mr. Cunningham would respond to their efforts. The thought was more exciting than even the sleighride. Perhaps all she had needed was to think about someone else for a change. She'd never thought that that someone would be Mr. Cunningham. She had been intimidated by him for so long, but after being in his house, she was suddenly seeing him as human—a person with needs and feelings.

The driver stopped not half a mile behind the house, where a forest of pines separated their property from Ravencross, where Julia and Esmond lived.

"Wasn't this one of your favorite places when we were younger?" Noah hopped out of the carriage and turned back to reach for Amelia's hand.

"It was the best place to play hide-and-seek." She stretched her hand to his. He surprised her by not taking her hand but taking hold of her waist. He picked her up and, in a rush, swung her down much too close to him. Her hand landed on his chest, and she laughed in surprise, her cheeks flooding with the pleasure of his hold on her.

Noah produced an all too smug grin. "I think we ought to play a game like the ones you loved as a child," he said.

"What sort of game?" She was reluctant to step back, but Wendy still had to climb down from the carriage, and step back Amelia must.

Noah assisted Wendy down next, although there was no lifting or close proximity involved. To them both he said, "I was thinking we ought to see who can find the prettiest pine bough to make a garland for Mr. Cunningham's mantel. And since we brought two axes with us, we should form two teams."

She saw where this was going and was about to object when Noah added, "Lawry, why don't you join Miss Park's maid and see if you cannot find a better pine bough than we can."

Wendy scoffed. "Not to offend, sir, but no one knows a good pine bough for decorating like the help. It won't be much of a contest."

Lawry laughed. “She has a point.”

“See here,” Amelia said, her mitten-covered hands going to her hips. “I would have you know that I have a talent for seeking in this forest, and I strongly doubt it pertains just to finding people.”

Noah nodded. “She is rather good at seeking, even if I cannot follow her logic to finding pine boughs.”

She elbowed him. “Let the contest begin, and we shall see.” Her competitive spirit had been roused, and she was ready to win. Who needed a chaperone for a few minutes in the woods? There was nothing at all to worry about.

The two couples split ways. Amelia headed deep into the trees, and Noah followed with an ax in one hand.

“Do you know where you’re going?” he asked.

“Of course I do.” The taller pines were farther out and likely had branches long enough to stretch across Mr. Cunningham’s mantel.

They had been walking for several minutes before Amelia spotted a branch she thought was acceptable. She stopped and turned sideways, stretching out her arms to get a feel of the size. Before she could put her arms down, Noah stepped right into them, wrapping his own arms around her middle.

“You don’t have drag me into the middle of the woods to ask for an embrace,” he said.

His smell, his warmth, his very being overwhelmed Amelia’s every thought. She sputtered a surprised laugh, searching for an ounce of decorum. Latching hold of her reason, she pulled back a few inches. Anything more seemed impossible. “Noah Brooks!”

He brought his head down, his gaze soft and melty and without any regret. “Was it another dance, then, that you wanted? Or perhaps something more?”

His nose was almost to hers. She wanted his kiss. Wanted it more than she could breathe. But she conjured up an image of Mr. Wilson and pushed Noah away. She pointed to the tree. “This one.”

A flash of disappointment crossed Noah’s face, and only a small smile remained. He followed her finger to the branch she had selected. “That long one on the bottom?”

“Yes.”

He frowned. “Are you sure?”

“I guarantee we will win with that one.”

He studied her. “It’s huge.”

“I know! It’s perfect.”

Noah scratched his head. “Listen. I want you to have what you want.”

Were they speaking of the tree or about them? Amelia gave a slow nod.

"In fact," he added, "I'm ready to sacrifice a great deal for your happiness." He started to walk backward into the thick branches. "Even if it means I have to climb through these thick branches to get that extremely difficult branch you selected."

She bit her lip to keep from laughing at his dramatics.

As soon as he was deep enough, Noah awkwardly hacked away at the branch. She hugged herself around the waist, unable to keep from admiring his strength. She couldn't imagine Mr. Wilson doing this for her. After a moment, Noah practically crawled back out.

She pointed past him. "Did you forget the branch?"

"I've got to pull it out now." He bent over and yanked on the end of the branch. He must have thought it was still attached in some way, because he threw his body weight into it, but the branch came soaring out, and Noah ended up on his back.

"Eek!" Amelia squealed. His chest moved, but his eyes were closed. She dove beside him, her arms going to either side of his shoulders. "Noah? Noah! Speak to me."

He opened one eye. "Must I? I'm savoring another embrace from Mel Park."

She snorted and hit him in the chest. "Are you well?"

They both shifted into sitting positions, the snow crunching beneath them. "I'm excellent. I just conquered that branch with you as my witness." He looked admiringly at the tree. "I cannot think of a time I have been prouder of myself. Not even when that difficult bill I worked on with my father passed last winter with an almost unanimous vote. Although, I might have pulled twenty different muscles."

She laughed at him. And then, remembering how he'd flown backward, she laughed harder. Noah's laugh soon mixed with hers. She gasped for air, her forehead falling into his shoulder. "I can't breathe."

"Please don't tell anyone about this," Noah begged. "I want to keep this achievement close to my heart."

She shook her head, her laugh taking up again. "Must I keep such a success from the others? They'll be equally proud."

Somehow Noah's arms had come around her again, and when she realized it, her laughter waned. She couldn't remember being happier all year than she was right now. This was exactly the way she had felt with Noah last Christmas—safe, cherished, loved.

He grinned, the perfect curve of his mouth drawing her eyes. When he reached up to tuck a curl behind her ear, the graze of his fingers sent a thrill through her.

"I told you I would sacrifice for you," he said. "There went my pride."

"I like you better without it," she said, barely breathing. This was where she wanted to be forever, right here in his arms. And for a sweet second, the fears of the future had nothing on the rightness of the moment. Their heads came closer and closer. She was going to pull away, but by the time she thought to, his lips were already on hers, and then retreating seemed impossible.

Noah tightened his hold on her back. He smelled like a mixture of pine and musk, an intoxicating combination. He kissed her gently at first, true to his personality. Somehow one of her hands found the back of his neck and the other his jaw. That touch elicited a spark that turned into a fire. Years of longing poured through her as she tried to convey the words her voice could not speak.

She loved Noah Brooks.

She'd always loved Noah Brooks.

His mouth moved across her jaw and back to her mouth until they were both breathless. When his lips moved away, it was too soon.

"You are wonderful, Mel," he whispered, his thumb gliding over her cheek and across her lower lip. "I am honored to have shared this moment with you." Gray hues smoldered in his soft blue eyes as he seemed to admire every feature she bore, not missing any freckle or imperfection. "You might not trust me completely yet, but I hope you will soon. Because I want to marry you."

"You do?" The words sounded silly and childlike, but she really was surprised. He did care. He cared enough to pledge his life to her and none other.

"I adore you," he said. "Which is why I am going to bring you back to the others and not kiss you again right now. You are everything to me, Mel. Everything."

He wrapped her in his arms, his hug as divine as his kiss. "I have just one request. Will you tell me who it is you choose to spend your life with by the end of the ball? I have a feeling Mr. Wilson has a proposal of his own planned."

She froze, thinking of Mr. Wilson for the first time since their excursion into the woods, and nodded against his shoulder. After this kiss, she could not continue to be divided between the two men.

"I want you to know," he continued, "that if you choose Mr. Wilson, I will leave the following day. I won't make you suffer my company."

For some reason, he was giving her time again. He had given her a year before, and she had hated him for it. This time one day would be a gift from him. There was no pressure to let their kiss command her thoughts, but in many ways, it was too late for that.

Her answer formulated easily in her mind, but she decided she would use the time wisely. She wasn't going to let her emotions lead her away from Noah, nor her head lead her closer to Mr. Wilson. She would follow her heart, and this time there was no question where it led.

Chapter Sixteen

Noah hadn't planned on getting Amelia alone in the woods or for their surprise kiss, but he did not regret either. By the time he dragged the pine branch back to the sleigh, he had already replayed the moment with Amelia in his arms a dozen times at least. It didn't help that she kept looking at him with those doe eyes or that she let him hold her hand.

"What is that?" Lawry asked.

Noah had to release Amelia to heft the branch into the sleigh. "What does it look like? It's the winning pine bough."

Wendy and Lawry burst into laughter.

"What is so amusing? Once we trim it a bit, it'll be just the size of Mr. Cunningham's mantel." Amelia stepped onto her tiptoes. "Let's see your offering, if you're so smug."

Wendy picked up an armful of small, evenly sized branches. "Do you not even know how to make a garland, miss?"

Amelia's cheeks pinked. "Um, no, I don't suppose I do."

Noah covered his hand and turned to the side to hide his mirth.

"Noah Brooks, why are you laughing?"

He straightened. "I assumed you knew what you were doing with this monstrosity."

She folded her arms across her chest. "You could have said something."

He chuckled. "I am certain we can use it for something."

"I am sure we can," Lawry agreed.

"But I declare us the winners," Wendy said, opening the sleigh door for them to climb inside. "And I will teach you how to tie a proper garland when we get to Mr. Cunningham's so you might have a chance at beating us next year."

The idea of the four of them playing this same game next year sounded wonderful. Noah helped Amelia inside, and soon the sleigh was on its way once more. He resisted holding her hand again only because he wasn't sure it was proper to do so in public until they were officially engaged.

As they approached the church, Noah caught the shape of a man in the distance. "It looks like Thomas is at the vicarage. In the graveyard, of all places."

Amelia leaned over him. "Is Alice with him?"

"No. Actually, I might have been mistaken. It doesn't look like Thomas." When they neared the path to the vicarage, he squinted. "Does that look like Mr. Cunningham?"

Whoever it was suddenly collapsed, disappearing behind a headstone. Noah slapped the side of the sleigh. "Stop!"

The sleigh lurched, and Noah held his arm out to keep Amelia from sliding across the seat. In the next second, he had the door open and lunged out of the sleigh.

"Noah!" Amelia called behind him. He knew without looking that she would follow him. It made him move all the faster so he might protect her should there be any blood or, worse, a dead body.

He darted down the slight hill from the churchyard toward the grave markers, his boots pounding into the snow. He weaved through the headstones until he was beside the fallen man. It was Mr. Cunningham, all right, and he groaned as soon as Noah attempted to lift him.

"Is he hurt?" Amelia asked, weaving through the markers to reach them.

"I am well," Mr. Cunningham said, his breathy response so different from his usual gruffness.

Lawry dashed past Amelia, taking up Mr. Cunningham's other arm.

"Thank you," Noah said, and Lawry nodded. Together the two of them helped Mr. Cunningham to the sleigh. Wendy helped get him settled inside, and Amelia took a seat beside Noah.

Mr. Cunningham was pale. Too pale. And he appeared older than ever.

"Let's take him to Fairmore," she said. "We can call a doctor there."

"No," Mr. Cunningham objected. "Take me home. And no doctor. I am just winded."

Amelia looked at Noah, who nodded and instructed the driver to bring the poor man home. A few minutes later they were in front of Mr. Cunningham's house, and Noah and Lawry assisted him inside.

It was cold again in the drawing room, but Lawry made quick work of the fire while Wendy rushed off for tea. Amelia found a blanket in a basket by the sofa and spread it over Mr. Cunningham's lap. Noah stepped back, assessing what to do. He settled on opening the drapes and lighting a few candles to brighten the room.

Wendy returned with enough tea and finger sandwiches for everyone. Amelia took a seat beside Mr. Cunningham and made certain he drank and ate a little.

"All this nonsense on my account." Mr. Cunningham shook his head. "None of it is needed. I'm well enough."

"Can't we call a doctor?" Amelia fussed over his blanket again.

"I'm not ill and nothing is broken," Mr. Cunningham barked.

Noah knew there was only one thing they could do for him. "Lawry, help me with something outside, will you?"

Lawry gave a nod and followed him out. A few minutes later they returned, their arms loaded with pine boughs and baskets of what Noah assumed were ribbons.

"What is all this?" Mr. Cunningham sat up straighter in his chair, color returning to his face.

"It's Christmas." Noah grinned. Those two words seemed to fill up the entire room with more light and warmth than either the fire or the candles.

Mr. Cunningham's perpetual frown softened, and wonder touched his expression. "Christmas? Here?"

His reaction surprised Noah. Was he afraid to celebrate Christmas? Lady Blakely had mentioned the grand parties she had attended here in the past.

Amelia seemed to pick up on the same observation and said, "Don't you say a single word in argument. We have spent all morning preparing, and we will need your help."

"I couldn't possibly—"

"You certainly can." Amelia opened a basket and pulled out a pile of red satin ribbon. "I assume you know how to tie a bow."

Noah put his fist to his mouth, in awe that Amelia would attempt to get Mr. Cunningham's cooperation in this particular activity.

Mr. Cunningham scoffed. "Of course I do."

"Then, let's get started." Amelia had a pile of ribbons in the man's lap before any objections could be made. "I insist."

Mr. Cunningham grumbled but measured a ribbon the length of his arm and snipped it with a pair of scissors. He had a perfect bow tied a moment later.

Amelia took the scissors away from Mr. Cunningham and replaced them with another cup of tea. "I insist you keep drinking."

"So much insisting. Is that all you young people do anymore?"

Amelia glanced at Noah, and they held back a laugh. Insisting seemed to be the only way to reach Mr. Cunningham.

Wendy and Lawry went straight to work on the garland, tying segments together. Meanwhile, Noah began hanging the bows Amelia and Mr. Cunningham completed wherever they directed him to.

After Noah hung a pair of bows on the corners of the largest window in the room, Amelia cooed, "It's delightful!"

One compliment from her, and he was ready to take up decorating as a profession. "Do you think anyone in Parliament would be impressed by my bow-hanging skills?"

"Indeed," Amelia said, pointing to a lopsided bow on the mantel. "It looks oddly like when you try to tie your own cravat."

Everyone laughed except for Mr. Cunningham, but at least he appeared amused.

Noah started humming "The Twelve Days of Christmas," and soon they were all singing it. Mr. Cunningham had quite the baritone voice, but he scowled at anyone who messed up a lyric, which Amelia did a handful of times.

After the pine bough was hung, the room and the joy within personified Christmas. Noah stole a seat beside Amelia. Her pleased expression produced an urge in him to kiss her again, but he restrained himself. Wendy passed around the remainder of sandwiches, distracting him from the constant pull of the woman beside him. They devoured the food while they visited. Gone was any divide in station or difference in age, leaving behind a unity of feeling and mutual respect.

Amelia brought up the story of how Mr. Cunningham had struck her with an apple when she was a child.

"I remember that," Mr. Cunningham said with a chuckle. "You were hiding behind a bush, and I thought you were a stray dog who kept coming around and eating my chickens."

"I was no stray dog," she defended with a scowl. "And I had a bruise on my leg for a month."

"Forgive me," he said with a look of contrition. "You learned your lesson not to hide from people, but alas, now you're barging into their homes and forcing them to celebrate."

Amelia gave a firm nod. "And we hope to force you to come to Fairmore tomorrow for Christmas dinner and my mother's ball."

Mr. Cunningham scrubbed his jaw with his hand. "Christmas dinner . . ."

"More courses than you can possibly eat and with all the trimmings," she added.

The older man looked about the room. "Oh, why not?"

Noah grinned in disbelief. This was a morning he wouldn't soon forget. Unfortunately, they must soon return to Fairmore. He didn't care to upset Lady Blakely by taking too much time with her daughter; nor did he wish to upset Mr. Wilson, who—even with his flat emotions—would likely be livid if they stayed away for too long.

Noah stole a glance at Amelia. Would tomorrow be even happier than today? Their kiss had been special, but he was not naive enough to think she would forget their year apart so easily. He had hurt her deeply by not committing to her sooner; he knew that now. It would take a miracle worthy of the Amorwich Legend, but Noah hoped Amelia would choose him.

Chapter Seventeen

Amelia couldn't stop thinking about Noah's kiss. She didn't just replay it in her mind, but she studied it and his words that had followed. Did he really want to marry her and not Miss Hampton? Her heart soared with the thought. And she trusted Noah, despite the long months that she had told herself otherwise. She'd known him for forever, and he was not a man capable of lying.

She aimlessly fingered the new gown Mother had insisted on having made for her for the ball—a white dress with a red overlay and matching red gloves.

Wendy began weaving a red ribbon through the curls piled high on Amelia's head and then added the slightest bit of rouge to her cheeks and lips.

Amelia stared at her reflection. "I feel different."

"How so?" Wendy asked, bringing out her dancing slippers.

"Like my life is about to change forever." A smile stretched across her face.

Wendy set her hand on her shoulder. "Did you speak with Mr. Wilson, then?"

Amelia's joy instantly deflated, and her smile drooped. "One of Mama's guests knows him, and the two were inseparable yesterday. I had no idea Mr. Wilson was so passionate about horse racing, but it was all he wanted to speak about. I did promise him the first set tonight. I will tell him then, even if I must risk someone overhearing."

She hadn't had a moment alone with Noah either, which bothered her even more. Did he regret his proposal? Did he still want to marry her? But she was sure that after a little time together tonight, he would reassure her again.

Wendy picked up Amelia's dance slippers and kneeled in front of her. "I know you have had your misgivings, but Mr. Brooks's year away from you seems to have deepened his affections. I believe he is desperate to have you."

Amelia barely suppressed a girlish giggle. She rather liked Noah's desperate side. Then she sobered. "What about you and Lawry?"

Wendy slid the slippers onto Amelia's feet but didn't meet her gaze. "He proposed."

Amelia held her breath. "And?"

Wendy sat back on her heels and sighed. "Lawry visited my family without telling me. I was angry at first, but I couldn't stay angry. He truly cares for them, and they care in return. He's promised to send a portion of his earnings to help provide for them. Can you believe how generous he is? I'm coming to realize that love doesn't remove every fear or reservation, but the right man loves you through them." A smile spread across Wendy's face. "I told him I would marry him."

Amelia couldn't resist. She threw her arms around Wendy. "I'm so happy for you!"

Wendy returned the hug. "And I you, miss."

"Perhaps," Amelia began as she pulled back, "perhaps there is a way you can continue to be my maid while you are married to Lawry."

Wendy's eyes lit up. "I hope for that same possibility."

Wendy's happy news carried Amelia down to the drawing room. She met Noah's eyes when she entered the room and thrilled at his appreciative stare. He stood beside Mr. Cunningham, who wore a sharp dress jacket, a red cravat, and neatly combed hair. Noah whispered something to Mr. Cunningham and started weaving around Curtis toward her. Mr. Wilson arrived at her side at the same time as her mother, his steady arm extending to escort her into dinner.

As eager as she was to be with Noah, she readily accepted. She and Mr. Wilson needed to be together for their important conversation to take place. With the formal place setting, her mother had placed Amelia between Mr. Cunningham and Mr. Wilson and across from Noah. At the top of her plate sat the sugar form of a dancing maiden. A delighted grin seized her, and she met Noah's gaze.

He winked in return, melting her into a puddle of happiness. It was all the reassurance she needed. She could trust him with her heart. He loved her. She was going to let Mr. Wilson down and accept Noah's proposal before all the attendees had finished arriving for the ball. Nothing was going to prevent them from speaking this time.

She turned toward Mr. Wilson, but to her dismay, he was deep in conversation with his friend. She waited for them to finish, even leaning toward him to get his attention, but Mr. Wilson was too enthralled by the topic of horseflesh again.

She smothered her frustrations and turned to speak with Mr. Cunningham instead. "Is everything to your satisfaction?"

"I haven't had a Christmas dinner like this in over a decade."

"Why not?"

Mr. Cunningham dabbed his mouth with his napkin. "I stopped celebrating Christmas when my Irene died. It was everything to her. I stopped living too."

"I cannot imagine losing a spouse, but it sounds similar to our response when Papa died."

"Yet you still found time to force your way into my home."

She laughed. "I had a little encouragement." She looked across the table at Noah, catching his profile. "It's easier to withdraw than face the hard parts of life, isn't it?"

He nodded. "I was ready to die yesterday in that cemetery. I thought it was rude of you to interrupt."

She set her hand on his forearm. "But now you are grateful you lived long enough to eat this delicious goose."

He chuckled. "Yes, and I think it's time to make some changes. This won't come as any surprise to you after what I confessed, but I haven't been an admirer of this world for some time now. Seeing the portrait of Irene in the center of all the Christmas cheer you gifted me is the first thing that has felt right in many years."

Warmth seeped into Amelia's chest, and her eyes pricked with tears. Christmas had healed him. And seeing Mr. Cunningham choose to be happy again healed her too. She hadn't realized until now that she hadn't thought of the reason behind the holiday for many years. She'd made it all about traditions and thoughts of Noah. No matter her own future, this was the kind of joy she wanted to make a part of her Christmases forever.

"I am so happy for you, Mr. Cunningham. Especially because I plan to have you attend our Christmas dinner for years to come."

Mr. Cunningham patted her hand. "Because of the holiday, instead of arguing, I'll just thank you kindly."

"Well done, Mr. Cunningham," she said.

The rest of dinner passed quickly, and it was time for the dancing to begin. The finest quartet in Amorwich serenaded the guests while they entered the festively decorated ballroom. Mr. Wilson took her hand for the first set, which happened to be a lively reel. The steps of the dance had too many turns for her to finish a sentence properly, and her gaze wandered toward Noah.

Despite her feelings of reassurance at dinner, she did not like the way so many women surrounded him. When the dance brought her closer to him, she saw his head tip back with a loud laugh. What had that pretty blonde debutante said to amuse him so?

All those months of fretting came back in an instant, flooding her with insecurity. After the song ended, she knew she must seize the opportunity to speak with Mr. Wilson. "Can we not sit out this next dance and talk?"

Mr. Wilson nearly smiled. "I was hoping to do the same." He weaved her arm through his. Her heart raced, but not in the same way it did when Noah was near her. These beats were stuttered with anxiety. Did Mr. Wilson plan to propose?

He passed the open chairs along the wall and led her to the door to the balcony. A pit in her stomach formed, but she did not object. This needed to happen. She could break her news to him better out here.

Whether she shivered from the cold or the lack of other people outside, she could not say. Mr. Wilson put his arm around her, catching her off guard. He hadn't touched her more than to thread their arms together, and she was entirely unprepared for anything more. He led her to the half wall and turned her toward him.

"While my attentions to you have been pointed, I haven't yet declared myself to you."

This was her opportunity. "Mr. Wilson, I have thought a great deal about our time together."

"As have I. We are well-suited."

They were suited, perhaps in station and affability. But she knew now that they weren't *well* suited at all. Every moment since Noah's proposal had made that clear. "I disagree."

He raised a brow, his demeanor barely cracking. "Pardon?"

"Do you feel particularly happy when you are with me?"

"Happy?"

"Yes. This last week I realized I don't make you happy. I don't make you laugh. I don't even make you smile."

"I am not one to show great emotion."

"But I believe you are capable of feeling it. I know I am. When I am with you, I feel safe, but I want more in my marriage than security. I want to be with someone who challenges me to be better, who knows my moods and how to pull me from them, and who loves me despite my many flaws. I want the kind of happiness that reminds me of Christmas." She hadn't meant to say so much, but it all came tumbling out.

He dropped his hands from her arms. "You are speaking of Mr. Brooks."

She stared at him, at his stoic brow and thin mouth, but his eyes gave her the first glimpse of vulnerability she had ever seen in him.

"Yes." She licked her bottom lip, suppressing the worries she still had regarding Noah, simmering just beneath the surface. "Thank you, Mr. Wilson, for being a good friend when I needed one. I hope you are not bitterly disappointed."

Mr. Wilson sighed. "A little, perhaps. But I am enlightened by your speech. I wish you well, Miss Park." He dipped a bow and stalked back into the ballroom.

She leaned against the half wall and hugged herself. Knowing she had hurt Mr. Wilson, she felt her excitement for the night fade. Exiting the balcony herself, she was greeted by a dazzling array of multicolored gowns, a cacophony of laughter, and glimmering candlelight beneath pine-covered chandeliers.

But no Noah. Where was he?

She searched the crowd, the knot in her stomach growing, until she finally spotted him. Dancing. With the pretty blonde debutante. Amelia blew out her breath, the timing of the moment undoing her. What if he had already changed his mind about her? She had been so certain last year too.

No. No, she was being silly. She needed to collect herself, and she would be well again. She turned to leave when she nearly ran right into Mr. Cunningham sipping his punch.

"Miss Park." He pointed his glass to her. "You look as if you're ready to leave your own ball."

She forced a smile. "I only thought to slip away for a moment." And then hide in her room the rest of the night while her insecurities preyed upon her.

"I'll join you. I might be ready for some change, but not this quickly. All these people are irritating me."

She took one last glance at Noah and his partner, hating how well they looked together, and accepted Mr. Cunningham's arm.

When they reached the ballroom entrance, he paused at the door. "Just a moment, Miss Park." He leaned over and whispered something to a footman and handed him his glass. "I'm ready now," he said. They took the corridor to the library, and once inside, Mr. Cunningham settled into a chair by the fireplace, and Amelia took a seat on the sofa across from him.

Mr. Cunningham drummed his fingers on the arm of the chair. "You know, I might be a cantankerous old man, but I have been around long enough to know when love has been thwarted."

She brought her fingernail to her mouth. "Love is . . . confusing."

"What do you mean?" The voice from the doorway made her whirl in her seat. Noah stood in the threshold, and he wasn't smiling like he had been at his dance partner. "Thank you for sending for me, Mr. Cunningham." Noah strolled into the room, his back straight and with some distance between them. He looked as he had the day he had arrived, like she had wounded him. And she knew then that whatever she felt affected him as much as it did her. Because he cared that much.

Chapter Eighteen

Worry built inside Noah with every step he took toward Amelia. Was all their progress undone? And why?

"Mel—"

"Noah, it's not what you think. I told Mr. Wilson no."

"You did?" His frown softened. "You did. That's wonderful!" He took a seat beside her and reached for her hand. She tensed, sending his hopes spiraling down again.

Mr. Cunningham cleared his throat, forcing Noah to look his way. "I hate to interrupt, but did I ever tell you that my wife, Irene, was a direct descendant of the Morgans who started this town?"

Noah blinked. "The couple behind the legend?"

Mr. Cunningham sighed. "Oh, it's not a legend, really. It's true. Irene and I came together at Christmas too, the same as you. After she died, I stopped believing in it, until you both came to my house to decorate yesterday. I saw the truth again when you, Mr. Brooks, looked at Miss Park. It was the same way I looked at my Irene. It was then that I knew I had to come to this blasted ball to ensure you two had a Christmas miracle of your own."

Noah shared a shocked look with Amelia before looking back in disbelief at Mr. Cunningham.

"Well, I believe my work here is done." He slapped his hands on his knees and stood from his chair. A grin passed over his face as he assessed them. Noah had never seen him so happy. Mr. Cunningham walked slowly to the door but paused before he exited. "I'm thinking of writing a book about the Legend of Amorwich. Perhaps I'll even include the two of you."

Noah turned back to Amelia, who gaped at the now-vacant doorway. When she met his eyes, she quickly dropped her gaze to her hands in her lap.

"I won't let anyone pressure you," he said. "But I do hope you'll tell me what's wrong."

"It's a year-old hurt. You've heard pieces of it already. I thought you were going to propose last Christmas. When you didn't come to London, I convinced myself that you had toyed with my affections. Noah, you broke my heart. I thought I was healed with Mr. Wilson's attentions, but I don't think I am."

Noah's stomach sank. He slid close to her and put his arm around her. When she leaned into him, he felt a glimmer of hope. "I wanted to propose last year. I did not think you were ready and threw myself into my research at my father's bequest. I've never regretted anything more."

Amelia lifted her head, revealing a single tear on her cheek. "Rachel believed you to be fond of Miss Hampton and urged me not to grow too attached."

"Miss Hampton? No, it is her father's friendship and expertise I've sought. He has been helping me in my research."

"Truly?"

"I swear. Miss Hampton is nothing to me. No one has ever claimed my heart as you have. I wish I would've confided more to my sister, but with her being your best friend, I withheld much of what I was feeling."

Amelia's eyes softened. "I was jealous tonight, watching you dance."

Noah squeezed his eyes shut. "Miss Rutherford is a cousin of mine. I told her about you this summer when her family came to visit. All she did tonight was tease me about you."

Amelia groaned and covered her face with her hands. "You deserve better than me."

He pulled her hands down and covered them with his own. "I could say the same is true in reverse, but it isn't about deserving. It's about choosing: choosing to love, choosing to forgive, choosing to change. I know I don't want to make the same mistake twice and spend another year, or even another day, away from you."

The smallest smile crept over her mouth. "Did you really want to propose last year?"

Noah reached up and wiped a tear staining her cheek. "Then and every day since. I am so sorry I gave you cause to doubt me."

"I am sorry I doubted." The sincerity in her eyes was a bandage to his regret. She threw her arms around him, drawing out a surprised laugh. Her gown was sleek beneath his fingertips, her face warm against his neck. He drew back, and she lifted her head, her dark lashes framing her mesmerizing hazel eyes.

"I will always love you," he whispered.

"And I have loved you always," she breathed back.

Their lips connected a breath later, his heart threatening to erupt with the sheer joy of her words and touch. Her silky mouth was just as sweet and wonderful as it had been in the woods. He moved his thumb across her smooth cheek before encircling his hand around to the back of her delicate neck. His other hand went around her back, holding her as he had yearned to hold her for so long. She loved him. Amelia Park loved him. And he would dedicate his life to being worthy of her.

The door suddenly collided with the wall, and Noah reluctantly pulled back. Rachel flew into the room, her brown hair pulled back in a pile of curls and her pink ballgown billowing between her long strides. "There you are! I've been searching everywhere for you two." She rushed to them, her arms spread wide, her husband trailing several feet behind her. "I wanted to be here sooner, but our carriage wheel broke, and then we had to ride in the back of a hay wagon, of all things. I cannot begin to tell you how utterly ruined my hem is."

Noah and Amelia stood just in time for Rachel to round the sofa and throw her arms around them both.

"What are you doing here, Rachel?" Amelia asked. "This is such a surprise!"

"I know! Isn't it wonderful?" Rachel pulled back but kept a hand on each of their arms. "I received your letter, and I had to come rescue you from my tiresome brother." She glared at Noah.

"You don't have to rescue anyone," Amelia said. "It appears Noah is madly in love with me."

Noah gave a firm nod. "It's true."

"He is?" Rachel crossed her arms. "You are?"

Noah grinned. "And she doesn't even find me tiresome."

Amelia nudged him, her eyes teasing. "Especially now that I have seen him chop pine boughs."

Rachel's sputtering mouth finally closed. "And here I thought Amelia had cornered you to tell you off."

Noah pulled Amelia away from Rachel and tucked her possessively under his arm. "I was assuring my jealous fiancée that she can trust me." He looked at her—his beautiful soon-to-be wife. "Always."

Amelia grinned. "It would help convince me if you kissed me again."

"Amelia!" Rachel scolded.

But Noah didn't mind an audience. Kissing Amelia was like celebrating Christmas over and over again in the best way. Besides, they needed more book material to give Mr. Cunningham. This particular Amorwich romance was to be the very best capstone to all the others.

About the Author

Anneka R. Walker is a best-selling author of historical and contemporary romance. With humor and an abundance of heart, she crafts uplifting stories you won't soon forget. She is the winner of the Swoony Award, the LDSPMA Praiseworthy Award, and various chapter contests. Her books have received praise from *Publishers Weekly*, Historical Novel Society, Midwest Book Review, and Readers Favorite. She graduated from Brigham Young University–Idaho with bachelor's degrees in English and history and hopes never to stop learning. She is a blessed wife, proud mother of five, lover of Jesus, connoisseur of chocolate, and believer in happy endings.

Subscribe to Anneka's newsletter at mailchi.mp/a278fdec4416/author-annekawalker and follow her on social media.

Facebook: @AnnekaRWalker

Instagram: @authorannekawalker